THE WINNOWING
BOOK I OF THE NAXOS QUARTET

PATRICK GARNER

First published 2019 by Aegis Press
Northborough, Massachusetts

10 9 8 7 6 5 4 3
Copyright © Patrick C. Garner 2019
Revised March 2024

Garner, Patrick C.
The Winnowing / by Patrick C. Garner
Print ISBN 978-0-692-18969-6
EPUB 978-0-692-18971-9

Front and rear cover artwork by Patrick C. Garner
Front cover photograph © Getty Images
Typeset in Baskerville

AUTHOR'S NOTES

The Winnowing is Book I of *The Naxos Quartet*, which chronicles the appearance of the ancient Greek gods in our world. All four books are stand-alone novels, but the reader is encouraged to begin the series with *The Winnowing* (Book 1), followed by *Cycladic Girls* (Book II), *Homo Divinitas* (Book III), and *All That Lasts* (Book IV).

———————

Unattributed poems are by the author.

A glossary of Greek deities appearing in this volume is included at the end of the book.

The characters in this story are not based on living persons. Only the gods and goddesses are real.

Comments and feedback are welcome. Please leave a review with Amazon. The author may be contacted at patrickgarnerbooks.com

CHAPTER 1

Only after the Day of the Pyres — the massive bonfires that obliterated the three — did I begin to reflect on the events of the last few years. Before that, all I could do was react. This narrative is my attempt to understand.

I used to think of the human condition as one of birth and death, the assumptive bookends defining life. Now I see the human condition as one of sex and death — for birth follows sex. Sex is the beginning, the wildfire that in its wet heat drives conception.

That's where this story starts. My role was decreed by forces that chose me to shelter the girls who are the early protagonists. The events were all planned, but not by me. For fate, or I should say, *The Fates*, ordained much of what occurred. Adding to the mayhem, the Olympic gods intervened repeatedly.

When the divinities decided to reappear in our time, they had not changed their ways. Deception, seduction and incest were second nature to them all.

You see, I was led to believe I was the father of the three girls. *I wasn't. We were not related whatsoever.* For years I provided for them without restriction. No matter, my belief was suddenly turned on its head by the gods. I was compelled to become the lover to two of them, both young women by then.

Blame Eros. Yes, I still *rage* at Eros and much of the Greek pantheon. I was used on the most base level. Not only were two decades my life devoted to a lie, I was robbed of my ability to react differently.

Call it a gilded cage, but what happened was wrong on so many levels that it can never be excused. It can never be forgotten. Upon learning of the deception, my reaction was *wrath*.

I should mention that my name is Jackson, or Jack Night. My business associates sometimes use my nickname — Jackknife, a compliment, as I'm considered good at what I do.

And you will see that Chloé, my presumed daughter, bore our child. *Incest?* No. *Then, a betrayal of trust?* No, again. For reasons that will soon become evident, neither of us chose our fate. Early events were mapped by Laine, her older sister, and aided by the divinities.

In the beginning I knew little about Greek gods (and I will not use terms such as *mythological* or *mythology*, as those words imply they did not exist.). The girls were an incarnation of the three Fates, but that information came later. The Fates in the ancient world were sisters — goddesses — who decided the lifespan of all individuals. Call it ancient predestination.

They were active for thousands of years before they withdrew from human interaction. Yet, they were not forgotten. Even today, some events are attributed to fate. Old phrases die hard, much like the Fates themselves.

When they pulled back from the world, they ensured the cycle of life and death would continue without interruption. Laine once told me their retreat occurred in tandem with a widespread drive against paganism. I'll go with that, but what precipitated their return? This question impels much of what I am about to record.

She would use the word *reanimate*. This does not mean they woke to consciousness after millennia. They had to be born a second time.

Be aware: the first chapters of this story are wound in a necessary (and I believe, unavoidable) haze of sensuality. We call the maddest of desire lust. It is not: it is fire in its essence. That one element drives our creation.

Fire: I was swept into it from the beginning and annealed by its heat at the end.

Chloé and I lived in a small town west of Altoona, Pennsylvania. I had not married her mother; she abandoned us after Chloé's birth. As I succeeded in finance, I bought a large property on the outskirts of that community. I preferred privacy, and the estate suited us.

My relationship with Chloé changed when she started college at a branch of Penn State in Altoona. The proximity allowed her to continue living at home, which she preferred.

If blessed with premonition, I would have distrusted events as they unfolded, but we were naïve. And deliberately deceived.

She was a freshman at about the time she began to … Before I elaborate, I note the first day of the changes began with a startling phenomenon. Working at home in my office mid morning, I became aware of the room filling with light, shimmering in its intensity. I set down my coffee, squinting into the warm glow surrounding me. At that moment Chloé entered the room, a luminescence around her. She wore panties and a camisole. I remember her squinting as well, and as she narrowed her eyes, she straightened a strap that had fallen from her shoulder.

Perhaps the golden light that pulsated about her was a foreshadowing. Perhaps it was simply a cosmic fluttering without significance. Yet, I recall the moment and her appearance as pivotal.

How do I present this dispassionately? Initially, her change was no more than dressing immodestly, something innocent enough. I did nothing to encourage the behavior. In fact, after the first week of her walking around the house half-dressed, I remember commenting about her having abandoned her usual sweatpants and tees.

Her feelings had always been fragile. When I said something one night like, "Clo, all you've worn around here for the last week is —" she stopped, frozen in place. I suspected I had overstepped when she turned toward me in tears and fled to her room.

Dismayed, I followed. She stood by her bed, shaking, hugging herself. I put my arms around her and said, "Sorry. I didn't mean to hurt your feelings." She turned toward me as I tried to comfort her. With her face tucked against my neck, she whispered, "I thought you'd like it."

"Chloé, you can dress any way you want," I said. She twisted against me, not sensually, instead burrowing in, folding herself into me, like always.

To my surprise she responded, "So I can get some prettier stuff?"

As I nodded, she kissed my cheek, her usual thanks, and pushed me away. "Then maybe I will." We walked back to the kitchen, the tension vanishing as fast as it began, with Chloé in her unremarkable underwear.

For months after that moment in her bedroom, I replayed her broken whisper in my mind — "I thought you'd like it." Within weeks of our small confrontation, she wore new things, prettier and costlier. She chose pieces with lace, something she increasingly favored. Lace highlights, howsoever small, were sewn into the curves of her new bras and around the edges of her panties. Black, russet, pink ....

Was she aware of my preoccupation with how her lips formed words, how her fingers opened like bird's wings? I found myself watching her absentmindedly slip a thumb below a bra strap and run it toward her shoulder, straightening a twist.

I concluded she was innocent, yet she had to be conscious of how she now violated the distances we always had maintained. For instance, she would sidle up to me and — inches away — ask something that could have been asked from across the room.

I knew my attraction was wrong, and that I was strangely losing self-control. Yet, I changed nothing, allowing the lunacy to envelop me.

One night as I sat at the kitchen table, she came in wearing panties and a demi bra. Instead of standing close and demanding attention, she slipped between me and the table, straddling my legs and putting her arms around my neck. The pieces looked new, another boutique buy. "Like?" she asked in the low voice she had started using. Then, "Have I become a flirt?"

For the first time, I leaned over and kissed the swell of her breast. I lingered, even letting my hands cradle her hips, examining her violet eyes. "Yes. And I like Chloé, the flirt. But let's be clear. If you're to flirt, you can flirt only with me."

"A funny rule."

"Every family has rules."

She smiled. "What if I never flirt with anyone else, ever?"

I kissed her again above her bra. "Me and no one else."

She pouted. When I said nothing, she said, "Should I stop?"

Instead of replying, I brushed her lips with mine. She breathed unevenly. Then I pushed her off. "Homework, tease."

She gave me a crooked smile, then put her arms around me, blurting, "I'm yours, see? I'll always be." My hands were high on her ribs. She let go of my neck and put her hands over mine, dragging them higher.

"Clo," I said, "don't." She leaned up and kissed me. I pushed her away and said, "Homework. Now." Her smile flickered and I watched her back as she left — her walk was confident.

The next day she came into my office after classes. She wore a sundress as violet as her eyes, square cut above her breasts. I sat at my desk and, as she had done the evening before, she straddled my legs. This time I sensed anguish. My mind raced. She'd gotten into trouble. Or been suspended. Or worse. "Okay, what's up?"

"Oh, it's nothing like that. English class. Stupid, I know, but I didn't understand a poem." She wiggled on my lap. "It just made me mad —"

"Do you remember it?"

"Sure," she said. "It's simple."

I must confess
I can't deny
heaven lies
beneath a cotton dress.

"What the hell?" she said. "Beneath? Like, under a dress tossed on my bed? Heaven if it's hanging in my closet? Come on!" Chloé never cursed; she was upset. And I recognized the poem's insinuation.

"You can't guess?"

"Guess?" she said. "It makes no sense. Who in their right mind would claim heaven's under a dress?" She glared and I met her eyes. She paused and then understood, becoming still.

I put my palms on her thighs. She put her hands on mine, her eyes impenetrable. She pulled my hands higher and said, "This?" I nodded.

"I'm so stupid —" She blushed. "You never said my … that that …"

"My negligence."

"No," she said. "I'm just dumb."

I pushed her away and said, "Go change clothes." She got up pouting, leaned over and kissed my cheek — a small thing. Deception, *seduc-tion*. Impossible that the poem was a setup.

And so I tumbled on, happily oblivious.

                                    ❧

The dance between us continued from her freshman year into her sophomore ... kissing, half-touching, innuendos as we said goodnight. A constant tension (as well as the innocence she emanated) drove me on: Clo, my violet-eyed fawn.

At Penn she focused on history, a topic I discouraged as impractical. I had attended a private New England college on full scholarship and studied finance. After graduating with a degree in statistics, I got a master's from Wharton in applied economics. When I graduated, a dozen firms competed for me. Consequently, I remained thoroughly committed to what I considered serious academic study.

At first, when Chloé finished high school, she agreed to my prodding about choosing a practical major, while admitting she had no particular focus. In fact, there were moments when she despaired of ever finding anything. To some extent, my degree worked against persuading her, as what interested me left her cold. But that changed in her freshman year. Shortly after her 19th birthday, she randomly picked up a copy of Graves' *The Greek Myths*. She read the two-volume set in a week, reread it and then began to read similar books.

After a few months, she had an extensive collection. In the evenings, we watched old movies that included cavorting gods; many she found historically wrong or simply hilarious. She became a savant of the period, gaining what seemed an obscure expertise, one which I continued to discourage, however obliquely. What would she do with an ancient history degree? I was ignored.

CHAPTER 2

O ne night she said, "It's your fate, you know."

"My fate?"

"To be mine." Then with certainty: "Your fate."

"Are you one of those Greek sirens, calling your man to an enchanted place?"

"Maybe," she smiled. "You realize, once you've heard my song, you can't resist." She hummed a simple melody, eyeing me. I put my hands over my ears and grimaced. "You're mine," she whispered. "You can't escape —"

We danced a dance older than Pangaea, none of it new. Except to us. Except, like the apple in that ancient garden, Chloé was forbidden. That I knew. Or at least believed. Yet she saw the future differently, utterly disinterested in what left me apprehensive. She became adept at pushing us along, each acceleration orchestrated with subtle confidence, each maneuver imperceptible, discernible to me only in retrospect.

Consequently, necessarily, I lived in Eros' thrall, somnambulant — vacuously unaware of the machinations. Admittedly, we were still feeling our way through a labyrinth, our decreasingly innocent journey prone to derail.

One day I visited a jeweler and bought an expensive necklace, something a smitten middle-aged man might buy his mistress. I recognized the similarities. And I didn't care. The woman helping me, once she'd wrapped the gift, said, "She must be very special."

❧

One night after dinner, Chloé smiled. "You remember Zoey."

"Sure. You saw her last week."

"She made us PB&Js." Her ankles were crossed in a lotus position and the crotch of her blue panties shimmered openly in the soft light. She raised an eyebrow. "Her mom said you were quite the stud when you were cruising."

"Cruising?" Surprised at the turn of the conversation, I said, "What a funny term. Do I know her mom?"

"Jane Louise. Or that's what Zoey's dad yells. Anyway, I didn't get the impression you were friends. Just that she knew about you."

"Sounds like she's embellishing. I can't remember ever being called a stud. Let alone a cruiser."

"Well, her words. She said you had a rep with girls around here. Sowed wild oats. That sort of thing."

"She's full of funny phrases, not to mention bullshit. I never had a rep."

"Yes, you did." She was solemn. "Tell me about those days." I purposely eyed her crotch which, in the shadows, made a lazy curve like a stroke of paint.

"Open up," she said. "This is serious."

"I dated a lot of girls. Sure, I got around. As you know, Justina, your mom, left us when I was eighteen. She and I were kids when we had you. I had a lot of testosterone to blow, and anger too —"

"Ever count them all?"

"The girls?"

She grinned. "As in, slept with."

"You're trying to nail me."

"Not *trying*."

"Zoey's mom did a mind game on you. I played around. I'll take that bullet. But a Romeo? I only liked girls with blue eyes."

"Not violet like mine?"

"No one's like you."

"Liar." She looked pretty, grilling me. "You're about to become a bad dad. Remember who you're talking to —"

"I stopped with that stuff when you turned nine. Maybe you were ten."

"I'm glad you brought that up. I never understood."

"I couldn't imagine bringing a woman home and having to deal with that. With you." I paused, then continued. "Remember the time I came home from a date and you'd been fighting with the babysitter?"

"The crazy lady you'd found. So mean. I hated you for that."

"Yes, you said I rescued you. After she left, I held you while you cried. I thought I'd never calm you down. That's when I decided to quit dating as long as you lived at home. I owed you that."

"So I'm yours, your only one?" she asked. As I nodded, she rose from the couch and stood facing me. "Would you have dated me? When you were sowing oats?"

"That's not an appropriate question."

"Don't lie."

"You're more beautiful than any girl I've known."

She kept those grave eyes on me. "Am I prettier than Mom?"

"Twice as. You've seen her photos."

"Maybe they didn't do her justice—"

"She was attractive. You're beautiful."

She blushed. "If you dated me, would you have slept with me?"

A mad question. When I said nothing, she whispered, "Sometimes you're an idiot."

A few nights later, she called me into her bedroom. "Will you always be here for me?" she asked. I bent and kissed her nose. She raised herself, saying, "You can't leave me, you know. You can't fall in love with someone else."

"You're the one who'll fall in love. I worry every day you'll leave."

"It's not our fate to end like that."

"Fate can't be foreseen."

"You're wrong. I know." She turned quiet, saying, "You don't get it. I'll never love another man. Not like this."

She wore a chemise she'd insisted I buy. Her soft curves glowed in the light coming through the window, moonlight dancing on her headboard. She slipped a hand behind my neck and pulled me down. She pressed my mouth against hers. She ran her fingers through my hair. Minutes went by. When I straightened, she whispered, "Promise me we'll do that again."

"Do what?" I said stupidly. I was in a small daze. A tipping point? I didn't know.

"Your mouth. What you just did. Promise me —"

And after that night there was more. She wasn't demanding, but she became skilled at guiding me here and there, drawing my hand lazily into her soft curves.

❧

Another evening in her room, she said, "I told you I'm yours. Totally. Forever. Yours. What does it take for you to understand?" She reached up to kiss me, whispering, "Yours."

She crawled onto her bed and motioned for me to follow. "Lie on me. Make it real." Closing her eyes she said, "I'll die if you don't —"

For the next fifteen minutes I moved against her, pressing — it all ending with her sudden cries. And then we lay still, her eyes dark, her hair glistening. "You should have taken me."

"I should have never gotten into your bed."

"You're wrong."

"Yes, wrong," I said, my fury rising. I pushed the sheets away and stood. "Have we lost our minds? What the hell are we doing?"

"You're loving me. You've always loved me —"

"As a daughter, never otherwise —"

Shaking her head, she rose on her knees in the bed and beckoned me closer, crooking her finger. And obediently, I stepped closer. She put her hands on my shoulders and whispered, "This is right. So right …"

Yet I was furious and ashamed. I was wrong. And unambiguously certain that these months of pleasure would collapse into some undefined horror. As if she read my mind, she said, "It's all unfolding as decreed."

❧

Afterward, I thought to myself, *Decreed.* Then, *What am I doing?* Still, I rationalized it all. If I broke it off, the emotional damage could be far greater than if I indulged her. She would tire of me soon. She would come to her senses.

Yet too frequently, she would whisper, “I need to be touched. I ... need … to be … touched.”

I was lost. Later, I insisted she go on the pill. But she said no — she was a “half-virgin” and didn’t need protection. One afternoon, with her begging me to touch —knowing “touch me” meant finding a yet greater ecstasy — I climbed on her. As I moved once again, she said, “That’s my *mons Venus* —”

But I didn’t want talk; instead I struggled to control myself. As we kissed I lowered myself. At some point she raised her hips in a crazy lurch toward that sensual heaven she so wanted — and for the first time I let her drive me in, into her taut heat. After minutes, after crying out, she came in what she later described as a “starburst.”

We lay for a moment, absorbing the act, full of each other. I wasn’t sure she was breathing; everything came to a halt. I whispered, “Breathe, Chloé.”

She inhaled and said, “At last, at last — now, do it again.”

Time slowed — one of the blessings of making love — and I lost track of how long we went on, becoming conscious only when she cried out again, her hips shuddering.

After it all, after the fire, as we touched, I said, “What if I just got you pregnant?”

She smiled. “Oh fertility.”

Her levity shocked me. “I’m serious.”

“So am I.” Placing kisses on my cheeks, she rocked against me until she fell asleep.

❧

That summer, lying beside me, she said, “I hated being a half-virgin. I couldn’t tell you, but I hated it.” She spoke sleepily and stretched. The curves of her breasts and legs were like waves. She caught my gaze and grinned. “ ‘Bet you can’t guess what I’m gonna say?” She doubled down. “I ... need ... to be ... touched ... by my outlaw man.”

Many of our mornings were similar, as if on a honeymoon. Once, when I tried to talk about the sense of miraculousness I felt, she dismissed me, saying "No — just destiny."

She gained confidence in us, and in this assurance came increasing composure. She was increasingly my equal. Indeed, her composure, always evident unless making love, was a delight. But lovemaking erased all of that. At those moments when she sought pleasure, she held back nothing, always a vulnerable girl.

I was a perfect foil. Although she called me the outlaw, she refused birth control. When I argued about the foolishness of it, she'd say, "Destiny."

꙳

Chloé's favorite topic at age seven or eight was her grandfather — my father — whom she never met. She could rarely hear enough about his exploits, and had photos of him around her bedroom. He was always in bright sunlight, standing beside one of his planes. He had been an early innovator in the computer field, patenting a half dozen electronic switches. Becoming wealthy, he quit the field at about my age to pursue his real passion, which was flying and restoring antique planes. At one point I think he owned five of them, several for parts, the others flyable and respectably fast.

As a kid I did a fair amount of flying with him, mostly in summers. My mother seemed a distant, although vaguely glamorous, figure. When she appeared for an occasional flight, she dressed with a long scarf and linen blouse. She rarely participated in his longer jaunts. Those were left for me.

I lost them on a fall afternoon after I had turned eighteen. They went up for an inaugural flight in a Cessna he'd completed the day before. The plane was a two-seater, or they would have insisted I come. I watched the flight from the small airstrip near our home. The plane was bumblebee yellow, and I remember it ascending in its small glory, watching my father rock the wings, then feeling sadness as it disappeared on the horizon. I think it remained aloft for six or seven minutes before the engine failed.

Their deaths left me wealthy enough to take responsibility for Clo when she came along eleven months later. In retrospect, I think Clo grieved more than I did at the loss, with her hero worship of the grandfather she never met endlessly endearing.

∾

Chloé and I continued in our haze. One night, I had a dream that would prove prescient, although in those early months I had no insight into its meaning. Nor would I for another year and a half. Only moments before the ceremony with Danaë did I understand.

In the dream, it was morning and we lay in a small cabin overlooking a meadow. We made love, and Chloé's nightgown was damp from the effort. Afterward, I propped myself up beside her and gazed through yellowed windows into the field. In the middle of the grasses, I saw a little girl dancing with abandon. Blue dress, blond hair tied in ribbons, laughing. I sensed instantly this was our daughter (a conclusion which proved stunningly wrong).

Without transition, Chloé and I then sat on a stream's mossy bank at the bottom of the field, the sky gray and the girl dancing animatedly nearby. I put my arm around Chloé — she wore only a cotton skirt. She pointed at the girl and yelled, "Look!"

The little girl now spun, her blue dress a blur, the ribbons a hypnotic whirl. Chloé knelt, reaching out, and the little girl, looking at me intensely, vanished in a flash of sparkles and dust. I woke sweating.

Chloé's side of the bed was empty. I smelled coffee. The dream was too real. I glanced out our window, almost expecting to see a small girl twirling on the lawn.

CHAPTER 3

S hould we care when wakefulness mirrors a dream? Near the end of summer, Chloé wore a crinoline slip, tulle with blue trim, the crinoline semi-translucent. She recognized I had fallen long ago for the lace and ribbons. This, though, was new. When I first saw it, I thought instantly of the little dream-girl's petticoat. Chloé's slip tied at the waist with a ribbon, like the girl's.

Nothing changed, our infatuation inexhaustible. The crinoline skirt became frequent nightwear. She'd often threaten, "If my daddy finds out what you're doing …"

Two months after we first made love, she informed me this was her 14th day. "I'm ovulating. I'm tender — everything needs love. I need you now, all night —"

A late afternoon, we lay in her room. Her skin aglow, her small breasts full. She whispered, "Ovulating girls need love. Touch me. Now and later. And again at night. I know you will —"

I am tempted to describe her as ravenous, but I think of the word's derivation from raven. She was no black-feathered bird with glossy wings. Rather, she was a girl who offered herself without hesitation.

&

I'm sure my uncle Bill, my mother's older brother, never could have imagined Chloe's transformation years after he and his girlfriend stepped in to help after her birth. They had lived down the road from us. Linda taught me the basics about babies and became, in effect, a surrogate mother to Chloé until we left for school. I was eighteen years old with an inheritance and young child in tow.

We'd visit them on holidays. Uncle Bill fawned over Clo. Occasionally, almost two decades later, when I had her deep in the shadows of our bed, dressed only in — using her preferred spelling — *le négligé*, I was conscious of what would be his inevitable disgust.

I still remember a conversation Bill and I had when she was only months old, and how he leaned toward me with gravitas, man-to-man, suggesting I give her up for adoption. I replied, "Impossible. She needs her dad."

Today, if he were alive, he'd say, "I warned you, Jack."

Tempus fugit. Time flies.

One night before the start of her sophomore year at Penn, Chloe said, "We're a couple, aren't we?"

Startled, I hesitated, saying, "I don't know. A couple?"

"Why not?" I saw her eyes watering.

"The word 'couple' implies public acknowledgement, as in, 'all their friends know they sleep together. So they're a couple.' "

"Well, don't we?"

"We do, but as far as I'm aware, no one knows."

She whispered, "So we should marry. Then nobody would hit on me."

"It's not legal to marry, but it's not illegal for you to wear a ring."

She clapped her hands in delight. "You should surprise me. Something sparkly …"

It seemed so simple, yet we couldn't do the normal things a couple did. Still, there might be an option. My consulting work allowed me to live anywhere. She had little clue how well I did. My major client was based in Chicago, while we lived 600 miles east. When I needed face time, I would use video conferencing or fly. If we moved, Chloé might live as my wife. She wouldn't even have to change her name. And no one would question the legitimacy. Our age difference wasn't rare. I had not broached the possibility, though. She seemed happy, but I saw walls closing in.

Weeks later she said, "You've forgotten something."

"I can't imagine."

"My ring. There's a Tiffany's in Philly."

That weekend we drove to the city. Soon Chloé wore her ring, a two-carat classic with a matching band. As the saleswoman ran up my card, Chloé slipped the ring on her left hand and gave me an insincere kiss. "You're such a sweet man. Wait until Daddy finds out what we've done."

We locked eyes. Yet, were I to admit the truth, her eyes were increasingly unreadable. I could penetrate to a certain depth, then encountered disquieting darkness.

That didn't stop me from foolishly considering her mine.

Back in our familiar world, our hidden estate, she reverted to her schoolgirl daytime ruse, followed by explicit evenings. Nothing made me happier. Yet, it was too flammable. Over dinner I asked her whether her friends had noticed the ring.

"Of course," she said. "All my girlfriends are, like, crazy envious. A Tiffany! Why ask?"

"Can you imagine what comes next?"

She appeared innocent. "No."

"If they haven't already, they'll ask, 'Chloé, who's your husband?' "

Wearing a pale bra trimmed in lace, she smiled, "Oh, that. No prob. I've told them a quickie thing happened over a weekend. A young exec. He travels far too much. But it's alright because I live at home. He's okay with that."

"He's okay that you live at home. With your daddy."

"Who loves me fiercely. I always say it's better not to cross my dad."

She'd spun a tale covering her through graduation. Ingenious. By then we'd have moved. "Did your husband knock you up before he left?"

"Daddy! Really! Well," she blushed, "he may have." She brushed away a tear. "We've been trying for a couple months."

"Who's been trying?" She was mixing up her men, imaginary and otherwise. I wasn't sure whether she was playing or upset. Seconds ticked by and she sat silently, polishing her ring with a napkin, watching me without expression.

Later in her room, she offered herself, saying solemnly, "No talk. I'm too combustible."

CHAPTER 4

Chloé continued her study of ancient — what she called classical — Greece. The texts she read became more scholarly. Two she recommended were, I believe, *Portrait of a Priestess* and *Women and Ritual in Ancient Greece*. I read neither.

Her professors were nominal scholars; Chloé wondered if she should transfer to New York University, which offered a more robust program. NYU conducted archeological digs in Greece, Kuwait and Cyprus. We discussed a move to the City, but she wasn't enthusiastic. Anything seemed possible, everything formidable.

Occasionally I would prod her to discuss her fascination with a period that seemed irrelevant. She would say toss-off things like, "Oh, a hunch I'm on to something." She had favorite characters, some of the names I'd heard but knew little about. She described what she called the "A" gods: Aphrodite, Apollo, Artemis, Athene. She was fascinated, too, by the Fates, warning me I had only so many heartbeats till I died.

Before classes one morning, Chloé remarked that she'd changed, her expression wistful, even puzzled. "Something's going on, and I don't know what." She laughed. "And too, my crazy love for you ... There are all these gods bouncing around in my head like I'm possessed. Obsessed with you and possessed by the gods — I wish I knew what was happening." She paused. "It's your fault. First you seduced me. Then the Greeks came."

"Who seduced whom?"

"Okay. One month I'm checking out the guys at Penn, the next none of them measures up to you."

"Who's the Greek god of love?"

"It's a *goddess*, Aphrodite."

"Perhaps she shot you with her arrows."

"That would have been Eros, her son. He does Aphrodite's dirty work."

❧

Neither of us was interested in a debate about society's laws or prohibitions. We agreed: what nonsense. Instead, we would create ashes of ourselves. Fate. Fire. For me, it seemed extraordinarily dangerous, and for Chloé, something preordained.

She liked to say, "Frequency equals quality." One night she said, "Erase my thoughts. I want Zen-love —"

"The French call it 'little death.' "

"I don't need a poet now —"

That night when she slept, she wore only the crinoline skirt. I needed sleep, yet she beat me to it, and I lay awake. Worries about relocation, why she wasn't pregnant after months — turning these thoughts around endlessly, I drifted for an hour. She kept shifting against me restlessly. Perhaps tonight, whatever barrier was between us would collapse under the fulvous moon. Maybe the key was that, if I took her, I had to will the child we wanted.

So I slipped into her. As I always did on nights when lovemaking was one-sided, I held her softly, rocking and chanting a sorcerer's incantation, "Chloé, Chloé —"

As if an angel asleep, being taken in all her heartbreaking innocence, she rocked back against me as she slept. And I responded, only half-trying not to wake her.

At some point Clo felt me and cried, "Oh yes —!"

Afterward, I dared not tell her my thoughts. If once again the loving came to naught, my confession might break her heart. Instead, I whispered, "Sleep, love."

"Lover —" she whispered, and we were lost in another night's darkness.

❧

The next morning Chloé sighed and rolled onto her side. "I had a strange dream last night." Her eyes shimmered. "I sat on a couch with a girl. I knew her, yet I didn't. We looked the same, except she had red hair. She had her hand on mine and we sat in a room where everything—chairs, the tables, walls — seemed to shiver."

After a moment she continued. "She put her arms around me and said we would be together soon. Then she kissed me. It felt … sisterly."

"Well, you don't have a sister. What else?" I said.

"She looked at me for the longest time, and said, 'It'll be a girl.' Then she vanished. I remember glancing at the couch and seeing the indentation where she'd sat. I saw a piece of paper on the cushion and picked it up. It said, 'You're the Spinner' in red ink."

I took her in my arms. "Better than, 'You're a spider.' "

She frowned. "One of the three Fates was called the Spinner." Seeing my incomprehension she turned away, saying, "Really. What the fuck?"

❧

That night in bed she whispered, "So we're gonna have a little girl." She smiled. "Once it happens, I want to move somewhere. We'll get out of here."

She held me for a long moment, tapped my forehead lightly with hers and said, "Okay?"

A little girl. I was astonished. Did we now dream the same dreams, see the same apparitions? I pulled her close and said, "Sure," my hands on her cheeks, my heart pounding. Her eyes were glazed. She moaned and slipped her hands around my neck.

Between semesters at Penn with three weeks free, Clo's focus was flirting and lovemaking. I remained enough of a cynic to know this could last only briefly, so I willingly abandoned deadlines and client demands.

Such fevers always break. I wasn't sure why our love felt so vulnerable, possibly because it seemed inordinately important. Or because Justina, Chloé's mother, had once come and gone in my life as if a ghost.

When we went to bed one night, she smiled, saying, "Aisa ... don't you love it?"

"An ancient town?"

"You are soooo slow," she said, pushing me onto my back, lowering herself. As she rode me, she said, "Aisa ... will be ... our daughter's name."

I don't know what came over me as I usually had impeccable control. That night I didn't. Chloé rode me for mere seconds, then I came as if in a wave of light. She cried out and I did as well, suffused with whatever had overcome us, a sense of something unimaginable occurring.

Later, Chloé stroked my cheeks, suddenly the adult between us, her eyes bottomless. To lighten the solemnity, I said, "Is Aisa with an 'A' or an 'I'?"

She giggled. "It's pronounced like Isa, but starts with an 'A'."

Dazed, I ran a hand over her belly, then lightly up her ribs. I tried to think logically. Real and unreal. Dreams were what —? I thought of the phrase, *Figments of reality.* Yet here we were, the two of us through an unaccountable alchemy, creating an imagined child. Looking into Chloé's eyes, I knew.

As we held each other, I replayed that mad climax. I took my Chloé in heat, oestrus. In her perfect receptivity, my child with child, with *my* child. An ancient brew: the fire of being from fire, from an ancient vivacity. I felt revulsion. And dread.

I could not have known that within seventeen months, the child would be dead, lost forever in a conflagration that swept away Clo, her sister and the child. That night in bed, such things were unimaginable. Guilelessly I said, "You know, too, don't you? What we've done —?"

Eyes closed, she whispered, "Yes."

℀

Afterward, still dazed I fell asleep. She never moved, except to lie against me as we fused. Light filled our room. I woke later, my strength back. My eyes still closed, I felt her near. She sat on the bed. "Miss me?"

"You'd left?"

She grinned — a Cheshire cat. "I showered. You should, too. I've made coffee and toast."

However innocent, she was the initiator, sitting before me, now with child. Her eyes sparkled. She whispered, "I've been *really* taken by my man."

☙

She missed her period. At ten weeks she visited a doctor who, after the usual tests, affirmed what we knew. Further, the test results were unremarkable. What we didn't know was that the tests were unnecessary; Laine would clarify that soon enough.

Chloé, in her crinoline skirt, remained an intoxication. "You know my orgasms are grander than ever, don't you?" she'd say. "There ought to be a law against men like you —"

"There is," I'd say. Such comments earned me an elbow to the ribs.

In retrospect, years after these events, I remain astonished at our blindness. I have described Chloé as naïve, as innocent — as if I had a deeper grasp of what occurred. But I didn't. In less than a year, our understanding of who we were was shattered. Laine transformed us — our guileless fantasies becoming fallacies. Naiveté and innocence, assumptions and convictions — all of it would end.

☙

Chloé stayed small for months. Frankly, I couldn't tell she was pregnant. No one would suspect, but that would change. She knew her friends at school would wonder eventually, as her husband — the enigma — had not been seen. There had been a delay, something about emergencies in branch offices, Hong Kong and Singapore.

Wisely, Chloé wanted out. She made calls to real estate agents, and spent hours viewing listings in distant towns. Once, she came close to choosing a condo in Philly, but wavered. The city was changing. She couldn't imagine our daughter having to navigate urban streets. Then, as weeks passed, Chloé shifted from high rises to country estates. "With enough land, we could own horses," she'd say.

"Not me. Everyone I've ever known who rides goes down. Bones break. And it's constant work to keep stalls clean —"

This dialogue became a pastime, the conversation between us almost memorized like lines in a play. "In the country we might raise chickens," she'd whisper, "and sheep. Lambs are cute. Or get a cow."

I'd pull her onto my lap and tease the swell of her stomach with kisses. "We like grass and trees and privacy, not chickens and cows."

"If not cows, then goats. Goats are smart. And they have weird eyes —"

*

Within the month, Chloé found a Colonial advertised as restored, circa 1810, barely post-revolution. A "charmer," the ad stated, and in the countryside an hour northwest of Philly. The stone house had six bedrooms, a gracious study, a mid-19th century greenhouse, and a carriage house, all on 53 acres in an area with similar homes.

It was expensive, but Chloé insisted we look. Within days we toured the property. The agent appeared to be about my age and Chloé introduced herself as Mrs. Night. We walked through the house repeatedly. Chloé lingered in one room, then another, then repeated her steps, memorizing the light, wall colors and ambience. The back of the house looked out over a wide meadow with a stream running in the rear along a woods line. I liked the natural landscaping, the sense of rolling fields, imagining hounds baying in a hunt.

The agent was rhapsodic, highlighting features that meant little to Chloé. He noted the house was a candidate for the National Register. The owner, he said, was an elderly widow who had updated the house and staged it in American Country style. Chloé asked if the furnishings were included.

He said, "Make an offer. I suspect she'd consider anything."

Clo said we'd think about it. Later, our conversation over dinner revolved around how we would maintain the house. Far too large for us, it was well over 8,500 square feet, with five full baths and an immense study I could use for an office. The master bedroom itself was 24 by 30 feet, with floor-to-ceiling windows overlooking the back meadow. The setting provided more privacy than our current home. As she said, her eyes gleaming, "We'll be in the middle of nowhere, camping all alone."

Before we finished dinner, I emailed an offer to the agent. Within twenty-four hours we concluded negotiations. Financing would not be an issue; I'd pay cash. The house was ours.

Clo promptly dropped out of school, commenting she could always transfer to Penn's campus in Philly. The school decision now left her at home and, given her pregnancy, I did her bidding.

At six months she showed only slightly. To my amusement she viewed our lovemaking as a threesome, always including the child, all of us joined in a cosmic dance. Did it make sense? No, but Chloé's utter conviction trumped my skepticism.

CHAPTER 5

One morning she woke morose and I hesitated to ask — her moods were unpredictable. Our usual conversation over breakfast was muted. After lunch, she walked into my office, looking broken and wearing only a crinoline skirt.

"My clothes don't fit." She opened her hands at her waist, showing me her size.

I put my hands on her waist. Yes, conceivably her waist had expanded from twenty-one inches to twenty-two, and how could I have not noticed? As always, I was culpable.

"And now I've gained seven pounds!" She cried loudly and I pulled her close. She started giggling, then she pushed away, opening space between us, and struck her fists against my chest.

"It's your fault," she cried. "I've never been this big. Never!" Her eyes flashed and she pulled me to her. Kisses later, the crisis blew over. Blameless, Chloé went on.

At her next doctor's appointment, she was told she would gain a pound a week. Her doctor said, "Even ballerinas show at the end."

To me, none of it mattered. If attuned to anything, I knew Chloé's moods. If she wanted to pout, or cry, or beg to be ravished, I gave in to it all. She remained needy but delightful — and she carried our child.

Although Chloé tired in the bedlam of our mobilization — or as she called it in a fake French accent, *le Mobilization* — she amazed me from the moment we said goodbye to our small town to the hour we sat at the dining table of the new manse.

The table that came with the house was double the length of our old one. Feeling ridiculous facing each other from opposite ends, we sat close. Her eyes glowing, she said, "Just us."

The move had gone well. Chloé had hired a local woman, a professional "organizer." When the movers arrived, the woman guided them, making snap decisions, showing them where to place the few large pieces we brought. And to my delight, Chloé was energetic, lighthearted throughout. The two women got along well, and at one point I heard them talking. "When are you due, honey?"

"About five to six weeks. Seems like forever."

The woman laughed. "You've got a good-looking man." She gave Chloé a mock frown. "He *is* good to you, isn't he?"

"The best. He adores me." Her eyes were bright. "And I adore *him*."

Hours after the woman left, an older man drove into our driveway. He reminded me of illustrations in a child's book of Ichabod Crane, the character from *Sleepy Hollow* — gaunt, leaning slightly, thinning silver hair combed back hard.

"Are you my new neighbor?" he asked.

"If you live nearby, I am, sir." I extended my hand.

"Well," he squinted, "I knew the former owner. She retired from a local bank years ago." Shaking my hand he said, "If you ever need anything, I'm about a mile away." He pointed north. "Tom Kendrick. Saw the moving van and thought I'd say hello."

We chatted, Chloé hanging back. Kendrick at last ran out of comments. He shuffled slightly. "The old widow would call me now and then."

"Did she have trouble? Or was she lonely?" I winked.

"No sir. She kept imagining she saw things in the back. By the time I got here, nothing to see." I shrugged and he continued. "Two hunters once, she said. Supposedly dressed in cloaks. Sandals. Hunting with old-fashioned bows. Nothing when I looked."

"She was lucky to have you around."

"The last time she called she'd seen a naked woman bathing in the brook." He laughed. "Can you imagine? If there ever was one, the beauty'd fled before I showed —"

When Clo and I woke the morning after our first night, I opened the windows to the field. A hound, lithe and gray, moved impassively through the grass, stopping to sniff. A neighbor's dog? It may have been twenty feet at the most from where I stood, and it turned to stare, its eyes insouciant, oddly serene, impossibly red. I felt vaguely menaced and stood taller, broadening my chest.

It turned. Something glinted in the woods beyond the stream, and the hound loped off toward the low sun and into the shadows of the oaks beyond the field.

Less than a week before Chloé's due date, our doorbell rang midafternoon. I expected no one and assumed a delivery. Instead, I opened the door to a young woman about Chloé's age. Nervous, twisting her hands together, she said, "Excuse me. I should have called."

Her nervousness made me want to reassure her. She had red hair and flush cheeks, the kind common to English girls. Her eyes were unusually blue, and her skin glowed in the light, setting off her sundress. She was an archetypal beauty, lifted from a pre-Raphaelite painting.

Smiling foolishly, I said, "Okay, so what can I do for you?"

From behind I heard Chloé approaching. Saying nothing, she stared at the girl and then at me, her face questioning. This was no friend of hers. I turned back to the girl, who said, "You're Jack Night, aren't you?"

Before I answered, she caught herself and said, "No, that's not how I wanted to start. Look, I need to talk."

Chloé said in a wifely tone, "Who are you?"

"Laine Lowell. You don't know me." She began to cry and I wondered if the tears were real. In a broken voice, she said, "I've been driving hours —"

I was scrupulous about privacy. Night wasn't on the mailbox. She'd worked to find me. I was tempted to end this now, send her away, but the girl shook, wiping away tears. Chloé shrugged; their dresses were almost identical.

"Okay," I said, stepping aside. Chloé led her to the living room and pointed to a chair. I followed, observing the girl's narrow waist. Fit, she moved with ease. We sat and seconds passed.

She sobbed, caught herself and half-smiled. "This might all be wrong. I could be crazy." She dropped her eyes.

Chloé whispered, "You need to tell us why you're here."

"I said my name. Laine."

"Yes," I said. "Lowell."

"Okay," she said. "… do you remember … well, she would have been young, like twenty years ago. A girl, Michele Lowell?"

Michele? — the name was vaguely familiar. Chloé stood awkwardly and said, "Can I get you something? A drink?"

Laine shook her head. "No, but thanks." I saw doubt forming in the girl's face as if she'd made a terrible miscalculation. "Michele Lowell. That means nothing —?"

I shook my head.

"You would have known her only briefly. I'm her daughter, Laine Low —" Her voice caught and she let out a sob, covering her face again.

Chloé spoke soothingly. "Lane is an unusual name for a girl."

She glanced up, shifting back and forth between us. "It's Laine, like E-laine, but no E. L-a-i-n-e."

I had a growing sense of dread. "What's this about?"

Her knuckles were white. Chloé glanced at me.

Twenty years ago? Michele Lowell? Then I knew. I hadn't given Michele a thought in as many years. I would never have remembered her last name, except for this girl saying it as if I should. Michele was one of the girls I'd played until I'd tired of their smell, or their smiles, or the bows in their hair. Michele would have been sixteen or seventeen. I suppose I knew her for a week at most. So what?

At the time I was full of myself and all the femmes from my little town were interested. Or so I thought. I remembered Chloé's comment months ago: I had been a stud. That's what they must have said behind my back. Not a compliment, but perhaps there was awe at my exploits. Laine's eyes were azure, a disconcerting blue.

"Okay. So how's your mother?" The comment was crass. She understood I wanted this to end.

"You remember her?"

"Barely, hardly. We were kids."

"A few weeks after my birth we moved to upstate New York. I think she wanted to start over."

"She's doing well?" A hollow question.

"No, not really." Her face was pale. "She's dead. Dead and gone."

I still felt nothing: people die. How did she expect me to react? Chloé watched me intently. I said perfunctorily, "I'm so sorry." Then, "You have to realize I haven't thought about Michele — about your mother — for decades. We dated a week. Or a couple days. I barely remember anything —"

"I get it," she said. She unlocked her hands and ran her fingers through her hair. "I should have guessed."

I stood. If she wouldn't, I would. "I don't understand why you're here."

"She died two weeks ago. Told me your name the day before."

My name? I didn't believe it. Where was this going? "I'm sorry but we should wind this up."

She ignored my dismissal and shifted her gaze to Chloé. "Is this your daughter?"

"How do you know I have a daughter?"

"Web research. You're easy to find." She whispered, "I know a lot about you. You're referenced all over the internet. A recluse, a financial genius."

I felt my anger rising. She continued, "Only one Jackson Night from the old hometown."

"Whatever you're selling, I don't want it. And I'm about to call the cops —"

"To say what?" she asked. Her tenor changed. "Say what? Say your daughter's come?"

She didn't take her eyes off me. Chloé covered her mouth with a sharp inhalation. I said, "What?"

"Mom always told me she'd had too many boyfriends. That she'd been a wild thing. I hated that. Before she died, she said she wanted me to know the truth."

"I don't … believe it."

"She said it was you. She said it had to be. She said she'd lied to me. That she'd never slept with anyone before —" Laine's voice broke.

I simply stared at the girl. Chloé sat forward, her eyes tearing. "You're my sister?"

Laine stood and took a small step toward me. A lock of red hair crossed her brow, yet I was caught in the intense blue of her eyes. I whispered, "This is crazy."

We took the last steps toward each other. She stopped, her cheeks flush and she leaped into my arms. She cried and laughed. I spun her around, holding her by the waist. Chloé joined us. We staggered around together in a primal dance.

At last, Chloé broke away, laughing, Laine grinning. I was pleased to see a lovely, intelligent smile. With half-closed eyes, she said, "Kiss? A tiny one?"

My wit, however dim, returned. "No, I never kiss my daughters."

Chloé squealed. "Liar!"

Laine stepped back into my arms and lifted her face. We kissed softly, for a half second. She whispered, "I've wondered about you all my life —"

Chloé's eyes shone and she rocked excitedly. Laine turned and said, "Sister, you're going to have a child!"

"Yeah, a daughter. She's about a week away. This guy," She pointed at me, "has backed me 100 percent. He's quite the father." Laine could not have caught the double entendre. Clo took Laine's hand and they turned, dresses swirling. She said, "We need a real drink! Celebration wine, Daddy! Make mine short."

I bowed to the two with a small smile and left.

Shit. I thought to myself. *What the fuck?* I mechanically went through the steps of being a host. Glasses, napkins, cheese, water, wine. What was happening? I knew nothing about this girl. We were celebrating and I hardly knew her name. *Laine.* Red hair, blue eyes, all as improbable as anything I'd encountered.

I found the girls sitting together talking. They smiled. I stopped, saying. "Okay, I'll admit: you've got the same mouth."

"And eyes," said Chloé.

"And chin," said Laine.

The similarities went beyond that. Both had the same body — slender hips, small breasts, tight waists. I kept that thought to myself, though. Instead I snorted, "But nobody has hair like Laine's. Were you born like that, girl?"

Laine gave me a simple, loving look. " 'Figured I'd inherited it from you. Ha! I'm crushed."

I poured wine and sat across from them. "Tell us about your mom ... What happened?"

"Oh," she said, her eyes changing instantly. "That."

"You don't have to talk about it."

"But I will. Cancer ... esophagus. She learned two months ago. Advanced, spread fast. She'd had no suspicion. Almost as soon as she knew, she was gone."

"Unusual."

"Carcinoma. She smoked ..."

"Laine, I trust you're taken care of?"

"What do you mean?"

"Money. Did she leave you anything?"

"Enough to find you. She had $600 in her account. And I do have the old car."

"So you're broke."

"Uh-huh." Her eyes darted between Chloé and me. "Don't like me now as much as you did before?"

I blurted, "Hardly. You're good here. But I have to know to help."

She sighed. "Yeah, I'm broke. I've got a couple twenties left. Enough for a half tank of gas and a couple meals." Without warning, Laine took Chloé's hand. "You're so pretty," she whispered.

"You're sweet, Laine. Right now, I'm a walrus. Daddy's putting up with me."

"You two are amazing. I can tell you're close."

I said, "That's an understatement. We've been taking care of each other for years." Laine looked at us with curiosity. "And you're going nowhere," I said, "until we get you on your feet." I stood. "I'll help you with your stuff. Give me the car keys and I'll drag in whatever you brought."

"You're saying I can stay? Even a couple days —?"

"Longer if we decide we like you."

She glanced back and forth between us. I said, "Joking."

"There's a suitcase in the trunk. That's it." She handed me keys. "You're sure? I won't stay long —"

Won't stay long. I questioned my sanity. Once I gave her a room, my little paradise with Chloé was over. Laine sat innocently. I extended my hand, pulled her from the chair and into my arms. "You're not going anywhere."

She held me as if she would never let go. I thought, *Identical to holding Chloé.* Two golden pears side by side in the sun.

I stepped back, aware of a ringing in my ears. I searched her eyes for something, anything duplicitous. I saw only tears. "Knock it off." I said. "None of that emotional stuff. You'll kill me."

Chloé still grinned and winked and said, "Dad, I've got to say, all the daughters you make are beautiful!"

"Chloé, what the hell do you mean by 'all'? Should I expect another to show up soon?"

She giggled. "I don't know, *stud.*"

Laine laughed. I was grateful for the levity and tried to take command, sounding stern. "Okay, Laine. You're been here for a half an hour and never asked about where to pee. Chloé, show her. And I'll get her stuff."

Later that afternoon, a storm appeared and a midsummer's rain pummeled the windowpanes. I turned on lights and said to Laine, "I should show you your room."

Chloé asked, "Where are we putting her?"

"The big guest room?"

"Good. Canopy bed. A door that opens to the meadow."

"Yes," I said. "Comfy." And I thought to myself, far from where Chloé and I sleep. Yet, I knew — in a matter of days Laine would guess. I faked calm. Chloé and I needed to speak. I wasn't about to sit with Laine and say, "Oh, your sister and I are lovers. We sleep in the same bed down the hall."

Laine asked, "Chloé, is your room near mine? There's so much to catch up on. I bet we could talk all night!"

"Nah, I'm at the other end of the house. Besides, this kid —" She tapped her stomach. "— is exhausting. I crash early." She grinned. "But you and Dad can talk."

Clo stood, pulled at the waist of her dress and sat on my lap. She wiggled until comfortable. "Right, Dad? As long as you aren't loud."

I put a hand on Chloé's side, trying to appear grandfatherly and felt Aisa kicking. "Thumper. At it again."

To Laine, we must have looked reassuringly domestic. I turned to her and said, "Why don't we all go to dinner before Clo crashes? There's a nice place a couple miles from here. If you didn't bring anything, Chloé can loan you stuff."

Laine blushed and said, "I brought a dress."

"This place is pretty upscale. Dark lights, candles, all of that."

Laine's face filled with mystery. On a hunch, I said, "Okay, I'll bite. You have something suitable?"

"You know the $600? Well, I —" She stopped. "Can I show you?"

Without waiting, Laine ran to her suitcase, opening it and pulling out a classic cocktail dress. She held it against her chest, delighted at our surprise, and turned the dress around so we saw the back. Black, it plunged in the rear, identical in cut to one Chloé had. Clo stared at Laine with fascination.

Laine said, "My fantasy while I tracked you down was, well, when we met, you would invite me to dinner. I wanted to be … pretty."

At a loss for words I took her hand. "Let me show you where to sleep."

Laine and I walked down the hall and I opened the door to the room. She stopped and turned into my arms. Holding her was identical to embracing Chloé. I felt traitorous. Why hadn't Clo come with us? Laine lifted her face and gave me a second kiss, which I found terrifying.

Everything seemed distorted, yet strangely exhilarating. Overwhelmed, I needed to find Clo. I hadn't been alone with her for far too long.

CHAPTER 6

Chloé worked in the kitchen and gave me a quick smile. "Did it go well, the two of you?"

"Yes, I suppose. Laine kissed me again. She seems a complete wreck." I put my hands on her waist. "Give me a kiss, a real one."

She turned her head and smiled. "I like her. What do you think? Tell the truth."

"Me? Totally confused."

"We look like twins."

"Except for that red hair."

"Well … if she had hair like mine, you couldn't tell who's who." She smiled. "Guess I wouldn't like that."

"Has it occurred to you she's smart, and she'll figure out our deal in time?"

"Our 'deal'?"

I whispered, "Ninety-nine percent of people would freak out. She will, too."

"Well, she'll have to know."

"Okay, Chloé, you want to tell her over dinner?"

From her expression she might have been fourteen, but the clueless innocence seemed genuine. She put her arms around me, resting her face on my chest. "I can't hide my affection. I won't. And you're right. She'll have this figured out fast —"

"Okay, your assignment."

Laine walked in wearing the dress. "Ta-da! Check this out!"

Chloé said, "Ta-da meets Ou-la-la. A hot babe just walked in!"

Laine's hair glistened, still wet from her shower. She said, "Hey, you're not ready. I'm starved." Her smile was triumphant.

I felt too comfortable with them and said, "Laine, those eyes should be banned. Bluer than blue."

She appeared hurt for a second. "Mom sometimes called me 'Baby Blue.' I only show these to people I love. Everyone else sees gray ... or that's what I'm told."

I slipped my arm around her. Chloé snuggled in on the other side. I kissed them, saying to Clo, "Okay, kid, you've got ten minutes to clean up or Laine and I leave you here."

Laine pointed at me, saying, "And you better get dressed yourself. I'm not going to a fancy place with a guy in shorts." Even in this warm haze, we had become too familiar.

Fifteen minutes later, we drove to the restaurant. I turned to Laine, "When did you last eat?"

"Hey, I told you I wasn't broke. I had donuts this morning, cheese and wine with you this afternoon." She said it lightly, but I wondered. On arrival, we were seated at a corner table and I sat between them.

Our drinks came and I raised my glass. "To Laine, our missing link —"

Chloé cried, "Yes!"

Laine shook her head. "It's like I'm on Pluto or something. This is all so weird."

Chloé gave her a solemn look. "What's weird, sister?"

"Being here, knowing I'm with family. There'd always been this hole I never understood. There had to be more, you know, but there wasn't. And now I understand. Does that make sense?" I felt her hand on my thigh and she said, "I want to hold hands." I put my hand over hers and turned to Chloé. "You want to hold hands, too?"

Chloé's eyes watered, and she said, "No, it'll make me cry."

Laine's hand twisted in mine, our fingers entwined. She smiled. "I'm still amazed." She kept her hand there until the waiter came for orders, as if afraid I'd disappear. Halfway through dinner, I asked, "Any boyfriends with broken hearts?"

Laine smiled and said, "Nope, never had one of those."

Chloé turned to Laine, "I don't get it. You're stunning."

"I don't know. Maybe I don't trust men. Mom never did. She had a couple boyfriends, but they all left her hurt. One stole jewelry. Another cleaned out her cash. One struck her after a couple drinks … I watched it growing up. Not for me."

Laine paused. "How about you, Chloé? You've at least had sex. That's more than I can say!" She laughed, and I thought, *She's still a virgin.*

Laine continued, "So, can I ask about your boyfriend? Obviously it had to be serious or …" She caught herself. "Well, you know what I mean. I'd hope —" She retreated, saying, "Sorry —"

Chloé smiled. I wondered how she'd respond. *Boyfriend.* These were infested waters. But she surprised me by reaching her arms out and holding Laine. I leaned back to give them room.

"Well," she said, as she sat back in her chair, "it's like this. I've always been a daddy's girl." She smiled broadly as if it was self-evident. "And no one's been able to compare to him. Remember I said he's the best?" Laine nodded cautiously. "Well, you'll see. He is."

"Chloé, you're dodging my question. I wasn't asking about *him.* You're a week away from having a baby. Are you still with the guy?" She paused, scanning Chloé's face. "Ah, my new sister's got mysteries. And her eyes shine."

Chloé leaned forward, glanced at me, and said emphatically, "Our daddy did it."

Laine's eyes shut and she covered her mouth. Chloé hissed, "Open your eyes and look at me." Laine did and Chloé said, "That's right: I'm Daddy's girl."

Laine glanced at me, releasing my hand, stood, then sat. Chloé said quietly, "But I'll share him with you. I mean, not in bed. But you have rights, like me. We're both his …"

Laine drew a long breath and said evenly, "Can I ask something?"

"Sure."

"Like, you sleep together?"

I intervened. "I realize this must be a shock."

"Shock on shock on shock," she said.

"One touch by Chloé led to another by me …"

"What bullshit," she said. "I'm sure that's how it happened. I mean, I've never even had sex and the sister I just met has been fucking the father I just discovered." She paused. "For how long? Did you wait until she was out of Girl Scouts?"

"We first made love a year ago."

Laine's eyes flitted between us, then dimmed. Chloé tried to take her hand and Laine angrily pulled away. Then Laine straightened and shook her hair. She turned to Chloé, her face blank. She examined her and commanded, "Kiss me, little sister." Chloé leaned forward obediently. I watched them kiss. Then Laine broke it off. Chloé cried, her self-restraint unraveling. She looked down, wiping her face. I now expected Laine to stand and dash what remained of her drink at me. Or use her fists. *Kill the monster*, I thought, *Kill the monster-father lurching brokenly in darkened woods.*

Laine shifted her chair and turned, watching my eyes. I noted in confusion that hers were a deep blue that went on and on into a feminine eternity. They weren't bloodshot like Chloé's; they were vast and clear.

She spoke, putting a hand on my arm. "Okay, you too." Again, the commanding voice. Our lips touched. Her hand gripped my arm, her other hand around my neck as she drew me closer, our kiss a strange, fiery thing. When she broke off, she said, "It's okay. What the fuck, we're all in love … Just not what I expected."

She raised her hands, her elbows bent in an odd, hieratic gesture, her palms open. Looking at me she said, "Gotta pee. Have a glass of wine waiting for me when I'm back."

Then she took Chloé's hand, lifting her to her feet. "We'll go together. Leave our father here to sulk —"

CHAPTER 7

That night Chloé retired within minutes of our return. She unzipped her dress before us and said, "Knew I'd be exhausted. You guys stay and talk." We watched her half-waddle down the hall.

"She's beautiful," Laine whispered.

I put my hand on Laine's shoulder. "Another drink?"

"Yes."

We went to the sitting room off the kitchen with its rocking chair and couch. I sat on the couch and patted the cushion. She sat, turning to face me. Tired, I kissed the top of her head. She smiled. "Do I have to worry about you seducing me?" Her eyes sparkled.

I laughed, the sound tired. "Hardly."

"Ah-huh." After a moment she said, "Do I get whacked if I call you 'stud'?"

"Yes. Try Dad." She moved against me lightly.

"Okay, stud. As Chloé said, we owe our existence to your astounding stud-ness."

"You can be hard-headed, can't you? You don't want to irritate me on day one."

"Once a stud, always a stud. That's what Mom said."

"You're lying."

"Okay, I guess I'm not good at that. Mom wasn't, either. I always suspected she'd conned me about not knowing my dad. I still don't get it, though."

"You said she was independent."

"Yes, I guess."

"Any university under your belt, Laine?"

"A couple semesters, then Mom got sick. I'm smart though. Don't imagine I'm a dumb-ass pushover."

"Never thought so."

"I test at 148."

"Big deal. My exact IQ."

"You're kidding."

"152, if I'm forced to be exact."

"Does a high IQ indicate a high libido?"

"What?!" I laughed.

"That's what Mom said when I got my test results. She said it as if dismayed."

High IQ or not, I could hardly form sentences. The day had been too long. "If you've got a high libido, you know it, babe."

"Well, I do then," she said. "High. Higher than high."

I studied her face, her eyes and slightly open mouth. I said, "Too tired tonight. I'm crashing as we try to impress each other. Time to call it quits."

A trace of disappointment crossed her face, then she smiled. "I found you, Dad! Walk me to my room?"

I stood and pulled her up. She kept smiling as we walked down the stairs to the bedrooms. I stopped at her door. She lifted her head and I backed away, saying, "So, goodnight." She pressed herself against me briefly, and turned into her room.

In my bedroom Chloé slept. I undressed and got into bed. As I snuggled, she murmured. I put an arm around her, exhausted.

In the morning, I let her sleep and pulled on a bathrobe. My second daughter sat on a stool in the kitchen drinking coffee. She said, "Hi, Dad."

"How long have you been up?"

"Oh, a while. Lots to think about."

"No kidding."

"Do I get a hug?"

I walked over and she stood, slipping her arms around me. "Um, still can't believe."

"Did you sleep?"

"I did ... Feels like I've known you forever." She wore a guest bathrobe.

"We might make an intellectual case for that," I said. "I mean, knowing me forever. If your life started yesterday, then you've known me forever. Well, at least for a day. Or something."

"Or something. I'm waiting to detect that high IQ .... Waiting, waiting!"

"No jokes. I'm not awake. Coffee?"

She reached for the pot and said, "How?"

"A little milk."

"Me, too." She surveyed the kitchen. "I'll help around here. You have to tell me what to do."

For the first time that morning, I observed her dispassionately. She hadn't combed her hair. Wild, it seemed a mass of fiery sedges, sharp-tipped rushes. I imagined briars hidden in her hair, golden ribbons mixed with burning locks, a wash of peppermint on her lips. She strode over, paused, closing her eyes. Turning her face up, she placed her lips on mine, whispering, "A morning kiss?"

Everything except Laine's body against mine vanished. Her lips opened as we kissed and I pushed her away, a flicker of anger stirring. I whispered, "I think I no longer trust you."

"Should I trust *you*? Remember, I don't trust men. Any men."

"I don't even know who you are."

"You like my kisses," she whispered.

"Kisses make you a dangerous girl."

I heard Chloé approaching. She entered the kitchen with a bright, "Good morning, everyone!"

I said with humor, "Contractions yet?"

"No, but I'm lucky after last night's cuddle."

Laine asked, "What happened?"

Chloé giggled. "Could have been my imagination, but he's a dangerous guy."

Laine smiled. "Dangerous is a popular word." Chloé gave her a puzzled look. Laine said. "That's what Dad called me a minute ago."

"Daddy," Chloé admonished, "don't be mean."

Laine said, "After a simple morning kiss."

I shrugged, the coffee kicking in. I said, "You'll learn to kiss. You'll get better—"

Laine put up fists. "Watch it, dude."

Chloé squealed again, "Daddy! No girl wants to hear she kisses badly!"

I stepped over to Laine and gave her a public hug. "Sorry. I can be slow."

She ground her knuckles into my side, smiling for Chloé. "Fine," she said. "But that's the last kiss you get." The knuckle stung.

Chloé smiled. "I'm glad you two can make up. I'm hardly awake and I walk into a father-daughter spat!" She giggled.

Laine smirked. "Don't worry. I'll learn how to kiss."

Chloé waggled her finger at us and said, "I expect you two to get along. Dad, you treat Laine like you treat me or I'll beat you up."

I laughed. "First, Laine wants to give me a roundhouse, and you're gonna beat me up. If you two get together, I'm a goner."

Laine said. "I like the sound of that. Who needs men?"

Scanning the back meadow I saw deer in the open field—a stag and four does—six prongs on the male. Odd, I thought. Deer bed down in the day. I'd seen an occasional one along the edge of the woods at dusk. This was a small herd, seemingly indifferent to the flooding gold of the sun. I said, "Deer!"

Laine and Chloé giggled, neither looking.

CHAPTER 8

Emails from clients accumulated and I reluctantly responded. The girls came into my office around noon, Clo announcing lunch. In the dining room, she said, "I had a couple contractions while Laine and I talked. But they've stopped."

Laine kissed her cheek. The two appeared to have known each other forever. They were exhilarated, joyful. Such intense camaraderie — all after a couple hours of talk.

"Laine needs clothes, Dad. I went through her stuff this morning and I'll bet she's had nothing new in years." She paused. "So we have to do something. I gave her my card. And orders to shop. Clothes, undies, socks, shoes."

I'd already reached the same conclusion. Laine wore jeans and a sweatshirt. I guessed those—along with her cocktail dress and the sundress she wore when she arrived—were all she had.

"Absolutely," I said, "you've got a huge closet and Chloé and I are fashionistas." I glanced at my khaki shorts and the wrinkled tee I'd pulled on. "We'll expect the same of you."

She smiled cautiously. "Maybe. I mean, I don't know whether I'll be here more than a couple days —"

Chloé cried, "Stop! We just discovered you —!"

Laine hugged her again and said, "No crying. You'll upset little Aisa."
I noticed she pronounced the name with a silent A, *Isa*.

I turned to Laine. "This place is yours now. It's not a temporary
squat, and no one throws you out."

"No matter what?" she said.

I paused: those intense blue eyes. "We're mad about you."

A smile flickered on her face, open, unaffected. "Okay," she said. "I
guess I'll hang out with my fam awhile."

Chloé tried to deflect it all. "Dad, take her shopping. Get us a pizza
for dinner. I'll text if anything comes up —"

"Okay, we go shopping in thirty. Whatever you need to do, Laine, do
it now."

"Yes, sir." She scooted off.

Chloé grinned. "I imagine she'll stay."

"So do I. And thanks. I can be dense at times."

"As in, 'Then there were two daughters' …"

"Yeah, but you're more than a daughter." I gave her a hug. "I'm
concerned about leaving you …"

"I'm good. You can goof off with her awhile." She whispered, "Make
sure she gets lots of stuff. Let her splurge."

"Got it."

"She has two bras—hopeless ones like my old schoolgirl stuff. She
went gaga when she saw mine. Who knows what she really thinks —"

From behind us Laine said, "I think you're the coolest. And your stuff
is to die for. What I think is I'm in heaven."

"How much did you hear?" Chloé asked.

"Oh, all of it. Enough that I know Dad'll have remorse if he doesn't
get me half of what you have."

Kissing Chloé's forehead, I offered Laine my arm. In the car, I turned
and said, "We'll skip the mall. There's a high-end area in the old down-
town with three or four boutiques."

Laine said, "You know, I've loved you all my life. There were times
when I hated you. But mostly, I dreamed about how this would be …"
She reached and took my hand off the wheel and entangled her fingers
in mine. "It's like I'm on a date."

I hated mawkishness. "Be warned: I don't do shopping well."

"She said you have impeccable taste. It'll be easy. Clo and I are identical — just pretend I'm her."

We pulled into a parking slot before the shops. "Are you into fashion?"

"I've never owned anything but hand-me-downs from Mom." For over three hours Laine bought clothes, shoes, silk scarves, even a shiny blue raincoat. She conferred with me on selections a few times, but had excellent taste. Finally, we approached the lingerie shop. "I'll do this alone."

She pointed across the street. "There's a coffee shop. Go." To sweeten the command, she kissed me on the cheek. Some time later she joined me.

"Success?"

"You'll think I'm competing with Chloé."

"You can get away with anything except competing with Clo."

"Taken as a warning."

"Coffee?"

"A smoked butterscotch frappuccino."

I smiled. "For a girl who's broke, you know what you want."

"I'm good at saving up nickels and dimes."

When I came back with her frap, I stared into fathomless eyes. "A drink for a girl who keeps secrets."

The innocent smile. "Are you toying with me?"

"Testing. I haven't figured you out entirely."

"Probing my defenses?"

"Easy as counting your ribs."

She pretended to shiver. "All eighteen?"

"Ah," I said. "'Got you on that. You better have twenty-four or you're no daughter of mine."

I saw a flicker of irritation. "You'll have to count them and let me know."

"Half your ribs are beneath your breasts. An embarrassing exam."

"I don't care." Her face was impassive.

"A challenge we'll save for another time. I never count ribs in a coffee shop. At least not a girl's."

She smiled. "God, I like you." She tossed her hair off her shoulders.

"You make me glow. No one's ever done that. Even with Mom, I felt like an accident."

I reached for her hand and kissed her wrist. Picking up pizzas, we drove home. Twice Laine asked if we could hold hands. She shifted in her seat, facing me. "Thanks for being so generous. I love it all. I'm overwhelmed. And a little high."

We found Chloé napping, but she woke and smiled. "Well?"

Laine crowed, "Success! I got lots of stuff. And he was great like you said he'd be." In her joy she whirled in a circle, an amazingly controlled pirouette, her arms out gracefully. It seemed vaguely familiar. She turned twice, her eyes never leaving mine, then slowed.

Chloé sat, her feet dangling over the side of the bed and said, "She dances, too," then clapped her hands. "We're the same size. Whatever you got fits me!"

Laine took Chloé's hand. "Come on. I'll show you everything —"

They went down the hall. In my office I scanned messages. Concentrating was difficult. Swiveling my chair, I viewed the meadow in the back. Part of my enthusiasm for the house was this sight: field, stream, forest. At the moment, no deer, no hound to return my gaze. A light breeze stirred the grass. As I looked I was shaken by a realization: the dance she'd done a half hour earlier was the little dream-girl's.

Minutes passed as I stared out the window. I knew, but knew nothing. The small brook beyond the edge of the grass, too far away for me to see, was there, the same stream in the dreams. Now Laine's pirouette … Did she know? I felt like an idiot.

My office door opened and the girls ran in. "Look!" Chloé squealed. "Have you ever seen anything prettier?"

Laine spun in a blue dress with narrow pleats. I saw yellow crinoline in layers and a flash of panties, her hair full of golden ties. Chloé clapped and after several pirouettes, Laine cried, "Dizzy!" and plunked into my lap, looping her arms around my neck. She whispered, "Yes?"

She put her face an inch from mine. "You like my dress, don't you?"

"Yes," I said. "Yes."

Chloé thought it all hilarious. Laine, though, kept staring at me. Chloé grabbed her hand. "Come on, we'll get the pizza ready now —"

I watched them leave, Chloé pulling Laine along. As I watched, time slowed and Laine's blue dress moved in a languorous spiral, twisting in a leisurely wave around her waist. The back of the dress lifted as she moved under the door frame, underwear flashing, salmon, almost transparent. Red hair, ribbons. Laine's eyes fixed on mine as Clo dragged her away. Then, the room quieted in the half light. Through the windows, I watched the meadow ... and remembered an old saying: *Tempus fugit, memento mori* — Time flies, remember death. A professor of mine, now dead, once scrawled the phrase across a blackboard.

I sat in a loose, hallucinogenic torpor. Or simply lassitude. The meadow, too, sang a clotted tune of lethargy, a mirror to the listless clouds overhead. If I'd had any sense, I would have brought Laine's visit to an end and sent her away forever, into the world, into the summer's fire and stifling heat.

CHAPTER 9

Dinner was memorable, but largely because Laine sat across from me with her cobalt eyes. My daughter, my lost and found daughter —

Her attention throughout the meal was on Chloé, the two of them animated. Laine was flawless, her composure perfect. Clo kept glancing at me, smiling. I was careful to be there for her. And although Laine rarely engaged me, I recognized us as locked in a curious contest.

Something had occurred a half hour earlier. Perhaps she understood. However, if she did, I didn't. That word reappeared, like an ancient cur with teeth exposed: *Dangerous.* I thought, *Perhaps I'm the danger, not Laine.* Perhaps we were all bewitched. Something inexplicable had occurred.

After every series of giggles, the girls embraced, laughed, hugged and gave high fives at their manifest brilliance. And I saw a new side of Chloé. Perhaps they were mere sisters, the combustion set afire by that alone. Regardless, I sat entranced, caught in it all. At one point in the dinner, Laine turned and said, "You're checking me out."

I thought my observations discrete. "Sure," I said, "I am."

Chloé said, "He does that all the time —"

Laine smiled. She had rung our doorbell less than thirty-two hours earlier. And now Chloé and I felt we had known her forever. I should have been more wary. Laine yawned and said, "I'm done. You guys outlasted me tonight." Chloé gave her a small shove and said, "Bet I beat you to bed!"

My watch read 1:30. "Okay, I'll close up. Goodnight, girls."

Chloé said indignantly, "You have to tuck her in."

Laine stood, putting her hand on my arm affectionately. "That would be nice. Give me a few minutes first." She left us there.

Chloé seemed enchanted. "Daddy, we're so lucky."

"Any more contractions?"

"Nope. Aisa's quiet."

"Good. You're a beautiful thing, Clo. I can't wait till we're a threesome."

"You mean foursome." she said. "Laine's gonna be here. I hope she'll stay —" She kissed me. "Now go and tuck her in. She's never had a real daddy."

I rolled my eyes. "I've been missing in action her entire life."

"You'll do. Just be sweet." She smiled and shoved me down the hall. Then I heard, "Dad?" I turned and Chloé said, "Take your time. I bet she'd like a story or something. There's a lot of little girl inside that one."

I shook my head. "I won't be long."

Laine's end of the house was almost dark, a single nightlight in the hall. I stopped at her door and knocked. She said, "Come in." Standing in front of the mirror combing her hair, she glanced and smiled. "I'm almost done!"

In an old tee, Laine turned, and I realized she was in one of my undershirts and boxers. She said, "Chloé's okay with it. You're not angry?" I took a step closer and she said, "All that stuff I bought earlier, and I forgot nightclothes."

"I thought you bought a couple gowns."

"Have to unwrap them, I guess." She said huskily, "I always wanted to wear my daddy's underwear." She corrected herself. "I mean, to bed." Then she flounced over and put her arms around my neck. "You don't care!"

"I don't." I found my hands on her waist.

"Remember I told you about my libido?"

"I remember indelibly. Sky high."

"It happens whenever I'm around men."

"Says the girl who trusts no man—?"

"Trust and libido are different things."

She pressed against me. I drew her closer, feeling her breathe. She sighed, "See? Heaven."

"We have to talk."

With a pout, she said, "No. Tell me a goodnight story or something —"

"What happened back in my office? Those turns?"

She averted her eyes, shaking her head. "You know."

"I don't."

"Guess I danced too fast. You saw my panties. You shouldn't have." She whispered, "You were taken by them, weren't you?"

"I wasn't."

"You were. Now *you're* the liar."

"That's not what I want to talk about." I glanced at the chair beside her dresser and saw the panties, laid neatly on top of the petticoat, there for me.

"Admit it. You love them—"

I paused and said, "Here's a dreadful cliché, Laine. But it's the best I've got. There, for a minute, in my office, time stopped. As you danced. And something happened between us."

"Oh." She shrugged. "Just one of those cosmic shifts." She raised herself, placing a sparrow's kiss on my mouth.

"Something … changed."

Her mouth now inches from mine, she said, "Why are you torturing me?"

"What?"

"You know." The lilting voice and glowing eyes: Laine, who did not exist two days earlier. She continued, "You have an obligation. Kissing lessons."

I thought of Chloé, who had admonished us. I was hers, not Laine's. She kissed me again on the corner of my mouth. "You have to make me un-innocent."

"That's not a word."

"If I used it and you understood, it's a word!"

"You know Zen combat?" She shook her head. I said, "Masters spar with words until one of them acknowledges being bettered."

"How does the loser concede?"

"With a deep bow." With a sad smile, I let her go, stepped back and bowed from the waist. Then I grabbed her, pushing her back and pinning her on the bed. "What I didn't tell you is they also revel in surprises."

"Oh," she said, breathing hard. I could smell a faint vanilla, Clo's cinnamon. She blinked and said, "God, you're fun. You realize I'm in love?"

"It's mutual."

"Well, now you have me anyway you want. I'm helpless."

"I may not release you."

"Chloé would rescue me."

"You're right. Her patience will eventually run out."

She pretended to wiggle against me. "Know what you should do?"

"No."

"Count my ribs. See if I qualify to be in the fam. Like a final test." She was impassive. "I love tests."

"You have such damned dark eyes."

"No, they're blue."

"Not blue. Fucking blue mysterious."

"Look, let's get it over with. Count my ribs. You know you should."

"And if you don't have a dozen a side?"

"Then, toss me out."

I released her hands and took her tee, pulling it up. Her chest was freckled. The freckles drifted like tiny orange stars down her chest, disappearing into the circular pool of her areolae. Salmon nipples, the color of her panties. Her breasts moved slightly on her ribs, trembling knolls, her eyes wide. "You better have twelve pairs. Let's see—"

"What a stupid exam." An insolent young girl's voice.

I placed my right thumb on her lowest rib. "One," I said, moving higher. "Two, three, four—" At six, I had already pushed into the lower rise of her breast. I met her eyes again. "You okay?"

"Did Chloé ever say you've got hot thumbs?"

"And you have endless freckles." She sighed. My thumb edged higher. "Seven ...." At this point my palm cupped her and I continued. "Eight, nine ...."

"She whispered, "Oh my—"

After a moment I said, "Twelve per side. You're a perfect girl."

She smiled softly. I pulled her tee down and stood.

CHAPTER 10

The next morning the three of us sat at breakfast, Chloé robed and Laine still wearing my tee and boxers. Chloé stretched. "So, how does Dad's underwear fit?"

Laine giggled. "Perfectly. Boxers are kinda sexy."

Chloé reached across the table and took one of Laine's hands, studying her fingers, then said solemnly, "I hear you're a perfect girl."

Laine flushed, her cheeks burning. "Is that what you hear?"

"Ah-huh. Lots of ribs and you wanted kissing lessons, too."

"Clo —"

"Don't 'Clo' me. I'm pissed."

Laine looked at me. I reached for the carafe. "Coffee?"

Ignoring me, Chloé said, "Even now, your nipples are poking out!"

Laine's eyes narrowed. "Okay, if you're going to start —"

Chloé cut her off, standing, her index finger like a pistol. "Don't think you can fool with him behind my back —!"

Laine appeared crushed. She stood, about to flee. Chloé said, "Got you, didn't I? Sit down —" She pointed at Laine. "Sit!"

Laine did so reluctantly. Chloé returned to her chair, continuing, "I guessed from the first night. I'm not as whip smart as you, but I knew what you thought when you found out we slept together —"

"Chloé!" Laine cried.

"I'm gonna go on," she said. "Ideas are in Dad's head, too. I saw it. You two merged like two streams into one big, happy river." She stood again, then sat. "But I don't want you to ever leave. That's right. Dad and I are mad about you." She turned to me. "Aren't we?"

"Sure." My heart pounded.

"What you don't see is he and I are forever. I mean, we're so tight no one can come between us. It's that tight —"

Laine blurted out, "I wasn't trying to —"

Chloé interjected, "Let me go on … I can't be jealous because there can't be a threat. We're forever. You know what that means?"

Laine started to cry.

"That means I'm rattling you. It's good to see I can."

Laine wiped her eyes. "I don't get it."

"It's okay. Dad can show you stuff. He's good. He's yours. He's yours because he's mine. We can share. Maybe he'll say in a couple months, you and he are forever, too. That won't bother me. Nothing splits us apart. I've loved him since time began —"

Chloé got up, lifting Laine's face and said, "This is the last time you'll cry about loving Dad." Clo kissed her, turning to me. "You told me she wasn't any good."

"She kisses girls better than she does men."

Laine cried, "Okay, okay, enough!"

"Laine?" Chloé asked. "Here's what I say. You and Dad love each other. It's obvious. It's what's right. I love you both and I don't care how you make it work." She stopped and held her lower stomach with both hands. "Aisa's kicking, harder now." Looking at Laine, she said, "Aisa will be your niece and sister, too."

"Crazy."

Chloé pointed. "It's all his fault. Hunk-of-man. An outlaw man."

I wondered if this was bravado. From behind, I put my arms around her. "Chloé, no girl shares her man. You'd be driven out of Nashville if you sang that song."

"I wouldn't share you with anyone. I'll share you just with her." Laine still sat. "We're sisters. And you're hunk enough for two."

Laine said, "Those are crazy lyrics, girl —" She went on, "I'm putting 'em to music, listen —" Laine sung,

Wouldn't share you with just anyone,
I'll share you just with her.
Laine and I are sisters, and
You're hunk enough for two …

Chloé clapped a rhythm, then both sang in a country twang,

Wouldn't share you with just anyone,
I'd share you just with her,
'Cause Laine and I are sisters, and
You're hunk enough for two …

At the end they squealed in delight. Chloé took Laine's hand. "Good. No, great. But poor Daddy …"

Laine laughed. "He'll be exhausted —?"

"Uh-huh."

"You claim he's a hunk of man —" Laine said solemnly, examining her hands. "Well, from my perspective that remains to be seen —"

I groaned. "Enough! I'm going downstairs." Back in my office, I almost locked the door. Instead, I sat at my desk, not bothering with work. I swiveled and scanned the meadow. A hawk circled the sky. And this morning I saw the stream, a first. There it was, meandering along the edge of the meadow: the view was that of my dreams.

Swept away by a vision of girls and meadow grass and brooks, I imagined Laine, fifteen years younger, in a mad twirl in that blue dress. And Chloé, before she became pregnant, lying on Laine's bed. And Laine's wild hair, a rash of fiery strands sparkling in the light, her feet moving faster and faster in the dirt.

Too many anomalies. Laine had adroitly dodged all questions, and knew I knew. These coincidences did not occur in reality, yet Laine was real. Frustrated, I got up and left the office. The guest room was several doors down and, as I passed, I saw movement. I paused and saw her at her mirror brushing. Her lilting, happy voice cried, "Hi, big guy!" Laine wore a pair of my shorts and a bra cut too low.

"Chloé loaned me the shorts. It's okay, right? We're the same."

"Am I invited in?"

"Always. Help me out!" She handed me the brush, freckles

descending into her ribboned bra, nipples pushing against the fabric's mesh. "I do 100 strokes a day. I'm at 70. Finish me, Dad."

Her hair absorbed the sunlight off the windows in a flood of gold. I pulled the brush through her hair, counting as I did. The force of each stroke made her sway slightly. I needed to brace us, and said, "I'll have a better hold like this —" I put one arm around her ribs, her hip pressed against me.

"Like my new bra? Chloé told me what to get. Before you and I went shopping. She said you like yellow."

"Laine …" I hesitated. "We should talk."

"You know," she said, "All this touching is getting me bothered. You stroking my hair, caressing me —"

"The blue dress, the little girl, the meadow —"

"Silly mysteries, Dad. Spirals that follow spirals into some old seashell. There aren't good answers to everything. And you're trying to outsmart the Fates. No one does that." She pushed me away. "You're at 122. I thought you'd never quit!"

She leaned up to kiss and said, "Are all kisses between a man and woman so soft? Do they ever kiss differently —?"

Her arms locked around my neck. I pushed her away. "I should check on Clo."

"No, she said I have you for the morning. She has baby stuff to do. And it's only 9:15. You're mine till lunch —"

"Then, let's take a walk. You haven't been to my meadow. I want to take you there while the weather's good. There's a stream, grasses —"

"I know all about the meadow." Her eyes flashed.

"Before we walk, look —" I went to her window.

Taking a step, shielding her eyes, she said, "I know the view."

"We'll walk to the stream."

"I don't want to put on a top."

"No need. There's little difference between that and a bikini. And there's privacy here. No other house for a mile."

She hesitated. "I don't like bees or snakes."

"I'll protect you. From everything bad."

"You're a good daddy." She leaped into my arms and gave me a kiss. Putting her down, I said, "Where are your shoes?"

She slipped on flip-flops and grabbed a straw hat. I leaned out into the hallway and yelled, "Chloé! We'll be in the back —!" From some-where she replied, "Okay!"

Opening Laine's door into the field, I pulled her along into the meadow. Midway I stopped, pointing toward an eight-foot circle where grass was flattened. I said, "Grass is beaten down."

"That's where deer sleep."

"No —" I realized instantly, although I had not seen it before. "That's from dancing. Someone doing spins and pirouettes."

"Deer, not dancing," Laine said.

"You know the view from the windows in your room?"

She spit out, "Where you and Chloé sometimes fuck?"

"No. Not there."

"Yes, you have."

"Laine."

"What?" The sun washed her face and chest. A light breeze lifted her hair, spinning it sideways. She stepped into the circle. "Is this what you want —?"

She softly turned. Only a professional with years of time on the floor could have had such precision. She did so a second time and kicked off her flip-flops ... a third turn, barefoot, somewhat faster. "Now a real one," she cried out. And she began to dance the identical dance I'd dreamed. Her hair flamed, the locks phosphorescent. I stepped back to avoid her arms.

As she spun, she eyed me, laughing giddily, reaching her arms toward the sky. Then she slowed, maintaining the precision. When she stopped, she sighed. "Got to catch my breath."

Angry, I left her there and walked to the stream. I heard her cry, "Hey, you!" but I felt only dread and saw the same mossy bank from the dreams. I was slipping back and forth from dreams to waking. The stream sang as it flowed around and over rocks. It was a foot deep, tea-colored and clean, a friendly, happy stream.

Then I heard footsteps and she mounted my back, her thighs grip-ping my sides and arms around my shoulders. She nibbled at my ear. I felt the mesh of her bra against my back. And as she toyed with me, she chanted softly, "Daddy, Daddy —"

I rolled her off and onto her back in the grass. Before she reacted I lay between her legs, pinning her arms back. She watched me and I released her wrists, saying, "Fake, phony, trickster Laine —" and tickled her. She fought back and a breast popped out of the half-cup bra as her straps fell. She twisted against me, laughing.

She laughed the same as she danced, her eyes never leaving mine. I played rough with her, pretending to count her ribs again. She fought, begging me to stop. At last we slowed, warily assessing each other. As she caught her breath, she stuffed her breast back into the bra, grinning recklessly. In the little girl voice she said, "I don't care!"

I pinned her wrists back again, pressing her down. Without hesitation, she started hip circles, her hair tangled, wild. I whispered, "All I missed in the field as you danced was your dress. Not the same without it and the petticoat. "

"In my closet. I'll wear them for you next I dance."

" 'Next I dance'? I'll wear them *next I dance*? That sounds Shakespearean —"

Her blue eyes drowned me. Peculiar. Only the light breeze through the nearby trees kept me anchored to reality. That and the pressure I kept against her mons. The sun splashed across her chest. My eyes wandered over her freckles. I noticed my khaki shorts, loose around her waist, now unzipped.

"Laine, who the fuck are you?"

"One of the Fates." The corners of her mouth turned up. "I'm here to protect you." I shook my head.

She said, "There's a downside you should know, a downside to being a virgin protectress. If I lose my virginity, I lose my power to protect. If it happens, that's bad news —"

"As simple as you being my long lost daughter, right?"

"Nothing's complicated."

"You don't even know how to kiss, and you're worrying about virginity?"

"We start lessons soon. One thing leads to another."

"I'm worrying about who'll be the teacher."

"Be careful," she said. "Be careful where you go."

I released her and propped myself up, looking around the meadow. I felt anger, a growing irritation. "You know, I should plow this place up. Get a contractor in here to rip it out. I'll pipe the stream. That would end this craziness."

She grabbed my shoulder and shook her head. "No. We can tease, but not that."

"Have I hit a nerve?"

She spoke casually, "I like it here. Out in the grass."

"Thirty minutes ago, you didn't want to leave your room."

"That was then."

I swiveled around. "I don't know. I've probably made a mistake leaving it like this. There's enough room here for a couple holes of golf or a tennis court—"

"You can't."

"Why?"

"This is …" She closed her eyes and whispered without a hint of humor, "You can't because once we've lain like this, it's become sacred ground."

"Oh?" She sighed. I squinted into her eyes: the blue there was the sky itself, reality, it seemed, defined by Laine. "How old are you?"

"You know."

"Twenty."

"Yes."

"You're not my daughter, are you?"

"No."

"No?"

"Yes. I am. No, I'm not. Yes, I am."

"Daughters don't seduce their fathers."

"Chloé puts a lie to that." She looked younger. Seconds earlier, I'd been mad with desire. But the girl I pinned now seemed all innocence. Her eyes glowed with love and trust—a nubile ingénue. Was there no end to the play, the veils and the fraud?

I felt watched and turned to the house. In the kitchen windows overlooking the field, I saw Chloé, a dark silhouette obvious in the glass. How long had she been there? She waved excitedly. I knew she understood I had Laine pinned. It would have been easy to be aware of my arousal, Laine's flushed cheeks.

I turned to Laine who said, "You're mine another hour."

"No," I said. "Game's over."

CHAPTER 11

We walked back to the house. Clo met us, saying, "You two look happy."

Laine dashed to her. "A hug!" and they threw their arms around each other. Chloé stage whispered, "Was he good to you?"

"He asks too many questions!"

Chloé glanced at me. "Have you been grilling Laine?"

An inexplicable dread came over me. "Possibly. I'm still putting it together."

They both laughed. The sound seemed to roar off the walls. Barely there, almost subvocal, it slammed into my ears. Had I hallucinated?

Laine's face became serene and Clo looked at the floor — and an immense silence prevailed. Laine leaned into Chloé and said, "I'm starved. Oranges and almonds?" She smiled at me, saying, "You must be starving, too." As if I were a child, she gestured for me to follow.

In the kitchen the two worked together. I sat on a stool watching. If Chloé were not pregnant, they would look identical. The patrimony seemed indisputable.

As I agonized, Laine turned and took a few fast steps into my arms: the seductive girl, plying sorcery. She must have sensed my unease and indeed, I doubted myself, wondering if I were being disloyal, caught in an amalgam of sensations.

On the one hand, I half-believed she was my daughter, half-convinced she was indeed a child of an old fling. On the other, the elements of her slow revelations seemed staged. I was reminded of Chloé's unveiling, the leisurely seduction, pressing step-by-step. Daughter or actor? And I admitted my deep discomfort at Chloé's consent, their instant camaraderie.

Laine slipped her arms around my neck and started blowing kisses at my ear. Chloé stood nearby. "Daddy, Daddy," Laine cooed. "Give me real kisses. You're not sincere. And don't say no."

I broke away, my senses bewildered. "You smell like oranges." Even my attempt at normal conversation was awkward.

Laine sighed, "Blood oranges," and ran her hands over my chest. "Feel my sticky fingers." She stepped away a foot and leaned against the wall, tossing her hair. "Daddy, we should play what-if. For instance, what if I'm *not* your daughter?"

I said tiredly, "You are."

"Yes, I am. No, I'm not. Yes, I am." Then she threw herself into my arms again, crying, "Oh, *Daddy*!"

Chloé placed our plates around the table. Her eyes half-amused. We sat and Chloé said, "Isn't it like we've been waiting for Laine all our lives?"

A strap on Laine's bra slipped down her right arm, and she pulled it up. "No," I said. "I never expected Laine."

"I did. I've been waiting for her forever."

"No you haven't."

"I used to dream about her." She glanced at Laine and smiled. Although incredulous, I recognized my protests as tedious. "Really? What did you dream?"

"Oh, nothing."

Laine caught my eye and shrugged. "In the next week," she smiled, "there'll be three sisters. Crazy, huh?" Laine now looked sixteen, with a scrubbed, fresh, young girl's pout. Our chameleon.

Chloé squealed, "The three Fates. They were sisters, too!"

I had the vaguest recollection of the Fates. Laine scooted her chair up to mine, and put one arm around my neck. "They were sisters, gorgeous like us. Goddesses, I guess."

"You guess?"

"Okay, they were. They were always topless, wore white skirts and ... they were all-powerful."

I said, "What did they do?"

"They decide how long everyone lives."

Chloé interjected. "If they want to end someone's life, they do. Snip." I was aware they were using the present tense.

Then, two things happened. Laine stood and pointed toward the field. "Chloé! She's come!" But Chloé didn't turn, groaning and gripping her stomach instead. I looked back and forth between Chloé and the window. Her contractions had begun. Even so, they were preempted by the appearance of a young woman in the meadow, standing in the dirt circle. She held a bow. Waves of long hair tangled with the arrows in her quiver.

Astonishingly beautiful, she wore a white tunic that stopped at her knees. It had multiple folds, cinched with a purple belt across her ribs. The tunic was cut modestly, loose at her neck.

My impression of her age was conjecture, but she appeared to be about twenty-five. In dark sandals with straps criss-crossing her calves, she wore a golden necklace, her eyes severe. These images, however briefly seen, shocked me.

Laine pressed against my side. As we watched, the woman stooped in the field and clapped her hands as if calling a dog. Indeed, a massive hound came loping up and circled her, its tail wagging madly. She stroked it, stood and turned away. Scanning right and left, she strode toward the woods with the beast. At the stream, she made an easy leap to the far bank and disappeared.

At that same moment, Chloé groaned again. She doubled over and stammered, "It's time."

My heart beat loudly. The sun, so brilliant earlier, slipped behind ochre clouds, its fire veiled. I felt a sudden headache. And heard a faint, goddamned ringing.

"Dad? Chloé's started. She won't last long —"

Laine helped Chloé stand, bracing her as they headed for the car. I turned back to the windows, surveying the field: it was tranquil, verdant in its summer flush. Two sparrows pecked at sand in the circle. Then, I saw the hound sitting on the stream bank watching me.

CHAPTER 12

Early that afternoon Clo gave birth to a robust and angry-fisted child. The attending doctor said it was the easiest and fastest delivery of her career, and opined Clo would be home within a day.

A nurse eased Aisa onto Chloé's chest. We walked into her room and Laine laughed, "It's done. The three are one!" Laine crawled onto the bed with Chloé and they nestled, Clo too emotional to speak. She listened while a nurse recited the hospital's policy of keeping mother and child overnight. When Chloé shook her head, the nurse said, "Yeah, honey, you showed us how to do it. Miracles or not, you're here for the night."

Then Clo slept. Laine eased off the bed and gave me a solemn look. "Jack, you don't realize what you've done." *Jack?* Her eyes were humorless. She ran her hands through her hair, tossing it back.

"Your hair's like fire, resplendent."

"I don't need a poet now."

"That's Chloé's line."

She glanced at Clo. "Such a sweet girl. Someone should put Aisa in her crib."

"Laine, that quote about a poet is right out of Chloé's mouth. From long ago."

"Yes, you were about to make love one night."

I tried to keep my voice low but I heard it rising. "If we're flaunting mysteries, what the hell happened in the backyard as Chloé started labor?"

Laine turned and put a finger to her lips. "Let's go home. I can't tell you anything. Or at least not everything. But we'll talk."

At home we separated briefly. When we met in the kitchen, Laine wore a camisole and boxers. My easy repartee was gone. As we faced each other momentarily, she said, "Pinot, please. Cold."

I scanned the field and brook. Nothing. The yard was already in long shadows. I got Laine's wine and poured myself a scotch. We sat across from each other and she said, "I like to hang out at old bookstores. There aren't too many left."

" 'Don't like the smell in those places."

"Entropy. The fate of all things."

I took in her camisole, lingering so she couldn't mistake my gaze. The thin straps over her shoulders were black. Her arms glowed in the incandescence. "Nice top," I said.

She shrugged. "You bought it for me."

"That applies to most of what you wear."

"Threw out the old stuff," she said. "Except my dresses. Anyway, bookstores ... A week before I left to find you, I browsed one called Cast Outs."

"Used books?"

"Yes. I found an unbound sheaf of poems, page after page."

I listened.

"Someone's old manuscript. A treasure. What's strange is the cover page. It's titled, *Cigarillos*, and unsigned. No author's name, no date. It might be a work by T. S. Eliot, or Mary Blow, the local baker's niece .... Odd, huh?"

"Poetry isn't my thing."

She appeared exasperated. "So I call the author Poet X."

"Laine, let's talk about what's going on."

"Sure."

"How do I put this?" She cocked her head expectantly. I said, "You're not what you pretend."

She stuck her tongue out, then ran a thumb under a strap. With her other hand, she lightly brushed her palm over her breast, smoothing the silk. "And you want answers —"

I nodded.

"The woman you saw in the field is a goddess. A deity. I mean, in the old sense." She grinned as if making a colossal jest, a real groaner.

I played along. "She *was* gorgeous."

"The woman you saw — you're saying she's hot?" She laughed.

"A local actress? A friend you brought along? I don't get it. No one would go to the woods dressed like that."

"She isn't an actress. She's a hunter. A huntress."

"Laine!"

"You saw the bow and arrows."

I tried a new tact. "Why is she here?"

"She protects us."

"First, an unsung daughter shows up. Who says she'll protect me. A short time later, a goddess makes an appearance, here to protect ... who? You?" We stared at each other. "Does she have a name?"

Laine stood abruptly. "Artemis."

One of Clo's A-gods. "Artemis. Why not Madison? Or Ashley?"

"Because she's Artemis."

"Why call her a goddess?" I thought about Kendrick's comments: in our backyard, the widow's claims, seeing hunters in cloaks, naked women in the stream.

"Because she is."

"You want me to take you seriously?"

"Of course."

"A goddess?"

"Artemis."

"Laine, gods and goddesses don't exist in my world. Nor prophets or soothsayers. That's all a salve for the lost."

"Goddesses have nothing to do with soothsayers." She sat, her limbs splayed like a starfish in exasperation.

"Aren't goddesses female gods?"

"Stop being so rational," she said. "Artemis is changeless. She's ancient."

I smiled again. "The woman we saw was about twenty-five."

She laughed. "I didn't expect more, but I hoped."

"That's a put-down?"

"Goddesses stop aging in their mid-twenties. We become immutable —"

I stood and turned to the window overlooking the field. I guessed I would see nothing, but pretending to scan the meadow, bought time. I turned to her. "Laine, you said 'We.' You meant 'They.' Get your damn pronouns straight."

"I did."

"You're my fucking daughter. You're twenty years old —"

She rolled her eyes. And giggled as if we were discussing a TV skit. Her eyes twinkled. "Daddy's inquisition."

"Shouldn't you level with me?"

"Shouldn't I learn to kiss?"

"What?"

"You've forgotten. Kissing lessons tonight."

"Laine, Chloé's in the hospital. How can you even talk like that?"

"It's okay. She said you would show me how. While she's recovering. Come on, we're alone —"

"So you admit this Artemis is a joke."

"Decide what's more important: talking or kissing," she said.

As I poured another scotch, I asked, "Wine?"

She shrugged. I filled her glass. My watch read 7:15. "We have time to talk."

"Lessons first. I'm insatiable."

"You're distracting me. Chloé calls *herself* insatiable."

"We're the same, both insatiable. At least she was."

I sighed. "Let's get back to goddesses. Lessons later. You said *We*. Not *They*."

Laine seemed blasé about it all. Finishing her wine she said, "Okay. Let's go snorkeling. Into the deep." She smiled and spoke rapidly. "A thousand years before Christianity, a small number of extraordinarily gifted children emerged. All came from a town at the eastern foothills of Mount Olympus in Greece. It's called Dion." She went on. "It was a brief evolutionary spasm. Some saw it as a paroxysm. Perspective depended on whether you were of the blessed. Or a father watching your child surpass you daily."

"Remember I studied finance. You'll lose me with 'evolutionary' anything."

"What I'm saying is that over a decade's time, a small, select group of boys and girls materialized in the Mediterranean. About 1,200 BCE. They …" She paused. "You're bored."

"I'm not. Go on —"

"They were gifted. But most notably, the townspeople realized they were … special. If they fell off a wall, nobody had to put them together again. They bounced up, intact. If an angry sheepherder hit one on the back of the head with a club, the child laughed. Then sent him tumbling."

I remained expressionless.

"Of course their families couldn't relate. They matured more quickly than normal children. Like four times faster. Inevitably the children banded together and left."

I smiled. She smiled back. "I've lost you, haven't I?"

"It's a history Clo would like."

"Did you tell her bedtime stories?"

"Yes, I'd make up things to put her to sleep … polkadot unicorns, purple cows."

"How old was she?"

"I told her silly stories as late as last year. If she couldn't sleep."

"Tell me one tonight!" she cried.

I said nothing. Bon mots seemed impossible. Laine played me easily. She continued with apparent exasperation, "The kids grew to maturity in five to six years compared to twenty for any other kid. To explain these children, the local tribe described them as gods. And goddesses. As the children exercised their powers, they visited various terrors on villagers who disparaged them."

"I'm not sure where we're heading with this."

"You wanted an explanation."

"So … what 'terrors'?"

"The cliché stuff. Throwing lightning bolts, turning maidens into trees, raping dewy young things, making springs burst from rocks. General run-of-the-mill mayhem."

"Is any of this apropos?"

"Artemis is one of those girls, a goddess — and one of the most important. In time she became the protectress of young girls, and of any goddess girls who had not grown to maturity. That's why she appeared today."

"And so, I presume, we circle back to 'We.' "

"Yes."

Silence hung between us. Of course, I instantly made the connection. The implication, as breathtaking as it seemed, was clear. Once again — this time, consciously — she ran a thumb under a camisole strap. I lifted my eyes to hers and said, "This goddess appeared because —?"

"Mainly because of Aisa's birth. Clo and I can protect ourselves. But our baby sister can't."

My ears rung. It was utterly absurd, Laine suggesting the three were somehow connected to a distant goddess. Or were goddesses themselves. And absurd to say a goddess — Artemis — was keeping them from harm.

"Why would any of you need protection?"

"It's complicated."

CHAPTER 13

S he said, "There's much more. First, there's reanimation. That's how
we've returned."

"As in, after a long night's sleep?"

"Yes."

"I'm glad Clo's not here."

"There's nothing she doesn't know. She's up to speed." She paused.
"Jack, I'll tell you more, but later. You're protecting us, too. So you have
to know, but I'm tired of you rolling your eyes. And I have to unwind."
She watched me, then whispered, "I hold my men to promises."

I'd lost all acuity. Clo crossed my mind, but Clo wasn't here. And she
appeared to have given permission … to Laine and me … to do what?
But before I could go on, Laine interjected, "Lessons. You promised."

"Kissing," I said, "is a risky game." Although nothing overtly had
changed, I suddenly knew this girl was not my daughter. She was not
even an aspirant. And I was but a diversion, mere entertainment. And
this long evening —? Likely, a tawdry detour in a longer game.

She looked at me and said, "None of what you're thinking is true."

"How do you know what I'm thinking?"

"I know!" she cried. "And I know what we should do! Pretend I'm a
sleeping princess and you're the prince. Give me a kiss to wake me from
eternal sleep —"

"A wake-up kiss?" She nodded. The upshot was kaleidoscopic: her hair, the violet camisole, her cobalt eyes. She waited, eyes begging. I bent and placed my mouth on her neck. She moaned as I kissed under her ear. She kept one hand on my neck and continued to make noises, shifting her legs. She tasted like Chloé. Then I kissed her mouth, playing her game. She yielded at once, opening, sighing, "Don't stop —"

"Who's teaching whom tonight?"

"You, me. Me and you."

After a time I broke away. "Have you awakened, princess?"

She closed her eyes. "Yes. From a terrible sleep. But now that I'm awake, I confess: I need more." Her eyes were sultry. "See, I missed your touch when growing up."

I let my hand drift down her ribs to her belly. She whispered, "Kissing lessons only. Only kissing lessons."

"What if I'm seducing you?"

Her eyes were fathomless. "I'm chaste. I'm a maiden."

"And a pretender. Someone else's daughter —"

"Not yours?"

"Not mine."

"So my visit to you and Clo has just been meretricious?"

" 'Meretricious'? You mean 'not it seems?' Who the hell are you? And out in the meadow, you used, 'Next I dance.' "

She half-pouted. "I'm a virgin goddess. We speak funny." She was flush with a lovely glow, her cheeks russet. I could smell a cocktail of fragrances, an unidentifiable bouquet. Even in the dim kitchen light, her freckles cascaded into her camisole in a seductive opalescence. I poured us a drink, and she assumed her droll, sad-eyed puppy look.

"Should I glance outside?" I asked. "See if Artemis is watching in the dark?"

"She's not here. She's guarding Aisa."

My cell phone chirped. A text. I swiped the screen and read, *They're releasing me at noon tomorrow! Can't wait to get away. —C*

I replied we'd see her then.

"A warning: in a couple months at most, Aisa will appear to be a one-year-old." Laine said. "There's no time for a normal childhood. Then in a year, she'll look four or five. By six, she'll appear nineteen or twenty. Don't be surprised."

"But Clo developed normally, no crazy growth … a normal kid."

"As did I, but we had time, and any acceleration would have made us freaks. Here, in this little Eden, Aisa can flourish without anyone knowing."

The chthonic ringing started again in my ears, although it seemed modulated—the tone changing, softening and directed by something I failed to grasp. I watched her carefully. She sat aimlessly thumbing both cami straps, her eyes closed, the fabric tight. The raw silk cast a sheen. She opened her eyes. "Earlier, I'd said it's complicated. I called it reanimation. I should have told you more. The word itself is less than clear." She paused. "It's a sanctioned word. It's how we define … re-intensification of life."

I raised my glass of scotch. "Here's to sanctioned re-intensification."

She ignored me. "Imagine an oil lantern. The wick is so low you have to strain to see it burning. Someone turns it up. The lamp becomes bright, reanimated."

"What are we talking about?"

Her eyes filled with tears. "We're talking about me, Clo and Aisa." To my shock her fist hit the table. "Don't you understand? We've been asleep! Now we're not —"

"*We?*"

"The three of us." She appeared furious.

"Reject, reject," I intoned. "I watched Chloé's birth. I was only eighteen. I've raised her since, been her protector every day of her life. Not some fanciful Artemis."

"You were chosen."

"Laine, we make a little headway, then we hit a wall. If I know anything, I know who I am. And I sure as hell am not 'chosen.' "

She grinned with tears still in her eyes, frowning prettily. "Am I being bad?"

After a long pause, I said, "Bad is good, good is bad. For instance, Clo likes to be spanked when she's bad. It's good."

"I knew that about my girl."

"Careful, you'll be over my knees before you blink."

She reached out. "Her, not me. I like kisses." She tapped her lips. "Here. Reanimate me. Wake me from this sleep —"

"I thought I'd done that. But if I failed earlier, let's reawaken a languorous girl." I kissed a corner of her mouth, reveling in the darting touches of her tongue. Her eyes closed and she started her little moans.

"Oh my," her voice vibrated. She shook her hair. Perhaps it was the dim light, but her eyes lost their uncertainty, almost as if an aperture opened in her pupils, an azure lens widening, blue again, cloudless, long-lashed, her cheeks undulating — I was lost in it all and told myself: *concentrate on her words, ignore the rest.*

As if she read my mind, she straightened, pragmatic. "And the time is —?"

I checked my cell phone. "About ten."

"Sit down," she said, pointing to a chair, her expression exacting.

She shifted, conspicuously, impenetrably businesslike. I struggled to take these twists seriously, to pay sufficient attention to avoid her disapproval. I suppressed my sarcasm, pulled a chair out and dutifully sat.

She hooked one of her feet around my ankle. Under normal circumstances I would have found the gesture charming. With intensity, she said, "Now I'll compress thousands of years into less."

I waited, conscious of the chairs, the painting of a pastoral landscape on the wall, our drinking glasses, Laine's ardent face. Every object seemed swathed in a translucent light, the effect that of an old tintype with its edges softly burnt from chemicals. I slumped in my chair, disinclined to listen, yet enthralled.

In a gesture more typical of a six-year-old, she wiped her lips with the back of her hand. "All of this, all I've described, however disjointedly, is a part of a whole. I just haven't made it easy for you."

"If you're saying you've given me puzzle pieces without a picture, I agree."

"You've gotten hints."

"Few."

"I've been evasive. The problem is that you won't believe me. Let's go back to earlier this evening, when I talked about those kids."

"Who were called divine by the unwashed."

"Yes. One of the original girls grew into a restless, dark personality. Imagine a girl from today with spiked hair and face tattoos. A derringer tucked in her bra. A hell-raiser with a bottle of gin half out her purse. A nose-ring or two. She was aptly called Night. Or at the time, Nyx."

"Night? 'N' or 'K'?"

"N …" She caught herself. "Sometimes the stars align."

I leaned forward and she said, "There's more. Nyx gave birth to numerous children, including three girls called the Moirai. Some of the children resulted from her coupling with other gods, some she generated herself. No matter how many kids, she looked like a kick-ass starlet." Laine seemed enthralled by this divulgence.

"This is or isn't a myth?"

"Isn't." A Botticellian beauty radiated from Laine's face, her lips, her cheeks, black lashes cradling her eyes — she was Chloé's opposite in intensity. "I'm showing you the puzzle's picture. That's what you want."

"Too slowly."

"There's more. I mentioned the Moirai?" I nodded. "They were later called the Fates, or Enchanters, or the Apportioners."

"Three sisters. I'm getting bits of this. But this all sounds like Disney."

"It's not. They were powerful. They controlled the fortunes of mortals and gods alike."

"What were their names? Chloé, Laine and Aisa?"

Standing, she said, "Klotho, Lachesis and … yes, Aisa."

That hellish ringing again. "I'm way over my head, girl."

She was dazzling, her eyes resplendent. "No, you're not."

"I'm to believe you and Chloé and even Aisa are these ancient goddesses, somehow revived."

She spread her arms out, saying, "Yes —"

I half expected her to levitate. She stared at me a moment. Inexplicably, she smiled. Then, in exquisite slow motion, she rotated her upper trunk, her right arm moving away. I watched her cock her palm against an unseen force, then release it as if from a spring and she slapped me. My head spun sideways. Reflexively, I raised my hands, expecting her to strike again. I tasted blood.

"Laine! What the hell —?"

She dropped her hand and slumped. Her hair fell into her face. Then she recovered, her feet apart, knees bent, hands out — a defensive position. I stepped back. She breathed hard, her eyes fluttering.

CHAPTER 14

"I t's bleeding," she sobbed, looking at my mouth. Then she was in my arms. After a split-second embrace, she pushed back. "I split your lip."

She kissed it lightly, running her tongue over the open break. I felt exhausted. I freed myself from her and sat. "Better that than a lightning bolt."

She moved abruptly to my lap and relaxed against me, softening into my chest and arms. I regretted the last hour or two, the indulgent, treacherous lessons, her attempts to explain herself. The cloying mysteries — the ridiculous story of ancient children.

She was an enigma, and tonight's events — this mad climax — a shock. Only inches away, breathing on my neck, she whispered, "You love me?"

As I returned her gaze I was overwhelmed. She seemed irresistible. "Do you?" she demanded loudly.

"Sure —"

"Love," she said bitterly. "Love. I don't know what that means." Her lashes were wet and I half-kissed her eyes, conscious of my lip.

She shuddered. "You still don't get it, do you?" To my silence she said, " 'Don't trust me? That's okay. We are not intended for love."

"We?"

"Yes, the 'We' who establish each person's lifespan, who ensure it runs its course and who snuff it out. I've tried to tell you in a hundred ways."

She tightened her arms around me. I allowed myself to roll my palms around the softness above her hips and said, "The three sisters, the three Fates."

"Our mother, our ur-mother, was Nyx."

"Yes, the bad-ass starlet. But that happened impossibly long ago. You cannot be that."

Her face seemed a sea under moonlight, tranquil, the anger, the anguish gone. I teased my hands around her ribs as if polishing an exquisite vase. She closed her eyes, rocked her head.

"Laine, for all I know you're just a girl, captured by some cult. That none of this is true."

Eyes closed she said, "I'm no one's captive." She leaned up and kissed my cheek. "Except yours."

"Sure. I've been chosen."

"Yes, you're chosen. To reanimate us from what became an endless sleep. You've unwittingly set the machine humming again."

"A necessary male."

"Our stud."

That faultless face, those high cheeks — demure yet implacable. I checked my rising anger. "All of this is fantastic. But I still have to connect the dots. I haven't. I'm only halfway there."

"I've left nothing out."

"Except why you disappeared so long ago." Her eyes were soft. I continued, "Humans always die. Who needs Fates?"

"Look, humans are always born and die because we created a birth-death machine, a biology-based algorithm to work steadily while we slept."

"Slept?"

"An elective retreat. Humans go into comas. Gods and goddesses do, too. Ours was self-induced. We decided to withdraw. It happened around CE 390, a dark time leading to darker and darker times —"

"The Fates and all the other gods just quit?"

"Yes, the Fates — and the male gods. The women — nymphs and goddesses — vanished incognito into wildlands in what's now France, Spain and Greece."

Before I replied my cell phone chirped. I read a second text from Clo. *Can't sleep. You guys awake?*

Talking.

Good, Clo wrote. *Aisa's sleeping.*

See you soon.

Be sweet to Laine, she continued. *She can share our bed tonight. xxx*

I texted a neutral-faced emoji, then turned to Laine. "Your vigilant sister. And she says you sleep with me tonight."

"What's hers is mine."

"Bullshit."

"Don't get caught up in the fictions of your time."

"Meaning —?"

"Morality. Our morality is amorality."

Circles crisscrossing circles. "You say the gods followed you into that long sleep, but not the goddesses."

"Imagine a weariness. Rest appealed to many. Artemis, the other goddesses and their attendants agreed to join us, but at the last moment backed out. They proved prescient. I woke again, but the male gods spiraled into an unrecoverable darkness."

❧

I was weary, deeply weary of it all and we agreed to stop. In the bedroom, without being told, she got into Clo's side of the bed. I smiled at her red hair, black cami, my boxers pulled half down her hips. I slipped in on the other side and turned off the bedside lamp. "This is exciting," her voice a whisper. "I've never slept … with a man."

"I should pull those boxers off, you tease." We whispered as if someone were listening.

In the quiet she said, "Daddy? Play any way you want, but we can't have intercourse. Don't make me break your arm —"

I took her by the waist, pulling her against me. She snuggled, whispering into my ear, "I feel you. You're aroused." Her voice was excited, and I took her bottom in my hands, teasing the cleft between her cheeks.

Pushing away, she turned on her back, opening her legs, an angel spreading wings. "I've never had a man on me —"

"You've forgotten outside? We did this by the stream."

"You're too literal. *Pretend* I've never felt a man —" I lowered myself, adjusting my weight. Even through the boxers I felt her, the heat seductive, her breathing uneven.

"Push now —" She moved in the circlets she'd learned beside the stream. "And can we kiss?" She giggled. "While we press?"

"No. My lip is killing me. Thanks to my ninja daughter."

"Oh god," she said with exaggeration. "Here lays a gorgeous and bothered girl. And her man says, 'Sorry, kisses out.' "

For four or five minutes we made pretend love — my captive, my enchantress moaning, bucking against me, her hands on my back, moans turning to cries, until she let out a small whimper.

"Oh," she whispered. I stroked her cheek and as she quieted, "What was that?" Then she smiled. "Oh … of course. Will Chloé be upset?"

"Didn't she give permission?"

"Yes. To do anything but make love." She gave me a suggestive glance. "That wasn't making love?"

"No."

She hugged me. "In the morning we'll open the blinds to the sky and birds. I want you to wake me with your hands touching everywhere. "

"At dawn. Now let's sleep."

She pushed against me and we spooned. Chloé, Laine, Chloé, Laine. In the dark—in the silence — the girls were indistinguishable. I kissed her and she slept.

❧

I woke at dawn to the smell of a cigarette. As I rolled to my side, I saw her against the bed-board, smoking. She said, "I know —"

"You smoke?"

"You don't mind?" She took the pack on the nightstand and shook one out halfway and winked. "Want one? We could be a twosome."

Cigarettes killed her mother. Or so she'd said. Her hips were inches from me, and I sunk my teeth into her thigh. In surprise she opened her legs and twisted away. But I held her firmly.

Putting out her smoke, she lay beneath me with a half smile — an archaic Greek kore, all the marble turned to soft flesh. I was wondering whether to pin her against the sheets when I heard a sound from outside:

a terrifying growl that cascaded into howls. I sprung off the bed and ran to the windows, pulling blinds aside.

In the center of the meadow lay an enormous three-headed dog, thrashing, arrows jutting from its sides. Each head was open-mouthed, tongues lolling, teeth caught in a sustained howl, each head writhing erratically. Its sides were bloodied, its eyes outraged.

On the edge of the meadow, only ten feet from the dog, stood the same young woman — Artemis? — white tunic, golden bow in hand, severe eyes. Her beauty mocked the beast's hideousness.

A dozen young girls stood beside her, all dressed similarly, each with a belt binding their tunics below their breasts. I guessed they were twelve to fifteen. Their expressions were inscrutable, the blank look of fashion models on a runway.

I felt Laine's arms encircle me from the back, her chest against my shoulder blades. The dog-thing continued thrashing in the grass, its howls weakening. It shook, then slumped against the ground, its eyes empty. In stagecraft impossible to orchestrate with such exquisite timing, a large crow swept in from a tree and perched on the carcass, glancing sideways and cawing into the dawn.

Artemis raised her bow skyward and released an arrow. The troupe — or the troop, and I wasn't certain what they were — turned, leaped the stream and sauntered into the woods. A number of the girls wore short tunics and their movement into the trees sent the thin material high up their thighs: they were bare-assed.

Laine still held me from behind and said, "All for you. And no, I wasn't warned."

I might have spoken or reacted in any number of ways, but I stood with my hands on the windowsill, continuing to watch the field. The beast lay still, the crow now driving its beak repeatedly into its blooded sides. Nothing appeared staged. A light breeze moved through the grasses, stirring the dry leaves of the oaks.

At that moment the only thing indisputably real was Laine, and I turned, her arms around my neck. We held until she whispered, "I'll make coffee."

"Just like that?"

She nodded, untangled and left. I turned back. Impossible: no dog now, but the ground was bloodied. A silence descended onto my sacred field.

I dressed and walked into the meadow, stopping at the edge. The immense silence remained. The wind had died. Grass was broken and dirt scraped away: long claw marks. I squatted, examining the ground.

Aware there could be no explanation, I stood, searching the woods, then backed slowly into the house. Before I opened the door the ringing in my head began. I stopped briefly, leaning against a wall and pressed my fingers to my head. I knew Laine waited upstairs, probably having watched it all.

As expected, I found her by the windows. Without speaking, I approached her: intense blue eyes, soot-black eyelashes. She gave me a small smile — only the corners of her mouth flickered. "What did you find out there?"

"Let's not play games."

"Oh?"

"You see, now I have to accept or reject all of this. If I accept it, my entire world — predictable and pleasant, explodes. And if I buy in, I become a party to ... something impossible."

"If you reject it —?"

"If I reject it, I reject you. Then you're out of here."

She watched me. "Me, Chloé and the baby, on the curb?"

The damned ringing again: I pressed my temples and closed my eyes. Before seconds passed, her lips brushed mine, her hand on my chest. Her kiss reminded me of my lip. She casually pulled my right hand to her breast. "We're yours. You're ours. Let's never talk about disentangling what has taken so long to engage."

I absentmindedly thumbed her nipple. She said, "You know you'll make me moan if you keep that up."

"Because you're insatiable."

"Helplessly."

"A three-headed beast just died outside. An everyday event."

"That was Cerberus. Or a facsimile."

"Cerberus?"

"A monster from the underworld."

"And so we circle back to last night's talk."

"Yes. Which ended when I slapped you."

"And what did you say the moment beforehand?"

She shrugged. "That we had decided to withdraw."

"Yes, exactly. *We*. Withdraw."

She smiled and pulled my hands to her waist. "We withdrew in the fall of CE 394, our exit precipitated by the acts of another monster — may as well have been that three-headed beast. Theodosius the Great, the Roman Emperor. He ordered the destruction of our temples, all non-Christian places of worship throughout the world. It was like *Kristallnacht* in Germany, except the stormtroopers were frenzied Christians."

"Theodosius?"

"Flavius Theodosius Augustus. Almost the last of a 300-year line of corrupt emperors. Mighty Theodosius. For a few years before and after, all our sacred groves were burned, temple virgins raped. Temples to Athene, to Apollo and his sister, Artemis, all brought down, the beloved statues smashed by the thousands, libraries burned. The highest civilization the world has ever known, one that flourished for two millennium, destroyed in mere decades in the name of the Christ."

"You lived through this."

"Oh yes. The three of us, the most powerful of all the gods. Even so, with all of our authority, we remained naïve, just the dutiful administrators of birth and death.

"His edicts became a sledgehammer precipitating what you now call the Dark Ages. The smoke and fires from that stupidity smoldered for at least a thousand years. Some would say it smolders still. A small consolation is that Theodosius died within a year of his edict, cursed by those of us he sought to stop."

I let her go, watching her rage.

"We despaired for humanity. Imagine an all-powerful despot today ordering the destruction of every record of philosophy, mathematics, science and technology … banishing all beliefs except those of his own."

"Horrific," I said. "But I still don't get 'withdraw.' If the Fates are so powerful, why didn't you stop it all?"

She smiled warily. "Our motivation to create order from chaos comes from believing the system we save has merit. By then, the majority of Romans believed in the cross."

CHAPTER 15

W e held and she ran her hands over my sides, pressed one palm against my belly, then ran both hands up my chest, moving against me, sighing, mewling her particular, alluring song. "— I'm just a girl."

I held her by the waist, letting my fingers play outside the boxers. She said, "For thousands of years we were regulated like the lives we monitored. We were diligent, disciplined. Clo spun the threads of life, I measured their length and Aisa cut them mercilessly. All simple self-control. How could it be otherwise? Sex leads to eventual death for each lover and their children .... It's the sauce of that unbroken cycle, sperm and eggs meeting in a bloody sea—"

"I get it," I said. "Enough. We all die. Sex is a catalyst. But if you are what you say — what you say the three of you are — why the interest now in something goddesses spurn?"

"Sex? Goddesses are needy, too. The Fates, though, are held to high expectations. We stay virgins so we can see life with purity." She made little circlets against me with her tummy, pressing each breast back and forth against my chest as she spoke. "With our return we've discovered unexpected … fire."

"Where?"

"In all the places fevers burn."

"Does that make you human?"

"No, for Aphrodite and others, love is all. Passionate love. Don't imagine sex is exclusive to humans. Perhaps —" She kissed my neck. "— it's a force that drives the universe."

She continued. "The expectation, the mandate for our purity remains. Aisa and I must be virgins. Clo was freed so she might give birth."

"And I am just a baby-maker?"

"Not entirely. Clo's passion, her love, is real. And, until I arrived a few days ago, she knew nothing about this. She had suspicions, but not a suspicion of being part of this … continuum. No suspicion she is who she is."

"Her interest in classical Greece?"

"I planted that. To ease the transition." She put a hand on my cheek.

"You're the intellect behind all of this, aren't you?" She nodded. "And the bullshit about a 148 IQ? What's a realistic number?"

"Immeasurable." She caught herself. "No, that sounded narcissistic. Such tests are not relevant."

"You mean you can run circles around me."

She snorted. "You see everything from a man's point of view."

"Virgins, promises, expectations. Let's put it to the test," I said, placing my hand on her stomach.

"No," she said. "I've told you. If I lose virginity …" Her eyes were wet. "you're the loser."

I felt her heat. She moaned something guttural, struggling to focus. "These are mysteries, Jack, even to us."

"Were you ever sick as a child? Measles, sore throat? Ever break a bone?"

"No. Impossible."

"Nor did Chloé," I said, remembering. "Free of every illness."

"Of course." I kept stroking her and her breath became more uneven. "Jack, please, I can't think —"

I stopped. She sighed, "You're always stopping."

We kissed until she broke away, gasping. "Have you noticed anything?" she breathed. "Your lip?"

"I'd forgotten about it —"

"I healed it, got tired of kissing the corners of your mouth." I touched my wound, the swelling gone.

"You don't need a mirror," she said. "Chloé will never know."

"That would have taken days to heal." She looked away. "How?"

"It was nothing —"

I released her and walked to the windows: a typical estate view … gardens, sinuous stream sparkling in the low-angled sun … tree tops moving in the wind … I turned and said, "What secrets don't I know, Laine? What else?"

With a half-smile, she pointed to a chair. "Sit."

I did, and she promptly straddled me. "What else?" She shook her head, tight with self-control. "There's so much … Chloé's dreams, for one thing."

"I would have known."

She shifted in my lap and pressed herself into my ribs. "Your conceit. The father who knew his girl so well."

"Go on —"

"Chloé started having them when her periods began."

I said, "I've never heard any of this."

"For instance, once, in her room she saw an immense hawk. Golden, swollen, it perched on a chair back, flexing its wings.

"A glittering, bejeweled band surrounded its head. And there was something prodigious about the bird, its eyes astute, the skin of its claws as red as smashed mulberries …

"She saw it afterward as a guardian. It became her secret, the hawk a gift at puberty. Still, she didn't grasp its meaning. In the morning, when she woke after that first dream, she walked to the chair where it had perched on the chair's pine back. Brushing her fingers over the wood, she felt scratches in the pine.

"In time it gave her instructions for your seduction." In a sing-song bird-voice she whispered, *Bless him with your softness, in the light when you dress and when you undress—*

I whispered, "The hawk was you?"

"Occasionally you catch on."

"So you came in dreams?"

"Yes."

"For how many years?"

"Eight."

"You would have been about the same age. And you're telling me you appeared as an immense hawk, issuing commands when you were twelve?"

"Our age is irrelevant. I keep telling you. You keep dragging out that weary rationality." She scrunched herself around in my lap, then kissed my chest. My unsullied daughter-not-daughter, incorrupt and cunning, chaste and calculating, whom I was to believe materialized as a hawk.

"In other words, you're twenty, but you're not. You were twelve, but you weren't."

Her hands linked around my back. "You're playing dumb even though you get it. I've handed it all to you on a platter, and you keep acting like a brainless reptile baking in the sun. What are they called? Ig —"

"Iguanas." I glanced at the clock. "It feels like eleven, and it's 8:30." I stretched, trying not to push her off my lap. "Got to stand. We've been at this far too long."

Languidly, she slipped off and pulled up the boxers. She blinked black eyelashes. "I promise to dress before we leave."

"Not necessary. Go like that. If someone gives you a funny look, turn them into stone."

She paused, watching me. "I love you, but you risk becoming tiresome."

I walked to the windows, checking. "Yes, I suppose. But … it's over-whelming. Three thousand years discussed so casually."

"You're a smart guy."

"I left out the part about being told the daughter I raised is a goddess, and another goddess, who calls herself my daughter, breaks the news that she's not, while squirming in my lap."

"There's an old saying: *it is hard for mortals to see the gods.*"

I touched my lower lip again—smooth. I noticed movement in the field. A stag ambled through the grasses. Six prongs with dark rub marks, the same one I'd seen earlier. A three-headed dog, then this. The low-angled morning sun shone on its fur. Staring casually toward the window with incurious eyes, it shook its antlers and walked to the brook, bending to drink.

"Laine! A buck —"

She joined me. "Artemis attracts them. She protects them and she kills them. Both. It's never certain which she'll do. An odd contradiction. They're known as spirit bucks. They die and reappear." The stag straightened and without looking left or right, leaped the stream and ambled off, disappearing into the browns and grays, the sun-flecked brush.

She pressed into me: the little voice, the touch, her arms around me. Her world: I was certain I was being indoctrinated.

"Laine, again, what happens if you lose your virginity?"

"You know. Even a single thrust."

"Too arbitrary."

"It is what it is."

"I can walk around the house, touch its sides, but no more."

"There are no other rules." Hands on her hips, she said, "But I do want more lessons, want you on *me* —" She stepped into my arms, letting me stroke her, all the while rocking herself against me.

I paused. "May we talk another moment?"

"Sure, but you're to be serious. No sarcasm …"

"I'm still confused about why you've 'reanimated.' "

"Jack, you agree there's a natural cycle, life and death?"

"Yes. Still, we'd all like to live longer, if we're healthy." I shrugged. "Personally, I'd take an extra twenty-five."

"Granted," she said, the comment matter of fact. She seemed serious, spoken as if I shouldn't be surprised. In her eyes, I saw immense love.

Unable to respond without sounding foolish, I rubbed the back of my neck. "You're kidding. I'm now to live an extra twenty-five years?"

"Yes, and in good health."

I felt a lightness. She whispered, "I couldn't stand that you'd die at 65."

"Now instead I kick off at, what, ninety? You're serious?"

"I might change my mind."

"I'm sorry, my questions must seem inane."

"They're not. For as long as there's been life, matter has animated and then broken down. It's a grand cycle: creation and destruction, yin and yang. Extremes that together generate equilibrium, and apart, spawn chaos. Nature has no compassion, but it follows ancient rules." She touched my hand. "But always, what lives, dies."

"Do gods and goddesses?"

"A few of us have been lost, but not from age. I've been forced to take down a god or two. Even our lives are not limitless."

"Can a goddess be killed, say accidentally?" I asked. She raised her eyebrow. "For instance, if you're hit by a car and you're crushed."

"Gruesome. Yes, that might do it. We're immune to normal diseases and aging. If we weren't, we'd be mortal. We're what I call a-mortal. We're not susceptible to death in the common meaning, but yes, we can be killed."

"A-mortal." I repeated my question. "Why are you here now? You told me the three of you chose to retreat from the world. Now you're back. Why?"

"The natural cycle of life and death is threatened."

I shook my head. "By what?"

"Science. Scientists." She frowned. "Science typically spawns incremental advances. It defeats this disease or that. Life's extended. We expected that, our algorithm takes small advancements into account. But in the last decade, many discoveries, including something called gene amplification, have begun to coalesce. For the first time for humankind, there's a probability that science will map the precise gears and springs that constitute the aging clock." She smiled indulgently. "And of course, when that happens, scientists will inevitably jigger the gears slightly, and off you go."

"Wouldn't this be all over the news?"

"The research is largely secret. Investigations are on-going in a number of institutes and universities. As you might imagine, individuals with wealth are frequently funding the work —"

"Their intent is to prolong life?"

"No, their intent is to eradicate death. What man has always dreamed is now within reach. I guess in half a decade, men alive today will be transformed into what fantasists call immortals. I realize it sounds implausible." She saw me smiling. "Maybe not immortals — even we are not — but humans whose lives will have no known end."

"The undying."

"No, not Hollywood zombies." Then she wiped her mouth with the back of her hand. "A new race. Deathless, everlasting — whatever you want to call it. Regardless, it cannot be."

"And your role —?"

"Come on, you're not that slow!"

"Be specific."

"If this occurs, the program we set into motion millennia ago will be shattered, the old assumptions gone."

"Death will no longer do its work."

"Death for humans will be a memory." She touched the tip of my nose with hers. "Nature, the source of life, is threatened. Remember the tale of Icarus?"

"No."

"A human boy who wanted to fly. His father made him wings of feathers and wax, warning him not to fly too high or the sun would melt it all. But Icarus ignored him, and ascended higher and higher in his joyous flight. The sun, Helios, scorched him in its anger, belching flames and fire, and he fell into the sea.

"Today, if we pushed the analogy, a modern, technological breakthrough would ensure the wax would not be affected by the sun's heat and the boy would soar with impunity: a winged immortal, a child who might fly into the sun and return unscathed."

She fluttered her hands. "Whoosh! An immortal race is born in defiance of Gaia, of nature herself. The time, you see, is ripe for Aisa to return with her dreadful scythe."

She grimaced. "In school, I came across an illustration, a Dürer etching from around 1500. Aisa appeared as a skeleton wearing a crown and wielding a bloody scythe. See? It was Aisa. In man's subconscious, we live on —

"And now we're back." She shrugged. "I need a smoke before we leave for the hospital."

CHAPTER 16

Ve had a few minutes before leaving. Laine crushed out a cigarette and sat in my lap. Almost simultaneously, my cell chirped: Chloé.

I can be out of here in 60. Come!

Then another: *Soon!*

I replied, *How's the babe?*

She didn't respond. The morning sun rose high enough now that scattered light came through the windows. Laine looped her arms around my neck. I said, "Your return is about ..."

"Balance."

I lifted her — she was as light and small as Clo — and turned her so that she straddled me, her legs wide and our stomachs touching. Then I stopped: music came from outside, a solemn tune. It rose and fell. "What now —?"

"Sacred music from the Eleusinian initiations. Very old."

"Eleusinian?" The tune grew in strength, its location shifting.

"Listen carefully," she said. "An *aulos*, a tambourine, conch shells —"

Conch shells? My heart hammered and light coming through the windows seemed afire. I lifted her from me and sprang to the window. The hymn faded and I scanned the meadow, the edge of the woods, the brook — nothing. The silence was broken only by the wind, the grasses bent into graceful arcs.

I turned to Laine. "Nothing."

"A melody as old as the gods. A tune for Demeter."

"Who is —?"

"A goddess. Demeter and her daughter honored a village near Athens — Eleusis — with annual festivals and great mysteries. The celebrations continued for 2,500 years. Until Theodosis. We talked about this — the Eleusinian groves were destroyed, the mysteries forever lost."

She put her arms out, beckoning me. I shivered, hearing the same chthonic ringing in my ears. "The advent of Aisa is causing this," she said. "We're magnets. We left and now we're back — the ancient energies, dormant for so long, move again."

"And in my backyard?" Her eyes were wet, her cheeks flush. I blurted, "Look, I apologize. Sarcasm on autopilot." I wasn't sure I meant the apology. But I could see she expected it. In reality I felt a dark anger at the constant surprises.

"It's okay. My dad, the babbling idiot …" I no longer had the composure to banter, or the tolerance to be civil. One of her nipples poked from the cami.

"Laine, we have to get dressed." Checking my cell, I said, "On the road in fifteen."

With a kiss, she said, "I'll be ready."

Leaving her, I went to the bedroom I shared with Clo and put on pants, shoes and a shirt. I then went to Laine's room. Four or five pairs of panties lay side by side on the bed. Several dresses were thrown next to the underwear. She half-turned, naked, her breasts in profile, and said, "You pick."

Officiously, uncomfortably, I chose a cream pair of panties. "These. Now a dress."

She picked up two, one with vertical stripes that zipped down the back. "This one," I said. "And you'll need a bra."

She slipped into the dress, her eyes flickering. "Perhaps Clo will let you undress me when it's time for bed," she smiled. "Who knows what that girl will want."

I parked the car at the hospital and turned to Laine. "I should be excited. I'm not."

She laughed brightly. "Even with a new daughter?"

When we got off the elevator, Laine took my arm. When I signed us in, the secretary saw our names and stood. "Mr. Night, would you wait a second?"

Laine and I exchanged glances. After several minutes, an older woman stepped from a back office and said, "Mr. Night? I'm Olivia. Could we have a word?" Billing, I thought. Then I panicked: had my relationship with Clo somehow been uncovered? And what if it had?

I gestured toward Laine. "This is my wife's sister. Can she visit Chloé Night — while we talk?"

"Yes." She pointed toward the elevators. "She's two floors up, room 416."

I followed the woman to her office. Before I could sit she said, "An accident occurred this morning."

"An accident?"

"One of my maternity nurses, an experienced RN a week from her 38th birthday, died on the ward."

"I'm so sorry."

"It's the circumstances that warrant discussion." She continued, "Betty, the nurse, picked up your daughter from her bassinet to carry her to your wife …" She paused again as if gathering her words. "And as she stepped forward, she slipped."

"And what the hell happened?" My voice rose.

"No need to panic. Your daughter is fine. But my nurse hit her head on a bed corner as she fell. She died from the impact."

"How could my daughter be fine? She must have fallen, too —"

"No. Your wife witnessed it all. Through good luck which I can't explain, your daughter fell into the crib. Not a scratch." She paused. "It's been chaos here all morning. Physicians, policemen. I thought your wife might be traumatized, but —"

I said nothing.

"She seems fine. Still, you'll want to keep an eye on her. An officer took her report —" She checked her watch. "— about thirty minutes ago. She's now free to go." She paused. "Oh, one more thing. I've logged your wife's delivery as the easiest we have ever recorded. Fast, apparently painless, no epidural, no complications. She and your new daughter are quite the pair."

I found them in their room with Laine. Chloé sat on the bed, her legs dangling. She was dressed in checkered summer shorts and a white golf shirt. Laine cradled Aisa, already gurgling and making faces. I gave Clo a hug and said, "Well, do I get to hold the new one?" The girls stared at each other as if one might say no.

Laine passed me Aisa, and said, "Don't breathe on her!"

Aisa stared at me as I walked her in small circles. Her eyes were black except for a scattering of gray flecks around her pupils. She seemed unusually cognizant and made noises as we strolled. Clo said, "She knows you."

I glanced at her, ignoring the absurd comment and said, "I heard about the accident."

"The nurse? Yes, well."

"You saw it happen?"

"She was a few feet away." A throwaway comment. She might just as well have shrugged or pushed her hair from her face.

I wasn't sure what to make of Clo now. She had withdrawn. The shift, perhaps not evident to others, was obvious to me. Her eyes were guarded, her face tighter. I touched her cheek. "And you're okay?"

She pushed my hand away. "Of course."

"How did Aisa avoid being hurt?"

"She could not have been."

"A fall like that?"

She shrugged. This Chloé was not my Chloé. Maybe childbirth had left her undone. Laine smiled carefully. Aisa kicked in my arms, fussing, the room otherwise quiet. "Okay," I said, "Then, let's get out of here."

Conversation on the ride home was brief. I congratulated Clo on the delivery, and she said, "Probably could have skipped the hospital entirely. Who knew?" Laine found that hilarious. Aisa slept and I kept my eyes on the road, afraid a deer or something wild would bound in front of us.

As we passed Kendrick's old colonial, I saw him in the front yard. He waved as I drove by, and I raised my hand.

A half hour later as we gathered in the kitchen, I said, "I'm still shocked about the nurse. It's not every day someone drops dead like that."

Laine said, "Aisa's sleeping?"

Chloé said, "Yes." She stretched. The weight gained over the prior months appeared gone, her belly flat. Only her breasts were larger.

Laine wandered over to Clo, her walk a slow, triumphant sashay, a samba. Clo grinned and took Laine's face in her hands and shook her. She whispered, "I did it. Like a snake shedding its skin."

Laine said, "Yes. We're intervenors once again —"

I felt like a stranger. The room seemed charged, almost electric. After a moment, I said, "I'll be in the back. 'Got to get some air."

Going downstairs I went through Laine's room to the door leading to the field. I paused in the space, taking in the bed and the line of panties I'd reviewed. With foreboding, I stumbled into the light.

The air crackled with the freshness that follows thunderstorms. It hadn't rained in a week. I stood twenty feet from the house, gazing around. The kitchen windows, where I half expected to see faces, were silver in the light, the room impenetrable. The stream beside the woods murmured as it broke over the stones scattered between the banks.

In the bower where I'd wrestled Laine a few days earlier, the low growth was still bent. I knelt at the end of the fragrant bed and smelled the ground: mint, crushed grass, wild sage. Overwhelmed with heaviness, I stretched out over its length, turned on my side and closed my eyes. The brook sang and I fell asleep.

The sun seemed far lower when I woke. I must have turned on my back because now Laine straddled my chest, whistling a three-note tune, her hands flat on the ground over my shoulders, red hair in my face. I laughed. "What the hell are you doing here?"

" 'Came to rescue you." She slipped off and lay on her side. She smiled. "Do you know your stream's name?"

"No —"

"Pegasus."

"Like the flying horse?"

She whispered, "No, Pegasus means flowing spring, pretty brook."

I turned her on her back and wrestled her arms over her head, pinning her. She sighed, "Do anything but kiss me …" So I kissed her neck, shoulders, cheeks. She sighed dramatically and said, "You're insatiable."

She still wore the dress I'd picked out that morning. I turned her on her belly and zipped it down. The dress pulled off easily. I lowered my mouth to her softness. She kept sighing and shifting, finally whispering, "I begged you not to. But no. Now at least leave my bra on, sir —"

I felt exhausted and overcome by it all. I reached behind her and unhooked her bra. "Is this what you begged me not to do?"

"Yesss," she moaned. "Oh please. Not another thing —"

And so we wrestled together, playing in the grass. When it ended she smiled, saying, "Pegasus watched. And Artemis, too."

"And her girls?"

"Yes, all hoping to learn a thing or two. Like being on a farm."

We lay on our backs watching the sky. In the late afternoon, I counted clouds. Two, six, now seven, intense blue everywhere that wasn't blanketed. The blue mirrored Laine's eyes. "Laine, Clo's changed."

She said in a low voice, "Yes, and you needed time to yourself. But you should know: Clo will no longer be someone you recognize." She whispered, "She's gone. She's Aisa's mother now — Aisa, the heartless. Mother and daughter, an indestructible two."

"The accident in the hospital —?"

"The nurse's time had come. Her thread was snipped."

Laine rose on her haunches, took my hand and tugged. "Come, we've got to face the fierce ones." As she stood, the sun sparkled, glinting off her arms as if she'd been rolling in diamond dust. I ran a finger over her skin: glitter, the type girls use to paint their faces, coated her shoulders and arms.

"What's this?" She smiled mysteriously and took my hand. Then, I sensed something watching. She said, "I feel it, too. It's not Clo. Look —!"

She pointed toward the brook. On the opposite bank stood three does, fifteen feet away, shoulder to shoulder, watching us with curiosity. We remained still. She whispered, "It's not as incongruous as it appears. Deer, young girls — we're equally inquisitive."

She bent and picked a small violet flower. "A gillyflower. Bend down," she commanded. I bent and she tucked it behind my ear. The deer had not moved and still watched, large-eyed. A breeze swept the field, and I admit every *thing* felt enchanted.

CHAPTER 17

Chloé nursed Aisa in a sunroom that overlooked a sweep of lawn. She could view winding shrubs, stone walkways and trees. I stepped behind her and put my hands on her shoulders. "Hi, Clo."

She glanced up and I ran a hand into her hair, something she always liked. "Aisa looks like she grew overnight."

"She did." Chloé twitched both shoulders in irritation, and shook off my hands. Laine came in, sitting on the leather couch, smoothing her dress. "Sit. We'll chat up Clo."

Chloé appeared oblivious to us. I said, "Clo, no problems nursing?"

"None." The clipped, irritated voice. She never took her eyes off the child. Now late afternoon, we had not eaten since returning.

I asked, "Anyone starved?"

Chloé shook her head, saying, "Where are you sleeping tonight?"

I must have appeared startled. "Hell, I'll sleep anywhere. I'd love to keep you warm —"

She shook her head. "I have to recover from delivery. An RN said no sex."

"That's not what I meant."

She was curt. "I may pass you off to Laine." Looking at her sister she said, "Why would I ever sleep with him again? I'm through with that."

Laine seemed unsurprised. I stood. "Why would we do anything differently?"

Laine intervened. "Ignore her. Postpartum stuff, whacked-out hormones."

"No," Chloé said, "I'm no one's child anymore. No one's love-child. No one's fake wife. I'm through with all that shit."

"Fine," I said. "We'll talk later."

"There's nothing to discuss." She narrowed her eyes.

"I'm getting dinner," I said. "Laine, I'll need help." I took her hand and we left. In the kitchen she put her arms around me, her eyes wet, but strangely untroubled. To my surprise she softly whistled the three-note tune from the meadow, adding a fourth note at the end of every stanza. "Laine — can you stop?"

She pursed her lips. "Thinking," she said after a minute, "that you might now be mine. Not sure why I'm in such a good mood."

"I'm being passed from girl to girl?"

"We're beauties," she said. "Don't complain."

As we made dinner, I asked, "Should I take her seriously?"

"Yes —" She paused. "By the way, my business with Clo is business, however serious. That won't be compromised by who sleeps with whom."

At dinner, Chloé joined us, but sulked. Aisa slept in a crib nearby. Clo said no to my offer to pour wine. "I won't be drinking." In jeans and a loose-fitting blouse, she stared at her food, but otherwise ignored us.

Another disturbing shift: Laine now wore Chloé's crinoline skirt and an eggshell camisole I hadn't seen. She'd excused herself earlier, and when I saw her walk into the room for dinner, I laughed. "Chloé's petticoat?"

"Yes. now mine!" While Chloé watched, she ran up to me, saying, "Hmm, I can't decide. Should I add a plié to my routine?" She turned in a circle, the petticoat ballooning lightly. When Laine bowed with exaggerated poise, I clapped and said to both girls, "Be seated. Shall we start?"

Our moment of levity had passed. Several times during dinner Aisa woke, complaining, and Chloé obliged. At the end she said, "The asparagus was over-seasoned. I hope it doesn't spoil my milk." Laine and I looked at each other with half-smiles.

As the two of us finished washing dishes, I suggested we walk in the back woods. "We have a couple hours of daylight, and I haven't explored anything beyond the little stream. I've never even crossed it."

She corrected me. "Don't say 'the little stream.' It's Pegasus." I got the usual fist in the ribs and she said, "When you cross it, you enter Artemis' realm."

"A magic realm?"

She paused. "No mockery … I'll change clothes."

"You'll want jeans, a tee-shirt and hat."

"Yes sir," and she scooted off, turning and saying loudly, "I'm excited!"

Before we left, I found Chloé in the living room with the child. "Clo?"

"What?"

"Laine and I may explore the back. Can I get you anything?"

She turned away. I waited, but had been dismissed. I wandered down the hallway to Laine's room and knocked. She opened the door, saying, "Never knock again. Always just come in."

She had been waiting. Blue jeans, a white tee shirt, a silver necklace — the tee too big and one of mine. I tossed her a red baseball cap. She turned it in her hands.

"I love the wiggly P," she said. "But I'll never be a Phillies fan."

"It matches your hair."

She pulled it on and studied the mirror. "It's not the *exact* color." I got a pout, then she leaped into my arms.

A narrow dirt path traversed Pegasus across a shallow portion of its run. I'd not noticed it earlier. We held hands, walking through the flow. Beyond the opposite bank, the trail wound northerly toward the rear of the estate. "The property goes back about a quarter mile, hits a stonewall and that's the property line. Or so I'm told."

"How long would it take to get there?"

"I don't know. Not as long as it sounds."

"Then, let's go."

I led at a good pace. We easily climbed hillocks and jumped the small pockets of wetlands, as well as a second, steeper stream. Laine squealed as she leaped from one bank and into my arms on the other side. The trail wound through an over-story of towering oaks and occasional pines. I guessed it all prime habitat for deer, fox and turtles. After ten minutes, we hit a stonewall running at a rough perpendicular to the trail: the property line. The stacks of flat stones were old, many startlingly massive. "Who could have lifted these?" Laine asked.

"Probably slaves."

"How long ago?"

"1780s, or earlier. Amazing, isn't it?" I scanned the adjoining property: wooded and verdant. The trail made an abrupt turn west and paralleled the wall. I reminded myself to study an aerial of the area. It appeared the woods extended forever.

While we paused she fumbled in a pocket for cigarettes, sticking one in her mouth and handing me matches. "Be a gentleman." I struck a match and she dipped her head toward the flame. Drawing noisily, she exhaled into the sky. "Time to wander back. It'll soon be dark."

Even in the late afternoon, the humidity felt high. Her tee was soaked and stuck to her skin. I brushed aside my instinct to hold her, and struck off down the trail, heading back. I didn't get far, perhaps twenty feet, before she cried, "Hey, you!"

I turned and she stood where I'd left her, arms out, expectant, and I returned. "Miss me?" she asked. That was Chloé's line. I picked her up and swung her in a wobbly circle. As I set her down, she said, "About Chloé … She's closed herself off. It's as if the channel's gone dark. For two decades, I've read her every thought."

"Stop. You're saying you read minds?"

"Haven't I said so?"

I'd suspected as much the other night. Too many signs. I'd ignored them all. I said, "Fine. Then can't you draw on all of that ancient wisdom to tune her back in?"

"No. She's gone rogue."

She suddenly crouched, grabbing the back of her thighs, then sprung up. In a piercing voice, her arms skyward, she cried, "Help! I'm alone in the woods with a man!"

"Careful," I hissed. "You'll wake Artemis. I'd hate to be her pincushion."

She smiled and took my hand. "The goddess knows me. She knows I make stupid jokes. I'm more likely to be shot for being a bad comedienne than you are for molestation." She looked around and said too casually, "I'm attending a conference in D.C. next week. I should be gone for less than a week."

"What?"

"For less than a week. Four days, I think."

"A conference?"

"On aging."

"Open to the public?"

"I'm able to get in."

"I presume it's not free?"

She appeared charmingly irritated. "Dad! If I needed help, I'd say so."

"This ties in with what we talked about, doesn't it?"

"It's a lot of researchers talking to each other. These are usually pretty boring."

"Laine, I've gone to fifteen to twenty professional conferences over the years. Several I wanted to go to, most I had to attend to maintain certifications. But they're all damned expensive. Hotels, meals, conference fees. The costs run into the thousands."

She rolled her eyes as if I were tedious.

"Remember when you knocked on my door dead broke?"

She nodded. "Sure do. Now take me home."

So I pretended to drag her by one hand down the trail for twenty-five to thirty feet and then let her go. After that she followed closely, whistling her tune.

When we got back, we jumped Pegasus. The meadow was still and Laine slipped an arm around me over the final distance. When we got to her room, she collapsed on the bed.

"Exhausted!" she sighed, then bounced up and pulled off her tee. "Bra's wet, too. Yuck—" She reached back to unhook it.

"I'll check on Clo. Want a drink?"

"Yes, I'll dry off and meet you upstairs." As I turned to go, she said in a little voice, "Hey, I love you —"

Chloé wasn't in the sunroom or kitchen. I went to our bedroom. The door was closed and I knocked.

"Don't come in."

"It's me."

"I know."

I paused. "You and Aisa okay —?"

Silence, then a louder voice: "Go away."

I left for the kitchen, angry. I could throw her out. She was old enough. There'd be legal issues over Aisa, child support. But Clo would do just fine —

"Don't go there, Dad. She may change back as abruptly. It's only been a day." Laine stood in the doorway.

"So you read everyone's thoughts?"

"When I need to."

"Well, turn it off when you're around me."

"I can't." She shoved me hard. "And I won't!"

A weariness swept me. Of course she knew exactly what I thought. That explained a lot. Only thirty-eight, I felt old. In the finance world, I was considered a semi-genius. Here ... I wasn't certain where I stood with either girl. Love swept in and out. What counted one moment didn't the next. Chloé would emasculate me, Laine shadow me.

She laughed. "You're inconsolable." I said nothing and she poked me. "If you don't smile, I'll punch you in the ribs."

I found myself laughing. She wore a pair of my boxers and a torn workout top. Her small breasts showed like quarter moons on either side of the top, freckles descending her chest. She smirked and said, "Do I embarrass you?"

"My tomboy."

"Who'll be spending the night with her tomcat."

"Hmm, will he succeed in seducing his ingénue?"

"Only at his peril."

I opened the liquor cabinet. "Laine, do you drink anything other than wine?"

"Whatever. Pick our poison."

"Gin and tonics." I mixed two and we sat at what had become our seats. I leaned forward. "Days ago when I saw Artemis and her girls —"

"They're nymphs."

"Fine. Her 'nymphs' in the back meadow. The girls wore no underpants."

"Panties."

"Bare-assed. Almost as if flaunting their behinds. I can still see their tunics bouncing …"

"You liked that and you want to know why you got a show."

"I admit the image intrigues me. Who would walk in the woods like that?"

"The nymphs, when they run with Artemis, take a vow to stay virgins —"

"A repeated theme —"

"Yet, they're sexually mature. If they're caught with a man, they're banished. Or sometimes hunted as if game."

"Why? That's crazy —"

"I suspect Artemis doesn't envision death the way you do."

Before I could speak, she held up her hand. "Let me finish. The vow the girls take leaves them wild at times. Wild with lust. Desire is heightened by the hunt. They often tear animals apart with bare hands."

"Charming. These are not girls from this time —?"

"Hardly. They have followed her for millennia."

"If they're that old, why are they not all the same age? What's ideal — twenty? Twenty-four? Instead, their ages vary —"

"She wants variety, not a tribe of identical Amazons. And she loves little ones."

"All these girls — thirteen, fifteen, eighteen years old — flashing asses."

Laine's eyes were radiant, her cheeks flush. "Their bare asses, as you put it, are meant to provoke you, to dare men to act. Don't. They'll kill you on the spot."

"Feral cats."

"Worse. Blesséd virgins in heat."

"Sex and death, death and lust." I drained the gin and tonic. "Where are we going with all this crap?"

She remained silent. Goading her I asked, "Will you wear tunics and go bare-assed if I want?"

"Yes, for you. And I'll bend over and waggle my ass." She picked up her empty glass and rocked it idly. I got up and mixed us another.

"And death's role for us?"

"There is no mystery. You will die and I'll go on. That is how it has always been. Old age will enfold you, the same as it does all men."

"You're such a charmer. I normally give death no thought. Now this house stinks of it."

She said, "You're my father and I love you. But I can only go so far."

"No discretion, huh?" I tried to smile.

She gazed into my eyes. "Have you already forgotten? I granted you twenty-five extra years. You'll be vibrant all those days."

"You really did that?"

"Yup." She set her glass aside, empty again. "A small skill. We've used it twice before. Special dispensation." Her eyes dampened. "I'd make you a-mortal if I could. But —"

I wanted to kiss her, yet any action felt inferior to the magnitude of her gift. "I should thank you. I haven't —"

She stood. On that moonless night, I found myself listening for sounds from Chloé or the child, but heard nothing. "Music?" She shrugged.

I turned on John Coltrane — a saxophone to end the silence. She laughed. "Here I am with my father, which made me think of my mother's — my original mother's — father."

"Family trees are not this family's forte."

"Oh, this is a good one. Let me tell you!" She sounded lighthearted for the first time since our walk.

"So, he was Phanes, a guy. Or maybe a girl. Who knows? The reason I say that is Phanes was double-sexed." She continued. "That face again, Dad! I'm gonna go on even though you're rolling your eyes. The old term is hermaphrodite — as female as male."

"Is that even possible?"

"Admittedly rare. When I imagine him, I imagine someone with gorgeous breasts and a huge cock. I guess it might have been more complicated. Phanes went either way —" She giggled, then her voice dropped. "She's coming —"

Chloé walked into the kitchen, looking formidable, her hair disheveled. Dressed in the same nursing blouse, now stained with milk, she glared at us.

"The earth mother," Laine snickered. "Have you looked in a mirror?"

"Shut up."

Laine growled and put her hands up in claws. Mediating between the two I said, "Aisa's asleep?"

Chloé turned and stared at me, then at Laine. She ran a hand casually through her hair, sighed and said, "I came to apologize. I've been impossible. I've changed. But that's no excuse for my behavior." She kissed me lightly, then put her arms out to Laine. "Forgive me. Both of you …

"Giving birth to Aisa gave birth within me to … the realization that so many of the things I've wanted over the last decade were wrong …

"You, Dad, I wanted you as my lover. So I seduced you. But what the hell? Even this house … sure, it's ideal for … whatever we've become. We're out in the woods, and you have endless money to make it work … I'm the one who pushed to find something in the countryside, but was that really me?"

She turned to Laine. "Yes, you know I know. There is nothing I don't remember, but you, you woke long before me. And you've maneuvered this. Chosen our mothers, picked Jack for his virility, maneuvered events, found this house …

"You even hid yourself from me when you first showed, masquerading as an abandoned thing. You had one goal — to get a foothold here, in the estate you chose long before Jack and I ever thought of moving from our little town …"

Laine replied, "There were secrets and now there aren't. If you know, you know. So what?"

"I wanted to hear you say it," Chloé whispered. The three of us sat without speaking. Finally, Chloé said, "Well, regardless of your shit, Laine, what I said earlier is true. Whatever was bright has turned dark. I'm fucking depressed. And Jack — I'm through with sex, I'm through with you."

I said nothing. She looked at Laine. "And I meant it, although I didn't say it nicely. He's yours, if that's really what you want."

Clo continued, "But how will you stay a maiden? One moment of passion and you'll be screwed." She giggled, then was serious again. "It never ends well when goddesses sleep with men. Jack's a skilled lover and can show you things you never imagined. He's smart, caring, generous.

But he's not a god." She stood and looked at me, "Can you leave us alone?"

Dismissed, I left. Partway down the hall I stopped, close enough to hear Clo's voice as it rose. "He'll grow old, his strength withering like all of them. What then? What then, Lachesis?"

CHAPTER 18

She was no Artemis,
a goddess who strode
about with a golden bow
shining as bright
as the new moon on a blackened night.
—*Poet X*

L ate that evening Laine jumped onto the bed, slouching on her back, still in boxers. "What are you thinking?"

Before I could respond, Laine turned on her stomach and cried, "I'm not good at this. I always know exactly what you think."

"Yes, then you know I'm questioning it all — you, Clo, the meadow, the stars in the firmament."

"You know I love you?"

"I suppose."

She turned onto her back. "Show me."

She sensed my caution. I bent and kissed her lightly, then ran my hand down her neck and onto her chest. Her eyes fluttered. "Goddess, how long have you been mind-reading me?"

"Don't ask."

I spoke sharply. "Laine —!"

"Okay … decades."

"So the stories about not knowing who your daddy is until your mother lay on her deathbed … None of that's true."

She hesitated. "None of it."

"Did your mom — Michele — really die a couple weeks ago?"

"Yes —"

"She told you about me?"

"No, but there's almost nothing I don't know. If I need to."

"Then you know you're intimidating."

Deflecting my comment she said, "When we sleep tonight, what should I wear?"

"You suddenly can't read my mind?"

"What I'm reading is, not these boxers. Or your tees."

"Tomboys are fun when they're climbing trees."

"I get it. In bed, at night, they dress like girls." I smiled at her, at the once-again radiant, luminescent Laine.

I said, "You see what I'm visualizing, don't you?"

"Yes."

"For now. If I were you, I'd change before your man is less … less agreeable."

She rolled off the bed and walked to the dresser, choosing pieces. She turned. "Are you going to watch?"

"I may."

She faced me, pulling off the top and pulling down the boxers. Amazingly slender, her body was that of a girl in her mid teens. She pulled a cami over her shoulders and after smoothing it, held up panties.

She said, "Every night I hope you'll help me put sleep stuff on." Smiling, she whispered, "Chloé's made a huge mistake."

"How did things go upstairs?"

"Clo? Well, she predicts my disinterest in you. You'll get gray hair, bad teeth, a walking stick. You'll be in a wheelchair drooling, while Chloé and I are dancing under stars."

I smiled, chagrined. She said, "Time bends, implacable." She seemed, while I held her in my arms, to warp all normal measures of it. Over the long hours of that night, time didn't stop or accelerate. Instead it became sinuous. Although I struggle to define the sensory changes, time ceased to mean the inevitable progression of one moment to the next. Instead it became fluid. The fluidity of time with Laine existed as a gyre, an eddy—random vortexes running counterclockwise on a river's edge. Or spiraling away as silent whirlpools.

Purportedly that night, I remained the tutor. Yet, she governed our actual play. It wasn't a matter of controlling the pace; instead she used our lovemaking (as she called it) as an example of tempo, something she manipulated easily. In reality, several things occurred. First, she delighted in "show and tell," although the terms in the phrase should have been reversed. She asked me to *tell* her what I was about to *show* her. And if I were too brief, she demanded I dally and explain.

For the concept of time not to crumble, there must be a succession of events — morning must shift to afternoon, afternoon to night. During these lessons, time started warping. In retrospect, I suspect she toyed with me. It didn't matter. We started comfortably enough. That is, each touch became distinct, separate from the last. Together they became a montage, but one where each fragment had no discernible bridge to the next, and no discernible rhythm tying one action to another. Each kiss existed in singularity.

That night was our first together with Chloé home. I had been Clo's lover for a year, and the abrupt shift in our relationship would take time for me to accept. I assumed Chloé as innocent until Laine appeared. Then I saw Chloé as a confederate. At Aisa's birth she became sovereign unto herself . Nothing could be clearer. We were reconstituted. And although my financial means supported their maneuvering, I remained peripheral to what seemed a mythic re-creation.

Physical contact? Laine replaced Clo. How much of this was collusion between them? Maybe none, perhaps most. Even though Laine's bedroom was at the other end of the house from Chloé's, Chloé must have heard Laine's cries. Yet, Chloé had no reaction; she acquiesced, if not blessed it all. I would never know. Even months later it was a taboo subject. Still, as I reminded myself, the two girls stayed in mental touch. Whatever one thought or did, the other knew.

Regardless, during that same night Laine and I slept only an hour. We spent the time — that ambivalent term — loving in fragments, slivered kisses and incautious touches, our intimate contact always short of consummation. In the morning, we awoke as if from deep sleep. To me, she appeared radiant, even guileless.

The four of us quickly settled into a semblance of normalcy. Chloé stayed aloof. I grieved half privately. Laine, on the other hand, seemed exuberant. And as predicted, Aisa grew at an accelerated rate.

A brief incident reinforced for me that the sisters were as exceptional as Laine described. On a woods hike, Laine slipped while crossing a barbed-wire fence, cutting herself. I stepped across the fence first, pushing down a top wire with my hand, swinging my leg over. Laine tried to imitate me, but slipped and caught her thigh on a barb.

Only a few feet away I caught her by the waist. But her thigh had a gouge about eight inches long and a quarter-inch deep. Blood filled the gash. I tore off my shirt and wiped the wound, compressing the bleeding. "This'll require stitches, a tetanus shot—it's a damned serious injury, girl."

She shook her head.

"Laine, when did you last have a tetanus?"

"Probably as a kid, I don't know." She seemed amused. I lowered myself to look closer, amazed: she was no longer bleeding. I was about to use my shirt as a tourniquet. But the wound was disappearing.

"Dad, I'll be fine. 'Sorry about my cry —"

I still knelt, rolling out her inner thigh for a better view. Only a minute had passed since her fall. I struggled to find the wound. Only a faint pink line remained. I said with irritation, "How the hell? I was afraid you'd go into shock ..."

She put a hand on my shoulder, saying, "Come on." So we continued our trek in silence. Extreme danger had passed in seconds. I was to recall the event in coming months.

CHAPTER 19

No Artemis with hounds & nymphs,
no orgiastic Aphrodite.
Who then could be the One?
An exemplar démodé,
she roamed the melancholy
country with malaise —
—Poet X

The next morning I did something long overdue. I explain my negligence by saying I remained shaken by Laine's arrival. Her initial assertion (how many of us encounter a child we weren't aware exists?), the bizarre sexual interaction between us, the goddess claims, Aisa's birth and the tension between the girls — all were an extraordinary distraction. After breakfast, I retreated to my office.

Earlier, while Laine and I still lay in bed, I rolled her onto her back, took her upper thigh and examined the area of the wound: nothing. I bent and kissed the location. And I remembered how she'd healed my lip. In that instant, seeing her thigh, I experienced a rare moment of objectivity.

In my office, I did a web search for *Laine Lowell*. I expected to find nothing of interest, assuming she'd spent her life in New York state. I'd find high school references, social media posts with the usual selfies. But I found none of that. Instead, I found pages of citations for scientific articles. Surely this was a different Laine Lowell, possibly a senior scientist in a government lab.

From a three-month-old article that Laine Lowell, PhD, co-authored, I clicked into a biography, which included a headshot. It was Laine, red-haired and in a business suit, a young professional whom I presumed now worked around the corner from me in a chemise and boxers.

Her CV recited that she graduated from Stanford, and obtained a combined master's and PhD from UCLA. Her focus was human genetics. It took me a few moments from the dates to calculate that she was fifteen when awarded her undergrad degree, and nineteen when she obtained the masters and PhD. The CV listed numerous awards, noting her full scholarships.

Before I copied Laine's CV into a desktop folder, I counted the scientific articles she had authored or co-authored in the last three years: eighteen. No wonder she recited ancient history and the nuances of paleobiology with equal ease. Her competitive comment a week ago about having a high IQ was no exaggeration.

I scanned the abstracts of the articles. Many of them dealt with cellular senescence. I searched for the term and found that CS (my abbreviation) results from DNA damage, shortened chromosomes and other factors, many controversial. These elements in combination theoretically reduce life spans. Some scientists speculated that if CS could be prevented, life might be extended. Others postulated that death itself could be eliminated.

The technical jargon matched my memory of her lectures: *For as long as there has been life, matter has been transformed from the inanimate to the living, then lost animation … A grand cycle … What lives, dies.* I saw her flashing eyes. Was Chloé aware of her sister's brilliance? I wondered, too, why she hid her academic achievements.

At the end, I looked online for genetics-focused conferences in D.C. The only likely candidate was at the Four Seasons. Sponsored by the Center for Biological Mechanisms of Aging, it featured a number of "prominent experts in the field." I opened the PDF describing the confer-

ence. The brochure had photos featuring three of the speakers. Laine
was pictured between two older men. The caption under her headshot
read, "Keynote speech by geneticist Laine Lowell," noting she was on a
sabbatical from the National Institute of Aging in Maryland.

Now I understood how she afforded the cost: the conference would
be paying her expenses as well as a stipend. To think she would be asking
for my credit card! I had, without hesitation, spent thousands to clothe
her. My sad, insolvent, motherless child. We offered her shelter and celebrated a homecoming. Now I'd discovered her doppelgänger. Did she
believe I wouldn't eventually know?

The remaining days before she left were largely eventless. We took
walks, Chloé mothered Aisa and I resumed work. The backwoods and
the meadow revealed no new mysteries. One afternoon the hound
appeared for a time. Laine called me to look. It lay on its stomach in the
center of the meadow, alert, its ears peaked in response to a sound we
couldn't hear, then put its head between its legs and appeared to sleep.
When I returned later it was gone.

Wednesday afternoon Laine packed her suitcase and gave us a hug.
"I'll be back on Sunday," she said. "And I'll stay in touch."

She was leaving in a fog of concoctions and pretense. I watched her
dress rise as she slipped into her car and adjusted her seat belt. She
caught my eye, pulled the hem down and smiled. As she left I thought,
The esteemed scientist.

"Wow them, babe." I almost said "keynote," but did not.

She gave me a searching look. "I will, Dad." She knew. Of course. I
half-smiled and closed her door. Before she backed out, she shook a
cigarette from her pack, struck a match and inhaled, nodding through the
glass with a brief wave.

I never imagined being lonely with my once-beloved Chloé, but I was.
Instantly. As Laine left, Chloé walked into the house without comment. I
followed but stopped, instead walking to the back and sitting by the
stream.

The meadow was quiet, except for crows in the distance. The afternoon sun cast shadows across the grass. At the stream I sat in moss where

Laine and I had wrestled. My thoughts wandered. I turned once and looked up at the kitchen windows, curious to see if Chloé watched: nothing. Then I didn't care. None of it mattered any longer.

Time passed, I suppose. I say that as the *linearity* of time remained uncertain. Whether due to Laine's examples or to circumstance, I didn't know. *Let it go*, I thought.

I stood, observing the woods, looking over my shoulder into the meadow, wanting something to appear, but nothing did. I was reminded of a toss-off line I'd read once: *it's almost impossible to overestimate the unimportance of most things.*

I walked across the meadow and into Laine's bedroom. A pair of panties, a note on top, lay on the bed. In looping script, the note read, "Don't forget me."

Disciplined, I walked every afternoon, and Laine called at night. When I'd ask about the conference, she would stay in character, saying, "Well, Dad, boring but I'm glad I've come." Our calls were short but supplemented by texts. I'd learn about the talks and her critiques, or about the presenters, and how she worked hard at being polite, given the shopworn theories. When I asked if her funds were sufficient to avoid arrest, she would giggle.

I spent most of my days focused on business I'd neglected. Ten-hour days were followed by late dinners, usually alone, as Chloé retired early.

On the third day of Laine's conference, Aisa started crawling. Now twenty days old, she progressed from rolling, to sitting and that afternoon got up on all fours and began awkwardly crawling between Chloé and me, falling and picking herself up. All the while she gurgled and laughed, her black eyes shifting between us. Aisa was now six to eight months ahead of any normal child.

When I had a moment to myself, I opened the door to Laine's office, a converted guest room down the hall from mine. I had provided her with internet and a computer and wondered, now that I knew her accomplishments, where she kept her real belongings. A professional owned books, a laptop, drafts of papers, all the requisite paraphernalia. I sighed, imagining a condo in Baltimore near her work. Was she married or engaged? Was the obsession with virginity part of some parallel ruse?

As I stood at her desk, I saw three or four handwritten pages stapled together. They appeared to contain random notes. I reminded myself she did nothing carelessly, the notes left to be found. I scanned the lines. Quotes, notes about chromosomes, people's names. A few doodles, one of the sun — a circle with little lines radiating from the center—and a childish sketch of a salamander.

A poem titled *Disclosure* caught my eye. Had she written it?

> *On the postcard, the marble kouros stands,*
> *torso white, the chiseled chin*
> *reminds me of him, familiar, exotic.*
> *I run my hand over the geometry of thigh—*

I saw another, shorter.

> *She stood combing. Thin silk gown hung down*
> *like lightwaves across a killing ground.*

The same page had a list of seven names, four men and three women, most followed by PhD. Colleagues? Each was marked with an X.

The notes, mostly words and phrases, were in pencil or ink and I assumed jotted down over weeks. Many meant little: *telomeres, cytokines, cellular death, Zeno's paradox, inflammatory actions re chromosomal regeneration* …

A final poem appeared near the end, perhaps a fragment.

> *Tant mieux: the ribbons*
> *of the rainbow.*
> *She makes a gentle statue,*
> *rainlight soft about her sides.*

I set the pages down, desolate in her absence. The office seemed barren, a laboratory room almost scoured bare.

CHAPTER 20

There is a river. It lifts you
up each night & floats you out
across its floodplains, over its muck & slippery wrack—
its waters carry you along at night,
float you back
before the dawn, before bird songs start,
before the terrible morning light.
—Poet X

On Sunday morning she called from D.C. "Dad, letting you know I'm about to leave!" She sounded light-hearted.

The morning was warm and a humid wind blew from the east. I wandered out of the house, down to Pegasus and took off my shoes. I felt foolish, but guessed Laine might approve. I saw a small flash, a movement in the pool upstream from where I stood: a trout tailing in the current, speckled with gold dots on a pale body. I never imagined the stream having fish. I took a single step toward it, and it startled into the silver reflections.

When Laine arrived, Chloé was nursing and I was in my office. I'd lost track of the hour and stood when I heard the horn. As she opened the car door, I ran out, grabbed her and spun her around.

During lunch all of us chattered about D.C. — traffic, hotel food, truck clattering that continued all night, the smell of meeting rooms — everything but the conference. Laine never mentioned her talk.

After her return, nights in bed rarely varied — "lessons" continued. And as on our first night together, we woke each morning after an hour's sleep.

One morning, I mentioned to her that Artemis must have disappeared. As frequently as I checked the meadow for activity, I saw nothing. Even the deer had vanished. Was Aisa strong enough now that the goddess' protection — I say "goddess" as I now accepted Artemis and even the sisters as extraordinary — was no longer needed?

"Oh, you miss her, do you?"

"Marvelous entertainment. And I miss the nymphs." My smile elicited a faint one from her.

"You never got close enough to see, but many of the girls have pointed teeth, sharpened to look like a shark's."

"Bare asses and shark's teeth?"

"Yes."

"A malevolent little band."

She shook her head at my irreverence. "They're still around."

A morning or two later, we woke and Laine said, "Remember my reference to my grandfather, Phanes?"

"Your original mother's father? Yes, what did you call him?"

"A hermaphrodite."

"With mixed up sex."

"A being fully male and female."

"Hard to imagine."

She wore her usual sleeping things — a pink cami and a pair of my boxers. As we glanced at each other, she idly ran her fingers through the cami straps. Her hair flashed russets and Valentine reds. As she watched my eyes, she shook her hair. Morning sun slanted into the bedroom, a wash of cinnamon. The flushed light stained the walls. I squinted. "And now it's dawn —"

She threw an arm around me and put her head on my chest. "I liked last night."

"Did we sleep?"

"Enough." She nibbled at my neck, a fawn working on spring leaves. "Do you have to work today?"

"A few hours," I said.

She shifted her weight and straddled me, her hands pinning my wrists. "You taught me this." As she whispered, her hair brushed my face, her breasts teasing my chest. "It's a good trick," she said. "I do whatever I want."

I might have thrown her off, but I let her play. Gradually, her taunting turned to kisses, which turned to touches, and with a roll she lay on her back, which I knew meant that I should please her. The oddly colored light added to the room's mysteriousness: Laine, a seductress who would remind me constantly that the inner sanctum was inviolate.

Later that morning as I finished a complicated spreadsheet, Laine wandered in, rolling her eyes and saying, "All work and no play." She wore a sundress, saw me stare and turned in a circle. I stood. "Turn around again."

She did and I said, "I wonder if that zipper works," opening the dress with a quick motion and slipping my hands onto her ribs. "Checking," I said, "That no one's stolen my favorite things."

We pressed against each other. "But those can't be taken. They're yours." She kissed me and again, as I expected, time started sliding and winking out, wrinkling and undulating. The extent of the vacuum was a measure of how much I loved her: in her wonderland, emptiness was a confirmation of love. And one thing did not lead to another. She had broken the cliché.

When we parted, she said, "You saw what I did?"

I shrugged.

"Obliterated time. For you. Soon I'll show you how we fly through days and turn them into seconds, how your years are minutes, if they're even measured." She kissed my nose. "But now it's time for lunch. Zip me up and come along." I turned her by her hips and zipped the dress.

My afternoon was open, and I decided to escape the endless confusion and disconnections. I picked up a book for the first time in years and read in the sitting room. Storms came through, each with heavy rain trailed by wind and lighter clouds — deluge after deluge.

Chloé and the child came and went twice in two hours. To my inexperienced eyes, Aisa might have been six months old. Chloé stopped to ask me something in her now blunt manner. She held the child and when she paused, Aisa swiveled her head to stare at me. Her eyes were disconcerting — she had an intense focus. I wondered for an instant if there had ever been eyes as black. I broke my gaze and turned away, pretending to casually answer Chloé with a pleasantness I hardly felt.

Laine herself seemed preoccupied. She brushed me off when I checked in mid afternoon. "Research," she said. "Busy now."

About four, she brought me a glass of wine. "For my guy," she said before wandering off. Another half hour passed and I put the book down. The house was quiet. The door to Chloé's bedroom remained closed, the kitchen empty. I decided to check email and, passing Laine's bedroom, heard familiar music.

She repeatedly insisted I never knock, so I entered. Laine sprawled in the middle of the bed, asleep. In a pair of my boxers and an old tee, she lay on her stomach, arms overhead. I heard music again, slightly louder — that same solemn, sacred tune we heard days earlier from the back. The rhythm: one-two-*three*-four, one-two-*three*-four.

Laine had closed the blinds. I stepped around the bed to the windows, pulling them aside. There, moving from left to right through the grass about thirty feet from the house, the hound skulked — lithe, muscled. But I saw more. There! — the movement of a young girl, then another. I shifted to the center of the window for a better view, opening the slats.

Staged against the wood's edge were at least twenty girls, all in yellow tunics tied with sashes, their backs to the house with the exception of one who appeared to be about seventeen. Wearing a primitively-made bear mask, the orange-haired older girl held a bundle of grain — wheat or barley — in her right hand, her face turned to the sky.

Between the girl and the others was a rectangular, table-high structure made from massive stones. On the slate top lay a long knife. To the right of the structure was a bronze tripod, and at its apex a circular bowl roiling with fire.

As I watched, Laine, now awake, slipped her arms around me, whispering, "The girls are called *arktoi*, or little bears. They serve Artemis. The grain is black wheat, your *Triticum aestivum*."

"This is quite the masque."

"No, it's real."

All moved to the rhythm of music made by several girls to the side. The musicians stood beside the stream playing lyres, tambourines and a rattle-gourd. The girls dipped and rose in synchronicity, raising their arms and singing. As they danced they threw their heads back and shook their hair. Many of the girls held branches overhead.

"What are the sticks?"

"Lustral branches. They're dipped in blessed water." Clouds moved at a high speed, the sky darkening. Rain was imminent.

From the right side of the meadow, six girls appeared from the woods dressed in brown tunics, black sashes tied high on their ribs. Black ribbons cascaded from their hair. They appeared ecstatic, dancing in circles, shrieking and coming closer and closer to the main group of girls, who parted to let them through. Their red tunics ended six- to eight-inches above their crotches. Their pale buttocks, lower bellies and thin pubic hair flashed as they moved.

The girls held two birds in each hand tied in pairs by their feet — twenty-four birds upside down and struggling, wings lashed against their sides with twine.

"And the birds?"

"Artemis requires sacrifice —"

"Sacrifice?"

"Yes. Exaltation, praise, adulation, dedication." She took my hand and said, "We'll go out to get closer. Don't speak —"

She pulled me out, turning twice to hold her finger to her lips. I followed, amazed at how close we were to the celebrants. Laine stopped paces away, and we had a direct view of the older girl who thrust the grain-bundle into the overcast sky.

The dancing became frenzied and the girls stomped bare feet to the music. We were so close I could smell their bodies and hear ragged breathing, see sweat and the wet hair of the closest girls. A brief shower raked the field. It was ignored and only the hound, still circling the celebrants, stopped and shook itself.

Laine put her hand on my arm and said, "Look —!" She pointed to the girls with the birds. They advanced through the circle of dancers and raised the birds as if in offering. As they lifted their arms, their tunics rose, their dresses a thin linen stained in streaks from the humidity and rain. Laine moved to the rhythm, the melody euphoric, increasingly intense.

Then the orange-haired girl elevated her arms and shrieked, "Eeeei-iiii—!" The girls bowed, scraping their branches on the grass before their feet, falling to their knees. Laine was motionless. Then I saw the masked girl accept a bird. She gave it a caress, pinned it against the stone and raised the knife. Pausing, she observed the girls surrounding her and brought the knife down hard. Laine moved against me and we watched the older girl systematically behead the remaining birds. She caressed each, pinning it with her free hand, then raised the knife and struck.

At the end, the girls rose and in a fervor, echoed the earlier shriek. Several collapsed on the ground. Out of the corner of my eye I saw the hound weaving among them, sniffing their backsides, growling congenially, shuffling about, moving aimlessly.

Abruptly, a girl closest to us turned and stared at Laine, her mouth opening in fright. I thought it odd that none of them noticed us earlier. The girl fell to her knees and within moments others turned and repeated her gesture. Even the girl in the mask looked and dropped her knife.

Laine stepped away from me and raised her right hand, her palm out as if quieting a vast audience. She spoke loudly in an unintelligible language. I marveled that she had gained in height and fullness. Still, I was cognizant enough to be amused. She stood before them in my boxers and top.

Laine looked at me and sweetly rolled her eyes, as if only I would understand. She turned back to the girls. "Rise! The goddesses are out today! Artemis hears you and accepts your gifts. I, too, now know you each by name and face. Stand and be gone! Enough! Enough of this!" She spoke in the same strange dialect but this time, inexplicably, I understood.

Laine gestured with both hands in exasperation: *Up, be gone.* The girls rose and fled en masse to the woods, their tunics tossing and arms flailing. One would trip on another and fall, others crawled in a frenzy. Only the orange-haired girl retained any appearance of dignity. Before she jumped the stream she pulled off the mask and turned to stare at Laine as if still in disbelief. Then, once across the stream, she ran.

Laine turned to me, saying, "No talk about bare asses. Show respect."

The field was empty except for the hound. It lowered itself onto the meadow, laying on its belly where the girls had danced. It licked one paw, then the other as if in disdain. As I observed the beast, it returned my stare with dead eyes, emotionless. I said, "The dog."

She clapped her hands and the hound sprang up, turned and gracefully leaped the stream. I saw a gray flicker or two as it ran, a flash of teeth as it looked back, then disappeared.

"The hound is Orthrus. He often appears two-headed. He is called the Two-Directional One, viewing the past and future simultaneously. You are lucky he comes one-headed. A good sign, as in that state he only sees the *now*."

She gripped my arm but I brusquely shook her off and walked to the stone table. The girls might be actresses, recruited from a local theatre group, but the altar would have been impossible to fake as each stone weighed hundreds of pounds. Equipment would have been needed to build it and there were no tracks.

The side of the structure shone with blood. Birds were lined one beside the other in rows, their heads scattered in the dirt. The tripod burned with a hot phosphorescence, undimmed by the light rain.

I looked across the field. A blue ribbon lay in the dirt, fallen from the head of one of the girls. I bent and picked it up. Laine hissed, "Leave every *thing* you find. None of these … are mere curiosities." I tossed the ribbon back.

She returned to the house and opened the door to our bedroom. I looked around a final time and followed. My ears rang, the sound rising and falling to the same rhythm as the lyres: one-two-*three*-four.

As I entered the bedroom, Laine pushed the door closed, her eyes as dark as Aisa's.

CHAPTER 21

She favored fluted folds, knife pleats,
skirts of bleached silk,
bleached silk blouses,
bleached silk scarves.
—*Poet X*

In the bedroom Laine braced herself against a wall, her luminescence gone.

"You're okay?" I asked.

"Yes," she said. "We do not appear in public."

"*We?* The sisters?"

"Yes. *We.*"

"How did they know you?"

She looked at me as if at a fool and shook her head. "Each of us is unmistakable. We're like rock stars. Or the personification of death. You saw their reaction. Hopeless fear." She used the phrase with me that she cast at the girls: "Be gone!"

As I opened the door, I turned and said harshly, "Get out of what you're wearing and into dry clothes."

I wandered upstairs. To my surprise Chloé stood at the kitchen windows. She didn't turn when I walked in. I thought, *Scotch*, and found a glass. "I'll take it neat," I said.

She turned. A rare Chloé smile. She wore nothing but briefs. Her breasts were slightly enlarged, nipples high — otherwise she appeared to have regained her coveted pre-pregnant grace, her belly firm. Their restorative abilities were phenomenal: I thought of the wound Laine incurred, how it vanished as I watched.

"The baby's asleep?"

"Yes." Another smile. "I bet you didn't realize our little hacienda came with an altar," she said, peering out again. "I correct that. Make that, *sacrificial* altar."

I poured scotch and walked over. She pointed to the massive structure. A dark stain blotted its heart, outlining the rows of headless birds. Rain fell. She put her head on my shoulder and said, "You're taking this well."

I avoided touching her. "No, I'm not. You obviously haven't been inside my head."

"I am when I want."

"I'd forgotten," I muttered, then said, "I've missed you."

She pushed against me. "She's prettier than me."

"What do you want me to say?" I distrusted it all. Reaching for my drink I said, "Aisa's well?"

She turned to the windows. "I'll tell you when she's not."

Another wave of heavy rain began. As I sipped the drink, looking away from Chloé, I heard Laine's voice, low and melodic: "The bird carcasses will be gone by dawn. Coyotes, crows and hawks."

I turned. She was effervescent and her eyes flashed. She had changed clothes, now in a navy blue dress, so long it dragged on the floor. Cut low, it hugged her breasts. Suitable, I thought, for a Hollywood runway, a vamp. "I haven't seen that before."

"You bought it for me." Her eyes steady, she ignored Chloé.

"Drink?"

"Gin and tonic."

That élan. The exhaustion had passed, a mere dimming in a foggy night. If I hadn't seen her in the bedroom a quarter hour earlier, I would never guess she could appear so beaten. I mixed a double as she watched. The sisters exchanged glances. Chloé shrugged: an agreement of some sort. Neither girl spoke. I sat in my usual chair and gestured to Laine. "Join me?"

She didn't move.

"Then," I said, "a question." She nodded, expectant. "Why are these … events … happening?"

"You know."

"Remind me."

"We're here," Laine said.

"So they come, moths to a flame … Old Kendrick said strange things happened in the back. Before you arrived."

With a sigh she said, "I should have been more subtle, should have anticipated the widow might see us. But I had to test the —" she hesitated, "energy."

She set her drink down and made a pirouette, one circle, rising like an egret. The dress shone in the low light. She half-bowed at the end and walked to the table, making exaggerated movements with her hips. As she sat, Chloé said, "Look at the girl walk."

I asked, "The nymphs we saw this afternoon — are they the same who appeared with Artemis days ago?"

"Different, the first nymphs were in their late teens."

"Of course." I went on, "Why was the event here? Why not further off, in the woods where no one would interrupt?"

"No one interrupted."

"Until the end. Until they saw you."

"Artemis is here because of us. Her nymphs follow wherever she goes."

"And the meadow?"

"It's what we call an *epikentros*, a place situated on a center. The Iroquois used this same spot thousands of years before this became Pennsylvania. The hillock, the oaks, the stream — the power was recognized long ago. The Greeks called such a place *omphalos*, the earth's navel. We're simply piggybacking."

Night fell and wind mowed through the trees. I had an urge to view the field. I imagined candles flickering, or lanterns waving, nymphs dancing with sparklers in the slippery grass. As I looked I saw darkness as black as Aisa's eyes and realized in disbelief that I wanted more, another spectacle. And another.

Chloé turned to leave. Laine raised her voice and said, "Next time, wear a top. I'm tired of seeing you uncovered."

She left and we sat in silence for a while, the air fresh, scoured. I found myself becoming almost buoyant, stupidly happy. Laine, too, flaunted quick, half-smiles. We stared at each other and laughed.

"You can't imagine what it took to get into this dress. I'll need help getting out."

In the light I saw nipples through the silk. "You go quickly from goddess to girl."

She shook her head. "Sounds like lyrics from a song."

❧

As Laine predicted, in the morning the carcasses were gone. Gone, too, the tripod, the knife and lustral branches. The altar remained, brazen in its mass. When I inspected it closely, flecks of blood were scattered in a wide diameter. Multiple strike marks marred the stone. To my surprise the ribbon I picked up yesterday still lay in place.

I felt someone watching and turned. Standing in the doorway of the bedroom, Laine waved — an odd, endearing gesture; we stood only fifteen feet apart. I motioned for her to join me. She sidled up and put an arm shyly around my waist.

" 'Morning, Dad." She smiled. "Kiss?"

I gave her a half one, saying, "Trying to make sense of what happened."

"You never relax." She walked to the stream, then turned. "I know you will. Go on, interrogate." She was barefoot, like the girls in yesterday's ceremony.

"The event. You said, a sacrifice to Artemis."

"Of course."

"Why not to you and Chloé?"

"No one sacrifices to us —"

"Wheedling favors, begging for longer lives?"

"Not a chance.'"

Laine stepped into the stream and balanced on a flat stone in the flow. "Look, we pulled a switch millennia ago. Now we simply watch who it takes, what it reaps."

"A good engineer would have built backdoors."

"That's retrospect. We weren't sure we'd ever wake. Or that we'd want to, or need to. The algorithm does its job."

"But now you're rewriting it?"

"Sort of." She leaped from the first stone to a smaller one and slipped into the water. "Cold!"

I offered a hand, pulling her to the bank. She slipped her arms around me. "I'm not awake yet … Gonna make coffee."

As she skipped to the house, I peered up at a hawk circling the meadow in loops. Staying in the field longer would be pleasant. I'd wait for Laine. So I slumped against the altar. Overhead the hawk wheeled lazily, its wings tilted, head cocked sideways. Without warning it raked abruptly to the side, making a rasping cry and dropped beyond my sight.

Then I remembered last night's dream: a hawk — but far larger. That dream-bird had been massive, an almost mechanical hawk, perched above me on a pine.

I had lain on my back on the edge of a river, in washed gravel, my feet stretched into a tea-colored flow. The hawk sat across and thirty feet above me. As I watched it swiveled its head from side to side.

It was three times the size of normal hawks, a vast bird with ivory beak, enameled eyes, its head shifting as if on a mighty bearing. Languid majesty, immense power. It spoke, a cry across the water: "You!"

I rose on my elbows. "Listen!" it cried, as if into a megaphone (I was bewildered that I understood its words). Bellicose, it rose on its wings above the pine, hung suspended, a winged cross darkening the sky. It moved closer, crying of a momentous bestowal. Then I knew: its flow of words was a gift I alone could hear, a message from Hawk to Man.

As it sang above me, I thought: 'No!' for the pivotal words, the gift it sang was all inane. I heard, *Aeaea aeaeao* — a looping, incomprehensible dream-wheel racing with an emptiness that left me cheated, aware of cowled time.

Then, it lifted higher, wheeling, accelerating away, no more than a soft blur. I lay in the river as if deaf, having retained nothing of its revelations — each prophetic word incomprehensible.

Uneventful weeks passed. However precious, our time seemed precarious, pointless. In those slow days I felt danger, never relaxing. I was fortunate to have work. Several contracts came in, all with gratifyingly short deadlines. Laine herself remained immersed in her "research," although to her credit, at least once a day she would drag me into the woods for a 45-minute walk where she'd sometimes stop, saying, "You know I've not forgotten you —?"

One afternoon we sat near the back of the property, the old stonewall visible about eighty feet from where we rested beneath a massive tree. Laine designated the tree as The Oak. When we hiked this area, we were obligated to stop and sprawl beneath its shade, the space between its swollen roots a perfect bed. On this afternoon, she wore my old khaki shorts and a random tee, and under the tee she wore a bra meant to — using her words — enchant me.

With her back against my chest, laying between my open legs, she played with my hands, dragging them across her belly. "I'm closing my eyes, but only for a minute," she said. And in seconds she'd fallen asleep, breathing softly. I ran my fingers over her legs. I treasured holding her like this. But eventually, after lingering in that sanctum, we would re-enter our old animation (the one confirmed solely by the arc of the wheeling sun).

And what was time, anyway? A giant wheel crushing the living. According to Laine, desperation to escape death's inevitability was what propelled medical research. Eliminating death would eliminate fear, and fear of death ran deep, immutable in men. Death took everyone — fathers, mothers, sisters, lovers, friends. To overcome it would be to overcome the hounds of destruction, the Fates themselves.

These goddesses would now preserve the sacred cycle. She woke in my arms, looking at me, her eyes stern. "Death," she said. "I can't leave you to your own thoughts, can I?" She shook her head. "Death *is*, it's a prerequisite of life. But be patient. I'll not leave you behind."

CHAPTER 22

You are looking in a mirror
that reflects nothing you have ever seen,
a cosmos of stars, swirling gases
where you have always had a face,
always eyes, ears, a pleasing mouth.
Now there is instead a blur, the hum
of hydrogen & helium.
—Poet X

Days after dreaming of the hawk, I invited Laine to hike, surprised when she said no. Working in her office, she said, "Go without me today —"

"Sure." I shrugged. "I'll be ready in ten if you change your mind." She didn't and as I started, the outside temperature hovered at 90. I hoped the over-story of trees would provide shelter. I was right: once I entered the woods, the heat dropped.

Taking my usual route, I intersected the second stream. Steeper than Pegasus, it twisted around scattered boulders. A narrow deer trail followed the stream. I decided to explore, assuming the path would disappear or enter thick brush. The stream itself got wider as I walked beside it, enough so that crossing was a challenge. Yet, the path stayed clear. I continued, seeing the stonewall ahead. The ground flattened and the stream's velocity slowed. As it did, it widened and flowed under the stonewall.

Curious to see my abutter's land from this view, I walked to the wall. There the stream entered a large pool. Shrubs blocked my view, so I shifted down the wall slightly. With a clear view, I startled: a half dozen girls bathed in shadows. Two more sat on the bank. In the middle stood a taller woman: *Artemis*.

Tunics hung on shrubs. Below the tunics, stacked with precision, bows and arrows shone. I remained motionless, crouching close enough to hear their voices. I was surprised I saw no sentry, but this little grove lay deep in the woods. Then, beyond the pool, in the woods, something glinted. Crawling along the stonewall, I tried to make it out while staying in view of the pool. Then I saw a man.

Holding binoculars he watched — a snoop, I thought, then caught myself. We were both spying, although my prowling could be excused as accidental. To my amazement the man stood, plainly convinced he couldn't be seen. He appeared to be in his 50s, a patrician with a wave of gray hair. In any other setting, he would have been imposing.

Within a moment, one of the girls on the pool's bank startled and pointed. All the bathers retreated to the edge, watching, covering themselves with their hands. Only Artemis stayed in the pool's center, watching. I lowered myself and saw the man, now obviously exposed, hesitate. I imagine his first instinct was to hide. But instead, he took a step forward, paused, then noisily pushed his way through the brush toward the pool. It proved a fatal mistake.

He raised his voice, blustering at the girls as he lumbered closer. "What the hell are you doing here?" Then, "You're trespassing, all of you!"

As he stumbled onto the far bank of the pool, he pulled a cellphone from his pocket. Its edges shown dully in the stillness. "Let's get a video of this whole drunken group —" He raised the phone. At that moment, Artemis pointed at him: the air crackled.

Instantly, he was wrapped in thin blue flames that mimicked the electrical dance of a Tesla coil. Hot streamer arcs of purple fire popped around his flesh. Delicate corona discharges sang, filaments shot six and seven feet from his body, his face gone, obscured in hot ribbons of light.

Artemis dropped her arm, the electrical discharges fading. A faint haze drifted in the man's vicinity, and when it cleared, an old, unsteady stag stood in his place. It looked around uncomprehendingly, fear shooting through its eyes. Then it bolted, running into the woods, charging into a tree, hitting it hard. It fell forward onto its forelegs, then stood and charged again.

Running into the tree was calamitous as it gave the bathers time to grab bows. Artemis and the nymphs followed it in a rush. The stag got no farther than forty feet before leaping a fallen tree. Gracefully rising with its chest high, arrows slammed in a tight circle into its ribs. As it started its descent toward the ground, its legs gave and it collapsed, struggling to rise, then buckled sideways.

In a flash the girls surrounded it, one callously opening its eye with her fingers before stepping away. All danced nervously around the carcass, bending and dipping their hands into the blood bubbling from the wounds. I thought: *blood-lust*, something I'd heard described, but never seen.

Artemis made a gesture with her head. Several of the girls stooped with knifes and ran a deep incision down its belly. I was close enough to see the stag's bowels disgorge. Another girl approached with a twenty-foot leather thong. The girls whip-tied the stag's front feet together, and threw the free end of the thong over a pine branch about ten feet off the ground. I heard laughter, whooping from the girls.

One of the nymphs hacked off a lower leg, chopping at the joint. A second girl pulled the leg out sideways, tearing it away. The leg freed with a start and was passed from girl to girl, each ripping the exposed meat free with her teeth, licking fingers and wiping palms on their waists and hips. They were smeared with blood, their eyes flashing with a wildness and camaraderie I found frightening.

Artemis barked a single word and six of the girls grabbed the leather thong, pulling the hacked stag up vertically so the carcass hung off the ground. Tying off the thong, they exchanged glances and turned to leave, their bodies muscled and lithe. Close enough to hear their breathing, I saw their triumphant eyes.

Then with a sharp whistle, one of the girls to my left at the pool gestured with her arm. I realized she was pointing at me. I stood in full view, separated only by the stonewall. I was not conscious of having stood.

All of them froze. No one raised a bow. I stared into Artemis' eyes, her gaze steady. After seconds, she turned without expression and all returned to the pool where they washed themselves, then pulled tunics over their heads and tied sashes into place. The youngest girls ran to retrieve arrows from the stag. As they passed, I was ignored. Once beside the carcass, they pulled the arrows from its belly. With the bloody shafts in hand, they returned to the others and left in single file. After a moment, the woods returned to silence. The three-legged stag swung from the branch.

Sitting on the ground, I started shivering, conscious I had seen Artemis naked, witnessed a savage killing and been allowed to live.

When I returned home, Laine was in the meadow, circling slowly on one foot in the center of the beaten grass. She wore a thin sundress with starfishes imprinted on its front. The sun cut through it, outlining her legs. As I approached, she smiled. "A long hike. I know what happened, but I'd like to hear."

"I took a couple side roads, ran into a few surprises. You know, the usual hike in the woods." She said nothing, so I said, "There was more. Things got sticky. Ran into some girls."

"I hope they dressed modestly. God knows, I don't need competition."

"I'm not in the mood to banter."

She brushed her dress off thoughtfully. "I'm sorry. I thought we'd chat."

"I need a drink."

In the kitchen, I told her what had happened. She listened avidly, nodding occasionally. As I finished, I said, "I still don't understand."

"That immutable law: no man sees Artemis naked and lives?"

"Yes, we stood less than fifteen feet apart. She has freckles on her chest like yours."

"You got an eyeful."

"Yet, I'm alive."

Laine sighed, exasperated. "She let you live because of me. She sees you, she sees me, not some wandering man."

I felt nothing and had nothing clever to say. Laine's eyes burned with intensity.

§.

Night came like every other. We talked and, close to dawn, slept an hour. I had always required seven hours — more during stressful periods. At first I worried, wondering when I would crash, but gradually accepted the truncated sleep.

I wondered if Laine needed sleep at all, or merely indulged me. Perhaps she represented a metamorphosis I, too, would experience if I spent enough time with her. And so I wrestled with what seemed irreducible mysteries.

The next morning, I wondered if I should report the incident to the police. But I caught myself. Doing so would begin a cascade of inquiries. The truth would never be accepted. Any factual report I might offer would be considered bizarre, a raving — and only I had witnessed what occurred.

Laine walked into the kitchen while I drank coffee. I smiled. She was dressed in my underwear. It no longer seemed strange. She shook her head. "I realize you had to work that out. And you had to reach the conclusion you did."

"I didn't know the man. A neighbor? Hell, these properties are so big you have to walk a mile to find the next house."

"He lived next door."

"He might have been anyone."

"But he wasn't. He was a wealthy man. Will you take me to that pool? I'll even take off my clothes if you ask —" She sat in my lap and put her hands on my shoulders.

"I'll take you there, but I'm not sure about the pool."

"Why?"

"For one thing, we'd be trespassing."

"Who'd know?" She was right and pressed on. "We should go this morning. I've never been down the trail you found. Come on."

"Not this afternoon?"

"Let's not be predictable. And it'll be cooler now."

A quarter hour later we stood at the trail intersection. Laine wore a black pleated skirt and a tee with a backpack hitched over her shoulders. Taking a hard left at the second stream, we walked downhill on the narrow path. I whispered, "The stream crosses under the wall in about forty feet."

"You don't need to whisper. We're alone."

I gave her a look. She was telling me no one would interfere. Still, I felt apprehension. As we approached the stonewall, I saw what remained of the stag hanging to the right. The pool glistened in its dark grove beyond the wall.

The deer hung stripped of its flesh, only its head intact, its bones and ligaments an odd, shining rainbow of whites, slick yellows and pink. "Coyotes?"

"Yes," she said. "Let's climb the wall and inspect the pool." The old stones were secure and we jumped it. As we approached she paused. "Listen."

I wasn't sure whether I heard wind through the trees or music. The sound faded, then increased slightly — a single flute playing Artemis' song. We stepped into the grove. Being this close seemed remarkable. The banks and ground closest to the pool were covered in thick moss. Laine said, "Take off your shoes. All here is sacred."

She took off her clothes, hanging the garments on a shrub, and smiled. "You, too." She was lovely in the dappled light and stepped into the pool, putting her arms out and laughing. I undressed and joined her. The water was cooler than I expected. As we stood beside each other, the tune continued.

We didn't linger. Dressing, she wanted to see the spot where Artemis had stopped the man. Nothing remained. I wondered about his binoculars and phone, half expecting to find them. At her insistence, she inspected the stag bones, crouched beside the blood stain beneath it, and examined the leather thong. Flies buzzed inside the beast's ribs and around its eyes.

"In a few days in this heat, it will look like a hunter's kill," I said.

"Isn't that what it is?" She stood and gazed into my eyes. "His time had come." She leaned up and took my lower lip softly between her teeth. When she released me, she said, "Now take me home."

&

Ten days after what now I thought of as the stag incident, one of my clients noted during a call that I lived in the same town as a hedge fund manager mentioned on national news. He told me Al James of James Investment Funds had disappeared. James and his firm managed $49 billion in state and local pensions. His wife reported him missing. A former employee stated James owned residences worldwide, and was caught in the past with the wife of one of his traders in the Bahamas. The press had already reached conclusions.

After the call, I went online and found a bulletin about James that included a photo, but the quality was poor. I read further that he was indeed a resident of the town, although the article didn't give an address. Known for his extensive art collection, he sat on the board of two museums. Artists in his collection included Matisse, Kitaj, Duchamp, Rauschenberg, Bonnard, Giacometti …

Another photo showed him surrounded by several young women at a party on Sea Island. He appeared to be in his early 50s, his arm around the waist of a girl. Artemis had eliminated one of the country's wealthier men.

A few minutes later, Laine came into my office wearing a new dress. She turned twice and said, "You like?" I pointed at the screen. She scanned my face and turned to the computer.

I said, "His name was James. A financier with immense wealth. And now with a grieving wife. National news is running the story."

"They'll never find him. Unless they go searching for the ribcage of a stag." She kissed my forehead and lightly whirled away.

On Friday, we were visited by two policemen. They introduced themselves as local and said they had questions. I invited them in. As they entered Laine joined us and raised her eyebrow. I pull my arm around her and introduced her as my daughter; it remained a convenient ploy. I heard Aisa crying. The older detective, a man about 40, opened a file and showed us a photo of James, noting that he was missing. It looked like something off a press release. Had we seen him in the last couple weeks? Were we friends? Had we run into anyone who had seen him? Had we met socially? Had we ever heard of the James Investment Funds? Did I have money invested there? Did we know his wife? The detective asked Laine this last question directly, presupposing they ran in the same circles.

We responded negatively to every question. Laine sat beside me throughout, her arm through mine. The younger officer, a man in his 30s, asked to speak to my wife — maybe she knew something. Laine quickly interjected that, although I'd never married, I was the best father imaginable. That she kept hooking me up with attractive women, but I remained unreasonably devoted to my daughters. At the end of her elaboration, she kissed my cheek.

The men stood and thanked us, saying they might have more questions and to report anything warranting attention. After they left, Laine turned into my arms. "Kiss me. Nothing I said isn't true. You're the best." Her eyes dampened.

"Will we see them again?"

She shook her head. "They got nothing here. They'll learn nothing anywhere. It'll play out in time. We know he ran off with his secretary."

CHAPTER 23

Nothing is analogous,
all inside out,
the sudden mutation
according to plan, or no plan (a random
thing, an anōmalia).
—*Poet X*

As this story has been largely sequential, I should note that a month and a half earlier, shortly after Artemis killed the multi-headed dog in my back meadow, I searched on-line under mythology. I remembered almost nothing from school. My introduction to ancient names and images was from Chloé, her movies and books. As Laine talked about her past, I repeatedly checked her stories.

My early research centered on Laine's claim that she, Chloé and Aisa were a reanimation of the Greek Fates, or the Moirai. The information she shared in our conversations seemed accurate. She described the Fates as the children of Night, or Nyx. Whether their father was Phanes was debated. All but an occasional scholar recounted them as virgins. Yes, the Fates could extinguish even the lives of gods.

A celebrated Greek goddess, Artemis had been conceived by Zeus and Leto. Her brother was Apollo. Famed in archaic Greece as a hunter, she protected — ironically, I thought — wild animals, as well as girls. A number of stories involved Artemis and stags, nymphs, hounds and hunting. She and Apollo were birthed on Delos, an island within sight of Mykonos, both volcanic outcrops in the Mediterranean. When their mother, Leto, sought a place to give birth, only Delos welcomed her.

Laine's explication about the Roman emperor Theodosius was equally correct. He had, she said, destroyed many of the sacred temples in the Mediterranean world. Under pressure from Nicene bishops, he approved a major purge about 360 years after Jesus' death. Numerous church figures were complicit.

Within a few decades of Theodosius' edict, the open worship of the old Greek gods largely ceased. Burnt sacrifices, public and private, were banned. State support of pagan worship, which had been extensive, ended. As Laine mentioned in our discussions, thousands of sacred groves, statues and temples were destroyed throughout the empire. In a final conflagration in the same period, the library in Alexandria, Egypt, burned for a third time in what was mankind's greatest literary loss. The period of CE 392 to 396, although celebrated by the Christian movement, was one of humanity's darkest eras.

I found nothing in my research indicating the Fates chose to withdraw or retreat from the world. I had to take Laine's word that all the classical gods retreated in the same period. I also found no prediction that the Fates would reappear. Scattered, secret worship of Artemis, Athene, Aphrodite, and others continued, but lost resonance in succeeding generations.

Laine's fantastical claims were bolstered by the reality of the unfolding drama around me, and the supernatural wellness of all three sisters. I had attributed Chloé's childhood health to my parenting. Now I rejected that. Laine's ability to heal wounds — both mine and hers — remained inexplicable (which lent further, almost undeniable, weight to her claims). And that shaman's trick paled next to Artemis' powers.

In the end the research was useful, but far from conclusive. Laine was aware, as she appeared to know all things, that I had been conducting my own investigations, as within a few days of my first searches, she said, "Did you expect me to lie?"

One night, I asked her if their DNA were somehow dissimilar, that is, if an a-mortal being — her description — was biologically different from a mortal. She thought the question farcical, but could tell I was serious. "Of course we cannot be the same," she said. "If so, we would be susceptible to the same illnesses as you."

Several weeks after our discussion and before the stag incident, I wondered to myself if having their DNA tested might reveal anything of interest. The girls had the same father, different mothers, and an otherwise unknown background. So I decided to proceed, aware that the tests would have to be surreptitious. Laine would be most likely to object. The lab I contacted required a spit sample, or cheek swab, which I thought possible.

I vaguely hoped that a DNA analysis might trace ancestry and confirm all three's Mediterranean origin. Still, I recognized that as illogical. These girls were not the original Fates. Their transference could only be of the original *consciousness* of the goddesses.

Regardless, I secretly ordered kits.

One Sunday evening during the period that our relationship still flourished, Laine and I lay in bed discussing random topics — the absurd allure of camisoles, endocrine disruptors, the Black Plague of the 15th century (during which she was comatose), and the plague that struck Athens at its height (which she watched unfold).

As that evening turned into morning, I found by chance that she played chess, one of my small passions. I wasn't sure where I'd stored my board and pieces, so our discovery led nowhere. We fell asleep about 4 a.m. I woke at dawn, aware during the brief time that I'd had another dream.

My dreams were more vivid now. This particular one was odd, in that it was overtly biblical. Perhaps it related to our evening talks, although I remembered discussing nothing similar.

In it, I lived in a desert and heard something outside my tent. I left my wife and children — my wife cried, "Jacob, be careful!" — and went to investigate. A man stood several feet from the entrance. As I straightened, he gripped my arms. We struggled. He had wings.

Despairing, I continued trying to free myself, growing tired. I demanded, "Who are you?" His head was hooded. Over his shoulder, I saw dawn. We had wrestled all night. He angrily released me and vanished. I fell to my knees exhausted.

As I woke, Laine stirred beside me and stared into my eyes. I recited the dream. "Jacob and the angel," she said. "Old Testament."

"What the hell —?"

She pulled me to her. "Getting upset when you wake is not allowed."

"I can't imagine what could have triggered that —"

She paused. "Not everything is rational."

"Yes, but why wrestling an angel?"

In a hushed voice she said, "Angels don't exist. They're an archetype, burned into the human psyche. There is no such thing … just fictions from pre-history, symbols that rattle around in the human unconsciousness."

"Big words for early in the day."

"Sorry. I'll make coffee if you wish."

"Laine, if I wrestled an angel, why was it so easy to … neutralize?"

"Jack," she said, "it wasn't real."

❧

The kits arrived in an unmarked box. Laine had said nothing since I placed the order. I carried the box to my office and opened it: four, each kit nine-inches long. Inside each lay a discreet cylinder for the sample. As I handled one, Laine opened the door and walked in. She wore a dress I'd never seen — a thin piece with pinstripes, demure enough for a 1950s teenager. She stopped a few feet away.

Seeing the kits, she said, "They've come! Shall I be first?"

As many times as I had anticipated her reaction, I was still surprised. She said, "One just spits in the tube —"

As she reached, I grabbed her wrist and pulled her into my lap. She squealed and put her face into my neck. I set the cylinder down carefully and held her with both hands. She moaned as I ran a hand up her ribs. Eventually I found her nylons and garters.

"Very girlie."

"Yes?"

"Why?"

"I wore them because I'm a maiden."

"Maidens wear garters?"

"Of course they do." She whispered, "I do. And I am."

I whispered conspiratorially, "I hesitate to even ask, but ... do maidens spit into tubes?"

"Should I use my tongue instead?"

"Can you spit decorously?" I handed her the cylinder.

She spit into it, then held it up. "Enough for science."

She handed it back and, following the instructions, sealed it and labeled it using the press-on barcode. She kissed my cheek and said, "You thought I'd object."

"I did."

She said, "You'll need help getting samples from the other two."

"I figured Aisa would be easy."

"Assume nothing. She'll know." She hesitated. "But I can get it. And I will. It'll be easy for me, impossible for you. And I can get Chloé's, too."

"Why would you help?"

"Because we're collaborators." She stood, taking the kits.

After lunch I asked Laine if she wanted to take a walk. She nodded and changed. We met in the meadow and set out briskly. The afternoon felt pleasant, the sky filled with cumulus clouds suspended in a blue sea.

Almost halfway to the stonewall, she said, "Remember yesterday's dream? You couldn't relate it to anything and none of it made sense because ... I created it." I stopped and turned to her. She shrugged. "And I misled you when you woke. You weren't wrestling with an angel."

My breathing slowed. "Oh? With whom did I wrestle?"

"Not an angel. Not a god. You wrestled Death."

"Laine! You're fucking with me. Why would you do that?"

"For the outcome."

"You mean, I wasn't defeated —?"

"You weren't. Death gave up and left."

I looked into her face. My hands trembled. "What do you mean?"

"Death has walked away." Her eyes teared.

"Laine, what have you done?"

"Something remarkable. I've done something … we've never done."
She covered her face. I wrapped her in my arms and stroked her back.
She appeared so honest when she wasn't playing. But at this moment, I
wanted to hear no more.

I said, "Let's keep going. I want to see if the carcass is still there." I
took her hand and pulled her along the path toward the back.

At the stonewall, we stopped and I put my arm around her. The stag's
remains swayed in the breeze, stripped of flesh, the bones shining as if
varnished. The head remained untouched except for its eyes, each a pit.
The surface of the pool shimmered in the breeze and Laine pointed,
saying, "I want to lie with you, there."

She took my hand. We helped each other cross the wall and stepped
into the grove. "Here," she said. "on the moss." As we lay down, she
pulled me to her. She was ecstatic, clinging. I found it all terrifying.

"Isn't this pool sacred?"

She looked startled. "So what, Jack?"

"I can't do this. Not here."

She looked hurt. I sat up, looking into the pool while she lay on her
back. After a moment I said, "Now continue. What did you do that was
remarkable?"

"Created an opening, a small portal. Don't ask more —" Then she
pointed behind me. "Look!" Across the pool, I saw a girl. She squatted,
her legs apart, a long silver bow in her hand, her face empty, her eyes
incurious. She reminded me of the hound. I guessed she was twenty-feet
away.

I turned to Laine. "A nymph?" She nodded, and I pulled her to her
feet. She took my hand and we returned to the stonewall, scaling it in a
single bound. I glanced back and the girl had not moved except to follow
us with her eyes. Once on the path, we took up a swift pace home.

I had a sense of elation that seemed unjustified, or at the least, incautious. I had not felt as reckless in years.

CHAPTER 24

Sea-borne: mountains
Rising from the steam.
On the gleaming
Islands, horned dogs leaping
At the necks of deer.
—Poet X

S everal days later Laine suggested we meet in the meadow. I was
working in my office when she leaned in. I said, "Five minutes. I'm
winding up an email." Moments later as I walked out, I looked up. The
sky was ashen, an even wash of gray from edge to edge. Laine wore jeans
and a light sweater. She was doing an odd yogic stretch near the altar. As
I approached, she straightened. I took her face in my hands. "Okay, now
what?"

She pointed toward the backside of the stone structure. We walked
over and sat with our backs to the house. Touching her arm was reassuring. She appeared happy and her mood infectious. She whispered, "I
have the samples, sealed to go. Let's do lunch in town. Yes?"

I nodded. "Why the whispering?"

"I've had to block them both on this. I've pulled down a tiny veil." She grinned. I understood. She'd won.

"Can't they read my thoughts?"

"I closed us both."

"Okay. Let's do coffee in that small cafe —" As if five years old, she clapped her hands excitedly and leaned over to kiss.

"Difficult getting the samples?"

"With Aisa, no. Once I walled her out, she was easy. Babies are always slobbering anyway. I took a scoop."

"Chloé?"

She pulled a cigarette from a pack and lit it, blowing out a lazy ring. "I tricked her. You know how she's always sipping water? I got a cup and put in salt. She drank and spat it out. I harvested what she spat. Sounds gross, but it won't affect the test."

"I'd have needed the military to pull that off."

"Yeah, it wouldn't have been pretty." She turned serious. "We have a lot to talk about. Plans, strategies … and I have surprises." We stood and once in our bedroom, she pulled the sweater off.

"Wrong color, don't you agree?" She wore one of Chloé's bras, dusky pink with a front clasp, the narrow straps black. "I might go braless —"

I pulled her to me and said, "No. And pick out a blouse."

She pouted and I left. Randomly, I thought of James and the bones hanging near the pool, steps away from Artemis' grove — and the phrase Laine had used when we lay there that kept rerunning in my mind like a popular song: *I've done something remarkable.*

❧

Aisa was 94 days old, her eyes piercing. The child now regularly called me *Da-da*. The night before, after dinner, she pulled herself up using a chair, then took a step before falling. She would be walking soon. But her physical achievements, as startling as they were, paled in comparison to her awareness.

Laine stressed repeatedly that the child was fully conscious. And I believed she was. My youngest daughter, the reaper: malevolent, malign.

Before Laine and I left for lunch, I found Chloé with the child. She gave me a short list of things to buy. To my surprise she said, "Remember, I gave you away. That doesn't mean you forget me."

I was unsure how to respond. She'd made her feelings clear months ago. Now I was being upbraided. I said, "Chloé!"

"Get hold of yourself. You look at her with love-struck eyes."

"You're exaggerating."

"I'm not. She even asks what lingerie you favor and then wears it." Angrily she said, "She must have half my bras."

I thought, *An absurd comment.* She sat in front of me wearing her old schoolgirl underwear, topless, oblivious to the ludicrousness of it all. I tried to give her a reassuring touch, but she pushed me back. "Leave. Leave me alone."

At 11:30 a.m., Laine and I drove to town. I thought of the ridiculous confrontation with my violet-eyed daughter. Laine shook out a cigarette from a pack and lit it, saying, "So why was Chloé upset?"

"You know."

She paused. "The truth is she's uneasy because she senses I've blocked something. She doesn't know what it is. She's not even certain I have. But she's suspicious."

"And I'm the fall guy."

"Screw her." She ran her left hand through her hair, holding the cigarette away, watching smoke race out the cracked window. She sighed, took a deep pull and turned. "No one is an expert in everything. You know what I mean?"

"No idea."

"You're a financial whiz, right?"

"Supposedly."

"From my research, one of the best. But you don't know anything about AI. Or Euripides, big data or the origin of *Homo sapiens.* You couldn't build a cellphone, explain quantum physics, or replace someone's aortic valve."

"Where are you going with this?"

"I'm like you. Ask me about genetics. Or cellular senescence. I can hold my own, but only in that specialty."

"It's become a complex world."

"Yes, and the new complexity presents problems I underestimated …"

She finished her cigarette and flicked the butt out the window. "There are thousands of labs and universities across the world, all working on disjunct solutions to life extension, even immortality, each headed by someone hoping their path will lead to a Nobel."

"Typical science."

"Multiple targets."

I kept my eye on the road. What she described was beyond me. Anything I said would be conversational at best. "We're minutes away."

She smiled. "Let's eat first. Then mail the kits. After that, you can hand your credit card to your girl."

"Sure you don't have a platinum?"

"Even if, you're buying."

I eased the car into the restaurant parking. "We'll do Italian today. They have decent wines."

Our table was beside a bank of windows shielded from the street by cafe curtains. We'd gotten lucky — it was still early and the restaurant was quiet. We placed our order.

Laine turned to me and said, "Like my blouse?" It was a simple white piece without sleeves or collar.

"You know I do."

"I like to hear you say it. Over and over works." Then her voice dropped. "I've concluded no one person, or even a small subset of persons, knows everything. Leonardo was an anomaly. But he lived 600 years ago." She put her hand on mine. "I thought I'd identify a dozen experts, eliminate them all and be done. But the ideas are too widespread."

"I am half following you at best."

"There's another problem. Let me put it like this: You can kill the man with the idea, but not the idea itself. At least not once it's in the wild."

Waitstaff brought our drinks and an appetizer. Over wine she said, "I was naïve to believe there was a single genius out there. Or as is often the case, two geniuses who don't even know of each other's identical work. Do you see?"

"I see the kill-list expanding."

"Yes. I now have ninety targets, not a dozen."

I saw her mind firing, but she caught herself and sighed. Our food arrived and the waitress poured more wine. Laine frowned, shifting her chair so she sat closer — we almost touched — and said, "One of the prongs will be publishing research that disproves the theory that life can be without limits. By research I mean faked lab results, stuff I conjure. You remember I said the ideas have to be squashed, as well as the propagators?"

"Do you want a critique?"

She gave me a puzzled look. "No, I'm thinking out loud. And giving you a sense of where I'm heading." Laughing she said, "But you, sir, are an impediment."

"Excuse me?"

"For twenty years I've focused on one thing. Now you've distracted me. Now I think about you ... as much as I do my challenges."

She laughed. "What did you call me once? A 'greedy girl.' Okay, it's true. Who knows why? I have so much of you, I hang with you all the time, I sleep with you. None of it's enough."

After lunch, we shopped. She bought dresses, a couple skirts, blouses, a red scarf, boots, and belts. At the last store, she bought bras — "I'm returning Chloé's to Chloé. She's so angry" — and several expensive camisoles.

We stopped briefly at the post office, mailing the samples. As we left she smiled. "You're good with numbers, right?"

"Try me."

"Affirmed with that expensive education."

I shrugged, pretending boredom. "No different than Stanford or UCLA."

"Let's not," she said, pausing. "I thought we'd have fun, but you're spoiling it. One last chance for you. Here are three numbers: 30, 25 and 32. What do they mean?"

I sensed a grand game. Were the numbers fractals? The sequence for a combination lock? I glanced at her as I drove. She said, "No more hints. 30 ... 25."

"How many guesses do I get?"

"Sometimes you're a dolt."

Then I knew: 30, Chloé's bust size, so probably Laine's.

"Your measurements?"

She grinned. We fell into a pleasant quiet. She lit another cigarette and exhaled. "I adore these cigs. I can get away with things that would kill the common girl."

CHAPTER 25

She was perfect in her own way,
able to speak as one who has
become conscious
when she had not.
—Poet X

The next morning I woke to faint music in the meadow, doubtless a harbinger: the same solemn, sacred tune. One-two-*three*-four. Lyres, I guessed, and a tambourine. Rather than rise, I lay beside Laine, listening.

She moaned lightly. I reached and touched her hip. My lover, I thought, who is not. A maiden who is and isn't.

In so many ways I dreaded these days ending, more than I dreaded the implementation of her plans. I remained enamored of her — an absurdity in itself. I knew enough to know it couldn't last — and to distrust every facet, however joyous. It was a strange, deeply imperfect love.

I remembered Chloé's characterization: outlaw love. How could I forget? Three months ago, I thought I understood love, accepted its madness. Love, a flamethrower, burning all before it. Now I wondered if Chloé were no more than a precursor to Laine, goddess superseding goddess, one stepping into the footsteps of the first.

The music continued, rising and falling. I drifted and thought idly of the DNA testing, imagining the hissing whirl of the double helix, what it would reveal. Laine moved slightly, turned her head with a small sigh, and woke.

"Morning," she said, her eyes still closed. She lifted her head. "Music?"

"For the last few minutes."

She sighed. "Artemis comes again; the music's an omen."

But it ended. I showered, shaved and dressed. The weather had turned hot again. I half expected the music to lead to something immediate, but it faded. After breakfast, I spent hours in my office without interruption. About eleven, Laine and I shared coffee upstairs, this time with Chloé. She still walked around the house half-dressed, being defiant or merely haphazard.

Finishing her coffee, Laine stood, inviting Chloé to hike. Laine offered to carry Aisa, but Chloé refused. Laine shrugged — "So, don't go" — and gazed at me. "Can you be ready in a few?"

I assumed our walk, earlier than usual, was a setup for something — Artemis or a gathering of nymphs. In our bedroom, Laine changed from a cami and pulled on one of my old tees. I grabbed a shirt as we left. The humidity was up. Laine strode into the meadow and said, "It'll be cooler in the woods."

But it wasn't. We became soaked within minutes. By the time we reached the second brook, she stopped. "Let's pause —"

I scanned the woods, curious. We appeared to have been followed by three or four crows. As we slowed, they gathered in a tall pine, making loud caws as they settled onto the limbs and shook their wings. I was unsurprised when the archaic music restarted. Girls, I thought, in tunics with lyres, somewhere nearby. But no one appeared. Laine gestured with her head and we continued.

She set a fast pace and I found my excitement building. We continued several hundred feet where we encountered a clearing. Several girls played lyres at its edge and ignored us. The music slowed to a few notes, still in that familiar rhythm: one - two - *three* - four ... At the edge of the clearing, to our right, was a stone bench. Laine pointed and we sat.

A manila folder lay on the bench. Stenciled letters read, *J. NIGHT.* Laine passed it to me. Inside was a theatre program, a single page printed on heavy stock.

The People's Theater
Today's Event:
"The Stag Appears In Wingéd Victory"
Starring
Artemis As Herself
Hunter 1, Hunter 2
A Stag, Crows, Does & Nymphs.
Music Provided By A Small Quartet.
Synopsis:
Artemis Tricks The Evil Hunters,
Causing Their Demise.

The program looked decades old. Laine put her arm in mine, saying nothing.

Except for the crows, the woods were quiet. I glanced up: more birds. Circling the clearing once, they swept into the opening, landing and shuffling dispiritedly. Laine squinted. The humidity soaked our clothes and her hair was damp. She took her hat off and ran her hands through her hair, her blouse stuck to her back.

A dozen nymphs entered the clearing, marching in twos. They stopped at the edge, and on a signal from an older girl, squatted and waited. An audience? Actors in the event?

Then, a gunshot rang out a hundred feet away. Laine put a finger to her lips: "Hush."

Within a minute two hunters in camouflage and high boots entered the clearing carrying rifles. In the middle, a short distance from us, they slowed, scanning the ground — one of them in his thirties, the other older. The younger man said, "The buck headed this way. With that hit, he couldn't have gotten far." Their voices seemed amplified.

The older man nodded. "Lost the blood trail. A clean shot, too."

"We'll pick it up again —"

The older man broke his rifle open, checking the load. The gun was double-barreled — a shotgun. He closed the weapon, jammed the butt against his shoulder and swung the rifle randomly, then lowered it, looking disgusted. The younger man said, "Let's separate, Clive. The blood'll be obvious." They disengaged, separated by about twenty feet, heads down, walking in parallel.

After seconds, the older man snarled, "Anything?"

The younger man shook his head. Seconds passed, then a large stag appeared behind them, followed by four does. The stag was six-prong, likely the same animal that had walked so confidently through our meadow. It stopped at the edge of the clearing. Laine pointed and at the same moment I saw its wound: a stomach shot. Blood soaked its lower belly, yet it seemed oblivious.

One of the does stepped forward, snapping a branch, startling. Both hunters turned at the sound. The stag bolted into the center of the clearing between the hunters, splitting the distance evenly. As it charged, they raised their guns.

The stag gracefully rose in the air as if leaping high brush. To my astonishment, they fired at the stag at the same moment, and as they did, the deer became Artemis, who dropped to the ground in a crouch. She was fierce-looking and squatted on her knees. I realized the two hunters had missed her entirely. Instead, they had shot each other. The older man grunted and pitched backward. The younger man stared at his own chest, at the wound — staggered and fell.

They lay without moving. Artemis stood, straightening her tunic. It shone in the sun as if woven from gold thread. She gripped a bow in her hand. My ears still rung from the shots. I stood and Laine pulled me down. "*No!*" The nymphs, who had squatted throughout, rose and rushed into the center of the clearing, gathering around Artemis, hugging, whinnying and beginning a dance: the same incipient frenzy as when James had gone down. I guessed what would follow. I turned to Laine to speak and she put her hands on my cheeks, then her mouth on mine in a sudden, frantic kiss, breathing raggedly. She seemed caught in the frenzy.

Then she pushed me away. I glanced at the clearing and saw nymphs in groups of four pulling the men by their feet into the woods. The shotguns lay where they fell. Artemis stood in the center with her back to us.

This time when I stood, Laine made a high-pitched whistle and Artemis pivoted.

Laine rose and the two raised their palms in the old hieratic greeting. The nymphs, mirroring the panic I saw at the sacrifice weeks earlier, reacted to Laine as before, falling to the ground. Artemis lowered her hands. Laine made an odd move, given the circumstances, and slipped her arm around my waist, pulling me tightly against her. I felt her luminescence, a lustral heat. Her eyes flared, her face flush. The nymphs remained scattered on the ground, whimpering. The crows frightened upward, drifting away.

Artemis took two decisive steps toward us, and I felt my stomach constrict. Laine snapped her palm up at the goddess, stopping her. Artemis was now ten feet from us. She smiled, untroubled, nodded and turned away. I heard her voice then, melodious, resonant. "Up, all you girls," she sang lightly. "Eyes down, away!" She spoke in a strange language, but I understood.

She turned one last time to us and with her right fist, tapped twice above her left breast. Laine spoke a monosyllabic word in response. Each woman was dazzling. Artemis left and I watched. I realized that she, of all of us, appeared unaffected by the heat.

Bizarrely, the four deer that had accompanied the stag to the clearing still stood on the far edge, watching. The goddess approached them, stopping within feet of the closest. Her back was to us but I heard her whistle, and the does turned and bounded into the woods, tails up. Artemis followed. I still held Laine — or Laine held me — and said, "I can no longer tell what's real and what isn't. Did two men die or is this theatre?" She said nothing. "Really, Laine, what the fuck?"

She felt feverish, her hands trembling now that we were alone. I forced her away, saying, "What just happened?"

"She wanted to speak to you. I stopped her."

"That's all?"

"Yes … you're not ready."

"And the hunters?"

"Their time had —"

"Bullshit. They're actors."

She pushed her hair back, her lashes wet, pupils dilated. I walked into the clearing. A shotgun lay in the dirt. I broke it open and smelled the chamber: the foul scent of burnt powder, an unused shell in the second chamber. Dropping the gun I knelt and examined a dark stain on the ground: blood, or an excellent facsimile. I went to where the second hunter had fallen: again, a shotgun. The leaves were stained. I guessed the man must have shifted on his belly after being shot. I squatted, looking around, buying time. The girls had dragged both men into the woods. Both would have continued bleeding. I stood, seeing dark streaks in the brush, interrupted in places, but consistent. The blood tracks ended after a few paces.

I faced the woods, increasingly convinced I had witnessed two murders. Or accidental killings. Or — I wasn't sure how to characterize what I'd seen. I turned to Laine. "Give me the theatre bill."

She did. I scanned it: *Artemis tricks the evil hunters* ... All of this planned, staged.

Laine watched and shrugged, reaching for a cigarette. She handed me matches and said, "Light." As she exhaled, I crushed the match and sat on the bench. She turned, stretched on her back, legs on the bench and put her head in my lap, her eyes glazed. She blew out another pall of smoke. The breeze carried it back toward us and she waved her hand into the plume.

I said quietly, "So, goddess, what was that?"

"Just a dream."

"A dream of guns and death. A replay of James and the mighty stag." She shrugged again. I said, "Will Artemis hang their skeletons, too? Let coyotes pick them clean?"

She inhaled hard and shrugged.

I ran my hand over her soaked shirt, her hot skin. She crushed the cigarette on the underside of the bench and closed her eyes. Moments passed. Neither of us moved. Then, two nymphs walked into the opening, their backs to us as if, by not facing her, they were safe. She whispered, "It's okay to watch. No engagement."

The nymphs continued to back in until one of them reached the first gun, and the other made it to the gun closer to us. Both bent as if on signal, and picked up the weapons. They glanced at each other, then, cradling the shotguns, walked briskly into the woods.

Laine swiveled and sat. "And so it's over."

I felt paralyzed. We were a party to murders. At the sacrifice beside the altar, birds died. In the back grove, James was killed — and savagely. I had no reason to doubt today's event had raised the ante. Were they redneck hunters, a pair of financiers, or neighbors like James amusing themselves while trespassing on my land?

She took my hand and pulled hard. "Time to go!" Once on the trail, she skipped, oblivious to my turmoil. A red-tailed hawk appeared ahead of us, circling. I thought, *He flies like Laine lives, utterly untroubled, and utterly aware.*

Like a child she dragged me toward the house with giant, silly steps.

CHAPTER 26

From the sound-proofed abattoirs,
sacred blood is washed away
with hoses into fields.
—Poet X

In the following days, Chloé remained dispirited, and Aisa mirrored her. As I observed them I appreciated Laine's poise. One night in bed, I asked her how she stayed detached with her on-going death-work. She repeated that her mission was not that at all, but instead conservation of the cycle of life.

As Einstein once remarked, reality is merely an illusion, but a persistent one. Laine mentioned on a hike, "I am the destroyer of illusion," which at the time seemed overtly portentous. After the most recent incident, Laine avoided discussion; she wanted me to reflect. The next morning, though, she turned effusive. The sun rose and she lay on her back, restlessly shifting. She said, "I still shiver, remembering it all. And I burned for you on that damned bench —" She gave me a half-smile.

"You were surprised by what we saw?"

She drew me over and we kissed, the act itself a subversive sleight of hand, a conjuring of desire. What was real? After a few seconds, she said, "See? That's what happened yesterday, elemental heat." She sighed. "Or maybe not …"

I drifted in the absurd bliss she summoned at will. She rolled sideways to face me and said, "A smoke or coffee? You decide."

"Coffee." She nodded, taking a cigarette anyway and left. As I watched her back, admiring her narrow waist, I thought of her teasing numbers: 30, 25 … So much authority and dominion in a petite girl's frame. Reading my mind, she stopped in the doorway. I thought she might speak, but she yawned instead, poking out her butt languorously. Then she was gone, the unlit cigarette hanging from her mouth.

Mid morning she called me to her office. "It's time you saw my plans." At her computer, she pulled up a file and double-clicked. "Here. Take your time. I'll be back —" She left and I sat. A polished stone she'd pulled from Pegasus lay to the right of the monitor, black, glinting with mica. An ashtray beside it overflowed with butts; a pack of cigarettes and a box of matches were stacked nearby.

On the screen, I saw a document. Like the work I'd found earlier on her desk, it was undated. Random notes were under the heading TIME.

- *Regularity of sun & moon enforces the* illusion *of linearity.* ★
- *Time may be sinuous or fractal — 50 years, 500 or 5. Few understand.*
- *Time moves in arcs, not lines … sinuosity, the curves of my hip, of any girl's — the arc of my thighs, of anyone's. Time is never straight.*
- *Therefore, T = Fluidity* ✔

In a section titled ANALYSIS, she wrote, "Same irreducible conclusion: killing the man won't kill the idea," followed by a Δ. Then, "Must combine extirpation with reports," which was followed by Σ. The section continued, but I generally understood.

A section titled TARGETS listed twenty-seven individuals with addresses, almost all PhDs. Included was the individual's affiliation with university or government labs. From the addresses, I counted at least a half a dozen countries, including Singapore, America, France, Switzerland, China, and Japan. The name of each was followed by an age, most older than 45 and three in their thirties. The first line, struck through, read, ~~Clive Kline, PhD, US, NHGRI, 54~~ *. Over a dozen names had similar asterisks. At the list's end, I read, * = colleague.

A paragraph labeled PROBABLE CAUSES read, *Anything credible: cardiac arrest, aneurism, injuries, accidents, poisoning* … The list went on and ended with, *anaphylaxis or whatever.* I made a mental note to look up the meaning of several terms. An untitled section was composed of apparent random thoughts:

Immortal vs. a-mortal. Discuss again with J. ✔
IMG Conference Seattle. Book conf London. Madrid's or skip?
Extend sabbatical?
Animal consciousness. animist
Athene missing, and,
What the f*k is love?

A middle column titled, QUESTIONS, included,

Chloé's role?
Dress with front buttons?
Aisa: 4 yrs = 18 ✔
Jack: 1-to-100 t.

A final section read, TIMING.

Extirpation → *18 months max. Roughly 2+/mth*
Completion: before my 23rd ★

Seeing "23rd" reminded me: I didn't know her birthday. I reread the document, guessing most of the abbreviations. As I finished, Laine walked in. She pressed herself into my back and nuzzled my neck. She wore last night's cami. I turned to her and she climbed onto my lap, shaking her hair. "Laine, what's the 1-to-100 t?"

"I show you my secrets and that's all you ask?"

"My name's attached."

"What if I planted it to distract you? What if it doesn't mean a thing?"

"With you, nothing is random."

"I'll tell you. But first you tell me."

"What?"

"That you understand the document."

"It's a mix of personal comments and a deadly to-do list."

"What else?"

"The list of names … will I read their obits?"

"If I'm good at what I do."

"Cardiac arrest or bad pork from local takeout."

"Yes." She slipped her arms around me and pouted. "You haven't complimented my cami."

"I'm distracted by other things."

She said, "Do you like dresses that button up the front?"

"As long as I'm the guy unbuttoning them."

"And if I say you are?" She kissed me from my mouth to my eyes. "What color dress that buttons up the front?"

"One that perfectly matches the color of your eyes." We kissed again — lazily, electrically. Her eyes never left mine. I said, "A question: 'immortal vs. a-mortal' ?"

"You and I talked about this once. You've forgotten? Chloé and I — all three of us — are a-mortal. We don't get sick, we don't age —"

"Versus immortal. One's killable, the other not?"

She nodded.

"And the list of names, all the PhDs?"

"Some colleagues. Others not. But no one works in this field without the rest of us knowing. Those who are close to a breakthrough are the one percent of the one percent, the elect. That's why the list is short."

"Each is …"

"Obsessively pursuing immortality."

"Should you call it a-mortality?"

"That's what it would be, of course. Death by violent destruction only." She smiled again, guileless. "For them, aging is a disease. Such a discovery would roil the ancient equilibrium. Imagine, first it would be the extraordinarily wealthy. In time, as costs fell, it would include every-one. Then, as the magic became a mere commodity, men would sprinkle the pixie dust on their favorite animate things. Horses, bonsai, parrots, Siamese cats, pyracantha."

Her confidence was unnerving. I noticed her eyes had turned a deep cobalt. She said, "Within a short time and except under extraordinary instances, death would cease to exist. The balance of life would be destroyed."

I put my hands on her shoulders, dug my fingers into her muscles. "Is Chloé a true co-conspirator?"

"This isn't a conspiracy." She viewed me with immense amusement. "But Chloé? She's not seen any of this."

I pulled her closer. "Laine, a non sequitur: when's your birthday?"

"Always my inquisitor." She shrugged. "March 20. It's a special date."

I shook my head. She frowned. "The vernal equinox."

"Nothing done by chance ... and can we say that about the two hunters?"

She shook her hair and ran a thumb under a cami strap. "Of the two, one was Clive Kline, a scientist."

"The name sounds familiar."

"You saw it on my list. I struck it out last night. See, Kline and his lab assistant came to a private hunt on a large estate in an enclave west of Philadelphia. Kline's an avid hunter and the invitation to hunt private land out of season was irresistible."

"I get it. Professionally, Kline was on the hunt for immortality and personally, for big game. You knew him?"

"Yes, we co-presented at the Washington conference. He was close to a solution. We had a private chat on the second day."

"And you concluded: snuff him out."

"I pressured my extremely wealthy father," she said with a trace of sarcasm, "to allow Kline onto the membership-only big game estate. I noted membership costs a quarter million plus a yearly fee. That you'd allow him access for a day. "

CHAPTER 27

Birds behind a shield,
Hidden in the field,
Birds like shadows on my heart,
Her words a strange performance art.
—Poet X

A t times, regardless of the undeniable evidence, I struggled to acknowledge that Laine was who she claimed to be. The negative associations with the term *goddess* were impossible to ignore. The world had abandoned belief in such beings millennia ago.

The sisters represented themselves as servants of nature, although any subservience seemed minor. Their relationship with nature seemed more symbiotic than submissive. Laine said she, Chloé and Aisa were the most powerful of the divinities. Regardless, however powerful, they were curiously needy.

I idly wondered if Laine's sexual hunger might be satisfied in dreams. Could we make love virtually and not violate the stifling stipulations she imposed?

"As much as you upset me at times," she said from behind me, "you are amazingly sweet. And to answer your question, there's an outside chance. A possibility. Shared dreams. We'll have to experiment, perhaps tonight."

I turned and she slouched in the doorway, wearing a pair of my old khakis and a tee. She said. "I'd like to try. And something else … the 1-to-100 t. Too obscure."

"Does the 't' denote test?"

"Yes." She walked over, hands on her hips. "Let's hike to The Oak. We'll talk. You can hold me there."

Within ten minutes we crossed Pegasus — after weeks of heat, it barely flowed. In the early afternoon, temperatures remained moderate. Laine whistled her simple tune and my thoughts drifted. As The Oak loomed ahead, I stopped fifty feet away, waiting for her to catch up. As she did, I swung her into my arms. "Stroke my back," she said. "Make us one."

We held for a breath, enjoying the quiet. Once beside the tree, Laine pointed to our spot. I sat, back against the trunk, and she joined me, saying, "Arms around me. Close your eyes. If we drift away, okay."

Aware only of her warmth and her breathing, I felt protective, conscious of her small size. The last thing I remembered before I slept was her hair below my chin, the ocean of freckles descending into her tee, a faint smell of cigarettes on her skin. Her last words, like a hallucinogen? *Stop thinking.*

So I slept, instantly walking an ancient road. Trees on the sides were black from fire, their trunks charcoaled and soft. Fields spread out ahead, cornstalks cut low. A tractor without wheels lay on its side. A few paces ahead in a ditch paralleling the road, I saw a body — a woman face down, her hair in a jumble to the side. Her arms were tied back with wire. A warm, light rain fell.

Abruptly, I stood before a warehouse. To its right was a rail-yard and train with open box cars as blackened as the trees. Smoke trailed from the locomotive's stack.

I walked into the warehouse, into a hall with dim lights near the back. Then, I stood at the end of the hallway, squinting into an open area with industrial lights. Fifty feet to the right, on the same side as the loading docks, I saw a cattle stockade holding dozens of men, women and children. They watched me, eyes dark, children crying.

To my left, Laine lay on a narrow bed centered on a raised dais. An intense light hung over her. Tied to the bedposts like a starfish splayed and roped into place, she wore a violet cami, the garment gathered above her breasts. She appeared to be unconscious. I tried to move, unable, caught in what felt like an invisible, viscous gel.

I was in a glassed room looking out on the scene. Laine lay on the left and the stockade was on the right. A hand-lettered sign hung between them, swinging on chains. It read:

38 WOMEN, 36 MEN, 26 BOYS & GIRLS

I added the numbers: 100. Above Laine a sign lowered that read,

★ 1 G o d d e s s ★

The light above Laine turned red and swung violently. Suddenly, above the caged men, women and children, metallic arms rotated out holding perforated canisters. Each can was stenciled, Zyklon B. I knew instantly: the gas used in the 1940s in Auschwitz, Dachu, Buchenwald …

Almost at the same moment, I saw movement again to my left. A metal weight on a cable now hung directly over Laine's head; it was stamped *LB*.

Before me on a table was a timer. LED numerals counted backward: 31-30-29 … A placard beside the timer read:

1-OR-100?
★ LEFT BUTTON SAVES 1 ★
★ RIGHT BUTTON SAVES 100 ★

A mechanism with two large buttons lay beside the placard.

I glanced at the timer: 24—23—22 … The Zyklon canisters trembled, the metallic arms shaking, while the light above Laine swung violently.

I looked down again: 18—17 …

The test, Laine's damn 1-or-100 test. What did they expect of me? Laine was plainly a sacrifice — that is, if I acted morally. Save the many, betray the one. Save the one, betray the many. For what angry god was I asked to wield a knife?

I glanced at the stockade. Many of the women were now on their knees.

The clock: 12—11 … a ringing sound that had started earlier grew louder as the seconds flashed. The ringing filled the warehouse, an electronic a cappella screeching.

7—6—5 … I looked up. The scattered lights throughout the building were blinking on and off. The ringing became unbearable. At 3—2, I cried, *Nooo* —!" and pounded my fist left: *Laine.*

She awakened me with small tickles. I felt like an ancient traveler, returned from a lost century. "How much time has passed?"

"While you slept? Five minutes." Relaxed and cheerful, she pulled my arms around her. "Hold me."

I looked at the ensemble of trees over us — birches, beeches and oaks, all moving gently. Laine nuzzled me, saying, "Today we should walk all the way to the stonewall before we return. Up for it?"

I said, "No. I want to discuss the fucking dream —"

She whispered, "Not so soon."

"The test, wasn't it?"

In a tiny voice, she said, "Yes … and I'm alive."

"But only a dream."

"More than that. We'll talk. Maybe later —" Then she asked, "Has the ringing stopped?"

"Yes. You knew?"

"Come on. It'll do you good to move." Her face looked beatific, her eyes clear. I noted the cerulean pigmentation of her irises, perfect circlets, flashes like warm geysers bubbling in the deep cones of her eyes. She had a radiance I'd seen only when Laine faced Artemis and they acknowledged each other's power. I took several breaths and gestured down the trail. "Let's see if I can walk."

Then we did, pretending nothing had occurred.

Later that day, Laine worked in her office, refining operational details, fabricating crooked research, spinning sophisticated inventions to destroy her peers. I left her alone.

Late afternoon, I received an email from the company conducting the genetic testing. It noted results would be sent by email within 48 hours. I deleted it. Chloé walked into my office. She carried Aisa, now three and a half months old. Charmingly, the child cried, "Da!" as they entered. Chloé wore only her usual briefs.

I looked her up and down. "Nice to see you, Clo."

She half-smiled and sat in a chair across from me.

"Is Aisa reeling off sentences yet?"

Chloé nudged Aisa and said, "Can Aisa talk to Daddy?"

Aisa stared, saying, "Me play Da?"

Chloé laughed and said, "On a human scale, she's at about sixteen months in speech development." She set the girl down and Aisa stood. Although wobbly, she walked toward me. I got on my knees and intercepted her midway. "Aisa's a big girl!"

"We play!" she cried. *We.* Her flat black eyes fixed on mine and she grabbed one of my fingers. I was granted a rare smile.

Chloé said, "Can you cover me for an hour?"

"Sure, we'll be fine." I turned to Aisa. "Right, baby girl?"

Our hour together was discomforting. Aisa appeared confident in whatever she attempted, her body not mature enough for the tricks she tried. For instance, she kept trying somersaults, and ending on her side — yet she still possessed immense self-assurance. I felt myself being measured throughout as she locked her gaze on me, eyes bottomless. Near the end of our time together, she stopped playing and said as clearly as if she were Clo's age, "I hate you, Jack."

"What —?"

She looked away and began singing, "La-la la-la laa-la—"

At dinner that night, conversation was tolerable; Chloé participated. For the first time, she inquired about our walks and bantered with Laine about their differing attire. She wore only a brief, while Laine wore a flowing dress cinched at the waist and cut daringly. Occasionally, I caught Aisa glaring at me.

Before dinner, Laine asked me to zip her dress. She was braless and showed me her boxers before stepping into the dress. She played the sloppy, tomboy beauty. Bright-eyed, she gave me kisses after I hooked the top.

"Chloé has dropped her barriers," she whispered in my arms. "Don't ask why, but we're now exchanging impressions for the first time in weeks."

"Free flow?"

"Not entirely, more like sunny moods, but I'll take it."

At a point during dinner, Chloé gave Laine a shove and Laine pushed back laughing. Then an elbow hit a wine glass and pinot spilled across the table. Aisa cried and Chloé looked apologetic. Both girls giggled. Chloé gathered the child, gave Laine and me a kiss, and left. Laine rose from her chair. "Can I sit on your lap?"

Taking her hips, I swung her around so she sat sidesaddle. She looked away. "Would you still love me if I weren't your daughter?"

"Is this another test?"

"You've already passed a big one."

"Let's talk about that now."

"Answer *my* question first." Her voice had the precision of a disinterested scientist. As I paused, she turned in my lap to face me and put her palms on my chest. "Oh, forget it," she said. "A ridiculous question."

"Laine, I love you whoever you are."

"You're sweet-talking me, Jackknife." The old nickname.

I sighed. "Will this discussion ever advance?"

"Probably not." She pouted. "If this were a date, I'd be bored."

"No doubt. Miss Immeasurable IQ goes out with Dull Boy."

"I almost laughed," she said. Then, "Well, let's kiss. That'll improve my mood."

"A bad mood?"

"I'm lying. I'm good, a good girl." My hands seesawed slowly up and down her waist as she spoke. "I'm not only your girl, I'm your rapturous girl."

"I might have pushed the other button and saved a multitude."

"You didn't though. You saved *me*."

"Which was the right thing?"

"Yes." She kissed me, tilting her head to the side. "Yes, but you can't be concerned with right and wrong. Such things are arbitrary."

"Fuck all moral principles?"

"Yes, they're tools of control for humans — like religious dictates."

"I used no logic when I punched that button. I just did."

"That's why I'm rapturous, idiot." I got a small fist to my ribs along with a frown. "An honorable man would have saved the many. I don't need an honorable man. I need loyalty."

"Why the test? You can already read my thoughts."

"The test probed your unconsciousness to see how you'd act if you didn't have time to think." She was soft and yielding as I stroked her sides. Between each of her assertions, she let out delicate sighs, then became serious. "Now ... do I have permission to edit your DNA?"

I stared at her. "What? Did I miss the segue?"

"I can re-engineer your genetics to extend your life even more ... Jack, I want you around. This is the only way."

Her question was unfeigned. Dumbstruck, I said, "Explain."

"Today's test was a turning point. Remember at the pool when I said, 'I've done something ... we've never done?' I primed things. But I couldn't go further until certain ... Jack, just say yes."

"Extend my life? For how long?"

"Do I have to say?"

"Yes, you have to be damned precise."

"As long as a-mortal is long."

"Become like you?"

"Yes. Otherwise, you'll be gone in a few decades."

"You're not kidding, are you?"

She lit a cigarette and drew circles with the smoking match.

"You've done this before?"

"Yes." A long exhalation of smoke.

"When?"

"Once before for a friend, a goddess. Now I'd be doing it for myself. Selfish, aren't I?" She kissed me again, then again. She touched the corner of my mouth with her finger. "You'd never know. I'd do it while you slept. Or while you daydreamed." She giggled. "But you have to agree."

"What happens?"

She rolled her eyes. "Humans have twenty-three pairs of chromosomes. Several billion nucleotide pairs are on the chromosomes themselves. The order, the genetic information includes instructions to telomeres. It's complex, but the order of coding determines life span. I rejigger it, expand the pairs from twenty-three to twenty-four. I'm minimizing the complication, but it's like anything. Simple when you know."

"And you want a yes?"

She covered her eyes. "Yes."

She'd already added twenty-five years to my life, which I half-assumed was a hoax. I had listened, but not pursued particulars of the gift. Now she offered me something vastly different. Rather than exhilaration, I was swept with apprehension.

"Laine, I can't say yes. I need time. I hope you'll understand—"

She looked hurt. "Overload?"

"An avalanche." I said, "Let's quit. Maybe this will all make sense tomorrow. Or maybe not —"

She stood, pulled me up, put her arm around my waist and led me to our room. I outweighed her by seventy-five pounds, yet she steered me without difficulty. I felt an unidentifiable hollowness. In our room, I took off my clothes and helped her unzip the dress, watching as she pulled on a top.

We got into bed and I said, "I need time."

She said, "But I already know you." Sighing dramatically, she continued, "You'll conclude you don't even know who I am, that I purport to be a goddess, that the evidence seems to show ... the three of us are ... unusual, possibly gifted. But you'll wonder if we're aliens. Or creatures from the deep lagoon. Or secret agents. You'll conclude that if you say yes, I'll make a horrible mistake, fuck up your DNA, and turn you into Silly Putty."

Rolling her eyes she said, "What else? You'll ask, what if I'm manipulating you? Or lying? You'll think what if ... this is all a setup you still haven't gotten your head around? What if —?" She giggled. "You'll ask, What if, what if —

"You'll go around and around in crazy circles, with what-ifs that you imagine are logical. You'll use logic. And in the end you'll still be lying here in bed wondering what to say."

She took my hand and put it on her waist. She kissed me. I felt the curve of her breast, and caught in the river of her gentle monologue, I languidly followed her voice. In the darkness she whispered, "Be with me forever. Please say yes."

I stroked her shoulders. "A-mortal ...Would I always look 38?"

"In the first months, you'd lose about ten years as the cells reverse. Then you'd stabilize. At about twenty-five."

"And changes to my intellect?"

She laughed. "A pleasant jump ... Jack, say yes. There's no downside unless you enjoy wrestling death. And losing."

Wrestling death: the dream. Then I remembered a film I'd seen. Near the end, the main character plays chess with Death; if he loses, he dies. Laine said she liked chess.

I said, "We should get a chess set. With old wooden pieces. We can play."

"Unless you say yes, I'll always beat you. I'd be bored after the first three moves."

I turned off the light, hours past midnight. She spooned and slipped her arm under mine, saying, "You've heard the phrase, 'Dead man walking'?"

I could feel her heat, fire radiating from her skin. I lay awake in that ossuary, our starless crypt in the enchanted woods, Laine's *epikentros*, her place of centering — and found her promises of eternal companionship, of deathlessness, impossible to believe or even comprehend.

CHAPTER 28

Why do the priestesses cry, Woe?
I speak as one
tired of their lamentations.
                              —Poet X

D awn. Light filtered through half-open blinds. Laine lay quietly. I had slept an hour, once again refreshed. She opened her eyes. "Morning, Jack. Miss me?"

I shook my head. "Woke seconds ago."

She didn't ask about dreams or whether I'd decided. She gazed at me, then rolled over and sat on the bedside.

"Take your shower. Meet me in the kitchen in about twenty." I watched her pull a tee on over the cami. She winked and left.

Eyes closed, I thought, *flux*, Laine's fluidity. The variability of time and facts … I drifted, musing on the pleasantness of walking daily. The weather appeared moderate, although lately predictions seemed less and less accurate, almost as if the government's satellites had failed. I liked the thought of that, all of them winking out.

And I thought of the email I'd received the day before: DNA results should arrive soon. I had an increasing sense of unease about it all. Sending off the samples now seemed a waste. *Whatever*, I thought. Why share results, except with Laine, who was too involved? She would know, and Chloé would not. I corrected myself. Of course she would, and so would Aisa: everyone would knew everything.

After coffee I excused myself. I had obligations, as did Laine. She agreed we'd walk in the afternoon. Chloé mentioned cleaning staff would come in an hour. And being alone felt fitting — I couldn't shake the sense of being only half-awake.

So I worked on business. Things went well and late that morning, I scanned emails. One contained the reports from the lab. I almost opened it. Vacillating, I considered deleting it. Then I compromised and dragged it into a desktop folder I'd named *Blunder*. As I half-expected, Laine walked in.

I thought she would challenge me, perhaps demand I open the files. Instead she said, "Do you approve?"

Hands on her hips, she wore a pleated skirt with a sleeveless blouse fractionally too tight. The skirt was cut mid-thigh — a stylish outfit, I supposed.

"You can't hike in the woods like that."

"Chic, huh?" She twirled once and came over, sitting in my lap. "Put your hands on my waist. You know how."

As I did she said, "Now on my ribs the way I like."

I lightly moved my hands from her armpits to her hips, varying the pressure. She moaned in appreciation and said, "Forever, please."

"Yes, of course."

She turned to look. "Yes? You will? *Forever?*"

I sensed myself swept unexpectedly into a warm heat, into a light the color of topaz, tupelo honey, amber. It bathed us, infused her eyes and darkened her hair. I became intensely aware of her smell, a young woman's pheromones, a seductive chemistry as primal as the loveliness of her skin.

She whispered, "Pull my skirt back." As I did I saw her slip, a thin crinoline. I pulled the skirt up and cinched it lightly at her waist so it wouldn't fall, the slip I uncovered thin enough to allow light through.

"I bought this for you —" and as she spoke, she leaned forward and kissed me. As was so frequently the case in these last weeks, time paused. Or perhaps it shattered, splintering into an utter vacancy. I slipped a hand to her breast, and we may have kissed seconds or an hour. Her irises were cerulean, a purer blue than usual.

Again she asked, "Forever?"

I knew exactly what she meant. To my shock, I whispered, "Yes. For you —" and we kissed again. I knew with certainty that logic — that is, logic as an analytical tool —had no place in this strangest of places. With my last yes, I yielded.

As she held herself quietly against me, in my arms, eyes closed, I felt a small shudder of emergence, an odd elemental birthing. After moments she said, "Genesis." I unbuttoned her blouse, kissing her, and she observed in that voice she used when satisfied, "Enough. It's done."

Naively, I asked, "What?"

She laughed and said, "I made it so. Moments ago. Now you're like me."

Other than an undefined lightness, I felt nothing. Yes, the slight grogginess had vanished, my mind lucid, keen with an unexpected clarity.

She said, "We should eat before we walk. Say nothing. Let's see if Chloé knows."

In the kitchen we made sandwiches. Before we set out plates, Chloé came in with Aisa on her hip. Saying nothing, she set the child down. Aisa walked with far more confidence now, crossing from Chloé to Laine, gurgling, pointing at Laine. Chloé folded her arms together across her chest and smiled. "At breakfast, there were three. And now, four."

She walked the distance separating us and put her arms around me. I felt her press against me for the first time in months. She looked sideways at Laine, then kissed my cheek with affection. When we separated, she had tears in her eyes. Laine said, "And?"

Chloé said, "And I'm pleased."

"Only pleased?"

"You know what you're doing, I suppose." They exchanged a look.

Laine said, "Don't underestimate his faculties."

For the first time, I read Chloé's thoughts, and heard them as if she spoke aloud. And similarly, I read Laine's. Chloé's mind was in turmoil, uncertain. Laine, on the other hand, swam in a dominion of love, utterly alert. The three of us gazed at each other, suspended momentarily in an unexpected tension.

Laine said, "Over the next months, you'll understand; all of this will become clear."

Why should we even use voices? I thought.

"Because," she said melodiously, "voices are like woodwinds, lutes, violins. They give us pleasure. Words are like touch, only aural, an amusement. And their use lets us blend in with all those around us who would be terrified if we were mute."

She put a hand on Chloé's shoulder and simultaneously gave me a kiss, publicly sealing what she'd done. I read her thought, *You're mine.* And I read Chloé's skepticism.

To my amazement, I processed the entirety of their thoughts effortlessly. My receptivity seemed to have quadrupled. I now handled thoughts and sensory input with ease. The narrow stream of data I once accepted as normal rose as a vast river.

After lunch Laine and I struck out for the woods, the light sharp against our sunglasses. In an old baseball hat and khaki shorts, Laine walked in pink trail shoes. I thought momentarily about the morning email, and Laine said, "Chloé and I know the results are in."

I shrugged. "Then you know I haven't looked."

Reveling in my new energy, I didn't want to be distracted by what felt like old news. She persisted: "We'll read the results when we're back."

"Sure." I didn't want to lose the new ebullience. And on this walk, I felt indefatigable, tireless. At one point we stopped, and sensing my zest, she danced around me with her arms out, laughing and holding my eyes as she spun. "There's so much you'll discover," she said. "This is just the start."

Down the path, we came to the clearing where Artemis had transformed herself from stag to warrior. Nothing had changed. I viewed the area, and hand in hand we sauntered to the stone bench, sitting in the shadows of the oaks. I sensed another being, but scanning the clearing, I saw no one. "Who?" I asked.

Then I saw Artemis. She stood at the far edge, about eighty feet from us, in her tunic and, as always, with a bow in hand. She gazed at us without expression. Laine stood and raised her arms in the usual greeting, whispering, "Stand."

"I can't read her."

"We each have the choice, always, of opening or closing ourselves to others. If we didn't we'd have no privacy. Artemis is choosing to be opaque."

"Like Chloé when she went rogue?"

"Yes."

"But for you, Artemis is open?"

"Yes."

Before I said more, the goddess abruptly nodded, turned and strode away. Laine said, "She wanted to see for herself. It's been millennia since this occurred."

"She came to see me?"

"To confirm, not evaluate."

"Confirm, evaluate—what's the difference?"

"The ability to observe without evaluating is a form of high intelligence. And yes, she confirms my work. She'll be open when you meet again."

"Open, closed. Games on games."

She smiled. "Could be. Now, Jack, it's your turn. Close me off."

As she implied, blocking her was effortless. To merely imagine shielding made it so. "Yes —?"

"Yes." She kissed me. "Now let me in."

She smiled and slipped her hand into mine. I sensed Laine's breathing, her leg against mine, a tree bending eight degrees northeasterly in the light breeze to my left, the colorless tone of a flat stone ahead of us, a thin band of lichens on its edge, the slight curve (like a sine wave) of the path we walked, the shifting chroma of the sky … and Laine's reaction: *Yes, yes.*

That afternoon as we returned to the meadow, Orthrus sat on its haunches midway between us and the house. As it detected us, it stood, hair bristling, barking as if at intruders. I saw mocha eyes and yellow teeth. Laine and I glanced at each other. I said, "Can't read it whatsoever."

"Nor can I."

Turning, I skimmed the ground for a weapon. At the stream, I picked up a large stone, feeling far more powerful than at any time. My sight was remarkable, the dog's eyes no longer indistinct. I saw the black cratered skin around its nose, gray lashes above its eyes. The stone was a perfect projectile. I could kill the beast easily.

Laine read me too well. "No, Jack. I can't say why it's here, but don't. The dog is as old as Chloé and me … I can't imagine why it's upset."

Orthrus advanced, taking several steps, shifting its weight, taking several more toward us, its eyes appearing infuriated. She bent and opened her palms. "Orthrus … Orthrus, come here —"

The beast stopped, looking uncertain. It wagged its tail, then barked again. It backed off several feet, emboldened, barking louder. Laine stepped closer, again using her little girl's voice. At last, the dog allowed her to touch it, to run her fingers behind its ears. When I walked up to the two, I startled at its size, its shoulders muscled and broad.

"Come on, Orthrus, let me know what's wrong," she whispered. Orthrus now wagged its entire rear, lowering itself onto the grass. Then, it lay on its back and Laine stroked it. Glancing up, she said, "It wasn't you at all. Orthrus is being maneuvered by Aisa."

"Aisa? Why?"

"Orthrus won't know. I suspect Aisa's testing her powers. Let's find out —" Laine stood and Orthrus jumped up on its feet at the same moment. She thumped its side with her hand, saying, "Good dog!" It sat, looking indifferent. Laine pulled me to the house. From the hall, she cried, "Chloé?!"

From another part of the house, we heard, "Yes —?"

"Where's Aisa?"

We bounded upstairs and found the child rolling with delight on the living room carpet. She appeared almost beside herself, and when she heard us enter the room, she got up on one knee, stood and wobbled quickly off. Chloé walked in. "What's going on?"

"Can you read Aisa?"

Chloé frowned, closing her eyes. "No."

"She commanded Orthrus to attack when we got back."

Chloé gaped at us. "You're okay?"

Laine interjected. "I had to stop him —" She pointed at me. "— from braining the dog with rocks. We almost had a shootout."

"Okay," Clo said. "I understand, We'll have a mother-daughter talk."

CHAPTER 29

Her red wet
Hair lies over
Her shoulder
Like razor cuts.
— Poet X

I went to my office, pausing to scan the meadow. The dog was gone. A single crow preened atop the altar. Nothing else moved. For the first time, I sensed the crow's thoughts: benign, a non-sentinel.

I closed the blinds. Peering from windows was now unnecessary. I focused on the areas outside, probing for sentient beings. I sensed the thoughts of snakes, amphibians along the stream, voles burrowing in the field and the cacophony, the pettiness, of birds. I trusted that control would come. Uncertain of the range of my new awareness, I guessed it extensive.

Of course, I realize now that in my euphoria I remained blind to what lay ahead. With almost no warning, I could not have anticipated the shattering information to come. The girls, though, knew. By 4:30 that afternoon, I finished work. With my new clarity, I produced analyses far faster. I was yet to affirm a-mortality, as Laine implied, but whatever she'd done felt like a gift.

Completing my work, I sent it out. As I did, I browsed world news. Still early, I was amused that, in my new state, I could be hungry. Yet, the girls had robust appetites and I should expect the same.

Laine came in carrying drinks. "Quitting time," she said. "Don't know about you, but I'm burnt out."

"How's it going?"

"Oh, reviewing plans, triple-checking data —"

"Sounds ominous."

"And finishing reports. They have to be irrefutable. They'll be peer reviewed and outside groups will try to replicate conclusions." She smiled. "But it's not difficult to make fools of them all." Then she asked, "How are you?"

"The same. Fucking euphoric."

"It's all my doing. What have I unleashed?"

I grinned. "Only time will tell."

"Yes," she said. "Time."

The rest of the day was routine, almost unimaginable after the momentous events earlier. I forgot the lab results. The girls said nothing. Our evening seemed domestic in its ordinariness. Chloé was cautious, yet charming, and Laine continued to hum with a heartfelt happiness I knew I'd created.

In bed that evening we talked. Laine continued to offer me instruction. She felt, given my adaptation, I would pass through the entire "transition" in a month or less. She also surprised me with a gift — a vintage chessboard with wooden pieces. She insisted we play, and told me beforehand we should block thoughts from each other. "Otherwise, I'll destroy you," she threatened.

We played four games in two hours. The tally ended two to two, much to my annoyance. I expected to take her easily. She played positional chess, recognizing patterns rather than memorized moves. I admired her aggression. As we finished the night, she pointed toward the window — "The sun is rising, golden today. That's good."

I rose and looked outside. "And we never slept."

"You'll see there's no need. Night is time to play or plan or rest, if you must, but you can now skip sleep."

"Amazing. I always resented it." I caught her by the arm. "But I still get to bed you when I want."

"Well," she said, "You *are* a man." She shook off my hand, saying, "That aside, this girl's present need is coffee."

She left, still wearing her bedtime things — gray running socks, an old cami and panties I'd never seen. As I usually did when she went upstairs, I rolled onto my back. I now read Chloé and Aisa's thoughts — Chloé breastfed Aisa, and the two made inane chatter, mother-baby talk. Aisa's speech patterns were increasingly sophisticated. Concurrently, Laine and I made contact, our thoughts synchronized.

I remained surprised at unexpected turns, but as they occurred, I maneuvered each with deftness. My confidence grew. With the equanimity came a certain tranquility. Anything felt possible. I also sensed with trepidation that this calm was predicated on Laine's presence — I now resented my weakness. And as the thought came, she responded instantaneously: *We are now as one.*

Late morning she entered my office in a mauve dress belted tightly at her waist. It ended above mid thigh, cut immodestly at the swell of her breasts. She wore pearls and a serpentine necklace.

"Like?" she asked. Then she spun, the usual pirouette. The dress lifted as she turned. I offered my hand and she stepped into my arms. We held, and then she pulled up a side chair and sat. As she did I realized her thoughts had gone dark.

"We should review the lab reports. You pretend they didn't come."

I glanced at her, surprised at her tone. "Why do we care?" She said nothing. I shrugged and turned to the computer, finding the attachment from the lab and double-clicked. A second passed as the files were extracted: three paternity and four genetic reports, each labeled with the subject's name. I skimmed, *LLowell_pat.pdf, ANight_pat.pdf* and so forth.

"Where should we start?"

She looked critically at the files. "Open *ANight_pat.pdf*. A good beginning—"

I clicked the file and we read,

CHILD NAME: *Aisa Night, female*

ALLEGED FATHER NAME: *Jackson Night*

CONCLUSIONS OF DNA PARENTAGE TEST: DNA PATERNITY— INCLUSION. *The alleged father is not excluded as the biological father of the child. Based on the genetic testing results obtained by PCR analysis of STR loci, the probability of paternity is >99.99% as compared to an untested, random man.*

It took me seconds to absorb the information. The key phrases were *inclusion* and *probability*. I was Aisa's father. "No surprises. What next?"

She seemed excited. "Okay— let's open your report, big guy. So who the hell are you?" A smile. "Click on —" She pointed at *J.Night_gen.pdf*.

A multipage report came up. *Jackson Night, male. Genetic Report,* the data almost overwhelming and divided into four subjects: Carrier Status Reports, Wellness Reports, Ancestry, and Traits.

I read the pages carefully. My ancestry was European. My "Maternal Haplogroup" was H3. I had a small chance that my ring finger would be longer than my index finger; it was not. I had a 5% chance of having curly hair; mine was straight.

Laine's thoughts remained dark. I glanced at her and said, "My turn to pick. Let's finish the paternity reports, then we can get into genetics."

She said nothing.

"Chloé first." I double-clicked on the file *CNight_pat.pdf*, and read,

CHILD NAME: Chloé Night, female

ALLEGED FATHER NAME: Jackson Night

CONCLUSIONS OF DNA PARENTAGE TEST: DNA PATER-NITY — EXCLUSION. PROBABILITY OF PATERNITY: 0%

The probability I fathered Chloé was zero. Really?

"How accurate are these?" I heard my voice rising.

"Very," she said, her face blank. "Consider these, in fact, error-free."

What the fuck? Impossible, if not absurd. I took a deep breath, calming myself. I thought: *Don't lose it, Jack.* This was likely one of Laine's charades. I'd play along.

"Okay," I smiled, "you're next."

"I'm next," she said.

I clicked *LLowell_pat.pdf*, and read,

CHILD NAME: Laine Lowell, female

ALLEGED FATHER NAME: Jackson Night

CONCLUSIONS OF DNA PARENTAGE TEST: DNA PATER-NITY — EXCLUSION. PROBABILITY OF PATERNITY: 0%

Her report was a carbon copy of Chloé's. I was Aisa's father only.

How could that be? It couldn't. Laine? Of course. I had concluded she was a mystery long ago. Her art was chicanery. But Chloé? I had raised her since birth; I'd been at her delivery. She *had* to be my child.

Laine said, "I'm so sorry."

I turned to her without speaking. She shook her head, then looked away. At the same moment her thoughts opened: the reports were factual.

Then, the door opened and Chloé walked in. Her hair tied in a ponytail, she wore dark mascara. My first thought was that she had aged ten years. She appeared immensely tired. And unlike Laine, she cried.

We looked at each other. She fell to her knees before me, her pain obvious, and buried her face in my lap.

CHAPTER 30

And Sabines with a crow on their flag (&)
Brennus came for the wine, liking its quality …
& inviting his wife to drink from her father's skull
—Ezra Pound, Canto 96

I made no attempt to block the sisters. Doing so wasn't necessary. I switched to a state of merely surviving. It was the 111th day following Aisa's birth, and Laine stood and pressed herself into my back. Chloé sat on the floor, her head in my lap. They read thoughts better than I, so they knew I had none. Instead, I was hollowed out, raked clean like an empty gourd. Not moving, for minutes we were silent. I finally said, "So, girls, I still haven't opened your genetic reports —"

I clicked Laine's first. The file read in eloquent simplicity,

SUBJECT NAME: Laine Lowell, female.
Anomalous results were obtained from the sample submitted.
Please call Charles Thrones.

I didn't bother looking at either girl. "Accidents happen. I'm sure

Clo's report is fine." Clicking *CNight_gen.pdf,* I read an identical comment. Aisa's genetic report mirrored the others.

I asked, "Were the samples spoiled?" Neither girl spoke, although I now read their thoughts: *No.* In the silence, I picked up my cell. "Let's call Mr. Thrones. He was kind enough to include his direct line." The phone rang and a man said, "Charles Thrones." I tapped speakerphone.

"Mr. Thrones, I'm Jack Night. I opened reports from your lab on my three daughters and the report for each states something about 'anomalous results'."

He said excitedly, "Mr. Night, I hoped you'd call! Do you have a minute?"

"Yes. Were the samples mishandled?"

"Hardly. But we encountered a problem —"

I explained I understood little about genetic testing, that he needed to keep explanations simple. He said he understood and continued, "Humans typically have twenty-three pairs of chromosomes."

"I know that much. Let's move on."

"The three samples provided contained twenty-four, not twenty-three. The chances of that happening are minuscule. And more intriguing for us, the pairings are identical and in a chromosomal order that has never been recorded."

"And the significance?"

"We're not sure, given that these results are unique. Are your daughters healthy?"

"Yes. Incredibly so. Why?" I felt Laine's arms around me, her mouth against my neck.

"Twenty-four pairs is often associated with development of various diseases such as Trisomy 13 and 18, Down syndrome, Triple X, Klinefelter's syndrome, and other illnesses."

"What is Trisomy?"

"It's also known as Edwards syndrome, a condition caused by an error in cell division—a meiotic disjunction. When this happens, instead of the normal pair, an extra chromosome results and disrupts the normal pattern of development."

I sighed. "And all these diseases show up, I suspect, at birth."

"Often before. They can be detected when testing the fetus." He paused. "What ages are your daughters?"

I realized I still viewed them as my daughters; I didn't correct him. *Fuck, fuck, fuck.* "One is twenty-two, one twenty-one and the third is three months. All appear disease-free."

"I'm not reaching conclusions, Mr. Night. But twenty-four pairs of chromosomes are almost always associated with cellular damage." I said nothing. "Could we get another sample from each?"

"Should I expect results to vary?"

"No, but we have more sophisticated testing we might conduct. Yours was the usual commercial analysis, run before we realized what we had." He paused. "As I mentioned, the pairings are identical and in a unique order. Our chief scientist remains intrigued."

"His name?"

"Her. Dr. Cashmore, Jane."

I wrote the name down. As I scribbled it, Laine thought, *I know her. A technician. Ignore.* I got a forlorn look.

"Thanks. It's unlikely. But I'll talk to the girls."

"I hope you do. We would waive all costs."

I hung up and lifted Chloé's face from my lap, gazing into her eyes: violet irises. Her pain was transparent, she was wordless. I kissed her forehead, took one of Laine's arms and pulled her around so she, too, faced me. Perhaps for the first time since I had known her, she looked subdued, even chastened.

To my shame I found her melancholy seductive. She glanced up, knowing my reaction, her eyes pale, powder blue. Like Chloé, she seemed otherwise devoid of thought. I released her arm and straightened in my chair.

Then I stood, forcing Chloé to sit back, all of us aware we might never recover from this. "I'm going upstairs."

They looked at each other, and although their minds were open, I read nothing. I shook my head. "Well, talk about a sudden glitch."

From the front windows, I could see the winding drive and expansive lawn, and was suddenly conscious of Aisa's thoughts. She followed the chaos from her playroom, and I realized at this point that all of us knew. I left for the kitchen.

Wine at noon? Yes, wine and figs and olives, an antidote to a poisonous snake bite. I thought, *Impossible*. And finally, *Fuck them*. And as I muttered *Fuc*——, I read Laine's instant response from wherever she skulked, *No* —

Somewhat later, I poured myself a second glass and she appeared. I looked away. Without asking, she took the bottle firmly from my hand, set it aside and pulled my arms around her. "Hold," she said.

"The charlatan appears, in appropriate disguise."

"Don't be cruel."

"You're a liar, Laine. Whoever, whatever you are."

"I'm Laine." She slipped into my arms.

"The deceitful, duplicitous Laine."

"I was wrong. All wrong ——" She rubbed her cheek against my chest. I'm still not sure what came over me, but I roughly ran my hands across her back, into her hair. I put my hands on her hips. She moaned, *You can't not love me*. As she gazed up pleadingly, we kissed in a skim of heat —

Bullshit. I broke off and took her arms. "What are you?"

"Chloé's sister."

"And who is Chloé?" As I asked, I thought, *She's my daughter.*

"You want to know?"

"More lies would be ideal."

"She was yours until I came."

"How could she not be? Fuck, I watched her birth."

"You never knew. Justina was … a slut. She slept around. You and a basketball player and a third man, who is Chloé's actual father. Justina encouraged you to believe what you wanted, and we reinforced the lies because you would be the best man to raise the child."

"So for twenty years I raised another man's daughter."

"Yes. And your affair was never incest."

So, Chloé was merely some girl. The child of a woman I barely knew. I was a fool who'd poured a fortune into a hoax. I felt a shudder of grief.

"All these lies — they're because of you, aren't they?" I took her face in my hands and she moaned.

"Are your claims of maidenhood another fraud? Are you someone's wife?"

No. That you were our father is the only lie.

I realized that I didn't know what I'd do next. All reasoning had vanished. I thought, *Equanimity, find it fast before you do something terrible* —

Standing before me, flushed, she ran her fingers through her hair. She stepped away, raising her dress, flashing me, then turned. We stared at each other, silent, thoughtless, lost in, I suppose, a strange nothingness

You love me, she thought. *You do.*

You're monstrous. I brought her up against me, all of my reactions primal. I didn't trust myself and she said, "Not so rough."

I pushed her away. "Go to our room. Hiking clothes. We're going on a walk."

She left and I looked out the array of windows into the meadow. Nothing moved, not even wind played across the grasses within my magical realm. I thought of Chloé, now with Aisa in the nursery, immense sadness cascading through her. I projected to her, *We didn't know*

—

If Chloé had a response, I would never know. I was blocked. Enough, Laine and I had a reckoning. I heard: *I'm ready.*

I opened the door to our room and found her before the tall mirror, brushing her hair. "You finish," she said. I stepped behind her, put a hand on her stomach and drew the brush down. She closed her eyes, her caution high.

"Kiss me," she whispered. "You can't touch me like that and then not kiss."

I circled a nipple with my thumb, feeling her respond. Angry, I stopped and said, "Time to walk. We have a —"

"Reckoning," she filled in. "I'm up for anything." She grabbed her baseball cap and said, "Am I proper?" She wore her usual khaki shorts, tee and hiking shoes.

Then she lifted her arms, expectant, offering herself. I took the tee and pulled it up and over her breasts, high enough that I covered her face with the shirt. "Maybe I'll leave you like this, helpless."

Okay.

CHAPTER 31

Dark mascara, moon-lit brows,
in a dress with yellow petticoat,
tea length, endless crinoline, tight
at her hips, blood-red bows
doubled at her waist.
—Poet X

We walked out together into the nonsensical brightness. The sun burned, scintillant, a slender dilation of bright sky separating us from a storm harrowing the atmosphere a mile away. I said, "Thunderstorm. Bad one, too."

"Is it coming this way?"

"Probably. Let's forget the walk."

"No!" she cried. "If it gets worse we can turn." Vacuously, ignoring the violence, we hopped Pegasus and set a fast pace down the trail. Within minutes she spoke. "Confessions, Jack?"

"We've had enough confessions."

She hunched forward, looking ahead as she walked. Quietly she said, "First, I'm sorry we can't make real love —"

I said nothing.

"Confession two: when I first arrived, a shattered girl who'd lost her mom, I shouldn't have lied."

"That you were my daughter."

"All of it. But if I hadn't lied, you wouldn't have let me stay —"

"You're right." I glanced in the direction of town — the storm, now with an anvil top, loomed closer. "We're gonna get slammed."

"Let's go a few more minutes, then we'll sprint back."

I guessed we had no time before being deep in mayhem. "Might be too late —"

"When we hear thunder, then."

"Brave girl."

"No, and I'm not through confessing. I shouldn't have hidden what I do — I mean, professionally."

"Yes, you'll burn in hell."

"There's no hell," she said. "Three: you were chosen from tens of thousands of possible men. You made all the cuts, but the final decision seemed doubly easy because you knew Justina. When she told you you were the father, you were too gullible. You wanted it."

"Gullible? There's a pattern emerging."

"It's one of your better traits."

We made it to the clearing. I scanned the area. Several deer were hidden to our left, but I sensed nothing else. The storm continued closing. "Laine, this is crazy. Look —" I pointed at the black underbelly of the cumulonimbus. "It's a fierce one."

"We haven't heard thunder." As she spoke lightning struck and instantly, a roll of thunder. She careened into me.

"I don't do well with lightning!"

"What do you mean?"

"Terrifies me."

I rolled my eyes. At an even closer strike, she clung to my chest, rubbing herself against me. *I'm sorry, Jack —*

We needed shelter. It had been years since I'd done anything so stupid. Outside the clearing and to our right, I saw a possible refuge, a small building or shed, set forty-feet into the woods. How had I not seen it before? Another streak of lightning. I picked her up — she clung to my neck — and carried her there. As we got closer, I guessed the shed to be decades old. Moss covered unpainted clapboards, windows were dark.

Lightning struck repeatedly and heavy rain began. We were soaked. At the doorway, I dropped her onto her feet. "Let's get in."

Grasping the door handle, I jiggered the latch. The door opened slightly, then jammed. Warped. I put my shoulder against it, pushed and it sprung open. We lurched inside, our eyes adjusting to the darkness. The shelter was larger than I'd guessed, perhaps twelve by sixteen feet. Not a shed, a gentleman's retreat, I thought, scanning the room.

To the left was a small table with chairs. There were double windows on the building's sides. An oil lantern sat on the table. Several backup lanterns hung off hooks. To the right of the table lay a cot, a thin mattress running its length. A blanket box sat at its foot. At the back against the wall were built-in shelves with books, a metal coffee pot, cups, a picture, cobwebs. As I scanned the interior, she kept pressing and whimpering, then pulled off her tee. "Wet."

I dragged her to the table. The lantern was quarter full, the wick exposed. A box of wooden matches lay to the side. I opened the box, struck a match and lit the wick. It sputtered briefly, then threw off a flame.

"What is this place?" she said, hugging herself. The thunder had lessened, at least momentarily. But the temperature had dropped by ten degrees.

"The widow's husband probably used this as a retreat."

Disinterested, she said, "Got to get dry —" She started zipping down her shorts and I stopped her. "First let's see if there's anything to wear."

The blanket box had a folded shirt, a pair of trousers, several bedsheets. If this had been the old man's getaway, he'd stocked it well. I pulled out the shirt and shook it — wool. *Here, this will do.*

A peal of thunder rolled through the woods. The violence seemed remarkable. I watched her fumbling with the wet bra — she couldn't unhook it. I helped and got her into the shirt.

Suddenly cold I took off what I wore. Lightning struck again and she leaped into my arms. Thunder followed. In the air's electrical thickness, she moaned, half-mad. "Cover me," she cried. Dragging me to the cot, she frantically pulled me onto her, hooking her ankles around my waist.

She pushed against me and her cries filled the retreat. Then she shud-dered, raising her hips, her thighs trembling like a hummingbird —

After, in the silence she drew me against her, whispering, "You should have taken me. I wanted you so much —"

I said nothing. Her treachery and equivocations remained remarkable.

CHAPTER 32

Black crows in the meadow
Across the broad highway.
It's funny, honey,
But my touch don't feel much
Like a scarecrow today.
— *Bob Dylan*

For the next week, dirty clouds hung from the blue sky as if a small child had pasted them up. Nights filled with glitter, stars glistering like fireflies, or the sparkles Laine favored now and then across her cheeks. The girls were often languid, and even though Chloé was nursing, they started wine at lunch, drinking until late night.

To my concern, Chloé invented a little song whose sole lyric was, *Ako-lou-thei*, the syllables repeated endlessly. She sang it with a world-weariness.

I asked, "What's it mean?"

Laine half-smiled, "It's Greek for *Follow me* —"

And Clo kept me blocked. An entire week passed in a melancholy punctuated by Chloé's pauses at windows, where she would stand, saying occasionally, *Look at the clouds*. Laine insisted I ignore her — "Her mood will pass."

One night while Laine and I lay in bed, I asked, *Who was your father? Chloé's?* Laine responded in a whisper, "No."

How are you sisters?

"Through our common psyche." *Once a mother common to us all — I told you, Nyx — gave us common blood. But when we reanimated, a physical blood line made no sense.*

After awhile I asked, *What do you mean by common psyche?*

Our spirit. Our psukhē. She kissed me, deflecting further questions. To distract me, she said, "You should kiss me all the time. You neglect me sometimes, you know —"

That's not true. It's far more difficult to fool me now.

She allowed nothing more, obviously bored with constant explanations. Yet, I was not content and asked again about the hunters. I recalled the older man's name: Kline. Ten days had passed since their demise. Again, Laine offered little explanation.

Later I searched under, *Clive Kline, PhD*, and found him listed as a scientist at the National Human Genome Research Institute. On the NHGRI website I scanned staff biographies. A key researcher, Kline had independently pulled in $60 million in federal grants and authored or co-authored dozens of papers. At the end of the biography, I read, *On leave of absence.*

So the NHGRI masked his disappearance with obfuscation. Or Kline was not one of the men killed. I walked to Laine's office. "The NHGRI shows Kline on leave of absence."

"Yes. They have no idea what's happened. He was there one day and not the next, their lead researcher, their rainmaker — poof." Then she said, "There will be many more like him — the deaths just won't occur nearby."

"Names on your list?"

"Yes. And it's expanding"

When does the culling resume?

Winnowing, a better term. Soon.

I gazed at her from the doorway. Sunlight slanted through the windows and left a slatted pattern on her back. As the seriousness of her task increased, she wore office attire more frequently, although I frankly preferred the camis and casual wear. Today, she wore a sleeveless blouse and dark skirt. A necklace hung at her neck and she wore a bow in the side of her hair.

I brushed my fingers through her hair. "Winnowing: it's unusual."

"Culling, killing, terminating. Winnowing's a civilized term for what must be."

❧

We managed daily walks, Laine often smirking. Her new focus was "refreshing" our new retreat. So days after the thunderstorm, we lugged out provisions, including wine, bottled water, extra matches, flashlights and clothes.

Throughout it all, virginity remained her citadel. Perhaps her continuing hostility was driven by ancient tradition alone — the sacred dictum: *the Fates are virgins.* But that mandate had already been detonated by Chloé. On one level I didn't care, but I understood that the constraint, the strictures, cut us both.

One late afternoon when we had walked as far as the stonewall, we stopped a short distance from Artemis' grove. After resting on a large stone, I sensed someone. *We're being watched.*

She smiled. "Weeks ago you'd have been oblivious."

"Who?"

She put a finger up to her lips. *Nymphs.*

How many?

Eleven, forty feet away.

I scanned the woods. She whispered, "Don't. Only look at me. They think we're not aware."

Aren't they terrified of you?

Yes. But they have questions about life and death. They are under orders to come.

Artemis put them up to this?

Of course.

A game, I thought. Artemis and Lachesis. How would the nymphs overcome their terror? As for me, I looked forward to seeing the girls again. Weeks had passed since an appearance. Laine took my hand. *Listen!*

Lutes played the archaic tune. She stood and turned toward the sound. I stared in the same direction and saw movement: two post-pubescent girls thirty feet away. They held hands, dressed in tunics. Wearing leather sandals lashed with narrow strips up their calves, both stared at the ground and stepped forward.

Behind them another two arose. They repeated the moves of the first. Further pairs appeared, totaling eight girls. They advanced, and I noticed three girls behind the group playing lutes. Laine had now raised her arms, her elbows bent, palms out facing the girls. For seconds, no one moved. Her arms dropped to her sides, then the eight shifted mechanically into a semi-circle around us, their eyes low. The musicians quieted.

The nymph facing Laine was taller than the others, sylphlike with delicate features, her hair tied in a topknot. She appeared almost feral, wild as if woods had always been her home. Covering her eyes with her fingers, she sang,

> *Goddess, forgive us for we dare to sing*
> *Of Lachesis, the One who measures out our lives,*
> *We come to ask forgiveness,*
> *Of the Enchanter, the Apportioner*
> *Who controls the fate of mortals and of gods,*
> *Of all beings who breathe these hallowed airs …*

The girls knelt together, placing their foreheads on the ground, hands and buttocks high. The tunics on several fell forward to their waists; they were bare-assed. Then the same girl rose and, keeping her eyes covered, sang,

> *The goddess Artemis sends us*
> *With questions only you can address.*
> *You, Lachesis, are the most*
> *Brilliant. Hear our request!*

Laine clapped her hands together, the sound explosive. The girls trembled, several shifting backward. "Enough flattery!" she cried. "Ask what you will!"

The girl asked, "May I stand?"

"Do so."

The girl straightened. She kept her hands over her eyes, her hair matted and her cheeks ruddy as if rouge had been scrubbed across her face.

Laine demanded, "Speak!"

The nymph opened her mouth, hesitated, then frowned and closed her mouth. Her top and bottom teeth were filed to points. I felt a small shudder. She tried again, whispering,

> *Oh Lachesis, brilliantly inventive,*
> *Heart relentless, courageous one,*
> *We ask why Death must come*
> *To good and bad alike?*

The goddess said nothing. Her silence and that of the girls became unbearable. At the precise moment too much time had passed, she laughed, crying, "All stand."

Several of the girls hesitated, and Laine spoke louder, "Now!"

The girls rose. Laine commanded, "Hands at your sides."

Their terror evident, at least half the girls wept and exchanged glances, while unable to obey Laine's command. She stepped to the girl closest, taking her face in her hands. "Look." Their eyes met. Laine walked from girl to girl, with the same demand and the same result. She stopped before the lead girl, took her face into her hands, and seeing the nymph still would not open her eyes, bent and kissed her fully on the mouth. After seconds, Laine released her savagely, pushing her away, crying at them all,

> *Death comes like this, this kiss,*
> *Harsh and unexpected.*
> *Some say its touch is bliss,*
> *Some that it comes undetected.*
> *But all must go so others come:*
> *I ensure Nature is protected,*
> *Parts and sum.*

The lead girl wept openly, touching her lips. Laine stepped away, raising her arms, elbows bent, palms out, and cried, "All of you: back to Artemis!"

They turned and fled, except for the sylphlike girl in tears. She remained, eyes down. Laine ran her hand behind her neck and into her hair, pulling the girl abruptly against her. Laine stroked her back as if calming a wild colt.

She whispered soothingly, "Are you Artemis' favorite?"

The girl shrugged.

"I'll bet you are —"

The nymph blushed and kept her head down.

"No one hides their thoughts from me," she whispered. "I know you pledged yourself to the Huntress long ago."

The girl gazed up at that moment into Laine's eyes, and said obstinately, "We have all given ourselves to the One. She loves us equally."

Laine smiled. "Go and find the others." Yet, as the girl turned to leave, Laine stopped her, grabbing her tunic from behind. The girl froze. Laine turned, lifting the girl's dress in the back and holding it high. She said, "Look, Jack. This is how Artemis maintains discipline."

The girl's buttocks were striped with red lines. She had been switched, as recently as last night. The girl stared at Laine, her eyes flashing defiantly. She had a tattoo, a blue dolphin, on her left buttock. With her free hand, holding the tunic high, Laine whacked the girl's bottom and sent her staggering slightly. The nymph stood, her back to us, the tunic down. Laine spoke softly, "Go —"

We watched her leave, shoulders proud, weaving a path between the shrubs until she disappeared. I asked, "What's her name?"

Timessa. She comes from a wealthy, prestigious family in Athens. Laine took my hand. *Say nothing more about what you've seen.*

CHAPTER 33

Thus & ever thus
Hekátē, sea spray
eyes gray, obdurate
protectress at the city gate.
—*Poet X*

Timessa. I couldn't shake her image, the defiant eyes and striped ass. Why had Laine kept her behind? And why had she made such an exhibit of the girl's punishment? For any young woman from our time, it would have been deeply humiliating. But the girl's acquiescence, mixed with a fierce defiance, argued otherwise.

Several days later, Laine expressed frustration with Chloé. "She's obsessed with Aisa. I get next to no help. Still, I'm moving the timing up."

She whispered, "Age used to be considered a time of gradual decline. Now it's considered a mere disease, something curable." She shook her head, ending the conversation. Four months had passed since Aisa's birth. Chloé seemed to have no intention of weaning the child. Laine was exasperated enough to say, "She gets off on it." In addition, Laine and I were blocked again. Over breakfast Laine said, "Remember Timessa?"

"Of course."

"I should never have shown you her ass. Still, she has an exceptional IQ."

"And—?"

"I'm desperate for help."

"That girl? She's like a depraved child—"

"Yes, and she's also a sophomore at Vassar who's on summer break."

"You're kidding."

"No. I might persuade her to take a semester off."

"Vassar? Is she here to take off her panties and run in the woods with a bunch of pubescent girls?" When Laine looked away, I paused. I wasn't sure whether she was serious or testing. But bringing the nymph here to help? Ludicrous. She wanted me to acquiesce? Laine shrugged and left.

A week later, Laine borrowed the car to run errands. When she kissed me goodbye, she used an improbable phrase and tapped my cheek: *Be a good boy while I'm gone.*

In her absence, I went to the front door, responding to a series of knocks. There I found a tall girl I guessed to be seventeen or eighteen. Dressed fashionably, she held a briefcase, her makeup impeccable. From her look she might have been a professional at a bank or a brokerage. Regardless, she'd ignored the No Soliciting sign at the entrance.

"Jack Night?"

I waited for the sales pitch — or to be served with a subpoena. I was reminded of Laine's first visit. Perhaps it was the girl's cheek bones or the Grecian nose, then it hit me: *Timessa*, in costume, but the same.

Confident she would obey, I spontaneously said, "Smile for me."

She hesitated, then smiled as if doing so was the easiest thing in the world. Her teeth were perfect. I said, "You've been to a dentist."

The broad smile abated. "Invite me in?"

I opened the door and she entered. She wore an expensive blouse and a dark skirt, black heels and, I guessed, stockings. She walked confidently into the living room. "Here?" she said.

"Sure."

We sat facing each other, and I asked, "How old are you?"

"You *are* abrupt," she said.

"Why should we waste time?

"Nineteen."

"You appear younger."

"Thank you."

"And you're here because —?"

"Lachesis thought we should talk."

"An interview?"

"I suppose."

"Am I interviewing you, or vice versa?"

She folded her legs smoothly and smiled. The room was so quiet I heard her nylons rub. "I am here for you to approve."

I ignored the awkward phrasing. "What exactly did Lai — Lachesis — ask?"

"That I answer all questions completely and openly."

"You know I am a-mortal?"

"Yes." She adjusted her legs again. "Yes, sir."

I sighed. This was Laine's doing, a setup. And why had Chloé not gotten the door?

"Would you like a drink?"

"Do you have white wine?"

"Do you normally drink this early in the day?"

"I *never* drink."

I stood. "Then a glass of wine."

"No, not really." She smiled and I sat.

"Timessa, right?"

"Uh-huh."

"Last name?"

"We have no last name."

"Okay ... Timessa, why should the goddess hire you?"

"Because I'm amoral."

"Amoral, not a-mortal?"

"Yes. But both."

"I've never heard anyone admit that." She shrugged, a shrug a six-year-old might make. Squirming in her chair she gave me a quizzical look. "Ask me something difficult."

"We'll work up to that ... Do you really go to Vassar?"

"Uh-huh."

"What happened to the shark teeth?"

"Caps." She smiled broadly to reinforce the fact. "You approve?"

"I'm not sure I approve of you whatsoever."

"This could be a conversation with someone's father. Can't you do better?"

"Are you intelligent or are you all attitude?" I thought of the tattoo on her ass.

She stared without expression. It seemed a look intended to buy time. After seconds, she put on a smile and pulled at her blouse, gazing at me. "I have an exceptional IQ." Laine's exact words.

"So you're amoral and exceptional."

She blinked. "Are you asking me to prove it?"

"No, I believe you." Then I looked at her. A minute passed. Neither of us spoke. She held my eyes. Another minute passed. Fascinating: she was amazing, never breaking my gaze. I smiled. "What's your major?"

"Molecular biology."

"I expected Greek studies." She wore the same non-expression. "Courses you've taken?"

"Genetics, protein chemistry, organic chemistry ..."

"Another question."

"Ask me anything."

"Are you Artemis' favorite girl?"

She blushed intensely. I had her. "Answer."

"Artemis loves us all."

"You mean all her nymphs?"

"Yes."

"But you're her pet."

"Favorite," she corrected, looking away. "I'm one of her fucking favorites."

"Good. No cursing. And no more equivocation when you answer, understand?" With markedly less assurance, she nodded.

"It's well known she likes her girls willowy. What's another word for what she likes? Lissome."

"That's not a question."

"No, it's not. I'm about to conclude you're eminently qualified. But ..."

She said nothing, and recrossed her legs, her cheeks pink. I felt I might like her better without the caps. I imagined working with her, front teeth glinting like ice picks, a lissome shark in the goddess' shark tank.

I purposely let time pass. Squirming again, she eased into what I guessed was an obscure yogic position, putting her hands under her thighs and arcing her back. The move pushed out her small breasts. She had to know the optics, yet her expression was one of boredom.

"Timessa, if we hire you, would you sleep here?"

"I would return to Artemis."

"You'd have to leave before dusk. And Lachesis works into the night —"

"Darkness doesn't bother me."

I felt relief. This was not a hostel. "Timessa ..."

She interjected, "Ask me anything."

"When we saw you ten days ago, you'd been spanked." She flushed. "You had, hadn't you?"

"Yes."

"Because you were bad, or because you like being spanked?"

"I was bad."

"How often are you bad?"

"A lot."

"Be specific."

"The goddess thinks I'm bad ... three or four times a week."

"Every other day ... And the dolphin on your ass?"

"Old." I saw the defiance in her eyes, heard it in her voice.

"How old?"

"About 2,400 years. A nod to Poseidon."

Poseidon, the sea-god. We stared at each other. She stood and shook her hair. "May I ask a question?" she said. I nodded. "If I work with the goddess, will I call you Jack?"

I heard a sound behind me: Laine stood in the foyer, resplendent in a white dress. Timessa looked stunned and fell to her knees, her head low.

Laine stood in her goddess stance, but seeing the girl's reaction, lowered her arms. She walked to Timessa and pulled her up.

Timessa stood trembling. Head down she whispered, "Oh Lachesis, brilliantly inventive, heart relentless —"

Laine covered Timessa's mouth with her hand and said, "No. If we're working together, you must speak to me as you do Jack. I'm not going to eat you, so stop groveling." Timessa half-straightened. Laine held her by the arms and pushed her a few inches away, gazing at her. Timessa closed her eyes.

"Remember what you forced me to do in the woods when you disobeyed?"

Timessa nodded, almost pouting.

"Now look at me."

The girl lifted her head. They regarded each other, then Laine hugged her, putting her arms around Timessa's waist. Laine controlled the embrace and Timessa loosened, slipping her arms around Laine's neck, clinging to her as if she would never let go. Laine stroked her back. I thought, *The taming of a wild thing*, what she'd done with Orthrus weeks ago.

Finally Laine said in a hushed voice, "You are Artemis' girl. And now you are mine, as well. Both of us will protect and love you." Then Laine bent and kissed her. This time the kiss was not aggressive; it was a sister's. Laine said, "Be here tomorrow. We work from nine to six. Do you understand?"

"Yes, goddess."

"Dress casually but neat. And to answer your earlier question, you will call him —" She glanced at me. "— sir. Never Jack. And your attitude, which I observed with great concern, will be respectful."

CHAPTER 34

Still, light emerges, rainlight null
desire opening through schisms
through apertures, primal mechanisms —
the whir of the double-ax that strikes the bull.
—Poet X

When Timessa left, passing the altar, crossing the stream and disappearing into the back in her overwrought clothes, I was glad for the favorable weather, wondering how this would play when it turned bad. She moved with a gracefulness that reminded me of runway models.

I asked Laine, "How long did you watch?"

Ten minutes.

"You're sure you want to make her a confidante?"

Laine slipped into my arms and moved against me. "View Timessa as an assassin. I realize that's difficult. But as she herself said, she's utterly amoral."

"She's tangled," I warned, "urbane, feral, amoral."

"She'll be loyal."

"How old is she really?"

"I don't know. I've been aware of her for millennia."

"And the story about Vassar?"

"A full scholarship, an honors student."

I sighed. "So, she's bright, loyal and without a scruple." Laine nodded. "How did things go in town?"

"Almost hit by a woman texting. And a guy your age tried to pick me up." She turned around. "Got to get out of this if we're hiking today. Zip me down."

Later we found time to walk, a pleasant hike. We got as far as the retreat where we affirmed that her passion hadn't ebbed. Then, when we were almost home, she said, "I want to warn you there will be more ... events." I eyed her. "It's Artemis —"

Ask her to end it now.

She wants you to see more things.

For instance —?

I'm sorry, Jack. You're still on a need-to-know basis for about a week —

"Why a week?"

"I can't say."

We continued along the trail, then jumped Pegasus and stood beside the altar at the meadow's edge, the sky overcast. I watched a half dozen birds hop erratically in trees. She held my hand and said, "Timessa starts tomorrow. She'll be punctual and busy for the first few weeks. Leave her alone."

"What do you mean, 'leave her alone'?"

"She's attracted to you —"

"What?"

"Yes, and I've made the stupid mistake of showing you her ass. A volatile mix. I honestly don't care if you dally with an occasional girl, but I don't want this one distracted for at least another month."

Timessa attracted? Absurd. I had been aggressive in my questioning, and on reflection, recognized I enjoyed toying with her. There seemed a subtle class structure in these machinations, and nymphs were in a lower echelon. "Sure — but you're the one who's been kissing her."

She leaned against the altar, and said cooly, "Jack, I've had a struggle in the last few months. My struggle has been letting your little attacks and offensive comments roll off. No one speaks to me like this, no one. No one *except* you. And even when I'm in your arms, when I should be at my warmest and most open, you'll say something and my first instinct is to strike you dead."

I'd kicked a rattlesnake. I thought of Timessa's fear. When Laine touched me, I recoiled. She whispered, "But I would never do that —"

Her eyes had softened but she no longer fooled me. She was seething. I wasn't terrified, nor would I ever fall to my knees. But I remained unnerved.

"When I turn my back, goddess, no bolts of lightning." I wheeled and left her there.

Perhaps that event marked when I first knew with certainty, however I sought to deny it, that my credulity, my easy guilelessness with this girl was gone.

And within months, affirming my instincts, all, in fact, would all be shattered.

❧

A few minutes before nine, Timessa arrived in old jeans, sneakers and a pullover, her hair in a topknot. She wore a poker face as Laine showed her around the house. We exchanged brief pleasantries in a hallway, and to a suggestion I made regarding use of the kitchen, she said, "Yes, sir." Her eyes were without a trace of yesterday's defiance.

Laine and I had spent a restless, dispirited night. She at last — and perplexedly — noted her relationships had always been with women — her sisters, her mother, school friends at UCLA — and never a man. Close relations between men and women were terra incognita to her. She never imagined being paired.

I said I understood, but that she was not to threaten me if I said something upsetting. I tried to explain that every couple has disagreements. Rarely does a relationship survive if one threatens the other with harm. And I noted I didn't give a damn if she were a goddess. After hours of quibbling about romance, we dropped the subject. Laine appeared disconsolate. We'd resolved nothing.

She spent the first morning with Timessa huddled in her office. At times I heard their voices and found the sounds a pleasantry. I usually worked in silence, and their chatter was almost familial, the soft voices reassuring.

That afternoon Laine invited me to her office to view an expanded strategy paper, an exploded version of the draft from a month earlier. Ninety pages, its categories were broken into units, components, procedures. Names were listed with business/university and home addresses, phone numbers, salient habits, immediate relatives and a recitation of known routines.

As I skimmed the pages, Laine sat in her swivel chair, sawing back and forth. Timessa stood to my left, uncomfortably close — in fact, close enough to rub against my arm when she shifted her weight from leg to leg. She appeared to be viewing the computer screen.

After she bumped me hard at one point, she said, "Excuse me, sir" with a blank expression. But she didn't move away and continued to touch me every fifteen to twenty seconds. Perhaps, I thought, she has no sense of social distances. Laine, usually aware of every interaction, paid no attention to our dance. After minutes, I said to Laine, "Could you offer a synopsis?"

"Page 84 begins an end-of-project summation. I'll have Timessa email you the entire file. I want your criticism. Tear it down, identify flaws. Even the best plans have defects. I need your critique."

"Fine. But this is massive."

"Understood. Drill into it. It's difficult for me to be detached." She frowned and paused, her conversational tone disappearing. "Timessa?"

"Yes, ma'am?"

Laine stared at her coldly. "Throughout the last six minutes, while I had my back turned, you played with Jack."

Timessa turned white.

"There's nothing you do and nothing you think that I don't know."

Timessa trembled but said nothing. Laine said, "Tell me why."

"I, I —" She looked away, then contorted her face as she appeared to be considering a reply. "I'm so madly attracted I couldn't help myself." She broke into tears. "I just wanted to touch —" Neither of us moved to comfort her.

"Timessa, should I send you back to Artemis?"

"Oh no!" she whispered.

"If you're working with me, you cannot be distracted."

She slipped to her knees and put her hands together. "Yes, I never meant anything like that."

"Do you love me?"

"Yes, ma'am."

Laine shook her head in irritation. "What should I do with you?" She hissed, "Jack?"

After yesterday's argument I knew better than to comment.

We did not hike that afternoon. Around six I watched Timessa leave through the back meadow, her gait happy. Chloé prepared dinner and we ate as a quasi-family. Clo continued to block us but we did not reciprocate, and I was not surprised when she said, "Trouble in paradise?"

Laine said, "Fuck off."

Several hours had passed since I left her office and I'd purposely shut off interactions between Laine and Timessa. I asked, "So, how was it resolved?"

"I dropped the issue and she worked."

"I did nothing to encourage her," I said.

"Yes. I can read her better than you. It's a girl thing, I suppose, but she's on fire. She worked well enough, but in her mind, you were touching her. All of the nymphs have been isolated for too long." Laine gave me a shove. "Jack Aphrodisiac. I may have to let her go. But I'd have to find someone else. And I'd have a difficult time explaining all of this to Artemis."

We sat in silence and I opened a bottle of wine while Chloé nursed the child. After I topped Laine's glass, she said, "You're amazingly quiet."

"Just thinking. I watched Timessa leave and she appeared happy."

"I gave her a hug and kissed her forehead." Laine continued, "She acted like I'd blessed her. It was all bliss and elation after that."

"Laine, you're still an amateur at this stuff. She thinks the hug was your blessing."

"No, not what I meant," Laine said, making a face.

Clo parroted her, saying, "No, not what I meant," and exited abruptly.

We made half-love unsatisfactorily that night. After a period of silence, Laine began to postulate about Pythagorus and an old rationalist she called Anaxagoras. I was largely lost throughout and unable to follow her nuances. The verities she expected me to accept, events she empha-sized as important, bored me. Her discourse that evening seemed oddly grandiose, an exhibition meant, I suspected, to impress me.

We played chess, as well — and for the first time I won all games. We were less than thirty minutes from sunrise. In the stillness I said, "And what do I do about Timessa?"

She shrugged.

I said, "Be precise. Don't leave me with generalities."

"Maybe she'll burn out if you play along."

"You don't realize what you're talking about."

"Make it a dalliance. She needs attention. That's all she wants."

"So, what are you saying? Are you throwing her at me? Clo threw me to you, you throw me to her —"

Laine sighed and turned on her back. "I'm not sure what I'm saying." Her skin glowed in the sunlight. She met my eyes. "Jack, I want the girl and so do you."

"No, you're wrong. I don't want the girl."

She smiled and pushed me away. "Then you'll figure it out."

CHAPTER 35

Entheos, archaic Greek
for one possessed by a god.

I spent too much time critiquing Laine's document. On the third day, in the afternoon, I emailed her a markup. I expected a discussion or debate, but instead she dismissed Timessa mid- afternoon and closed herself off. Several hours later and an hour before dinner, we hiked and she kept her feedback brief: "Excellent assessment. Timessa was differen- tial. Your comments are trenchant. Thanks. I get it. No need to talk."

I had purposely avoided Laine's office, working in isolation. Despite my efforts, on the second day, shortly after lunch, Timessa entered my office. Her visit appeared surreptitious and as she came in, she closed the door. I smiled. "You know the goddess misses nothing. She will know you're here —"

"Is there anything you need —?"

"No innuendoes, Timessa."

"Sir?"

"You should return to work." She wore a mid-length dress cinched at her waist with a belt. She toyed with the buttons at the top of the dress, gazing at me and said, "Do you like my dress? It buttons down the front."

I stood and said, "You're taking immense risks."

She pouted. In a lilting voice she said, "Okay, then. 'Guess I'll see you later —"

I told Laine during our walk. She seemed disinterested. As we entered the meadow, I saw the bronze tripod. It had been missing since the event months ago in the meadow with all the girls.

The tripod stood beside the altar. At its apex was the same circular vessel. Today it was empty and I pointed. "Yes," she said. "You're not surprised?"

☙

I watched Timessa as she left that afternoon. Her easy gait had a small flamboyance. Perhaps she supposed — I thought of Laine's reference to the girl being on fire — this would all lead to something. I also noticed that without fail, two or three nymphs would greet her on the far side of Pegasus, hugging before turning into the woods, which I found reassuring.

The next morning during breakfast, Laine mentioned that Timessa would be coming close to noon, so we might have a quieter morning. I remained suspicious of her pleasantries as the preparations in the meadow continued. Now the bowl atop the tripod was stacked with a yellow, resinous wood. A basin sat in the altar's center.

By ten the coolness ended, the sun climbing. My quick glance into the field yielded only the sight of crows dancing nervously in the grass. They seemed edgy but I was anticipating, unable to focus on work. There seemed a general disquiet about the house. I also ran across Chloé shortly after breakfast. She and Aisa walked hand in hand, Aisa taking large steps. She'd dressed the girl in a white ballet dress.

I said, "That's quite the piece."

Chloé smiled, itself unusual, and said, "I'll be in the yard. Aisa needs to learn to walk in grass."

I wasn't sure why she had chosen this morning. Her thoughts were opaque, as were Aisa's. I asked if she needed help. No, they'd manage alone. A quarter of an hour later, Laine came into my office where I puzzled over a spreadsheet. Like Aisa, she wore a white dress, hers of loose, flaring silk, semitransparent and ankle-length.

She curtsied. "Silk and delicacies."

"Is there an occasion, or are you merely being lovely?"

"May I sit in your lap?" I swiveled, pushing the chair away from the desk. She sat, snaking her arms around me. The archaic tune Laine whistled on our walks rose like a specter from the meadow. She stiffened at the sound, and said, "It's begun. A celebration today of certain things, which will consist of dancing and acting by players wearing masks and archaic clothing, all staged for your edification." She giggled. *Memorized lines*.

"Tell me I'm presentable." She stood and turned. She was shockingly beautiful. As I inspected her, she put on a golden necklace of woven leaves. I guessed it was ancient. The music grew louder.

We stepped into the field and before us, to my amusement, were dozens of little girls. Several did cartwheels, while others ran around each other squealing, none of them more than eight. All wore white dresses like Aisa's.

The tripod's smoke coiled off in spirals of burning cedar. Behind the altar stood the orange-haired girl who had earlier orchestrated the sacrifice of birds. Again she held a bundle of wheat and grasped a long knife, observing with the lucidity of a teacher the chaos of children before her. Behind her an enclosure, perhaps four-foot square, was covered with a shroud.

Beside the stream nymphs played lutes and a tambourine. One broke away and walked into the chaos of girls. She shook a tambourine overhead. The little girls stopped, turning to face her. The tall girl with orange hair lowered the bundle of grain. As if conducting an orchestra, she motioned with her hands, calling, "Two lines, two lines!" The girls, rehearsed, scurried to face the altar in rows.

Laine and I stood on the meadow's edge, unnoticed or ignored. She took my hand and whispered, "Expect the unexpected. This becomes a bit violent." Oddly, she put her hand before her face, palm touching her nose, masking her identity. She said, "You, too. We remain mysteries until I signal otherwise." So I imitated her.

Timessa appeared, towing a large ewe by a rope. Like the little girls, she wore white. As she entered the field, she barked something to the girl behind the altar. Timessa showed her teeth: points, the exemplar of a savage, Laine's new girl.

She steered the ewe awkwardly between the lines of girls who stood soldier-like in rows, staring robotically ahead. As she got closer to the altar, the animal bleated, collapsing and rolling on its sides. Its cries became desperate. Only Timessa appeared aware of its anguish. She kept righting it and pulling it along.

I saw Chloé at the edge of the field. Like Laine, she had a hand before her face and wore a white dress. It had been months since I'd seen her fully clothed.

Once Timessa was beside the altar, the little girls ran up and tied the ewe's legs together. It cried pitifully and Timessa pinned it to the ground with a knee in its ribs. The orange-haired girl pulled its head back. The knife glinted and she passed it to Timessa.

After a sudden upward jerk of the blade, Timessa thrust it down. The animal thrashed and cried momentarily, then sagged into the grass. Holding a bowl beneath its throat, the two girls collected the pulsing blood. Some splashed over the animal's fleece and splattered Timessa's dress. Her moves appeared ritualistic.

With the bowl full, the tall girl held it at face level. She moaned, swiveled and poured the hot blood across the altar's top. Almost simultaneously, the little girls started to chant. The lutists accompanied them. Timessa stood, her dress bloody. She looked vaguely intoxicated. Laine glanced at me, saying "Watch!"

At the altar, Timessa and the other girl stepped apart, leaving a passageway from the altar's front to the rear enclosure. The shroud was pulled aside. From the darkness Aisa emerged, blinking in the sunlight, in the white dress I'd seen earlier. She squinted, then walked with surprising confidence forward and between Timessa and the other girl. She stopped and observed the little girls.

Timessa picked her up at the waist and set her feet-down, legs wide on the ewe's carcass. A light wind whipped her dress. At less than four months old, she appeared in complete command. Laine squeezed my hand. Aisa's bare feet turned bloody.

As she stood, all the girls dropped to the ground. Timessa, the tall girl, the musicians with their instruments — all bowed. The child looked across the meadow, then hesitated, put a hand to her mouth and sneezed. Seeing her mother, Aisa waved and Chloé nodded.

Aisa raised her arms in the goddess gesture Laine used — elbows bent, hands high, palms out. To my shock she cried in a strained voice, using complete sentences,

> *There is a goddess*
> *With a baby's breath*
> *Who wields the power of death.*
> *Who cannot guess?*

Aisa lowered her arms. I whispered to Laine, "What the hell are we watching?"

"Aisa's coming out party." What I saw of Chloé's face was masked. Aisa appeared euphoric, singing out,

> *My eyes are black,*
> *I might attack.*
> *Avoid my glance.*
> *Now, dance!*

The little girls jumped up and began cavorting. Laine squeezed my hand again and whispered, "Hijinks. But this isn't done."

As she spoke, Aisa wobbled and sat on the ewe. She glanced around and noticed her dress, now smeared with blood. I expected her to howl, but she laughed and pushed her fingers through the fleece. Around her the little girls went mad.

The orange-haired girl hoisted her up and placed her on her shoulders. Aisa, now higher than anyone in the masque, gestured to the sky with her arms. I had never seen such animation. As I watched, Laine gave my hand another squeeze, released it and left my side. She joined with Chloé and the two walked toward the altar. Chloé took the child from the girl and set her back atop the ewe.

Facing us, the three stood together, palms out before their breasts. I had never seen Chloé, her face still blank, pose like that. The wind through the meadow had increased, blowing their hair back and flattening their dresses against them. Blood stained their clothes. I thought: *the Fates*.

With the exception of the three, only I continued to stand. As Laine had demanded, I kept a hand in front of my face. All the nymphs prostrated themselves in the direction of the goddesses, writhing or cringing in the field. A movement beyond the stream caught my eye: *Artemis*. I dropped my hand.

She stood wide-legged on the far bank, a silver bow in her hand. Sixty feet away, she was unclothed. I had once seen her naked in the pool at the grove. Now the goddess showed herself audaciously, her stomach muscles taunt. She scanned the scene, glanced briefly into my eyes and left. I felt an odd flash of sadness.

When I looked back to the meadow, the sisters had disappeared, as had Timessa. The orange-haired girl still stood by the altar, her tunic and hair wind-whipped. And the little girls now stood again in lines, facing her without moving, their dresses stained from the grass. The girl at the altar turned her face skyward and shrieked. An older nymph paused, clapped two short sticks together, and led the girls away, all holding hands, across the stepping stones in Pegasus and into the woods.

The tripod continued to smoke in the wind. I half expected the ewe to stand, shake itself off and lumber away.

The wind rose, strong enough to sting my cheeks. Walking to the altar, I found the bloodied knife and bowl, and felt transported to an ancient time. Looking up I saw a lone nymph, perhaps fifteen, squatting beside Pegasus, watching me. She was dressed modestly, a white flower threaded in her hair, angelic cheeks flush.

She spoke softly, her voice melodic,

The goddess Artemis' explication:
Everything is moving at speed.
There is no longer need
for explanation.

CHAPTER 36

Previously I spoke, a maiden, but now lie silent,
Bound here by the Fates.
—Epitaph on the tomb of the priestess, Hierophile

T he house appeared empty. I methodically walked from room to room. When I finished I stopped at the bathroom beside our bedroom and found the door locked. I suddenly knew: it could only be Timessa. Annoyed, I knocked.

"I'll be another minute. Sorry, sir —" I heard the shower running. Where the hell was Laine? In my office I found a note on my desk in loopy script.

Jack! An emergency. I'll be in Tokyo
and Singapore a week at most.
Then back to you!
I've given T endless tasks.
If she bothers you, send
her away. (Oh, Chloé

& A are out, but back tonight.)
More as I have time.

I felt that same loneliness — first Artemis vanished, now Laine. My anger rose and I caught myself, thinking of the adage: *Those whom the gods wish to destroy they first make mad.* Even so, I found myself alone with a wild girl whose intent was far too obvious. I had no interest in her enticements. And the clear permission I had from Laine to "dally" was preposterous.

Timessa stepped into the office. She wore one of Laine's pleated skirts, her hair wet from the shower. She had pulled on one of my tees without drying herself.

"Sorry, sir. I hope you weren't surprised. The goddess ordered me out of the dress. It's ruined. She laid out what I'm wearing. It's for me to wear."

I gazed at her for seconds. Physically, she matched Laine and the clothes fit her perfectly. I stood, saying, "Why didn't you dry yourself?"

"I didn't want to linger, sir. I was afraid."

"Of what?"

"That you'd be mad."

"Timessa, what do you want?"

She fell silent, then replied, "Nothing, sir."

"Come here and sit." I gestured to a chair across from mine. She walked over and sat. Reminding me of our "interview" from days earlier, she crossed her legs and smiled carefully. Her pointed teeth glinted. Obviously she felt no need to hide them now.

I looked at her legs. "No nylons today?"

"No sir."

"Timessa, define amoral." Her reaction was unmistakable: she visibly relaxed. I had altered the tension. She thrived, I suspected, equally under sexual or intellectual challenge, however inexperienced she may have been. Now we might begin a cerebral discussion.

She said pedantically, "Amoral? Being laissez-faire about sexual and societal matters. Contemporary culture, in its blind corruption, condemns amoralists."

"Is there a right or wrong?"

"Amoralists do not judge."

"Is that all there is to amoral?"

"Humans say amorality is purely the absence of morality. Deliberating anthropocentrically, a stonewall, for instance, is amoral. The stream beside the meadow is as well. They have no *moral* code, no societal standards. They solely 'are.' "

"You told me being amoral was one reason the goddess should hire you."

"Yes, sir."

"Are all notions of morality meaningless?"

"Are you speaking of moral nihilism?"

I smiled, ignorant of the term. "Could be. Tell me how you'd define that."

She crossed her legs again, a slow, deliberate gesture, a small flash. The game was on. I couldn't imagine working this afternoon. We'd kill a little time.

She shrugged. "Moral nihilism refers to the view that nothing is intrinsically moral. An example would be killing someone. A moral nihilist argues doing so is neither right nor wrong."

"And that's your position, I presume?"

She laughed lightly. "I have never thought about it. Sir."

"Do so now."

She paused, "Yes, that's it."

"Good."

She seemed puzzled by my response. "Morality, sir, is constructed. It's arbitrary. What is moral one human generation is not the next. Amorality, on the other hand, is timeless. Sir."

"Isn't that relativism, not nihilism?"

She appeared delighted. "It's wonderful, sir, being able to talk like this."

"Yes, it is. I do have a related question." She nodded. "Why did you show me your panties moments ago?"

Again, she flushed. I seemed able to push a few buttons on this complex creature. "I want to please you. Sir. You like to see them."

She might have lied, "I wasn't aware, sir." Or have said, "Would you like to see them again?" Or asked, "Should I remove my skirt, sir?" Now she waited.

I might have pushed this in any direction, and anything seemed acceptable. She presented herself, waiting. But still, for me all of this seemed too effortless.

"The goddess says she left you work."

"Yes, sir."

"It's been pleasant talking, getting to know each other." She squirmed, trying to anticipate. "I'll work until about six. Can you do the same?" She nodded. I stood, dismissing her.

She surprised me, leaning forward, leaving a small kiss on my cheek, lingering an indiscrete interval, lips soft, then turned and left.

ॐ

Unexpectedly, I might now have as much as a week to myself. I had deflected Timessa's advances without effort. And Chloé never asked anything of me. Laine's absence would mean I had leisure time. I found myself suddenly insouciant, even blasé about Laine's disappearance. A few hours had passed, and I was already tasting freedom.

My cell phone bleeped.

> *Landed LAX. Next leg Tokyo.*
> *O I wish this hadn't happened.*

I glanced at the time — 3:18, about the hour we usually hiked. I looked in Laine's office and saw Timessa standing at Laine's computer. "Do you ever sit?"

"No, I stand, sir. In the woods no one sits." She smiled. "I squat to eat or pee, sir. But otherwise …"

"I thought it might be pleasant to take a walk."

"You'd take me?"

"I'm inviting you."

She looked delighted. "Oh, I'd be thrilled!"

"We leave in ten."

When I returned she had an easy smile. I took her hand and led her out to the meadow. She was barefoot and shrugged when I noticed. "I'll be fine."

The fire still burned in the tripod as if it had just been fed, and in the middle of the field sat the hound, Orthrus, in its dangerous two-headed iteration. Timessa whispered as we stopped, "One head looks into the past and one to the future."

"I know."

We took a step toward it, Timessa reluctantly. The hound bristled in warning, growling so deeply that the ground vibrated. I guessed if Laine were here, the beast would be docile.

I held the girl's hand and focused thoughts toward the beast: *Move. Now. You are my guardian, as well.* It frowned and raised its paws to its head, scratching against its ears. I repeated the command, *Step aside. Protect.* Orthrus whined, slinking away to the altar. "We're good."

"What did you do, sir?

"Told it to move. And protect."

We leaped Pegasus and took the trail into the woods. In moments Timessa asked, "May I speak?"

"Yes."

She glanced sideways. "Why did you invite me?"

"We'll be together a week. I thought it might be pleasant to walk."

She smiled. I looked behind her toward the house and saw the beast sitting in the path, a one- or two-second sprint away.

"Come on, I like to keep moving." She nodded and we picked up the pace, continuing till we came to the clearing. I glanced at the shack and it seemed to be suspended, patiently waiting for supplicants to enter its realm. "You watched when the hunters shot each other?"

"Yes. I helped drag the older man away."

I was tempted to interrogate her, but resisted. Any further discussion seemed a continuation of a loop that exasperated me at every turn. "Let's head back."

She looked at the shed, almost spoke, then nodded.

At home, I checked the time. "Do you have friends meeting you at six?"

She appeared surprised I might know. "Yes, but should I stay tonight —?"

"No. Return to Artemis."

"Yes, sir." I might have read her thoughts, but chose not to. I had work and wanted to shake off Timessa's small spell. She was sweaty from the hike. I could have put a hand behind her head and drawn her close. Instead, I turned her around and said, "Go."

An hour and a half later she peeked into my office to say she was leaving. I barely acknowledged her, waving her off.

CHAPTER 37

They say the strong force of fate awaits
even those who offer prayers to their god.
—*Poet X*

After breakfast Laine sent a text confirming her arrival in Tokyo. Half the lines rhymed.

Dearest J,
At a conf today.
Tokyo, then lab-related stuff.
Can't say more.
Will message you when
I leave for Singapore.

I started work, checking the time: 8:55. Within three minutes, Timessa arrived, said, "Morning," and went to Laine's office. We worked without contact until lunch, when I invited her upstairs to eat. She looked pleased.

Chloé left us alone. I heard Aisa talking briefly and otherwise I felt we were on a quiet island in the wing of a grand hotel, left to our devices. Timessa wore a pink summer dress cut modestly, her hair tied in her favored topknot and strung with colorful ribbons. I thought she must have spent time putting it up and complimented her.

Tempted to press her about yesterday's event, I assumed Artemis rehearsed it, assembled the players, wrote Aisa's declarations and managed the stagecraft. Timessa had played a key role and would know all the backstage details. But to probe, I would be violating an undeclared understanding among us all. I confined myself to saying, "The celebration for Aisa seemed unusual. All those girls."

She nodded and smiled, volunteering nothing.

"Were they recruited from a local preschool, or a kindergarten?"

"Sir?"

"The young girls. They came from somewhere."

Timessa shook her head and fiddled with a small necklace she wore — it had a single pearl. "I cannot, sir."

She sat before me, an utterly amoral young woman willing to touch and kiss and, I presumed, give herself to lovemaking. Still, she persisted in bafflement, and responded to my simple question with ambiguity.

I walked to the windows. There in the meadow, near the altar, sat the two-headed hound. Was the beast a conduit between Timessa and her goddess? If Laine were here, she would read my thoughts and comment. But Timessa sat blankly, awaiting guidance. Not having heard her move as I viewed the field, I was surprised when her arms encircled my waist. It was Laine's move. She pressed herself into me with a small moan.

"Timessa!"

She jumped back. I turned to face her. "You're beguiling, and frankly, fascinating. But I'm not sure what that hug meant." Her gaze was steady. She played with her necklace. Then she smiled, winsome and endearing. "I know I'm awkward, sir. I'm sorry for that. Still the same, I hope we can get to know each other." She continued, "I realize I'm graceless, even gauche —"

"You're here to do Lachesis' work. That's your duty, not getting to know me, whatever you imagine that means."

"Yes, sir." She abruptly turned and left.

I stopped her with my voice. "Timessa!"

She turned. "Sir?"

"Be ready for a hike at four. You'll have to change from that dress."

"I brought nothing else, sir."

"We'll find something." She nodded and left.

I rejoiced having her gone. Awkward seemed a poor description of her lovely machinations. Saying, "I'm graceless, even gauche," sounded like an old pickup line. Curious for Laine's reaction, I texted,

Your girl T is flirting.
I'm beating her back. Comments?

An hour later she responded,

Perhaps she needs a spanking.

I tried to read the humor but there appeared to be none; she understood too much. I had instant flashbacks of what we had seen weeks earlier.

Laine didn't respond to my followup texts. I was on my own.

Back in the office, I stared out my windows into the field at the hound, then walked to Laine's office.

"Timessa?"

"Yes, sir?"

"I'm cancelling today's hike. Too much going down."

"Tomorrow? If so, I'll bring a change of clothes."

I should have emphatically said no. But I didn't. "Yes, we'll see what tomorrow brings." I was grateful she couldn't read my thoughts. I paused. "How's work going?"

"Well, sir." She'd anticipated a walk, but took the cancellation dutifully. As she spoke, she ran her thumb inside her necklace, side to side.

"Let me know before you leave tonight." She nodded and I went upstairs.

The day had fractured, and I'd accomplished almost nothing. I considered leaving the rest of the week, flying somewhere to see a client. Getting away made immense sense. Yet I struggled with even that. Did I want to leave? No. And I resented Laine doing so. Had she planned this weeks ago?

Too, I suspected I partially understood Timessa's attraction to me: Laine warned me I would, over a short period of months, be spun backward in age by about a decade. That meant a rebalancing of hormones, a remix mimicking the youthful physique of my twenties — which might also explain my constant arousal. Laine, always steps ahead, would have known. So why would she have left me with this girl? I couldn't believe she wanted any change in our relationship. I recognized I had gone from wild years in my teens to almost two decades of abstinence while I raised a child: philanderer to monk. Then I'd ricocheted from Chloé to Laine, a stone skipping from pond to pond. I was hopeless, a fool. I received a brief text from Laine.

Didn't mean to be flippant
on my last. Sure she's mad
about you. Just treat her as
an innocent ... whatever.
I'm forever & she's not.

As I reread the text, Timessa leaned in. "Sir?"

"Yes, Timessa?"

"I can't get the goddess' requests done and leave by six. She's insistent. I may stay later, with permission, sir."

I didn't want to deal with her, but given Laine's admonition, I was gentle. "Yes, of course. However long —"

I responded to Laine's texts with something upbeat. Then, with the extra time, I replied to business emails. I also scanned financial markets, pleased to see an uptick in stocks. Around eight, Chloé announced dinner. I hadn't given Timessa a thought in hours. How the hell would she walk home through the woods? It was not as if I might drive her there. I looked into the office and she startled at my voice. "It's after eight."

She picked up her phone and looked. "Got away from me."

"How are you getting back?"

She glanced at the window and shrugged. "You don't want me here." She made a goofy face. "Guess I'll find my way."

"No, you'll eat dinner with us and I'll show you a room."

She hesitated, then said, "Yes. sir. Thank you ..."

"Finish what Lachesis needs and come upstairs."

An hour later the three of us had eaten, and Chloé stood. I quickly asked, "Do you have anything to loan Timessa for sleepwear?"

She glanced at the girl and said, "What do you normally wear?"

"Oh, whatever."

Chloé smiled, "Then she can wear whatever." She left, whispering loud enough for Timessa to hear, "Don't stay up all night. Or I'll have to tell on you —"

Timessa and I sat for a few minutes, then she said, "More wine. Sir."

How much had she had? I filled her glass, asking, "You're not drunk?"

"Hmm, don't know." She grinned, her sharpened teeth showing as she smiled. "If so, I'll just say stuff I shouldn't. Sir." She reached and touched my hand. As she did her pink dress opened slightly in the front.

"What were Lachesis' requests this afternoon?"

She stared. Her gaze went on and on. I wasn't sure whether I detected woozy or mellow, or whether something else drove her. She was impenetrable. I'd never paid attention to her eyes, but noticed tonight they were a darker violet than Chloé's. "T, I asked you a question."

"You called me 'T'."

"I like that, don't you?" She nodded carefully. I said, "A nickname. Now, my question: her requests ... all emergencies?"

"Lachesis has begun the operation. As you saw in the document, it begins in Asia."

"Details?"

"Six researchers. What she's begun should be finished soon. First Japan, then immediately, Singapore."

"By the means she projected?"

"Exactly, sir." I remembered it all: accidents, heart attacks, food poisoning — apocalypse by ancient formula.

"So it's started."

"It started with James a few months ago."

"I thought he stumbled onto Artemis' bath."

"He was invested heavily in startup companies involved in life extension."

"I see. Then, the other two, Kline and his assistant …" She said nothing. As we exchanged looks, she reached up and undid her topknot. Her hair tumbled over her shoulders. She pulled out the ribbons and shook her hair.

"Do you mind if I take off my shoes, sir?" Without waiting she twisted them off. She gazed, smiling, throwing her shoes aside. "The next few months will be crazy ones."

I smiled, saying, "I've avoided the precise details. The network she's developed in each of these countries — is it functioning?"

"Yes. And that's my main assignment — coordinating surveillance, creating a matrix on each target's habits, determining the most effective extirpation."

"All in a day's work."

"Sir, may I comment?"

"Yes."

"You know I live by no moral code. For millennia our band of girls has mostly played. It's been extraordinary. There have been tradeoffs, of course. But we do as Artemis wishes, largely blown by the wind and her whims."

She placed her hand higher on my arm, her dress opening. I saw her breasts clearly, delicate cones capped in pink. "Now she who measures our lives asks a favor in return. Lachesis' mission is magnificent. I will do anything she asks."

She paused. "Do you need sleep, sir? Like you did before you changed?"

"About an hour. And you?"

"Four or five."

I glanced at the clock: midnight. "Let's find you something to wear."

CHAPTER 38

Now rain is down,
As, too, her clothes like a tired child's.
Wind stirs candle flames;
Through our open doors, storms.
—Poet X

After pouring more wine, I left her at the table, promising to find nightwear. In the bedroom, I gathered a pair of my pajamas, choosing to ignore Laine's numerous camis. Returning, I sat across from her and said, "Here, best I can do." She fingered the offering, smiling faintly.

We spoke for some time about Vassar and how she despised Pough-keepsie. I had little to say and admitted I had never seen the place. She flirted briefly, saying she'd show me around if I visited; she'd hide me in her dorm room, a suggestion she thought hilarious. She confirmed she planned to skip the next semester to focus on the "mission."

"I'm here," she said, "for at least as long as the goddess wants."

Eventually, I stood and said I had work, that she needed sleep. I noted

I usually rose around six. She said she did as well. We'd have breakfast together.

I walked her to the second guest room, showed her extra blankets and the lights. After pleasantries, I left for my office, frankly glad to be alone. My work progressed well and after some time I quit to read. Laine had given me a volume on chess strategy and I took it to bed. As I worked my way through examples, I heard a knock. Timessa leaned into the room, only her head and shoulders showing and said, "Sir?" I startled. The house had grown silent and I assumed she slept.

"A problem, T?"

"Can't sleep." She looked tired, and I detected nothing more. She kept herself largely hidden, which I found amusing. I saw the pajama top and wasn't sure why she'd come.

"T, just relax."

"I know the problem," she said with a shrug.

"And—?"

"I need to cuddle."

"No." And I thought to myself, an emphatic *no*. "We're not sleeping together."

"Can I explain?"

"Make it quick. And look — if we're talking, come in here." I found her hiding annoying.

She said, "You're sure?" I pointed at a chair beside the bed. She walked in wearing nothing but the top. Her hips were narrow, tanned and her legs muscled. Her pubic hair was light, a semitransparent brushstroke against her mons. She stopped several feet from the bed and said, "I sleep naked. Even this top itches."

"Don't make a big deal of it."

"Right." She sat in the chair, legs together and hands folded primly. "Now, can I explain?" I thought of Laine, and what she'd think, suspecting she'd be amused.

"Since I was little, the goddess holds me when I sleep."

I smiled at the image. "You and Artemis cuddle?"

"Yes."

"You're a favorite." She nodded, and even though I mocked her, part of me was incredulous. "I suspect the goddess wasn't there for you at school."

"My dorm mate was."

"You slept with your roommate? Every night?"

"Yes, you've seen her."

Her roommate must be one of the nymphs. "Would I know her if you described her?"

"She's the tall one with the orange hair. Philippa."

I lay propped up against pillows, and studied Timessa.

"We call her Filly."

"And the two of you hold?"

"Spoon." She shook her hair and rubbed her eyes. "It's the only way I've ever slept."

"Then you've got a problem if you think it'll be you and me."

"Can we try? Please? I'd sleep on one side. That's all." She pouted and tried to look as if I'd already said no. Imitating Laine's little girl voice, she said, "I've got to get a couple hours or I'll be a fucking wreck."

I tired of the parley; it was two in the morning. And I remained incredulous that I was negotiating with this girl. "Can you sleep if I read?"

She shrugged as if she'd won. "Uh-huh, if you put a hand on my waist. Let's try."

I motioned toward the bed. She rose and demurely pulled her top down as if to cover herself; it stopped above her hips. I made room and pointed, "That's your side. No talking, complaining or wiggling."

"Yes, sir." A ghost of a smile crossed her lips, and she slipped in beside me, under the single sheet, turning on her side. As I watched, she closed her eyes, whispering, "Will you be mad if I say something?"

"Depends."

"Okay, forget it." She shifted slightly and pushed the sheet off her hips. Time passed and she said, "Hand on my waist, please?"

"Fine, but no more talk."

I put my hand in the hollow between her hips and ribs, fighting the sensory feedback crashing in: heat, silken skin, a leopard's light musculature, softness, the rising and falling of her belly as she breathed. She had a faint luminescence, her skin flush and radiant. I studied her legs. The reading light exposed her small cheeks. In the incandescent light, I saw multiple stripes from what must have been a last spanking. They appeared fresh. No wonder she preferred standing when she worked.

As I fought every natural impulse to stroke her ribs or hips, she fell asleep, her body visibly loosening. In the shadows, the tattooed dolphin on her closest cheek seemed to move; perhaps she had flexed her muscles while asleep. Maybe I simply imagined it.

And now she slept in the harbor of my bed, safe again. I swore under my breath at the situation. Having her here, however innocent, felt otherwise.

Then I instantly detected a spectral presence — Orthrus. The hound lay against the door to the meadow, in the grass, breathing evenly, aware I was aware of it.

Orthrus was our sentinel, under the stars, the one or two-headed one, a wraithlike beast heeding only Artemis' commands, here to watch over the girl.

≈

Shortly before five that morning, I set the chess book down, aware I should sleep. Timessa lay beside me, muttering softly and shifting lightly, a leopard cub in sleep. I turned off the light and avoided contact. The sun rose an hour later and I sat, amazed to see the girl beside me. I slipped out quietly.

She came upstairs twenty minutes later, happy and revived. To my surprise, she ran over, thanking me for "everything." She remained in the pajama top, her hips uncovered, and I said, "T, here in my house we walk around in the common areas with pants, or a skirt, or at the least panties. Come back when you've dressed." Three minutes later she returned, in shorts and a top. We scrambled eggs and made coffee. I didn't linger and went to my office. She seemed joyful. I had never seen her so upbeat.

Downstairs I scanned my phone: texts from Laine, the time difference between Philadelphia and Singapore twelve hours. It would be about seven in the evening there.

Dearest J
In fancy Singapore
which makes Philly
look so old. Work going well.
Yr arachnid, L

My spider? If so, a black widow on the prowl.

I concluded that my self-reflection was unproductive. And I knew enough to know that, whatever I concluded one moment, I dismissed the next. My new goal: eyes open, senses alert — watch myself as much as everyone else.

Business, I knew, was always an antidote: I would impress clients, et cetera. For the next four hours, I massaged numbers and made occasional portfolio adjustments. The market seemed always to move my way; investments soared. I recognized the time as being one of those rare moments when one entered a zone where nothing imperfect existed. Time vanished there, work flowed without gravity's impediment.

Close to lunchtime, T walked in. She stopped several feet away and said, "Haven't seen you in hours."

"How's the work?"

"The goddess is pleased. At least she says so ..." She paused. "If we take a walk this afternoon, I'll stay in these shorts. If not, I want to change."

Then she did a strange little hop and skip, stepping closer. She seemed ecstatic. "Now," she cried, "sitting in your lap!"

With that she leaped the couple feet between us, landing on me softly, as lightly as a small bird swept in on a breeze, settling in a hush, and slipped her arms around my waist. "You should pay more attention to me," she whispered. *Laine's words.*

I let her stay and put my arms around her. I might have pushed her away, but was curious: she knew better. She remembered the admonitions. What did she want? She pressed herself against me, letting her fingers flutter on my back. In an even softer voice, she said, "Pay attention to me, sirrr —"

I took her arms and pushed her back. Neither of us spoke. Her eyes were glazed and she burned without disguise. If she had spoken at that moment, she would have said, "Take me, take me —" but she didn't.

She was testing, perhaps certain, now we had spent the night together, that I would be hers, her mind full of images of us spooning, her yielding and crying out, making love — and doing so with someone stolen from an absent, mighty goddess who had left me in her care. I reminded myself, I held a nymph, a being sheltered for millennia.

Perhaps she was genuinely as naïve as she appeared. And if so, why did Artemis now allow her to roam outside the ecosphere?

She saw my eyes clouding, closing her out and she cried, "I wanted to say last night — but you wouldn't let me — I love you." I heard despair. She stared into my eyes, then whimpered, "Have I been bad, sir?"

The old conditioning: if she erred she would be punished. I kept my grip on her. "Maybe you have, T. But I'm going to be lenient. No spankings —" She appeared relieved. "That's not how we relate."

"But I've been bad —"

"Sometimes being bad means you get a hug." Her long lashes were wet, her eyes tearing. "And no crying when you're here." She sniffled, trying to stop. I pulled her close and said, "Put your arms around me. No talk now."

She did. I let time pass, letting her sob then catch herself, sniffle and rub her nose against my shirt. She had few social niceties, and fewer inhibitions. A nine-year-old in a nineteen-year-old's body. Without pushing her away, I said, "Now let go and look at me."

She sat back, contrite. I said, "Timessa, I have something personal to ask."

"Yes, sir."

"You don't have to answer, understand?" She nodded. "You've told me Artemis regularly spanks you?"

"Yes, sir."

"Don't tell me it's because you're bad. I've shown you now how bad can mean a hug instead." Again, she nodded. "I saw your … bottom … last night. When were you last switched?"

"Two nights ago."

"If this goes on constantly, and has for years —"

She interjected, "Forever —"

"Why is your bottom not scarred?"

"We heal fast, sir. What you saw last night is already gone —" She slipped off my lap and turned, dropping the khaki shorts to her ankles, bending over. She wasn't wearing panties and her cheeks, which last night had been lined with angry marks, were silken.

She turned, her shorts still around her ankles. "See?" She smiled, inanely innocent.

"Pull up your pants." She did so with a small shrug. "There's something else, T. You have a duty not to be distracted. Not by anything. Your work comes first and last."

"Sorry, sir." She frowned. "Can we still walk today?"

"We might." She gave a thumbs up and left in an exaggerated march step, posture straight, one foot mechanically set before the next, arms moving in opposition to her legs, the perfect nine-year-old tin soldier.

CHAPTER 39

It was all downhill,
Petiole, ellipsoidal,
Auriculate: just what leaves delineate.
—Poet X

I skipped lunch and worked steadily. T offered to bring me food; I declined. An hour later, I received a text.

J, trouble here. Don't worry.
I'm fine. If you hear news, ignore.

Timessa was in Laine's office. We exchanged glances. "What do you know?"

"Things got complicated," she said, "but the goddess is okay."

"And —?"

"She says she'll be in touch —"

I went back to my office, pulling up the BBC world news. Under Top Stories/Asia, I read, *Possible Terrorist Attack.* The article described an explosion ripping through a lab at the National University of Singapore, leaving twelve dead and injuring four. An investigation was on-going and authorities would not speculate about the cause. The article noted the laboratory was one of Asia's leading centers for gene research.

I checked again with T: nothing. Her phone chirped and she looked down, reading out loud,

> *Have bumped my flight forward a day.*
> *Departing Sing for LA.*
> *Review sections 36—44.*

"And those sections are—?"

"The implementation sections." My phone chirped and I went to my office to read,

> *Pick me up in Philly.*
> *Will send details shortly.*
> *All's well. Stop w/ ?s.*

So, silence till she returned. I checked the BBC again: no updates. The *Times* was quiet as well. Then I found a local on-line source, the *Singapore Reporter*, published in English. An article noted that an explosion had struck laboratories at the university's science center around 10:15 that morning, releasing toxic gas from tanks stored in a back area. Investigations were on-going, deaths higher than initially reported. The toll had risen to sixteen, with eight seriously injured; the campus had been evacuated.

Somehow, I had rationalized the deaths in my backwoods. I still did. Now there were more, and I expected in the near future, more again. Singapore proved the unexpected, no matter the planning.

I had not seen Chloé all day, nor heard a noise from Aisa. Unusual, but not rare, as Clo often retreated to our old bedroom for the day. Scanning the estate, I sensed the hound lying beside the stream. And, of course, I read Timessa's intensity: she was implementing a series of prearranged instructions, one leading to the next, focused on the goddess' dictates.

Laine had pulled a chaos switch. I suspected the Singapore explosion was intended for a few individuals at most. She couldn't have known about the gas — its release incidental — or expected collateral damage. Inevitably, there would be similar unexpected accidents in a future location, in another land. I imagined a car wreck planned for a professor, the collision taking out two sons she ferried to school, children unexpectedly on-board. Or a virus spreading beyond a brilliant scientist's lungs, jumping to his wife when he coughed.

Incidents of war? There is an ancient rule — what strategists call the principle of proportionality — which, at best, serves as a rationale for the deaths of innocents lost under attack. I acknowledged, now that the wheels were spinning, peripheral lives would be lost. Laine operated outside any norms, outside of laws. Like any co-combatant, I faced a choice: pick up my gun or leave.

Another text came in. I flicked on the phone. Timessa, a first.

May I visit?

Yes. I felt tired, worried about Laine and sick of speculating. T came in and I pointed at a chair.

She said, "Just need a break."

"You and I both." As much as I resisted, we were suddenly comrades in an enigmatic war.

T said, "I've already messaged my friends not to come. The goddess needs me here. And new orders just in — I'm to look out for you." She smiled, shark's teeth gleaming in the dull light. "That means," she added, "I'll stay again tonight."

We spent a long moment staring at each other. She seemed solemn, almost ruminative, her eyes dark. I broke the silence. "Have you ever been anyone's muse?"

She laughed. "I don't think so." She added, "Sir."

"I may make you mine."

"What are a muse's duties, sir?"

"Essentially, a muse provides an artist inspiration."

"You're an artist, too?"

"Hardly. Perhaps I'm a financial artist. But still, you might inspire me to achieve even greater things." She said nothing, but her eyes flashed. "Your duties as a muse would not conflict with the goddess' demands." I was toying with her and knew she wanted to agree. She would have agreed to anything I asked.

"When do I begin?"

"Now."

She grinned and said, "What should I do first?" Then she whispered, "Sir, I thought muses went around without clothes. I'm okay with that."

"No, you'd be a distracting muse. I might have to fire you. Besides, you might be a terrible muse. We won't know until you start."

"But, I've already started," she said. "I'm the goddess' right hand girl and now a muse!"

I smiled. She whispered, "And we sleep together, too —"

CHAPTER 40

Your hair floats, your lips blur.
In sleep your fingers cock
as if they wrestle back
great birds.
—Poet X

Shortly after dinner, I looked in the mirror. Never particularly interested in my appearance, I rarely did so. But while we ate, T had said, "You hardly look older than me tonight."

Now what I saw startled me. The gray scattered through my hair in the last years had vanished. The laugh lines that gave me gravitas were gone. My skin glowed. If asked, I might have guessed my age as twenty-five. Laine had predicted I might lose ten years or more in three months, which I had dismissed as fantasy.

T and I split up after eating, each of us working independently. Around eight that night, I received texts from Laine, all brief. One included her flight schedule. Curious to hear if Timessa had additional news, I checked in. She stood at her computer, but without her khaki shorts. "Too hot for pants?"

She gazed up innocently. "I'm not in a common area, sir."

"We'll find you panties for tomorrow."

"No, now I'm your muse." She leaned over to me before I could react and stole a kiss, fleeting but brazen. "I like best … being a naked muse."

"We'll have to negotiate with the goddess about that."

"But she's not here."

"Anything new from Singapore?"

"Yes. All work."

Around midnight Timessa came into the bedroom, tired and saying, "I'm showering." I nodded and ignored her. She left and returned twenty minutes later, a towel around her hips. She stood a foot away and said, "I'm crashing earlier. Please do whatever you did last night. Sir." She unknotted the towel, tossed it onto the chair and got in beside me. I placed my hand in the hollow above her hips. Identical feedback as the night before: heat, softness, sensuality, girl-fire. She whispered, half-asleep, "Am I inspiring, yet?"

I ran my hand up her ribs and down her hips. "You're inspiring, but you're on muse-break at the moment. Go to sleep."

To my surprise — obediently — she closed her eyes and slept. I read for hours and turned off the light. I was afraid I'd wake her, but didn't and I drifted off. I guessed the time to be about four, earlier than I usually quit.

I woke at six. As I shifted, stretching, she turned on her back and opened her eyes, her legs casually undone. We must have looked like young lovers waking in the early dawn. Light flooded the room and she smiled softly. I kissed her forehead and said I'd be upstairs. She nodded and turned on her side, away. I covered her legs and hips and left.

Laine's first text that morning noted that, given what occurred in Singapore, we were switching to encryption, using something called PGP. She linked instructions.

I made breakfast and Chloé wandered in with the child. She smirked, "My, you look young. Suits you, sort of —"

"Missed you yesterday."

She glanced at Aisa and said, "The little girl's school day, wasn't it?" Aisa grinned and pointed a finger at me as if she saw something wicked. I said, "What?" and she scrunched her eyes, making a face.

Chloé said, "We're doing accelerated learning. She's best when it's concentrated. If I could be half as smart."

Timessa entered the kitchen dressed in shorts and a wrinkled tee. "Where's the coffee? Hi, Aisa! Morning, Chloé!" She gave me a hug. "Thanks for a great night!"

Chloé smiled indulgently. "He didn't keep you up all night?"

T blushed and I intervened. "Hardly. It's imperative nymphs sleep well or they're wrecks." Chloé was merciful and dropped it, and we sat around making small talk.

T looked up, "Phone's vibrating. Goddess messages. Gotta go."

Although I, too, had emails from Laine, un-encrypting them held no appeal. Possibly I resisted the extra seconds it took, resented her demands. I selfishly had viewed the next few months as an opportunity to explore my new prowess, but Laine's priorities seemed to trump my own. I remember thinking that I still had twenty-four hours before she arrived.

Late morning, T appeared in my office. She had changed clothes again and shed the shorts in favor of a diaphanous skirt. She still wore the tee, now rolled up to her ribs and knotted in the front. When she saw my face she said, "I checked with the goddess. These are okay." She stopped and with her arms out bounced lightly on her feet. The sheer skirt drifted up and down.

She said, "So you need to touch me, and I thought you might like this skirt."

I tapped my thigh. She appeared surprised and came and sat. I put an arm casually around her as if we regularly held. "But have you checked with the goddess about sitting in my lap?"

She flushed, making an exaggerated grimace. "No, sirrr."

"Do you imagine you won't be caught?"

She rolled her eyes and said, "You should do what I want."

"*I* should obey *you*?"

"Yes and touch me, too. I'm so soft and pretty and you know you should —" She put her head on my shoulder and sighed. I moved my hand across her back, digging my fingers into the muscles between her shoulder blades and down her spine. She pressed herself into me, appreciatively humming. Then to my shock she began to cry.

I slowed and she whispered, "Don't stop—"

"Did I hurt you?"

"No. I thought no one except the goddess could ever make me feel like this."

"And how do you feel?"

"Loved." She burst into louder crying.

I continued for a time. She finally stopped whimpering. I straightened her and gazed into her eyes. "T, you have work."

"I love you, sir." Her eyes softened. I knew her sentiments were those of a twelve-year-old. Love for her was golden — touch and sunsets and warmth, escape from the wildness of running with Artemis — and I knew myself incapable of being the object of that love. I put my hands on her waist and lifted her up and onto her feet. She lowered her chin to her chest as if a child.

"May we walk today, sir?"

"Today? Consider it a date. At four. And you'll have to wear something other than this —" I grabbed a handful of the slip. "Understand?"

She smiled. "Yes sir."

"And panties."

"We don't wear them, sir. Unless we have periods." She paused. "They get torn too easily in the woods."

"Otherwise nymphs go bare-assed?" She blushed and nodded. I let her go, giving her a gentle whack. She yelped and did her tin soldier march, striding out, back straight.

I skipped lunch, preferring to work. My business day had gone from seven or eight hours to four, and in the last two weeks, three at most. My output was far higher than in the past. I suspected my transformation was almost complete.

Throughout the afternoon, I'd given T no thought. Now she returned for our hike wearing one of Laine's short pleated skirts, bare-chested. I said, "Get a top. We're not going out like that."

"I want to be a good muse."

"Good muses do as they're told."

"Muses are often like this around those they inspire. I looked it up."

"You're lovely, but no. Pretend you're at Vassar. Now go on, be good —"

Pouting, she left and came back in an old golf shirt. As we left I scanned for Orthrus, and not sensing the beast, focused on where it hid. I found it, pivoted and saw a head partially exposed behind a stone. I pointed a finger-gun at it and said, "Pow."

T said, "Don't get him going. No one knowingly pokes a nightmare, sir."

"Yes, but I hate being dogged." She took my hand as if I were naughty and pulled me away and toward the stream.

Twenty minutes into our walk and 500 feet from the back stonewall, we encountered a girl standing in the path. The path was almost entirely shadowed under the massive oaks and she stood with her legs apart in one of the few areas where sun pierced the leaves. She wore a tunic with sandals laced to her knees. I stopped and gestured to T, who said, "Good! She said she might come."

The girl's hair was orange. "It's your friend, Filly." She nodded and two ran toward each other, arms open. I advanced, glancing left and right. I sensed no one, but it seemed unlikely Filly would come alone. With the exception of a light breeze, the woods were quiet.

T pulled her toward me. "Philippa, this is Jack." Filly nodded.

"May I call you Filly?"

She turned toward T.

"I've told him many things," T said. "We've even slept together."

Filly appeared startled. "You ... then you're —"

"Oh no, Filly, he ... well, just touches me."

I noticed the girl wore a long knife on her right side, secured in a worn scabbard. She seemed remarkably confident. Filly turned and met my gaze. "Timessa is special. Very special to us all."

"Which means?"

"She must be treated well."

"Is that a threat?"

"Should it be?" She turned to T and they exchanged looks. She went on, "Timessa needs clothes, which I've brought." She peered down the path. "They're over there. If she's to stay with you, she cannot wear the goddess' clothes. And we are about to have our periods ..."

The reference again. "That's why you've come?"

"And she wanted us to meet."

T still had her arm around Filly. I said, "Since you haven't answered my earlier question, I assume 'Filly' is what you prefer."

She ignored my question, saying, "Let's get off this path." Turning, she walked down the trail and we followed. She stopped and reached behind a tree, producing a satchel. "Clothes —" She frowned and closed her eyes. Almost at once a narrow path appeared through the woods. It meandered in a rough perpendicular to the trail and into what appeared to be a beech grove paces away. She smiled at us. "This will do. "

We turned and walked into the opening, the beeches old and in a circle, the center a grassed flat with scattered leaves. Filly sat and crossed her legs as if meditating. She pointed to a spot for me. I was aware I was ceding control of events to her. She shook her hair; it was dyed red at the tips. Like T, she, too, had a tattoo, hers a two-inch spiral on her neck.

As I sat across from her, I noticed her tunic bunched on her thighs; she didn't cover herself. No panties — she purposely exposed herself. T stepped between us, and surprising me, pulled off the golf shirt. Without explanation, she said, "I'll sit here." She took Filly's hand, whispering, "My favorite beings, both here today."

Filly squeezed the girl's hand, looking at me. "Why is Timessa special? Because she, more than any of us, has the capacity to love." Filly paused, keeping her eyes on mine. Then, she pulled T's head onto her lap, stroking her back and running a hand through her hair. She leaned close to Timessa's ear. "No comments while I talk about you, understand?" T nodded and closed her eyes. Filly continued: "She's utterly innocent, which enhances her capacity to love. Am I clear?"

I nodded. She continued, "The rest of us are unruly, distrustful. But Timessa has never been like that. She's a romantic."

"And —?"

Timessa sat and interjected, "And Filly is the *wisest* of us all."

As I met Filly's gaze, I was unexpectedly swept with a strange sense of nausea. Her gaze was darkly primal, threatening. I eyed T, who now sat like Filly, legs crossed and crotch open under her skirt. Why?

I thought, *Perhaps they give it no thought whatsoever, given their disdain for social mores.* Primordial emotions, sexual ambiguities, the iconic ∇ at the thigh's intersection, all leavened by an exasperating inscrutability —

"Justice and stability drive us," T said, "They are the core of the goddess Lachesis' work. And both are Filly's obsession." She blushed, I presumed at her forwardness.

"First," I said, "let's drop all the third person references." They shrugged. I imagined children saying, *Whatever*. I turned to T's friend. "Filly, if we are to continue, let's not compete. I'm an ally."

T looked at us and whispered, "Yes, no arguing between you."

Filly said, "There will be a full moon tomorrow night."

"So?"

The girls stared at each other. Filly said, "All of us have our periods then."

"*All* of you?"

"Yes. Since the beginning we have been in synchronicity."

"Goddesses, too?"

T added, "Of course not!"

Filly continued, "That's the only time we wear panties. Red ones."

I almost laughed, but their tone was utterly somber. "Red?"

"The sacred color." Without warning, Filly touched my cheek. "I have not said so, but all of us love you —" They laughed and at that same moment, I sensed the oddity of being beside two girls with teeth honed into triangles, whose groins were as enigmatic as Pythagorus' geometry.

Her hand remained on my cheek and I pressed it lightly. "It's an honor to meet you, Philippa."

T smiled happily and said, "Now, Filly, tell him more."

Filly looked at me for concurrence. I nodded encouragingly and she said, "Throughout existence there has been a certain proportion of fire, earth, air, and water in the world. The four elements. Things are made and then unmade. A natural law keeps the elements in balance. Similarly, there are a multitude of living things, each struggling to outdo the next. Am I being clear?"

T said, "She's being too formal — and too modest. Filly introduced this concept millennia ago. To a man in Ionia. Tell him, Filly."

"This man she mentions — I intended for him to have our knowledge. Many human ideas have had a similar origin. We were generous in the early days."

I nodded, assuming she would elaborate. "And the man?"

"Anaximander, a Greek from around 550 BCE. I met him in the hills of Miletus, in Ionia. He wooed me, wanted me as a lover, but instead I became a mentor. He was a runner, later becoming one of the first Greek thinkers. Our relationship was secret, as women were not allowed outside the home. He was a quick study and in time grew famous throughout Greece."

"Anaximander?"

She said, "Ana-zim-ánder."

"A new name."

"Yes, he's remembered now only in academia."

"I presume he attributed the notion to a god."

"No, I stressed to him that justice — the harmony of nature — is greater than any god. Or goddess. When the natural balance is under threat, the world itself is at risk." She smiled. "He claimed the idea as his, knowing I would never challenge him."

"So today," I said, "when humans threaten to defeat death itself, they become a menace to that ... equilibrium." They nodded.

CHAPTER 41

Euripides, who died in Macedonia,
taken down by dogs,
was on a walk.
You, too, walked through time.
Light flickering on your cheek
— your eyes sublime.
—Poet X

We spoke at length, the two girls elaborating on their roles across millennium. They seemed intent, no matter how they recrossed their legs, on keeping themselves exposed. I remembered Filly's comment: Every *thing* has a purpose.

After an hour I ended our discussion. T mentioned that the goddess had shifted tactics due to the "Singapore incident." The *James* and *stag incidents,* and now the *Singapore.* Had I read the goddess' morning messages? I admitted I had not.

Filly cocked her head. "A change?"

Timessa said, "She's switching to the virus."

I asked, "Virus?"

T said, "Something once used against blasphemers." She took my hand. "When the gods started exercising their powers, skeptics arose who said the gods were frauds or tricksters. A virus was loosed against them. It's not contagious so it was a perfect weapon against skeptics. And now, possibly, scientists."

Filly added, "Yes, the gods would not tolerate blasphemy."

"This virus still exists?" They nodded. "How fast does it act?"

"After contact, a week or so."

"Symptoms?"

T sighed and turned my palm up, drawing spirals in its center. "At first the victim becomes hyper-energetic. Suspiciousness sets in, then an inability to focus. Their mind wanders. They hallucinate."

Filly became excited. "She means they slowly lose their mind."

"Is there an antidote?"

"No," T interjected, "As the symptoms worsen, most eventually commit suicide. The goddess' brilliance, though, was remembering the virus is not infectious. With care, we can take out targets one by one."

I said, "And so the winnowing may continue."

T shuddered. "Yes. Selective winnowing."

Filly stood, handing T the satchel. After hugging her and touching my cheek, she left, sprinting away. We returned to the house where I decrypted Laine's messages. In the last, she reminded me to pick her up.

A half hour later, Timessa appeared at my office door. "May I enter, sir?"

As earlier, she wore the diaphanous skirt without a top. I responded, "Yes, but I have no time to play."

She entered and sat on the corner of my desk, looking away. I studied her profile, her aquiline nose and long neck. Her legs kept beat to a rhythm only she could hear. I returned to my work.

After ten silent minutes, I said, "T, have you completed the goddess' requests?"

"No, but you need me here."

"I don't."

"I know when you need me."

I paused. "Explain."

"You've asked me to be your muse. I am, sir." She smiled. "I'm pretty and you find my beauty inspiring."

"T, muses don't pose. They inspire by their presence."

" 'Presents'?" she said. "Then I'm your present."

"Just like that?"

"Always, sir. Whenever you want."

I stood. She gazed into my eyes and I put my hands on her waist, saying, "What shall I do with you?"

"Sir?"

"I'm the goddess'. This relationship we have — yours and mine —"

"Is one she approves. Sir." She put her arms around me. "Just take my gifts."

I took a deep breath. "And what are those gifts, Timessa?"

"Me. I have nothing else."

"If you give all of yourself, you lose your innocence."

"But, sir, my innocence is what prevents me from knowing love."

"No, that's not it. You can be madly in love and retain your innocence."

She shook her head. "Then I am."

"You're what?"

"Madly in love. Sir." Her eyes clouded. "You see what I'm saying?"

"Timessa —"

"Please don't call me that. I'm *T*."

"Look, we'll work until dinner and after, we'll continue talking. No working late tonight. We eat in an hour. Understood?"

She nodded and slipped off my desk, saying, "Okay. Then, we talk tonight."

❧

When I scanned emails, I found one from a firm I didn't recognize: Manson Real Estate Management. The email was sent to direct abutters of the James estate by an associate, Sally Ketchum. In two brief paragraphs, she announced the availability of the James property. The land abutted mine for 1,200 feet. Her letter noted the estate comprised 133 acres, and included the main "cottage," a 16,400 square foot home with an accessory carriage house, stables, a large greenhouse, and other amenities, including a squash court and pool in the basement. There were tennis courts in the rear, a theatre and a fully-stocked "safe room." Its extravagance far exceeded mine.

The asking price was as imposing as the home. But, I immediately recognized the advantage of combining the two properties into a single entity of almost 200 acres.

The letter noted no offers would be considered for a week, although inquiries were welcome. Inevitably I thought of Artemis and Filly and the nymphs encamped in the back of the property — the sacred grove was deep in those woods. Attached to the notice were several pages of exterior and interior photos. Drone shots showed the grounds from overhead. Intrigued, I saved the email.

At dinner T dressed modestly in Laine's skirt, which she offset with a crisp white blouse. Chloé and Aisa didn't show. I felt tired, itself unusual, and avoided drinking. As we finished, T said, "Our talk?"

I stood. "Meet me when you wish." On a whim, I stopped by the office briefly. Viewing the meadow, I saw the hound nearby, its eyes unblinking. I went into the bedroom and stood restlessly. Then I sensed her behind me. She was now in red panties. "Full moon?"

Her eyes went dark and she held out her glass. "I want to get drunk but nothing's happened. One last." I filled her glass and handed it to her as she sat on the bed. "I want to talk business. Sir."

"Goddess business?"

"And this and that."

"Fine," I said, "and I have questions, too." She smiled guilelessly. "Mine first, T."

"Yes!" She sounded eager.

"The virus Filly spoke about … created from scratch by the gods? No one understood biology then."

"No, discovered by observation. And it's not a virus at all — it's a fungus. From an oak grove in Greece west of Thessaloniki, between the city and Mount Olympus. One of us noticed almost 3,000 years ago that deer eating acorns from the trees went berserk. A pitiful sight as they're such gracious things."

"Something on the ground or the acorns themselves?"

"The acorns. They carry a pathogenic fungus. And it's found only there. Sessile oaks, a genetic subspecies of *Quercus petraea*."

"How will this work? Will the goddess persuade her colleagues to mix acorns into their arugula?"

She sighed. "Are you aware the acorn is a big ovary?" I shook my head. "So sexy when you think about it. The acorn's female, its sex external."

"What's the delivery system?"

"The fungus grows under that little hood at the top of the acorn, under the pericarp. Did you ever pop them off as a kid?"

"Sure. Underneath it's silky slick."

"Right. The fungus is there, on the inside of the cap." She smiled, excited. "So, the goddess has already ordered about seventy-five —"

"Ordered from whom?"

"Those of us who live near Thessaloniki."

"Nymphs? You aren't the only ones?"

"We're scattered in small bands across the world." She watched my eyes. "There are many of us, sir."

"Fine. But you haven't explained how the toxin is transferred."

"The goddess is working on that. But essentially, mechanics aside, the acorn is delivered and the recipient fingers it. The hood is barely attached to the top and, at the slightest touch, comes off. Everyone tries to put it back. No one can resist. And they make contact with the fungus as they fumble with the hood."

"Ingenious."

"Far better than plastic explosives. Or Zyklon B."

"What did you say?"

With a smile she bounced up and down on the bed. "Zyklon B!"

"Which is —?"

"A gas used by the Nazis."

My dream months ago: Laine tied to a bed, a cage full of people about to be gassed, canisters of Zyklon B trembling above their heads. "There are not many people who know about that."

She stared blandly.

"Timessa."

"Sir?"

"You constantly amaze me."

She giggled. "You're so easily amazed. Sir." She shook her hair and gave me a long, languid stare, then said, "I'm glad you met Filly."

"She's obviously a good friend."

"What else?"

"What else what?"

"Do you have other questions for tonight?"

I laughed. "Many. We'd be up weeks if I asked you all that's on my mind. But one last, a comment about nymphs —"

"Sir?"

"Have I told you how appealing you are when you smile?" She covered her mouth with her hand.

"First you found my teeth repulsive. Now you find them ... not?" She dropped her hand. "So. Do you want to kiss me, sir?"

I sat beside her on the bed and as I watched, she moved closer and put her head in my lap. I stroked her side and arm. She abruptly put up a hand and said, "Wait! What's the time?"

"About 2:15."

She sighed, sat up, struggled out of her top and skirt and got under the sheets. "Thanks, a good talk —"

Amused, I put my hand on her waist and she slept within seconds.

CHAPTER 42

We sail swiftly to our rest,
the words from our mouths lost,
our god du jour determined solely
by century & geography.
—Poet X

A
s I woke, I realized I knew how to deliver the acorns. No need to create an elaborate ruse. We would instead have a colleague send one to another colleague, peer to peer. Everyone in this arcane field knew each other. A small package from a friend would elicit no suspicion. I imagined a card enclosed with each gift that might read,

Big Oaks From Little
Seeds Grow.
Here's An Acorn For
Someone I Know.

A simple note would suffice. The small packages would be sent from an appropriate university town. An immediate downside, though, was that, rather than the elimination of researchers occurring over several years, it would have to be compressed into weeks. Otherwise investigators would identify the toxin, determine the method of delivery, and screen all mailings to all scientists in the field. But those were details.

Timessa still slept beside me, her breathing even. I slipped away. Sometime after I'd finished my first coffee, she came up, and minutes later, Chloé appeared with Aisa beside her. T wore a tunic neatly pulled down to her thighs.

As we ate Chloé said, "I approve of your idea. Brilliant."

"Delivering the acorns?" She'd been scanning me. I'd left myself open, and wasn't surprised.

T said, "Have I missed something?" I took her hand and said, "We've got things to do downstairs, and I'll get you up to speed. Before I pick up the goddess."

"Can I go, too?" she asked.

"No."

Chloé mocked her, however lightly: "Can I go—?"

I left, dragging Timessa behind me. Aisa suddenly shouted, "Now *dance*!" and we turned. Aisa looked angry. I quickly blocked her.

Turning into Laine's office, T smiled and touched my hand. In my own office I tried to shake off the girl's scent, her sensuality as blatant as an exotic flower. Opening my blinds I saw swallows and swifts overhead. And as usual, although out of sight, I knew the hound lingered beside our stream.

I had two encrypted emails from Laine, one confirming her flight, and the other citing random thoughts on what she projected for the coming week. I glanced at the time — an hour left.

I hadn't been in my office ten minutes when T came in. She walked to where I sat and pulled her tunic off, her eyes nervous. I sensed nothing but an endless burning heat. She let the garment drop and said, "So little time before you leave. We should spend it here —"

Surprised, I said nothing. She put her hands on her hips.

"Tell me I'll be your muse even when the goddess returns."

Although I could not anticipate what Laine's return would bring, I said, "Yes, a muse is a muse. The goddess knows."

"Can I sit in your lap?"

She had dropped "sir." I distrusted my instincts. And I knew Laine would be looking into my eyes within hours. I stood. "We have thirty minutes for a brisk hike. It may be our last."

I gently whacked her ass and said, "Get that tunic on. You're coming with me —"

Pegasus ran high and as we crossed it, our shoes got wet. T took hers off and left them on a stone in the sun, saying, "Where will we go?"

"Don't know. We'll explore." We set off leisurely, neither of us speaking. After only minutes I got a text. Normally I left my phone at home, but today I knew Laine was airborne, and I needed to be available. The plane would now arrive at 9:50.

I had time to leave for the airport, but nothing more. T took the change well, appearing stoic as we returned. The drive was without complication and I parked at Arrivals. Laine sent me texts as she landed and as she came out to ground transportation. I spotted her, almost indistinguishable from a dozen other young women. She wore jeans and a nondescript top. We hugged. I put her carry-on in the back and we headed home. She cracked her window slightly and fished out a cigarette. "Feels like three days, not six hours since my last."

"You're an addict."

"I suppose. But for us, smoking has no effect. Oh well —" She took a deep drag and exhaled toward the window, grinning. "Jack, you look about my age. I'll bet you're ripped."

"Ridiculous, huh?"

"I like."

"You weren't stopped by security?"

"Nope." She spoke about the operation, how it had been botched, how her extensive research had failed to reveal the gas canisters. In retrospect, she wasn't sure her on-the-ground resources should be faulted; the canisters had been moved the night before to a nearby room.

Regardless, she affirmed her shift to the fungi. We discussed my idea about presentation, which she approved at once. And she concurred that the acorns would have to go out as a batch at the same time to all recipients. As we talked about pitfalls, she shook out a second cigarette.

I mentioned the unexpected offer for the James estate with its extravagances.

"Can you afford it?"

"Yes, with a stretch."

"Then we should," she said. "I'm not certain the exact use we'd make of the combined estates, but it's a rare opportunity."

I got an uninhibited smile and agreed to make an offer, perhaps later that day. We shifted into a rambling discussion about Timessa. I explained I had tried to deflect her interest by making her my "muse."

"Do what you want — she's still a child," Laine said. "The question remains how to manage her."

We shifted into a discussion of Chloé's moods. Laine shrugged — her sister was hopelessly preoccupied. And the operation would continue, with or without her. Being thorough, I recited meeting Filly during a walk. We laughed at the girls' crotches.

"So you looked?"

"Of course."

"They're a fetching pair."

"You're laughing at me."

She smiled. "You're typical and they know it."

"All the changes you've wrought have had no effect on that."

"You imagine that occurred by chance?" she giggled. "I like knowing you're always half-aroused." As we entered town, I mentioned Filly's comment about the nymphs' synchronized periods.

"Yes, very tribal. That tradition began so long ago I hardly remember. You can imagine how the sight inflamed the occasional shepherd who spotted them in the wild. Some of this behavior we indulge."

She took my hand. "They are utterly loyal, and their *esprit de corps* is essential. Timessa, like Filly and the others, would die for you without a thought. As would the hound you so dislike."

As I maneuvered in the slower traffic, I asked, "We have five or six minutes alone at most. How would you have me handle T?"

"Let me watch your interaction."

CHAPTER 43

*There's no beginning, and
no end of a wave.*
—Laird Hamilton

Within minutes of our return, Laine shut herself up with Timessa. I followed the dialogue as Laine made no attempt to close herself. Inevitably, the conversation shifted to T's behavior. As if in anticipation of the meeting, T wore a humble tunic ending at her knees, her hair in a topknot. She expected punishment.

"He made me his muse."

"You accepted?"

"Oh yes!"

"That's an honor. What does he expect of you?"

"That I just *be*."

"The highest honor of all."

Laine told her to continue as she had — yet, always and without exception, her ardor must remain secondary to the mission's demands. The girl agreed, overwhelmed and surprised by the goddess' apparent sagacity. The conversation ended with Laine emphasizing that I remained hers, that any relationship the girl and I developed was temporal, a dalliance — Laine's indulgence might be withdrawn at any point.

Then the conversation shifted to mission details. Plans would be jiggered; the focus now would be on quality testing of the Thessaloniki acorns. They would coordinate the mission, but inevitably others would be recruited. The girl's apprehensions dissolved. As they finished, Laine gave her a hug.

Shortly after, Mrs. James' real estate agent called, suggesting a tour. She noted the availability of a video showing the house and grounds. The owner had recently ordered a thorough home inspection; the house was in exceptional condition. I asked for a video link; we might want to walk through later. I also asked if the seller would agree to hold the property. The agent made no promises, yet, within thirty minutes I had her email assurance that the property was on a twenty-four hour hold. She included a video link.

Laine joined me to watch. The video started with a long aerial shot that swept across a slate roof with multiple double-brick chimneys, eyebrow windows, copper accents, and a dozen lightning rods. A male narrator described the house as a 1924 Tudor-style castle with stone exterior and French roofs. We laughed as the camera panned along a moat that surrounded the building; the waterway, at least twenty feet wide, had ornate fountains in each corner. The drone panned over the rear of the house where landscaping included a shrub maze framed by a low wall. In the center of it stood a life-size statue. Laine cried out in delight, "Aphrodite!"

The video transitioned to a woman standing at the front door. She welcomed the viewer, then began to stroll through a wide foyer. She meandered through the house, pointing to various features. A fireplace in the massive living room was "a French original," imported from Trouville where, she noted, Claude Monet had painted masterpieces. Our hostess said the dining room windows could be Tiffany. The kitchen was updated in the last year and the heating/cooling system recently replaced.

Amenities were exactly what I expected from someone of James' expansive ego. For instance, the master bathroom was, in fact, two large, adjoining baths, effectively a his-and-her doublet. A gold jacuzzi on a cedar plank landing was centered between the two and backed by a curved window looking over the rear maze; the interior walls were copper sheeting. The lowest level housed a squash court with changing rooms. A pristine lap pool took up the remaining basement area.

After fifteen minutes, the woman walked outside and recited the obligatory "rare opportunity" pitch. As the video ended (with the drone panning away to show endless woods), the narrator intoned, "For those of you enamored of Hollywood's famed goddesses, this estate was owned briefly by one of the greatest, Marlene Dietrich." A glamour shot of the actress flashed on the screen.

At its conclusion, Laine asked again whether I had the cash. When I nodded, she said, "It's large enough for the entire tribe."

She shook a cigarette from a pack on my desk. I found a match and struck it on the side of the stone I'd found. Laine paused as the tobacco flared, inhaled and said, "Yes, grandiose. It's perfect."

❧

After dinner Laine took me into the bedroom and lay on the bed. In the low light, the freckles on her neck and arms and shoulders cascaded like gold flecks down her chest. She whispered, "I endured a week without you, Jack —"

We kissed, time fracturing as it so often did, merging once again. We kissed and she teased me with her hips.

A light knocking on the door interrupted us. From the hallway, Timessa said, "Sorry. Can't sleep."

"We'll be right there." Laine turned and whispered, "Take care of her, Jack —"

So I rose and pulled on pants and opened the door. T stood with her head low and I said, "Go on. Back to your room." There, she pulled off her top and slipped into bed. Knowing the routine, I stroked her waist. I felt her breathing calm. She softened and within minutes, slept.

When I returned to our bedroom, I sensed the hound in the meadow, lying under the full moon, its mind empty. I said, "Orthrus, always there —"

"You will have all its senses shortly. And more. You've changed far faster than I anticipated."

I knew she was right, yet I remained annoyed at her intransigence and secrecy. We slept an hour. I dreamt briefly of hunting with Orthrus. The hound made giant loops in the field before me, constantly flushing birds from the underbrush. As it did I took shots with a bow, missing each bird.

When I woke, I looked out. The hound sat beside the altar; a crow perched on its back, motionless. Smoke crackled from the tripod. Laine opened her eyes. I asked, "The theater continues?"

She shrugged. "Artemis. But then who knows."

So another scene would unfold — today or tomorrow or next week.

After coffee I went to my office, tapped my computer and read emails: no reply from the real estate agent. The markets were turning south due to a banking crisis in Italy; my currency shorts rose in response. I sold them and reinvested the funds. It was still early and I realized I didn't care if I acquired the estate. The purchase seemed frivolous, an inexplicable and gaudy jewel for Laine and all the savages. She walked in. "You're preoccupied."

I shrugged. "I feel like a surfer riding a twenty-story wave."

"It's an endless wave," she said. "A crazy rolling wave that sweeps across islands and estuaries and continues on and on. Didn't I warn you?"

A small ping from the computer: I checked — the real estate agent. Laine looked over my shoulder as I scanned the reply. James' wife had countered my offer, bumping it up a mere 5% with an additional condition: she wanted to close within thirty days. We hadn't even walked the place. I swiveled to Laine. "So who's maintaining the damn moat? Not me —"

"Let it grow algae." She continued, "Counter her counter with 3%."

"You're tough. She'll reject it."

"She won't." She was so certain that I did so. Within another hour, I had an acceptance and a PDF of an Offer to Purchase signed by the seller. I read the signature: Pauline James. She wanted out — and Laine wanted in. The estates would merge in less than a month. Summer was ending and the timing felt good, a fall acquisition half-exciting.

I called the legal firm I'd used for the current house and spoke to a partner, telling her I needed an immediate title search and representation at closing.

Then I sent the agent a note:

Suggest a time tomorrow to view the property. I may be accompanied. If any staff are employed to maintain the premises, ask the most senior to attend —

CHAPTER 44

They were perfect opposites,
he, the electrode — she, the electrolyte.
— Poet X

L aine worked in her office wearing a stylish dress. I noticed her
cheekbones, silver glitter smeared in a long arc on her cheeks. Then
something else: movement through the back window. Stepping to the
glass, I opened the blinds. Smoke drifted lazily from the tripod. Orthrus
sat atop the altar, sphinx-like.

In the surrounding grass, crows strutted randomly, rushing at each
other, brandishing their wings. I scanned the woods and beyond: no other
sentient beings of note. I heard the stream babbling, although I had
never had such acuity.

Orthrus swiveled its head and stared. From her desk, Laine whispered, *Don't engage.* I understood and stared back at the hound without
thought. I felt empty, yet cognizant. Orthrus insolently looked away.
Laine said, "See? You won that round. Oh, and the James purchase —
Artemis knows. She sends congratulations. And she has named the
combined properties."

"Has she?"

"Yes, it's to be called Aegle," Laine said, "like eagle. It means dazzling light." *Oh?* I thought, *and not Eden?*

Then she turned. "There's more. Timessa, show him."

Timessa reached behind Laine's computer, grasped a small glass cylinder and straightened, holding it in both hands. I saw an object rolling in the bottom.

"Careful," Laine said, squeezing my arm. "Our first acorn. From the *Quercus petraea*, a gift from our Greek brethren, fallen from a glorious oak."

I stepped closer and T turned the cylinder. A shiny acorn wobbled back and forth, capped with a checkered hood. T said, "Fresh from Thessaloniki."

"And if we touch it we go mad?"

"We're immune. Otherwise though, watch out." Laine smiled. "This first one will be used for a dry run."

"Where's it going?"

"A colleague of mine at MIT. Dr. Chura. She's had a good career, nominated once for a Nobel, and is now too close to certain breakthroughs."

"No sentiment on your part?"

Her eyes narrowed. "None. From now on, we're all assassins."

My cell rang — the agent. We could walk through the property this afternoon. The owner was in New York.

&

Clo, Aisa, Laine and I drove the short distance. I remained surprised at the pretentiousness of the building as I pulled into the circular driveway. A woman greeted us, introducing herself as Sally Ketchum. I introduced the others without elaboration. I instantly took a dislike to Ketchum as she intoned, "Fortunate you made the offer when you did, Mr. Night. I've already had two enquiries from foreign buyers."

I glanced expectantly at the door. She smiled. "Let's look at your prize."

As we started up the steps, a young woman appeared on the lawn, striding briskly toward us. She was in a white blouse, a high-waisted brown skirt cinched with a wide belt under her breasts and in boots, fashionably militant. She looked familiar, but I assumed she must be in Mrs. James' employment. To my surprise, Laine cried, "Art!" and the two hugged. The goddess Artemis strode up and put out her hand. "Jack, good to see you again." I noticed her necklace: woven barley ears, dull gold. Her hair fell in waves.

"I wasn't sure you'd make it."

"Jack, I'm always punctual." She gave me a piercing look. In my scan of the nearby woods, I detected a dozen nymphs, the hound nearby: she was punctual and took no risks.

All of us entered the house. James or his wife had done a magnificent job. Much of what we saw did not suit my taste, but the rooms were, without exception, generous. After touring the living quarters, we descended to the lowest level on a commercial-grade elevator. The squash court appeared unused. I had played in the past and a well-used court showed smears on the walls from the high-speed balls. Instead, this court looked like an exhibition space. The dressing rooms were immaculate. We made a quick inspection of the pool; it, too, appeared unused.

Outside, Ketchum offered to walk us through the immediate grounds. Artemis said brightly, "I'd like to see the maze. Isn't there an old statue there?"

Ketchum said, "Yes, a last-minute addition. Not my taste, but —" She caught herself. "Mr. Night, you asked for a staff person to attend if you had questions. Let me call him over." She placed a call, turning her back as she spoke. Almost instantly, a man appeared. She said, "Mr. Night, this is Alec." He bent at the waist rather than shake hands. He was extremely young — unusual, I thought. Wearing a large beret, his thoughts were obsequious.

She said, "He's worked here for some time. I've heard only good things."

"I appreciate him being available," I said, "but have no questions at the moment. Possibly later." Ketchum looked surprised.

Artemis interjected, "Does anyone want to join me? Let's solve the maze!" She might have been any young woman in her mid-twenties. I admired her — theatrical, her stagecraft was impeccable.

I told Alec reassuringly that we'd talk later. He nodded and stood aside as our group followed Artemis toward the back. Within moments

Laine and Artemis wandered into the maze. I saw their heads and heard their shrieks and laughter as they hit dead-ends. The maze was not immense, but carefully scaled so that finding the center was a challenge. I noticed the statue in the middle: marble and of exceptional beauty.

As they got closer to it, I heard Laine say, "Look!"

Artemis replied, "No, can't be."

"It is."

"Aphrodite."

"Yes, but an original."

"It's a Phidias, isn't it?"

"Impossible. They were all destroyed."

"The ivory filagree. And the gold wreath in her hair —"

I turned to Sally to see if she followed the conversation — no, she was unable to hear them. She said, "Are they lost yet? I'd never walk into that thing. Serious claustrophobia."

I smiled. "They're big girls. We'll give them another minute." She shrugged as if this happened every day. I again listened. Artemis said, "Aphrodite must not be aware it's here."

Laine whispered, "This is crazy — James couldn't have known what he had."

"What would a knowledgable collector pay?"

"600 million? It's utterly unique. I saw this in the Agora 2,500 years ago."

"We thought it was lost."

"This would be the only Phidias original in existence. James' dealer must have thought it Roman. Or some 19th century copy."

They held hands before the statue. The three of us were aware of each other's thoughts. Artemis was obviously a connoisseur; she considered Phidias, the artistic mastermind behind the Parthenon, the greatest sculptor to have lived, Michelangelo a mere imitator.

I sensed their awe, saw the two of them bow to the statue and turn. They wove their way back holding hands. When they came clear and saw us at the entrance, Ketchum glanced back and forth between them. Laine said nonchalantly, "Well, been there, done that!" She appeared charmingly bored. Artemis looked like she'd rather be anywhere else. She said, "A lot of work to maintain this place."

That reminded me. "Who cleans the moat, the general grounds? Mrs. James must have a small army here."

"Two local landscape firms. Alec will get the names for you." Sally was finished and said formally, "It's been my pleasure. If you need a second view —?"

As if she read my thoughts, which I knew she could not, Sally continued, "And yes, there's another hundred acres we haven't seen. But that's not in my wheelhouse. If you want to explore, Alec knows the grounds. I hear Mr. James spent a fair amount of time out back."

She smiled, turned without comment and shook my hand. I glanced back to the residence and saw Alec in a window.

As Sally drove away, Laine and Artemis hugged in parting. I noticed a lone figure standing at the far end of the lawn near the maze. She had to be a 100 feet away. An orange-haired girl in a tunic: it was Filly, a bow held casually in one hand. She waved and in a restrained gesture, I returned the salute, uncertain whether I was meant to see her. Then I caught movement to my side as Artemis walked up. With a firm grip, she took my arm — the grasp of a warrior — saying, "Soon, I will measure the extent of your change."

She released me and turned away. Alec had not left the window. I hoped he'd not seen Filly, who looked remarkably out of place in her tunic and sandals, a flower child.

CHAPTER 45

At the equinox a comet splits the evening sky
No one dares say the omen
is a manifestation of all that's awry,
and there are sky-
blue handprints on every wall
to ward off the evil eye.
—Poet X

Timessa found a glassblower in Taos who crafted small containers. Each came with an ingenious hinged lid and inside, a tiny pillow of satin with an indentation in its center, perfect vessels for a lover's ring — or a lethal acorn. At their arrival, T carried the boxes to Laine's office. The drama was building.

Ominously, last night's darkness had been split by a meteor. As Laine and I watched it arc across the sky, she held my hand and whispered, "*Komētēs.* A sign of all that's wrong. These appear so rarely. No one knows their cause."

I looked at her with surprise. "Laine, that's not true. First, it's a meteor, not a comet. And they happen constantly, dozens a night."

She whispered, "Not true. There's so little you understand." She left me there. I heard the door slam. To my disquiet, Orthrus sidled up, wagging its tail cautiously and watching me with red eyes. The giant hound pushed itself against my leg and rasped almost imperceptibly. I sensed no threat. In the dark, having the savage beast beside me seemed oddly comforting.

Squatting, I took its massive single head in my hands, scratching its ears. "Not double-headed tonight, old pal?" Its thoughts were machine-like as always, without judgment. Yet, now I was greeted as if I were one of its only friends. As I scratched, I noticed its warmth, far hotter than a dog's. It seemed to be burning with a heat that matched its eyes.

After a moment, I stood and Orthrus walked to the stream. I sensed it settling between stones near the bank. The sky was jet-black and punctured with stars. Venus was the brightest. I knew Laine lay in our bed waiting. Her anger had passed as quickly as it occurred, yet every instance left me anxious. She must have known.

That night, late, Timessa came to our room and without asking, slipped into the bed between us. Laine and I stroked her side. She whimpered, turned onto her belly, her fingers between her legs, and instantly fell asleep. Laine smiled, continuing to stroke her, and said, "She's just a child."

The next day, I watched as Timessa took the Sessile acorn and popped off the pericarp, then remounted it with a mild adhesive. "The glue has a neutral base," she explained. "It won't affect toxicity." She now wore glasses and nitrile exam gloves—strictly a precaution, Laine emphasized.

The adhesive T applied would bind the cap to the acorn's body during transport, but the cap would disengage at the slightest touch. We took a short break for coffee and Laine dictated a personal note to accompany the gift. Using a pen Timessa wrote:

Louise, I thought of you when I found this during a trip hiking
the Grand Tetons. Perhaps one of the gods meant for me to collect this for you!
Just rub the polished sides — a great stress reliever. — Layla

Laine turned to me. "Layla is a friend of hers from Cornell. She vacationed in the Tetons two weeks ago." She continued, "Chura played a key role in decoding the human genome a few years ago. She's now engaged in rearranging fragments of DNA from within the helical structure. It's masked as science employed to eliminate diseases. She won't say so, but she's aiming for much more."

Timessa would mail the gift. The two implemented a detailed protocol which included avoiding fingerprints and using a fake return address. The first package would be mailed tomorrow from Elkton, Maryland, a small town 40 minutes from the house.

Laine noted that Timessa had a driver's license. "If you'd rather she not drive, you can. Whoever goes needs to be at the post office as it opens."

Now mid morning, Laine suggested a hike, something longer than usual to further explore James' back land. We would have lunch after; Timessa would continue to work in our absence. In addition, T would track the larger shipment of acorns, which at this date should be between Greece and the United States.

In our bedroom, she pulled off her camisole, and I watched as she shrugged on a top and shorts, and put her hat on backward. After she slipped on shoes, we left for the meadow. I caught a glimpse of the hound fading into the woods. The tripod's smoke bellied out into the sky. I guessed the temperature at 80, the sky cloudless.

Laine took my wrist and pulled me toward the stream. We balanced across the usual steppingstones, then proceeded over the trail at a faster pace. When we arrived at the clearing, she pointed toward the shed, the refuge we had used repeatedly. "There. I need a drink."

I eased the door open. Nothing had changed. A thin light poured through the windows. When she entered I closed the door and slid the bolt. "I'll get water."

"No."

"You said you need a drink."

"Yes, of you, alone, here, without Timessa lying between us." She wiggled out of her shorts and said, "Come on —"

I picked her up and carried her to the cot. She seemed languid, loose and yielding. She lifted her hips as I took off her remaining clothes. "Now," she said, "do those things you do so well —"

We spent thirty or forty minutes making our anomalous half-love, and Laine came repeatedly. She seemed unconcerned that Artemis or a dozen nymphs were likely near. In many ways these moments felt unique — it seemed our hideaway was not in Pennsylvania, but in a distant corner of a wooded cosmos where nothing else existed.

An old poet once observed that bliss is ephemeral. And indeed, we had commenced our endgame. I was unsuspecting, trusting and unaware that this final hour would end all pretense. Even Laine may not have understood.

At some point she said, *Isn't this what love is?* She must have guessed my reaction, that her sentiment was a cliché, every lover's ardent belief. I said nothing. At the end, as we lay spooning briefly on the narrow cot, I whispered, "My transformation is done. You see it, too."

She whispered, "Jack —"

"And so I need no mystical protections. Or sanctimony about virginity —"

Even as I spoke, I understood the irony: she was a purveyor of death. In a soft voice, she said, "Jack, I warn you. Not about sex but about this: Artemis has created a final test. When it occurs, consider it like a hazing. I don't know how to explain, but you will be confronted with a situation and must make a decision."

"Another 1-or-100 test?"

"Higher stakes. And you must choose correctly."

"Or what?"

"You won't be allowed to … continue with us." She looked resigned. "You'll have to leave. Or if you don't, we will."

She rolled away and sat. Yawning and smiling as if we had discussed nothing of importance, she said, "Anyway, gotta dress —"

Although her comments left me with the old emptiness I had thought might be forever gone, she seemed sweet, attentive and — as I realized later — dangerously, even deliriously, manic in her attempt to appear normal. But for a few short moments, I reveled in the haze that follows embraces and detected nothing amiss.

Opening the door, I followed her into the sun. She turned and, putting her arms around me, said, "So much of what we accept as real is artifice."

"Like Artemis' theatre?"

She gave me a strange look. "Sometimes I forget how far along you've come —" Then she released me and stepped away.

Filly appeared, suddenly stepping between us, her orange hair afire. She put a hand on my arm and said officiously, "Follow me. Now. Artemis commands."

I could have thwarted whatever plans she had. I glanced at Laine, the empty face, her stance that of a goddess before believers, the radiance summoned so easily.

She hissed, "Go with her. You may see me later. In other circumstances."

CHAPTER 46

One thing makes wrong right: power.
—*Euripides,* The Phoenician Women

Filly's pace was steady and she gripped a bow in her left hand, her tunic thin and red, cut short, tight on her hips. She wore a smaller version of Artemis' golden-leafed necklace. Orange hair, red dress, gold flashing around her neck — watching her, I thought for the first time, *She's become like Orthrus,* her mind blank.

I recognized I might be going anywhere, even to my own sacrifice. But Laine had given me warnings that I would be tested. I also sensed I may have become more powerful than any of these beings guessed. I felt a calm mastery. And I cautioned myself against conceit.

As we approached the stonewall separating my land from the James estate, I said, "Filly, there's nothing to discuss?"

"No."

She bounded over the large stonewall effortlessly, and I did the same. Months earlier I would have crossed it carefully. I felt as loose as a leop-ard. We bushwhacked toward the pool where I had seen the nymphs bathing, skirted around it through the grove of trees, and picked up a trail that paralleled the brook and wound deeper into the woods.

As we slowed, I tried again. "You owe me an explanation." She said nothing and quickened her pace. I stopped. "I've had it. I'm turning back."

She stopped too, stepping close. "Sure, you can do whatever you want. I am here for Artemis. Nothing more. In that role I escort you. But be not mistaken: you can leave."

No "sirs." She pushed her hair back with both hands, her eyes catlike, her pupils black dots. "I do not pretend to control you. To even suggest it is a blasphemy."

She turned as if disinterested in my reply and continued down the trail. When I remained, she turned. "Yes or no?" Her voice was angry. I studied her eyes, and motioned her to continue, then I trailed behind.

We continued for minutes, then approached a large clearing. I remembered nothing like it in the aerials of James' estate. We were still far away, yet the girth of the opening was impressive. The path led directly into its core. At eighty feet I saw stonework, what appeared to be tiers of rectangular marble. Closer still, I saw curved, tiered stones.

Stopping at the edge of the clearing, Filly grimaced. Rows of marble seating surrounded me, rising to a height of sixty feet or more and sweeping in a three-quarter circle. We stood on what appeared to be a wide, stone-floored stage. I knew at once: an amphitheatre, and an ancient one, the stones worn from years of use, chipped and yellowed. My first thought: *impossible.*

As I gawked at the massiveness of it — a structure on property I was about to buy — Artemis stepped onto the stage and said, "Welcome to Aegle."

She appeared as the primeval goddess, dressed in a flowing peplos — an ancient gown made from a thin linen that fell in precise pleats to her ankles. A leather belt was cinched around her ribs and criss-crossed between her breasts. Her face seemed luminous. Any other being would have fallen to their knees before her. Yet, the same calmness I felt when Laine released me to Philippa moved through me now in an endless wave. I sensed we were the protagonists in this play — if that's what this was to be.

"It's Greek, isn't it?" I gestured at the amphitheatre around us.

"I've always been a fan," she said.

I glanced behind her at a narrow one-story building made from wide planks. The facade had twelve doors, each capped with bronze lintels. Between each hung a torch; the torches were bolted into the facade. In the center of the building, a single word in massive letters was carved into a larger plank:

PATHOS

"Greek," she said, "for emotion. In the beginning it encompassed joy and pain, exhilaration and despair. Today it's been reduced to mere piteousness. A shame. Here, though, its meaning is the ancient one." She took a step away.

I asked, "Do gods have such emotions?"

"You know they do."

"Yes. And what is the most powerful of all our emotions?"

"Rage," she said.

"Not love?"

"Homer understood. The first word in the *Iliad* is wrath. Rage cleanses our souls. Wrath propels us to action. Rage affirms our love."

Had I erred in following Filly to this fantastical place? I said, "Goddess, this theatre —"

"You are free to go at any time." She took another step away.

"I may leave. Still, I'd love first to view more of this old ruin."

"Not ruin — a working theatre."

"It's remarkable."

"I hoped you'd approve."

"We should discuss how you created this." I swept my arms in an arc.

"Yes, of course, if there is ever time."

" 'If'? Ah, I get it."

Who was the hunter? I smiled. "Now tell me of the coming play. The drama, as that's what I presume it is to be."

"I will be challenging you."

"A test?"

"I prefer now to call it a provocation."

"Not a trial?"

"Have you done something for which you should be tried?"

The gold necklace shifted below her neck. Like Laine, she appeared radiant, although Artemis' radiance was almost prehistoric. Her entire being seemed luminescent, as if she stood under a viscous, copper light. I said, "Aren't we all guilty of something?"

"We are not."

"Doesn't passion drive us into reckless acts?"

She said nothing. I found myself wanting to break her confidence. Looking around the amphitheatre, I said, "Be honest. Is this all for me? Or has it been here longer?"

"It's about thirty-six hours old."

I took two steps toward her, resetting our original distance. "When does the play begin?"

"Oh, it already has."

Lifting a hand overhead, she waved her arm around as if stirring honey. The time was mid- afternoon, yet her gesture triggered a darkening sky; night began to fall. She continued the circular motion and the sky grew darker still. Within seconds the sun vanished and the theatre lay in shadows.

"Nyxxx —!" she cried, and from somewhere behind the structure I heard an inarticulate howl that echoed among the empty marble slabs. As it faded, the torches on building walls flickered to life. Artemis dropped her arm and gave a signal to her side.

Filly appeared, now without her tunic. The light from the torches sent shadows across her naked belly. Red panties rode halfway up her hips — her only clothing, yet I knew the moon was no longer full. At the same moment, a floodlight projected a beam up into the highest seating in the theatre, illuminating a handmade disc, a cutout painted cardboard moon tacked onto a 2x4. The light lingered long enough for me to correlate panties and moon. Then it switched off.

Filly stood beside me. She must have come up in the dark, and said in a voice stripped of emotion, "Follow me." She stood waiting, her breasts high and her belly rippling. Everything stood for something. Signs and symbols, metaphors and allegories: if I didn't understand now, I might yet.

She took my elbow and led me forward. A flight of stairs descended to a wider aisle. We walked together and she steered me to the center of the seating. I saw a dais with a low curved seat large enough for two. A thin purple cushion stretched its length. Filly said, "Here."

She waited while I sat, then sat beside me, her hand resting on my thigh. I stared at her and she looked back. Her lips were moist and her neutrality had vanished. I felt pulled into a wild place, and in the darkness her gaze was so intense I turned away.

Almost immediately a long line of nymphs came down the aisle from the stage. They danced, skipping as they advanced toward us. At the sound of a whistle, they scattered into the seating behind us. I calculated there must have been forty to fifty girls of all ages. Unlike Filly, the youngest wore the usual tunics, carrying lustral branches which they piled beside the stage. But the older girls were naked except for red panties. All wore pearl necklaces, and the oldest girls had bright rouge smeared across their cheeks. Their appearance was whorish, yet they exuded guilelessness and a convincing naiveté; Artemis was masterful at this.

Filly squeezed my thigh. "Sir, watch the stage." Consciously or not, she moved her hand higher up my leg. "Look —!"

Stage lights now projected onto three girls arranging chairs and other props. The girls wore silk dresses — the lights shimmered softly off the material. They had their backs to us, and then turned to the front, their faces behind red masks. Each mask had round eyeholes, the mouths cut with an archaic smile.

Filly said, "They are Kore."

"Maidens?"

"Blissed ones."

"Not *blessed*?"

"Both." The three came together in the front of the stage, linking arms. From the darkness on the right, Artemis appeared and sat to the side on a throne-like chair. Like so many of the objects used that evening it, too, was red. As she settled onto it, she snapped her fingers and three hounds appeared. Artemis snapped her fingers again and they sank in a tight cluster around her. These were smaller dogs than Orthrus.

A young nymph leaped onto the stage from the same darkness that had concealed Artemis. In a frock, she looked thirteen, her hair tied in a topknot. She carried the goddesses' bow and arrows and presented them. Artemis took the offering and dismissed the girl. Filly interjected, "Instruments of execution."

I glanced at her and looked away. Her eyes had the same wild intensity. She said, "Now the plot."

The three girls unlinked their arms and leaned stage left, chanting,

We sing, Muse,
of Athene, Artemis, Aphrodite
and the Fates —

Their voices rose and they leaned stage right.

For these goddesses
have brought order to chaos
and light to dark —

"Each girl is thirteen, hand-picked by the goddess," Filly said.
"Pubescent?"
"Just."

Each goddess is pure,
bathed in celestial lights
and pointing us toward righteousness ...

The girls straightened, linked arms again and sang,

Except for two.
One has long stumbled from the ways
and one strays even as we sing —

Filly said, "They refer to Klotho and the brilliant Lachesis."

She sought out my hand and dug her fingers between mine. The girl's
voices rose an octave,

One became a lover
and one wants to lose
her virginity.
For these abuses
to the order

we present their cases
For your adjudication,
Oh goddess
who delights in hunting
And protects all girls
from harm.
May you judge without alarm.

I took a distinct dislike to events. I thought of Artemis and Laine as friends. Then I reminded myself this was nothing more than a masquerade.

From stage left, three nymphs appeared, each carrying a lyre. They struck the strings of the instruments, the scale discordant.

Filly leaned closer, "The frames of the lyres are tortoise-shell. The music they play is Dorian. You may find it harsh. Music echoes pathos. I cannot predict the tone —"

The music played for less than a minute, rising shrilly near its end. The three-girl chorus cried,

Now we present
the first of the two
who broke the rules!

Filly pointed down the aisle to our right. Two older nymphs carried a girl on a cot. They wore masks and passed in front of us, abruptly turning at the wide stairs and ascending the stage. As the procession passed, the girls in the chorus assembled a wooden frame, and leaned the girl in the cot against it. She was lashed down, the cot situated so she faced the audience.

Weren't the Fates the most powerful of the gods? This faux Chloé was plainly a stand-in, but did it not mock the Fates to even stage this trial? Again, I assured myself Chloé and Laine had sanctioned this. Filly whispered, "The first is Klotho. Listen."

The chorus faced us.

Klotho, once a celestial star
seduced her father

> *without regard to order.*
> *She spurned righteousness*
> *for licentiousness,*
> *dressing like a tart to frighten us.*
> *She must be abridged,*
> *her actions sanctioned,*
> *her wings pinned.*
> *Now she has arrived,*
> *the one who is depraved.*
> *O goddess, judge as you are inclined!*

Artemis stood. "Who brings the charges?"

As she sat, one of the musicians set aside her lyre and cried loudly, "I am the prosecutor!"

"Your charges?" the goddess said.

The prosecutor strode forward and stopped before "Klotho." She carried a tablet and read drily, "Klotho, one of the Fates, is charged with having committed incest with her father, the act not accidental, but repeated and deliberate — a seduction resulting in pregnancy. While filled with child, she continued her wanton acts, making love with frequency ..."

She paused, running one hand through her hair and straightening herself. Pointing at Klotho, she cried, "Loathsome goddess, bound to promises of purity, you have fallen to a dreadful place. I charge you with violating vows! I ask the court to strip you of all powers and to replace you with one able to set an honorable example for us all!"

Her voice echoed from her mask. She turned to Artemis and waved her files. "Oh goddess and protector, I have recordings, photographs and videos documenting each day through the endless months Klotho perpetuated her incestuous acts. The documentation is thorough and complete without exception. My files represent thousands of hours of what can only be described as ... outrageous acts."

She seemed vaguely embarrassed and curtsied. "I apologize for my choice of phrases, your honor. I cannot find a less offensive means to label the deeds of the defendant."

Artemis waved her hand dismissively. The girl bowed and returned to the musicians. She recovered her lyre and the three played a brief, discordant tune. Artemis rose again. "Who defends the accused?"

Filly responded, "I do, goddess!"

"Present your case."

Filly bent and whispered, "Watch —"

She mounted the stage and bowed to Artemis. Putting on a mask, she put a soothing hand on the shoulder of the faux Klotho. The stand-in wrestled against her ties and Filly stroked her arms a moment.

She spoke from memory. "My defense will be brief, as the prosecution's case is without merit and should never have advanced. First, the accused never slept with her father. She does not even know her real father. Her mother misled the man who raised Klotho, causing him to believe himself the *paterfamilias*. He was not. Testing affirms my declaration, regardless of what Klotho and the man believed. Therefore, incest did not occur."

Filly paused, looking back and forth between Artemis and the girl serving as prosecutor. She exuded confidence as she stressed her points. "Second, Klotho knew not that she was a reanimated Fate until informed by our beloved Lachesis, an act that took place only months ago. If you are not aware you are a goddess, and not aware of a goddess' promises, can you break your vows? Laws you do not know you cannot break.

"Since the appearance of the brilliant Lachesis, Klotho has ceased all sexual acts. She has abandoned them and spends her hours raising our beloved Aisa. And she regrets the year she spent in that man's bed … I say before this court, she is pure and these charges specious. I plead you find my client innocent."

Filly bowed to Artemis, then lightly touched the arm of the prisoner. Her small breasts swelled forward as she bent. How much of this was simply for the tribe's entertainment?

Filly bounded down the stairs and leaped onto the seat beside me.

"Facts are facts. Klotho is innocent as fuck." She was panting and gripped my hand again, slipping her fingers between mine, her eyes black. She pointed toward the stage.

Artemis rose. As she had done at the start, she raised her arm high, circling it again. Within moments the sky, which had been black, filled with stars. I recognized the Milky Way, a Big Dipper, and soft, swollen nebulae swirling in pastels.

She lowered her arm and cried, "The court will briefly adjourn ..."
Everyone on stage exited. The stage lights dimmed; only the torches
provided illumination.

Filly put her arm around my neck. "It's okay if we do this now." Her
mouth tried to find mine. In the dark I felt her breasts against my arm,
and she pulled one of my hands between her legs, muttering, "Yes oh yes,
please yes —"

I pulled away, saying, "Filly! What the hell —?"

She whispered, "Kiss me while all the others watch. Kiss me now. I
want everyone to see."

She was frantic, so I bent and kissed her, letting the kiss linger long
enough that it wouldn't appear a mistake. Then I let her go.

"Thank you ... Few nymphs are ever eyed by a god. The number
kissed can be counted on one hand —"

Stage lights rose. Artemis leaped onto the stage. "The judge has delib-
erated. Before I issue my verdict, I wish to poll the tribe."

Overhead, lights wove back and forth across the audience. As I
looked for the nymphs' reaction, I noted many of them rocking up and
down, their eyes glittering. The older girls showed pointed teeth.

She continued, "You heard the prosecution. And you heard the
defense. You have weighed the evidence."

She paused and the ellipsoidal lights begin to crisscross Artemis.
Alone on the stage, she continued, "A hand count of those who find the
defendant ... guilty!"

A girl in her early teens sprang up and counted hands. She finished
and, bowing to the goddess, cried, "Nine!"

"And votes to acquit?"

The girl rose again and counting, turned and said, "Thirty-nine!" She
tucked her tunic neatly under herself and sat.

Sweeping her hands overhead as if to vanquish the stars she had
created, Artemis concluded, "This is but a play. The goddess Klotho is
not Klotho. The real Klotho remains untried. Given that, I find the
actress innocent. And I congratulate Philippa for her work. Come up
here ... you'll always be my little bear, my *arktoi* —"

She reached out and Filly mounted the stage. The two embraced.
After seconds, Filly returned. I felt the play had sputtered to an end.
Anything further would be anticlimactic. And I felt my mind wandering.

I remembered an old song my father used to whistle: *Is that all there is?* Filly wiggled up against me. She pointed toward the stage.

Again, the goddess was radiant, almost afire. I felt an odd intimacy with her. She seemed the perfect persona for a judge, but if the pace of her theatre did not pick up, I would drift. I remained puzzled about why I was summoned. I knew the circumstances underlying the accusations better than any of them.

And I wondered why this show excluded Laine. In my conjecture, I lost awareness that Artemis had raised her hands, palms up, staring at something above the highest seating. When I noticed, I saw the paper moon, a spotlight on it once again, the disc swaying on the highest row.

In the hushed darkness, Artemis announced in a hoarse voice, "Act Two!

CHAPTER 47

She bent to give the child a kiss,
A light incense
in the arc of her breasts,
her eyes black, her mind numb,
vexed at what she knew would come.
—Poet X

The same nymph who counted votes ran to the stage and lit a match. She held it high for seconds, looking into the night, then bent and lit a fuse. As she stepped back, a firework exploded from the stage into the night, its projectile tailed by a shower of sparks. The glowing ball paused at its apogee, seemed to drift sideways, then with a crackle burst into a shimmering cascade of lights. Flares floated overhead, a mass of fireflies, then descended and faded into darkness. The nymphs broke into applause.

From one of the revolving doors in the rear, a tall blond woman emerged and walked toward Artemis. Her stride mimicked a fashion model's. She was barefoot and dressed in a white gown that fell below her ankles, her narrow waist emphasized by a golden sash, and her breasts covered modestly. I guessed her to be twenty-five. She walked to Artemis, who announced loudly, "Aphrodite!"

The nymphs applauded.

Filly whispered, "The goddess of love!" Her hands fluttered restlessly.

Stage lights blinked on and off, the applause stilled and a second woman emerged. Unlike Aphrodite, she was muscular, intimidating. As she stepped on stage, she stopped and glared at the lights. Then, almost angrily, she moved toward the goddess, her dress sequined, her hair tumbling to her shoulders.

Artemis said, "Nyx!"

The entire audience went silent. Filly sought out my hand. Nyx, as Laine had explained, was the primeval mother of the original Fates — a myth, I assumed. Yet, if this being impersonated a primordial deity, she did so convincingly. Nyx would be the oldest of them all, preceded only by Gaia. She was reputed to have created many of her children through parthenogenesis — self-fertilization.

Artemis picked up a mask, slipping it on, as Aphrodite and Nyx did the same. They faced us, the masks expressionless, circular holes replacing eyes.

Artemis said, "These two are judges for the final act. I will break a tie."

She swept her arms like a scythe — her dress billowing as if buffeted by winds, then demanded, "Out with the accused!"

From the end of the aisle, a procession appeared. Four older nymphs carried a single cot, then another four carried a second. Tied with ropes, a young woman lay on her back on each. The nymphs wore masks. Their pace was synchronized as if soldiers on a sacred march.

I felt nauseous. Filly turned her face into my chest as I recognized the first of the accused: Chloé. She lay passively, her eyes closed. The nymphs carrying her stopped before Artemis.

Then, I recognized the girl tied to the second cot. Laine's red cheeks and hair were unmistakable. Her eyes, too, were closed. Were the two drugged? I couldn't imagine them agreeing to this humiliation. Rapidly — and in motions obviously rehearsed — the nymphs tilted the cots and tied both women to the wooden frame. They faced the audience and opened their eyes.

Artemis declared, "Each of you is accused of crimes against the tribe. You agree to submit to trial?"

Together they said, "Yes."

"And you agree to consent to the verdict of this court, which may result in one or both of you being stripped of powers and privilege?"

Again, an affirmation.

Artemis continued, "Your powers are many and this court shall not continue without your acquiescence. Reiterate your consent —"

Yes.

Artemis turned to Aphrodite and Nyx. "The trial begins." Then to the audience, she announced, "As well as being the jury, the goddess of night shall be the prosecutor, and Aphrodite, defending attorney."

I stood angrily. "Stop! What trial allows opposing attorneys to also be a jury? No court would allow such travesty!" My voice echoed against the stones.

The goddess stepped forward and smiled. "This court understands your concerns, but you are new to our ways. What appears prejudiced is eminently fair. What appears one-sided is not. Think: their mother has been appointed as prosecutor. What mother would accuse her children of crimes they did not commit? And the defending attorney is the goddess of love, sympathetic to all passions of lust and mad desire. What seems unbalanced instead is ingeniously impartial."

She paused, then said harshly, "I will tolerate no further outbursts. Shall we continue, or shall I banish you from court?"

If I challenged her, I might derail it all. It was theatre regardless. I held eye contact with the goddess, then sat. Filly pressed against me.

Artemis remained quiet for seconds, then said, "I recite the charges."

She gazed at Nyx and Aphrodite, then at Chloé and Laine. Rising, she spoke, "Klotho of the Fates is charged with having committed incest with her father, the act not casual or accidental, but repeated and deliberate — an act ending in pregnancy."

From my seat I yelled, "False! And the accusation is the same as that made earlier!"

Artemis continued, "Lachesis, likewise a goddess of the Fates, is charged with having committed crimes of passion, of lasciviousness. Such acts are prohibited ...

"In addition, both goddesses are charged with repudiating purity and embracing lust." She paused and looked around. "These are the charges. Let the trial proceed!"

Nyx stepped forward and pointed at both girls, her voice piercing, alternately shrill or rasping. She spoke as if deep in a cavern, a smoker's voice from antiquity. "I am Nyx, and my children have included Sleep, Doom and Death, Darkness and Dreams — and to my shame, the Fates.

"These two, prisoners of this court, are my progeny, both now miscreants and seed gone bad. One fucked her father until full with his child, the other grovels in the same man's arms. I remind the court these two once were honored among us, examples to all. Now I, their mother, grieve at their acts and tear my hair."

She paused, tossing her knotted hair to the side.

"They might be forgiven if their errors were singular. But they are not. Their actions have been continuous and premeditated.

"With sorrow, I repeat: Klotho, my once beloved child, became a seductress. Lachesis, the brightest of all, writhes daily in her self-made love bed, moaning in ecstasy. Enough! I have filed proof of these acts. Documents include testimony of many nymphs whose reputations are impeccable. I ask this court to strip the two of power, as they have shamed us all."

She stepped back and nodded pleasantly to Aphrodite. The goddess of love in turn bowed to the audience, allowing a long silence before she began. Unlike Artemis and Nyx, she removed her mask, tossing it aside. I had never seen such beauty.

"I am Aphrodite, goddess of love. I know pleasure and I know the secrets of procreation. Do not be blinded by my beauty, for I remind you that many equate beauty and truth as the same.

"Nyx's accusations? They are spurious. She is blinded by an odd frenzy. We know about Nyx, don't we? She exemplifies anger. She is darkness itself. Although she birthed many, consider the children that erupted from her belly: Sleep, Death, Doom, Darkness, Dreams. She exploits frightening corners of the mind, and creates turmoil wherever she treads. Do we trust her to fairly describe the deeds of these beloved goddesses —?"

She gestured toward Laine and Chloé. "No! Darkness begets darkness. Nightmares haunt us. Death extinguishes. Nyx cannot escape her shadows. She is a creature of the gloaming. Is she qualified to judge these girls?"

Aphrodite answered for the audience. "No!" Her white gown floated up like bird's wings on an updraft, then settled slowly about her ankles.

"My dears, what are the alleged crimes of these girls?" Aphrodite gestured broadly. "They fell in love. Love! For this, Nyx condemns them to infamy?

"Oh, my —" She smiled knowingly.

"No one knows love and desire as well as I. Love, my children, is marvelous." She raised her arms.

"But desire! Where does it originate? Ah, remember my emissary, Himeros, who is my son — and Zeus' child. You call him by his nick-name, Eros, a winged cherub, an enchanter …

"And what does he do? Why, my bidding. Remember, too, that neither gods nor humans are immune to his assaults …

"You may ask, does this matter? Yes … because I sent him to hunt down each of these two. I commanded, 'Make the Fates insatiable; fill them with an endless lust —' "

She paused and bowed.

"All this is my doing. I directed the child-god Eros to infect these virgin goddesses. His arrows, tipped with my potion, pierced Klotho and Lachesis to the heart, causing each to fall madly for the man-god who sits among us now —"

She swiveled and pointed at me. We exchanged looks for the first time. She coyly glanced away.

"Their flirtations with passion, their derangement, were Eros' doing. Was harm brought upon the tribe itself? Let us examine Nyx's accusations. And I'll be brief now that this court knows my connivance in these so-called crimes …

"First, Klotho is accused of seducing the man whose seed brought Aisa back to this world. Nyx calls it incest! But Nyx twists the truth, as the man is no more her father than fire is the architect of rain. But we will put that momentarily aside. Maybe the issue is seduction. Really? Did Klotho seduce the man, and if she did, what outcome resulted that offends us so?

"Why, the outcome is Klotho's progeny, the beloved Aisa, whose birth completed the contemporaneous triad of the Fates — the very thing we have long awaited."

Suddenly, Aisa descended onto the stage in a wicker basket from overhead — a *deus ex machina*. Spotlights followed her descent. She stepped out of the basket and was hugged by Aphrodite. The audience of nymphs applauded loudly and Aisa's black eyes scanned the stage, lingering on her mother. Aphrodite took her hand and led her to a bench. Nyx angrily turned her back.

"Now the child — the goddess Aisa — watches these proceedings, wondering, Will they treat my mother fairly?"

Aphrodite paused dramatically. "Let us continue to our inevitable end. Was this outcome an outrage to our kind? Was it the abomination Nyx claims?

"No! The goddess Klotho coupled not with her father, but with a man who was himself deceived. No incest occurred, no familial love …

"The pregnancy that resulted brought us a rebirth of the Fates, two of whom lie here now, willing to have vile accusations thrown against them in their innocence. The third goddess, Aisa, has come at my request. All are here before you, and though they are more powerful than almost any other god or goddess, they submit to our will, knowing that truth will prevail, that madness — the madness of Nyx's accusations — will be banished from our records, stricken from our chronicles …

"Last, I briefly argue for the brilliant goddess Lachesis. She is accused of what? Of groveling in this man's arms —"

She again pointed at me. "— and pleading for release from her desires."

Aphrodite laughed. "Many, perhaps most of you, wonder, What is this 'release'?"

Artemis stood suddenly and commanded the audience, "All nymphs younger than fifteen are to turn away. Do not look or listen!"

Half the nymphs stood, turned and covered their ears. The goddess looked at Aphrodite and said, "You may go on."

"So, I ask," Aphrodite said, "what is this 'release'? Nyx, who has slept in countless beds with countless lovers, knows it well. This release is desire which inflames our legs and bellies and drives us to seek a sweet deliverance, a final rush of trembling joy …

"Is this a pathology or disease? Not at all. It is the physical manifestation of love itself. And why would I have sent Eros to infect the brilliant one? Because the virginal vow she took leaves her incomplete. Rather than ensuring she is 'pure,' the dictum that she stay a virgin strips her of compassion for those who love. It leaves her — how shall I say this? — half-baked, a mere shell.

"Can you imagine the Fates judging those who love, yet not themselves fully understanding love? It has always grieved my heart. After their reanimation, I seized a chance to complete their fullness and grant them enlightenment. Klotho has already gained those insights: Aisa is all the proof we need."

She gestured toward the child. Aisa cried out, "*I'm bored!*"

Aphrodite responded, "I'm winding it up, dear child. Just another moment." She turned to the audience.

"Lachesis seeks those same insights. Indeed, in the fullness of time, she may discover that for those who have left childhood behind, virginity contradicts the laws of nature …

"I tell you as the goddess of love: one cannot judge lovers without having loved … and the goddesses who decide life and death must know love, too …

"In sum, Lachesis' so-called crimes are the admirable desires of every blessèd young woman who wishes to be complete …

"Yet, I remind you, Lachesis remains a virgin, however much she has explored love's edges. Her caution, her devotion to her vows, has prevented the man from — speaking euphemistically, in the old tongue — plowing her furrows. The accusations the goddess faces are false …

"Beyond that, remember it was Lachesis who knew that the Fates must return, and who chose sexual union as … shall we say … the most discrete path. Then I added the component of lust to what she considered expediency …

"I, Aphrodite, have brought these two to where they are this day —"

Nyx strode up to Aphrodite and shook her fist. "Sly words of a whore! These arguments seduce the court no differently than this man seduced my girls! Shame on your sullied portrayal of love, Aphrodite —"

Nyx signaled with her hand and a sign stretched across the stage, reading

★ *T h e G o d d e s s e s* ★

It seemed familiar. At the same moment, a yellow light lowered over Klothos and Lachesis. The lights turned red and swung violently in the silence. Of course: The 1-to-100 dream, the test, the same props.

An orange incandescence bathed their bodies.

More movement, now to my left: Two immense metal weights dropped, stopping above each girl's head, swaying in the lights, the weights attached to carabiners.

Artemis cried out, "All nymphs now watch!"

As the youngest turned toward the stage, several gasped. Lights were now directed at Chloé and Laine, and for the first time I saw their expressions. Chloé appeared incredulous, Laine impassive.

Nyx cried out, "What mother should be forced to take her daughter's lives? Better I take my own. Yet, I will do your bidding if the court finds them guilty as accused!"

Artemis raised her hands, "No decision shall be rendered until the goddesses affirm or rebut the accusations! Let the accused defend themselves."

CHAPTER 48

And so I step up, into the darkness within;
or else the light
—Margaret Atwood

Neither girl spoke. Artemis pointed at Chloé, demanding, "Do you deny Nyx's accusations?" To my shock Chloé shrugged. Since Aisa's birth she had been melancholic, but now seemed willing as a Fate to resign her own fate to some reckless destiny.

Hearing no response Artemis turned to Laine. "You?"

Laine's voice rang out across the amphitheatre. "We both deny. As Aphrodite states, we are innocent. Look at the word carved into the building behind us. *Pathos*. Even the Fates have emotions, and ours are no different than any god's. Or any nymph's. Or any mortal's. We, too, hunger for love.

"That Eros pierced us after we had taken vows is, by Aphrodite's confession, indisputable. Hence we made no willful decision, as Nyx charges, to flaunt those vows …

"Instead, we were swept away. Until you have been caught in riptides, you cannot judge. What is desire? It has no past. It is a creature of the present, a thing that makes sweet promises about what's to come …

"All rationality vanishes. Desire promises bliss. Klotho and I could not resist Eros' seduction, nor can any god, or nymph, or mortal thing. His spell overwhelms us all …

"Klotho and I agreed to today's trial believing in its equity. Nyx argued in her conclusion that we should be stripped of rank. Or even killed."

Pointing at the massive weight, she said, "Look: over my head hangs Death …

"And if we are so betrayed, our current mission — the same that precipitated our reanimation — would abort. Chaos would ensue. Nature itself would collapse. This court would risk such chaos to satisfy Nyx, the mother who never showed us a moment's love, never comforted us in her arms? I am stunned this trial continues. Aphrodite's confession alone should cause charges to be dismissed —"

She stopped and sighed. The entire theatre quieted.

Nyx stepped between the girls and Artemis, spreading her arms with contempt. "These lies disgust me. Life is far from simple, but living it well requires discipline. These two mask their low desires and blame other gods for failings. 'Oh dear, Eros made me do it!' 'Oh dear, it's Aphrodite's fault!' Ungrateful to the end, they even blame their mother!"

Artemis stood. "Enough! Nyx? How do you rule?"

"*Guilty.*"

Artemis turned. "Aphrodite?"

"Innocent. The blamelessness of these two is so obvious that to argue otherwise is mad. You are the wise one among us, protector of foxes and deer. Of the innocent, of young girls. Observe these two —

"You know their story well, of how Eros at my bidding pierced them with irresistible lust. It would affect you equally if I bid him send you love. Do not judge these two as if they had a choice …

"I agreed to play this part, and you assured me of its fairness, as you assured these two. End this now —"

Artemis shook her head. "Of course, of course. Then, we are tied." She removed her mask, shaking her head. "Shall I break the tie? No, I abdicate."

As the nymphs gasped, she raised her hands and spun them in loose circles, signaling something new. A horizontal wire, more slender than the one from which the weights were suspended, dropped from overhead. On it clung twelve large birds, a purplish glow emanating from their wings, their eyes orange orbs.

Artemis gestured to the twelve. The birds fidgeted, side-stepping on the wire in a restless cha-cha. Grackles, I guessed, or primeval crows, or emissaries from a darker time. Ingenious theatre, but to what end?

"So I have appointed a jury and their decision will stand. These jurors —"

She pointed at the birds.

"— have watched the entire proceedings from above."

I was incredulous. A backup jury of birds? Had Artemis gone mad? The center bird rose on its wings, then descended to land on Nyx's shoulder. It nibbled her ear gently and Nyx half-smiled, lightly clapping her hands. After a moment, it returned to the others.

My anger, so long in check, exploded. I muttered, "This is fucking mad —"

Filly, twisting her fingers in mine, said in a tiny voice, "*Wish them away.*"

I glanced at her. "What?"

"They're Nyx's birds. Wish them away!"

Yes, obvious. I was hardly powerless. I turned to the stage and squinted at the center bird. I thought, *Vanish* …

Without a flicker, the bird disappeared. Filly said, "*Yes!*"

I squinted at the leftmost bird. I thought, *Vanish* — and it too disappeared with a faint pop. I laughed and did the same to the bird on the right: *Gone.* Artemis' "jury" was now nine.

Filly grinned and nodded, bouncing. "Yes, yes —!"

Several of the nymphs behind us pointed and giggled as each bird disappeared. Artemis and the others were unaware, preoccupied with securing Chloé and Laine into a vertical position to face the birds.

Nyx was the first to notice, crying, "No —!"

By now, many of the nymphs were laughing. I waited until everyone on stage looked up. I made another bird vanish, then another, *pop, pop,* only seven left. Filly was giddy and I had to keep nudging her to be still. Hands on hips, Artemis studied the audience, but said nothing. She noticed Filly. As if a parent speaking to a child, she said, "Philippa?"

At that point I stood: no one else would be punished. I said, "She's not involved —"

I waved my hand toward the remaining birds, wishing six of the seven away. They vanished, leaving a single, orange-eyed bird swaying on the wire. It nervously stepped from side to side.

"So you see, Artemis, I, too, can play at this. So much for a jury of birds. A poor joke anyway —"

She rose in her majesty, commanding, "Return the jury!"

"Impossible," I said. "The birds are scattered, atoms on the breeze —" I paused. "Goddess, are you not aware that I, too, am a conjuror? Watch again as there is more —" I waved my hand and the cords securing Chloé and her sister disappeared.

Artemis knew she'd lost control — yet I had no interest in humiliating her. What else was possible? I visualized the pool in the sacred grove, moss blanketing the banks. Yes, a fitting destination. Artemis there, cool water swirling at her hips.

She, too, vanished. I merely imagined it. For a brief moment I saw her standing alone in the pool. Oddly, she appeared ebullient.

At her disappearance, a number of the nymphs shrieked. Even Nyx appeared stunned. I assumed her dangerous, her mind impenetrable, but I had momentum and would maintain command.

Earlier in the trial, as I watched the objurgations and silliness of the prosecution, I unexpectedly detected a wrinkle in the amphitheatre; the structure was, in fact, a mirage. If I squinted I could see through the stones and the props and the stage itself. The creation was Artemis' wizardry, a mere simulacrum.

I felt my powers expanding even as I explored them. I decided to vanish a portion of the marble seating: *gone*! I could erase it all if I chose. I turned to Nyx and said calmly, "Maybe I'll obliterate the floor under your feet. Or turn you into atoms like those birds from hell —"

Raging, she pounded a fist into the weight above Laine's head. I said, "No more of that." I vanished the weight. She stared, suddenly uncertain. Ripping off her mask, Nyx jumped from the stage and strode away.

Then Aphrodite stood before me, her beauty overwhelming, her golden hair and eyes glowing. She cried and reached her arms out saying, "I'm so happy!"

Chloé and Laine joined her, laughing as well. I didn't understand their elation.

"So this —?"

"Is what you had to do," Laine said. "I couldn't do it for you. We had to confirm you understood what you've become."

CHAPTER 49

Who remembers Polygnotus of Thasos
the greatest painter in Athens
at that time? Wherever he went
he was maintained at public cost.
Now everything is gone,
His marvels, like the gods, lost.
                    —Poet X

Later that afternoon at the house, sitting against the altar, I said to Laine, "I never imagined any of this."

"I have a surprise for tonight. And remember, tomorrow you go to Elkton."

"I'll go without Timessa."

In mock shock, Laine said, "She's your muse! How could you not bring the girl?"

"I expect the muse phase to pass."

"Not likely. She's so proud of you. You're a hero to all of them."

"Filly deserves credit."

"Oh?"

"She suggested I vanish the birds."

Laine smiled. "She may have handed you a sword, but you used it with finesse."

"And you," I said, "can't dodge Aphrodite's snare."

"Pardon me?"

"You've been outed. Eros shot you through and through. You can't shake his honeyed spell. You're mine."

"You're delusional."

I rolled my eyes. "Don't fight fate."

"No lectures, please." She stretched. "Besides, I'm afraid you'll get me pregnant."

"Dumb argument. You're buying time. You can't escape."

"What if you do?" Her eyes were merry.

"Use divine contraception."

She snorted. "We have a dinner party tonight. A bright Elysium. Coming?"

"Is that your surprise?"

"Yes, a celebration for today's epiphany. You and me and a couple girls. If we're lucky someone'll bring a bottle of wine."

"Formal dress?"

She whispered, "As a matter of fact."

At seven we went upstairs. Artemis' trial had been transformative. Laine called my discoveries an "epiphany." Yet, they paled in comparison to the encounter I was about to have — one that would, within a short time, reshape my life again.

When we topped the stairs, I saw Timessa and Filly walking from the kitchen to the dining area, both fashionably dressed. I realized I had never seen Filly inside a house, let alone in modern dress. As she passed, she smiled.

Laine stopped at the entrance to the dining room, saying, "Before you're taken from me, kiss." As we did, Chloé wolf-whistled. Laine smiled, "Knock it off. You gave him up —"

She linked her arm in mine as we entered. The first person I saw was a beautiful woman, her dark hair lustrous: *Artemis*. She stood at a three-quarter angle to us, wearing a cranberry-colored skirt and simple blouse. She might have been at a stylish summer party. I noticed heels and the golden necklace she'd worn in the theatre.

She was the last person I expected; Artemis turned and smiled warmly. I said, "I owe you an apology."

"Oh?"

"I destroyed half your theatre and sent you to oblivion."

"I created it for you to raze. And I'm overjoyed you sent me somewhere that I love." She stepped closer and asked in a stage whisper, "You had your revelation. Has Lachesis had hers?"

Laine said, "My caution may save us all."

Artemis smiled. "Lighten up, my dear. Aphrodite was correct to send Eros on the hunt for your uptight little ass."

Laine took it well. "Artemis, you're a virgin yourself."

"But I'm not sleeping with a man."

Laine steered me to Timessa, who passed us glasses of wine.

"We're leaving early for Elkton," I said. "Be ready by eight."

T said, "Of course. Sir."

Filly walked over, smiling demurely. "Can I go too, sir?"

Laine shook her head. "No! Too much risk."

Several nymphs I recognized walked in from the kitchen carrying trays of food. Although pleasantly dressed, they appeared uncomfortable. Another followed with a casserole and a fourth, a striking girl I had never seen, entered with a platter. She glanced up and I smiled, thinking, *Beautiful enough to be Aphrodite's twin —*

Artemis lit candles and Chloé turned off the overhead lights. Instantly, the dining room became magical, swirling with young women, candlelight and laughter. Artemis clapped her hands and exclaimed, "All be seated!"

As we did, I saw an empty seat. "Someone's missing —?"

Artemis said, "Indeed. The beautiful one has yet to come." She cried out, "Aphrodite, Venus, Astarte! Appear, Goddess, whosoever you may be tonight!"

A sudden flare of light appeared beside the empty chair, followed by a small back-flash and a cascade of sparkles. Out of the swirling, Aphrodite appeared, her blond hair in waves, laughing in delight. "Oh, I'm late!"

Artemis rose and said, "Join us, beautiful. We're having a symposia tonight. You, as honored guest, choose the subject."

Aphrodite sat gracefully and said, "Thank you. I hardly have to think. For tonight's gathering we discuss virginity. It's obviously on our minds."

"I object," Laine interjected. "The subjects of symposia are philosophical. Your topic hardly rises to our expectations."

"My dear, I see I'm rubbing a sensitive spot — not to make a pun — but I view the topic as apropos. Oh, my glass is empty!"

One of the nymphs, the striking girl with golden hair, poured her wine. As I compared the goddess to the girl, I wondered who was more beautiful. As the nymph turned to retreat, Aphrodite grabbed her wrist, saying, "Jack, this is one you haven't met: Arethusa." She smiled at her revelation.

The girl blushed and bowed toward me. "My honor, sir."

The goddess said, "They call her Dolphin. She's a legend. Ovid, the poet, called her Alpheias. She was nearly raped one night, but escaped thanks to Artemis. She remains a virgin, aren't you dear?"

Arethusa froze. Artemis whispered, "Leave her out of this."

Releasing the girl, Aphrodite said, "How delicious. We have Artemis and Lachesis and a gaggle of nymphs — all supposedly as pure as an ocean breeze. And in contrast, we have Klotho and myself, playgirls, worldly know-it-alls ..."

Clo stood and said, "I have no interest in *any* of this —"

She turned to leave and Aphrodite rose. "To cut and run is cowardly. You would leave me with all these pietistic females? Only you and I can speak with experience. You've tasted love. The others can only guess —"

Chloé hesitated. "If I stay, you must take the lead."

The goddess said, "Then, it's settled. Our topic tonight is 'Why Virginity?' And given that I picked this little controversy, I'll begin ..."

She put a hand on my shoulder. "Symposia, Jack, were private parties held by men in separate quarters of their homes thousands of years ago. You would call them banquets, I suppose, but the men drank, debated. Of course they had servant boys attending them, and lovely courtesans. After a few hours, the party would break down into a dreadful debauchery."

Looking at the many young women in attendance, Aphrodite said, "So many virgins here tonight ... What *is* virginity, my dears?"

In the silence, the goddess continued, "Is it physical? Is it ensuring the precious maidenhead stays intact? If the latter, most of Artemis' nymphs lost that millennia ago as they pursued deer and game or played seesaw on fallen trees. And if not for the hymen, how are we sure there's been no coitus? My sisters, we are *not* —"

Artemis whispered, "I know if one of my nymphs breaks her vows."

Aphrodite said, "But that is only because their minds are transparent to us." She continued expansively, "Is it true that a girl who is chaste is ignorant of sexual pleasures?"

To my surprise Chloé spoke. "Not completely. There are alternatives."

Aphrodite said, "Self-love? And is that desirable?"

"Yes," Artemis said. "They remain innocent."

"Still, my dear, your nymphs run down deer, cutting them apart while they're alive, tearing off limbs, eating raw flesh. Is that innocence?"

"Not the same."

"So the ignorance is of sex alone? That ignorance makes them innocent?"

"Yes."

"And is innocence something we covet? I speak of the innocence of the chaste —"

Laine said, "Do you mock us, Aphrodite? And when does love-play cross a line? Does climax without coitus do that, or must penetration occur?"

From a back wall, Arethusa said, "If I may ... What is coitus?"

Artemis glanced at the others and said, "I have protected her."

Aphrodite smiled. "Child, coitus is from the Latin, *coire*. It's a societally polite way of referring to intercourse, penetration. You do understand, don't you?"

Arethusa blushed. "Yes." As Arethusa spoke, she glanced at me and I felt an unexpected frisson, a small unveiling — and I was startled at the risk she took.

Oblivious, Aphrodite redirected the conversation, saying, "Lachesis asks an excellent question. Does virginity imply innocence? Or can there be something in-between? And if there is, for instance, foreplay, does that end innocence, yet leave virginity intact?"

After a sip of wine, she continued. "As the brilliant Lachesis asked, does climax without coitus disqualify one from being a virgin?" She winked at Laine and pointed at me. "She asks because she has this man ride her every night. And she's relentless. How many a night, my dear?"

"Not the question," Laine asserted.

Ignoring her, Aphrodite said, "We speak of the most secret place, the *sanctum sanctorum*. Did women name this place?"

The goddesses together said, "No."

"Of course not. It's an invention of men. For us it's our groin. It has an explosive potential — Lachesis understands its sweetness. But its *sacredness* — that's a male invention, a concept constructed to control women."

Laine said, "At what point does love-play cross a line?"

Aphrodite spit back, "A line? Who cares about a line?"

"But this has always been our way," Artemis interjected.

"No," the goddess said. "I was born from raw sex. From the start I was a nova of lust and love. As was Nyx. We preceded you. Virginity is not 'our way'."

"Then why have you been silent about this so long?"

"Silent? I have sent Eros on thousands of errands. What seems new now is only that I chose to point his arrows toward Klotho, then Lachesis. They were the first goddesses he'd pursued for years. I left the rest of you to your righteousness."

Her voice barely audible, Laine said, "Why did you choose us?"

"You heard my explanation at the trial. The child Aisa had to be conceived to complete the triad of Fates. Your sister would never have slept with this man —" She pointed at me, "— if I hadn't infected her with leg-trembling lust."

Laine said, "I don't believe you. It was my influence, not yours. Show us your Eros. I think he's a myth."

The goddess said, "Himeros lives in the shadows, in the shadows of shadows. He waits for his targets to sleep before he strikes. But you, Lachesis, do you now admit virginity is … a mere fetish?"

I noticed Chloé crying but had little to offer. She opened her eyes and said angrily, "Our love was *real* —"

Artemis stood and said to the nymphs, "Consider all you have heard in the last hour as mere squabbling. Reach no conclusions. I should have shielded you from this —"

Aphrodite responded, "And consider Artemis' apologies to be a poor defense of an empty tradition. More wine —!"

Arethusa appeared distraught, yet filled glasses. I repeatedly glanced her way, assessing my sudden sense we were connected by some unexplained bond — was it intuition, premonition? As I studied the girl, Laine's hand lay on my arm, casually possessive.

"Indeed," Aphrodite continued, "Virginity equals ignorance, awkwardness, ineptness — an undesirable and graceless state. Is there any science affirming that virgins benefit from virginity? No. Love without sex is imperfect love. I would go further and suggest virginity is a savagery, a relic of patriarchy."

Laine shook her head. "No, you're too harsh. It isn't that. The Fates have always held to purity —"

Aphrodite laughed. "Purity? A twisted word. Our fate is at risk if the two of you represent what's pure! Klotho, a virgin? No. And you, Lachesis, do you consider your nightly trysts to be the normal behavior of a virgin goddess? Purity, indeed!"

"You say we were snared by tradition millennia ago?" Laine asked. "Who established these traditions?" She tried to sound reasonable but I knew her well enough to know that she, like Chloé, had been shaken.

Aphrodite shrugged. "Zeus and his sons. And good riddance to them all —"

I said, "Good riddance?"

She laughed cautiously. "During reanimation a few years ago, none of the gods awoke. Zeus, Apollo, the rest — likely gone to dust. We are all women. We are the last. That's why your coming has been extraordinary."

In conclusion, Aphrodite smiled, saying in a rush, "I do miss Dionysus. Oh, that one could party!"

Everyone at the table laughed. I turned to see the reaction of the nymphs behind us. Arethusa looked at me again, her eyes probing.

Aphrodite took Laine's hand and said, "Whether you're still a virgin is unknown. Shall we ask your sister? She's experienced. And she knows every muscle of the man you say you love —"

Chloé said, "Don't include me in this."

"That cannot be," said Aphrodite. "No one here is as qualified. You must measure your sister — and the man — for I'm certain you hear them playing late at night."

"Okay, okay." Chloé smiled sweetly at her sister. "Are you still a flower, Laine?"

"A flower?"

"I'll ask differently. Has Jack deflowered you, my dear?"

Laine glared. "No."

"Yet, he makes you come."

"Yes."

"It's good, isn't it? What he does —"

Laine said nothing. Chloé twisted her mouth. "I'll answer for you if you won't. Yes, it's fucking good. I hear your cries. And I know his play, his touch. I remember his breath, his kisses in my hair. I remember his hands and how they moved in the dark."

Aphrodite sighed. "Oh, merely listening I'm getting hot …"

Chloé waved her hand scornfully. "The question stands. Are you a virgin? Virginity is purity of the body — and the mind. And in your imagination, he ravishes you at night. Penetration is a mere formality. If you claim virginity, you're a fraud."

I heard Timessa gasp. Others smirked. Aphrodite calmly said, "Love and lust lead to enlightenment. Lachesis, my dear, I suggest you learn to enjoy yourself."

Laine covered her eyes. Aphrodite stood and moved to her side, removing Laine's hands. She lifted one hand to her mouth and kissed the inside of her palm. "I hope you forgive tonight's frankness —"

Arethusa caught my eye again. For a brief moment I was probed. We connected for seconds before she looked away.

Releasing Laine's hand, Aphrodite's eyes swept the room. She said, turning to Arethusa, "What do I desire, dear?" Arethusa nodded and brought wine. As she did, Aphrodite caught her, spinning her around and holding the girl against her hips. She whispered, "And with whom will you sleep tonight?"

Then Aphrodite laughed, letting her go. She caught my eye, motioning me over. Arethusa left the room, looking back at the two of us. The goddess said, "Jack, you have so much more to discover." She twirled a finger through her locks. "The extent of your dominion may surprise you."

"Goddess, isn't it strange to be in this advanced world that is, in ways, more primitive than what existed in your glory?"

"In my glory? Millennia ago? In the time of burnt sacrifices?" She examined me. "What do you know about sacrifices?"

"Nothing. It's not taught in schools."

"Animal sacrifice. Giving thanks to us for favors. A priest would sever an animal's artery and drain the blood. After roasting the meat, the fatty portion would go to men, and the sinews to gods. Bulls, horses, sheep, birds. The more valuable, the more we honored the immolation.

"Back then we called it holocaust, or in Greek, *holokaustos*. The word was usurped, repurposed for the horrors of your time."

I watched her and she whispered conspiratorially, "Now that I have you to myself, let me ask — why do the nymphs refer to you as 'Sir'?"

"Lachesis' rule. She demanded formality."

"You understand its derivation?"

"'Sir'? Of course. It's a traditional way of addressing a respectable man."

She laughed. "And its inference?" I shrugged.

"You haven't given it a thought?" She sighed dramatically. "*Sir*, Jack, is derived from the word *sire*. Do I have to teach you everything?"

"Sire is related to horses, right?"

"Sire refers to a bull or a stallion. Specifically, to a huge male kept for breeding. All of Artemis' nymphs grasp the meaning. Sire: a euphonic cousin of *desire*."

I smiled. "You're saying they laugh behind my back, imagining me as … a breeding stallion."

"For the goddess. As you were for Klotho."

"Now I feel the fool."

"Thank the brilliant Lachesis who made you a mockery."

We looked at each other a moment. She asked, "And your opinion: is virginity a barbarism?"

"If you're seeking agreement, yes."

"But you're not to be trusted, as you have one thing on your mind. The same thing drives all men. Sir."

"Never trust a sire when there's a mare in the stable?"

She laughed. "Has your transformation changed your performance?"

"We are equally direct."

"You prefer a double-entendre?"

"No. You're asking if my ability to perform has improved?"

"I suspect it's far better. Nod if I'm correct." I nodded and laughed.

"If Lachesis ever gives you the shake, look me up." She kissed my cheek, then paused. "You know what they say happens once Aphrodite kisses you?" I shook my head. "They say you're forever hers."

At that moment Laine shimmied between us. "No," she said. "He's mine." She placed my palm above her breast, locking eyes with Aphrodite. "You wouldn't understand —"

"Ouch." Aphrodite patted her cheek and kissed her. "Now you're *both* mine."

"Stay away." Laine took my arm, pulling me aside. "You have a trip in the morning. We're done here." She left me to give Chloé a parting hug.

During her few moments away, Arethusa appeared beside me. "A pleasure meeting you." I smiled and she continued, "Philippa speaks highly of you."

"I've never known a girl named Dolphin —"

"I'm a sea nymph. I used to serve Poseidon."

"Your ears must have been burning tonight."

"More than my ears are afire." I was surprised as she touched my arm and whispered, "We'll have an opportunity to work together soon." Her beauty was distracting as she eased her fingers down my arm.

Laine walked up and said with delight, "Arethusa!"

The girl bowed. Laine said, "I'm glad you and Jack have talked. Any chance of you staying here tonight? I need to speak with you — maybe over breakfast? Jack and Timessa are running an early errand and we'll have time."

Arethusa smiled mysteriously. "Of course."

"Jack, can you show her one of the extra rooms?"

I nodded. The three of us talked for a moment, then Laine said, "You two go. I'll close down here."

My party, and I'd been sent away. The girl looked at me. Unlike any of the other nymphs, she had dark, flickering parts of her consciousness I knew were masked. But was that possible?

At the room, she took my hand. I felt entangled, immobilized. Abruptly, her eyes tearing, she turned and closed the door without a word. I stood momentarily, then shrugged off the interaction. Nymphs were mercurial; Arethusa could be no different than the others.

Later, once Laine and I were alone in our room, she frowned, *No talk*. The conversation I assumed would be a continuation of Aphrodite's symposia did not occur. Timessa never appeared, so I read until almost five.

When I finally turned to sleep, Laine was sitting on the bed, still awake, staring blankly. I felt exhausted, weary of it all. My easy, guileless acceptance of this being was at an end. Something had perished, and whatever was left had no more substance than an apparition. If I were to use love as a measure, I felt like a fool — I was clearly Aphrodite's tool, an instrument used to seduce two of the three Fates. Now that I knew, I thought it ingenious. Yet, I would never look at Laine without seeing Aphrodite's hand.

Even with my new prescience, I could not have imagined the pending chaos. Although I was now *metamorphōsis* made flesh — a thing made into a completely different thing — I still could not predict the future.

CHAPTER 50

Before I rose, I dreamed I stood in the meadow. The sun was pale, an albino eye and I looked into it, squinting. Timessa, Filly and the lovely Arethusa were near. T, with exaggerated awe, pointed at a monstrous Laine who stood across from us beside a marbled monolith, its sides polished bright. Rising from a pool of water, it stood fifty feet high. Her image was reflected on its mirrored sides and a fog clung to the water's surface. Flecks of orange erupted in the mist.

The goddess wore a cloak as red as cochineal dye. She shrugged once and the cape fell from her shoulders, wrapping her ankles in a slough of silk. Naked, she looked up and lazily tapped the monolith with a fingertip. It splintered into leaf-sized pieces that floated toward us in extraordinarily slow motion, each fragment razor-edged. The inside of the monolith appeared molten, a nauseous boiling hell. Laine stood impassively as a massive roar hit us.

Arethusa cried, "Jack!"

I raised my hand, palm toward the heat. The shards wavered, then meandered back, reconfiguring themselves — puzzle pieces clicking together until the monolith was whole. Laine turned toward us, staring without expression. She appeared somnolent, languorous. The forest behind her, the stream and the grasses were a monochrome. I felt someone's touch, and when I looked, I held Arethusa.

Her voice, subvocal, was melodious: *Jack, be my sonnet, and my hymn.*
Her hair shimmered as I shivered.

I awoke bewildered. I scanned the house. Laine, Chloé and T already were working; Arethusa slept. I thought about the past weeks and of Laine: love, lust, strictures, pseudo philosophies, cloying surprises, half-truths, constant workarounds to avoid reproach —

When I reflected on the last twenty years, I knew I had always been as amoral as T. Societal mores and tradition are a comforting fraud. Yet, each new civilization is convinced of its superiority over the last.

Too, as Aphrodite implied, virginity is another talisman, but nothing more. Like any restriction, it's an impediment, a harsh bit in the mouth, a harness to restrain wild things. Last night's symposia illuminated our own struggle. I now knew Laine had suffocated lovemaking's thrill. And Aphrodite's admonitions would never break through that adamantine shell.

My waking revelation (whatever the dream's significance): I didn't care. *I didn't care.* I caught myself. It was too early in the day for this. I already felt restless. In a short time, I would be in Maryland mailing the first of the deadly gifts. T and I would be an incongruous team.

I met her in the hallway, dressed in a suitably unmemorable pair of shorts and top. "We leave in an hour," I said.

"Yes, sir." Her eyes glistened. "Should I wake Arethusa?"

"If she sleeps, she needs to sleep." I exited upstairs, thinking, *Arethusa*, unable to make sense of what had happened between us the night before.

As I made coffee, Laine walked into the kitchen, clearly preoccupied. T followed her, carrying the small box, a ten-inch square package. Her hands were gloved.

I reached out to examine the box and Laine said, "No, you'll leave fingerprints."

Timessa tilted it for viewing. The label read, *Dr. Louise Chura*, and included her MIT address. The lettering was in a woman's hand — Timessa's, I guessed, as Laine would not have allowed her own.

Laine said, "Leave. I'll keep my cell phone on."

Navigation announced our arrival and I slowed, pulling into the post office. To my amusement T put on large sunglasses and covered her hair in a wide hat. She said, "There'll be cameras inside."

"Smart. I'd never recognize you."

She left the car and bounded up the stairs. In minutes she returned, empty-handed. As she climbed in, she pulled her hat lower and squinted. "Without a hitch!" I backed the car out and we left.

On an empty stretch of road, she casually tossed the hat from the car. "Stupid disguise."

Breaking the silence, I said, "You say Artemis knows your every thought —"

"Of course."

"You don't miss the loss of privacy?"

"Oh no, it's liberating. To have nothing to hide is to be utterly free."

Her argument was Orwellian, that used in totalitarian countries — and increasingly in so-called democracies: hide nothing, be free.

In so many ways these girls lived an idyllic life — exciting, relatively safe, free of disease, constantly sheltered. Yet, they willingly accepted restrictions contemporary women would find outrageous. I glanced at her, noting her smile and said, "What are you thinking?"

She said, "I wonder about sharing myself with a man I love. You know …" Her voice lowered. "… Coitus."

"T, it's no big deal."

"What?"

"Intercourse. It's as much about intimacy as anything else."

"If it's not such a big deal, why the big deal?" she asked.

I laughed. "You've just made Aphrodite's argument."

Admittedly, I was startled by her ardor and said, "It seems to be etched into our genes that neither man nor woman, god or goddess, is complete until they've fucked."

"To be crude." She blinked. "Sir."

Timessa sat in a ball, leaning against the passenger door. The back of my neck tingled. I felt vaguely like Aphrodite's surrogate, sowing doubt. The rest of our ride was in silence.

CHAPTER 51

During the next week, I refocused on the closing for the James estate, now ten days away, rarely spending even an hour on business. In the last months, I had become increasingly wealthy. Financial speculations, regardless of their risk, fell my way. I'd been lucky in the past; now I seemed unable to lose (and reminded myself repeatedly that overconfidence mows down every gambler).

I was less attentive to old clients. When a firm in San Diego offered me a lucrative gig, I politely declined, claiming to be too busy. In truth, I sensed leaving Laine's war room would be an error. In addition, Arethusa now worked with Laine and T. Laine's casual *I don't care if you have an occasional dalliance* seemed an augury, as I found Arethusa attractive.

Laine herself frustrated every affection. We repeated the same patterns: bedtime meant I read, while she sat staring into space. I slept an hour, never sure if she slept at all, as she was awake when I quit, and often in her office when I woke.

Our closeness had been shattered by the trial and Aphrodite's symposia. Neither of us had the energy to reconcile. One evening I accused her of being pigheaded. Her anger flared, then when I muttered, "and obstinate," she blocked me.

One morning eight days after the Elkton mailing, Laine joined me for breakfast. She seemed upbeat, her clothes mirroring her mood. I remember her in a cotton blouse and a similar skirt. I was bemused when she reached out and touched my hand, saying, "How's it?"

"Disheartening."

"That bad?"

"I'm an idealist. I hold us to rationality," I said.

"As if we're machines programmed to be reasonable."

"Yes."

"You need a no-nonsense girl." She laughed. "Gods are cerebral, yet illogical. A long life doesn't guarantee wisdom."

I paused, studying her. Morning freckles glowed on her cheeks and flowed down her neck. "You're lovely."

"Do you want to unbutton my blouse?"

"Perhaps."

"I've been unbearable. I'm sorry."

"I'm hardly faultless. Blame the stunning Aphrodite."

"She whose logic is impeccable."

"And we can't forget Eros …"

She stood. "May I sit in your lap?"

I swiveled and she sat, putting her arms around me. "Hold me, hold me —" Then she rose abruptly and said, "Within a week the packages go out en masse —" She stopped. "Jack, the closing's on track?"

"Yes."

She leaned over, kissed my forehead and left. I didn't realize, but that fifteen minutes together was one of our last half-pleasant moments.

I walked to the window overlooking the field: crow games were on-going and to the side lay — I sensed it before I saw it — the two-headed version of Orthrus, in a deep shadow by the altar. The beast's absence during the last week had puzzled me. Now it had returned, and in its most ominous visage. Lazily, it stared with both heads, its eyes indifferent orbs, the omnipresent, dead lens of security cameras.

I went downstairs, then through our bedroom and into the field, the sun crisp and the air cool. The crows scattered noisily as I strode into the grass. Orthrus lay still, unperturbed. I bent to scratch it, aware of its immense body. "Hey, old friend, why two heads?"

It uttered a low growl of pleasure as I worked fingers behind its ears, switching from head to head. I thought of the mythos — that with its two heads it gazed simultaneously backward and forward through time. "And what do you see?" Its thoughts were as anodyne as its eyes: it projected an insipid stupidity — and a vague savagery. I might as well have been stroking an alligator.

As I stood, I sensed others at a distance: the voices of nymphs. In seconds, a dozen tumbled into the sun. In their midst, Artemis, a huntress today, with her younger girls, none older than twelve.

She raised her hands to shoulder height, palms out in the ancient greeting, which I returned. I probed her and read nothing. She'd turned off everything, exposing only her instant observations. As I scanned her, she responded, *You, too, can choose what to reveal.*

What I choose now is to be open, Goddess.

It is not all or nothing. For instance, turn off your memories from last night.

To my amusement, I hid them selectively. First showing them to Artemis, I hid them as easily.

See, she responded, *what you can do to objects you can do to thoughts. Vanish what you wish.*

She stepped closer, stopping within feet. The nymphs gathered, sitting in the grass. *There are other things. Remember your dream of the monolith?*

How would you know?

Until you choose to close yourself, nothing is hidden. She spoke. "The monolith exploded when touched."

"Yes. When touched by the goddess."

"And in your dream you willed it back." She paused. "That is the opposite of what you did to my amphitheatre." She paused again. "There you vanished parts, and in the dream you reassembled."

"You're saying I can do either when awake."

"Yes." She stopped speaking, expecting me to follow her thoughts. *It's nothing anyone else can do. It's your gift alone.*

She smiled, a rarity. *And there's more. For example, remember Aphrodite appearing at last week's celebration? She arrived in glitter and smoke. Those are cheap tricks we have used for millennia. Magicians saw girls in half, and we materialize from the aether.*

She wore the usual leather strap cinched across her ribs. Several of the nymphs shifted restlessly, already bored. The sun rose and Orthrus backed into shadows.

She said, "When we appeared as … gods, a few of us could transform ourselves into other things." Again, the bewitching smile. "A river-god named Alpheus could become water. Athene assumed the likeness of warriors, Apollo a vulture. Aphrodite would appear as a simple shepherdess, if she wished to seduce a traveler. Of course, Zeus became whatever he wanted — a swan, fish, a shower of gold, rolling thunder — he used disguises to debauch young girls. Or to gain advantage."

"Can you do so?"

"Among us now only Athene and Aphrodite can transfigure." She paused again. "Until you. Now there are three."

I shook my head. "Me?" To my irritation, I heard a light buzzing in my ears and felt dizzy: a precursor. A flash of anger rocked me. I stepped back from her. "Artemis, stop. These changes never come with warning —"

She leaned down and stroked one of the nymphs. "Look at her, Jack, at her sweetness." The girl smiled angelically. "Observe her flushed cheeks and braided hair." Artemis stood. *Now be her, become her. Do it now!*

I thought, I'll indulge the goddess, imagining myself, however absurd it seemed, as the angel-nymph. As I did, I felt a slight tingle and glanced down. Barefoot and in a tunic, I looked down on a girl, hair falling across my eyes. The young nymphs giggled.

Curious, I put my small hand between my legs — indeed. Almost involuntarily, I danced in a rough circle, squealing. Then I did a cartwheel, showing off.

"Jack!" She clapped. "Now return!"

I was stupefied. Return? I imagined "Jack," felt the same tingle and knew I had shifted again.

"You can now do as you wish and appear however you want. You've been able to for weeks." She folded her arms. "But enough of that. Now Arethusa. You've dreamed of her and she of you."

Was it obvious? The goddess smiled, "Has she told her story?"

"Arethusa? No, and if I were smart I'd avoid her."

She laughed. "Thousands of years ago she bathed in a river, only to be spied by Alpheus, the river god. He set a trap for the girl by becoming water, or I should say, the river became Alpheus. He waited for her to shed her clothes and bathe. Of course, he wanted her. You've seen her — what man would not? As she bathed, she sensed his presence in the water around her thighs. She fled. I hid her in a deep mist so she wasn't taken by this lecher-god —"

Artemis paused. "You too, Jack, can appear as whatever you wish. Whenever you want."

I envisioned a large bear, closed my eyes and trembled. The girls jumped back and even Artemis stepped away. I felt my immense bulk, growled and raised black paws, slashing at the sky. Then, I imagined myself as a single-headed Orthrus. With a tingle I became the dog. Eying the double-headed beast beside the altar, I barked twice. Orthrus rose warily onto its feet, its hair bristling. I returned to myself and as I did, looked at my hands: a man's. The nymphs broke into applause.

Artemis appeared indulgent. "Use artifice discretely."

"If I changed, say, into a crow, would you know it was me?"

"Not if you block your thoughts. That's why I showed you how. If used with cunning, you can fool us all. No one needs be aware that you, Jack, are here."

"I can appear to you as Timessa and you wouldn't guess?"

"Remember: the thoughts of nymphs are always open. To all gods. If she appeared and her mind was not the mind I know, I would suspect you instantly."

"But if I appeared as Aphrodite —?"

"You might fool us all." As if my sister, she gave me a shove. "I hold you to a high standard, Jack. Don't waste the gift." She smiled at the nymphs who duly sat around her. "Rise, girls, with a happy heart. We must go about our tasks —"

Without farewell, she strode into the woods, stopping at the stream, nymphs at her heel. On the bank Artemis turned, looking toward Orthrus and whistled, two fingers between her lips. The beast rose and trotted to her, then all of them disappeared.

Watching their backs, I said, "Au revoir —" suddenly alone. I heard Pegasus burbling over the stones along its banks. I walked to it, reflecting on Artemis' tale of Arethusa and the river god.

Imagining a small pool slightly downstream of the crossing, I closed my eyes. When I looked, a lovely pool had appeared. It was about three feet deep with banks and a sandy ramp descending to its waters. A perfect bathing pool, I thought.

I wanted to be impressed with myself, but felt vaguely like a poser. Nothing in my life had come as easily as this. A movement to my right caught my attention: a crow settled onto a low limb. Ah, the irony. I raised my voice and cried, "Aphrodite?"

The crow rustled its wings. "Or are you Athene, back from wandering in a broken world, come to prognosticate?" It swiveled its head and looked, eyes red, beak a bruised mauve. Issuing an unearthly screech of irritation, it lifted on its wings, drifting away.

&.

In the house Laine and the nymphs were in a state of excitement. As the goddess paced, Timessa hunched over a computer and Arethusa took notes. Twice, Laine stopped and punched a fist into the air, elated.

"Okay, what's going on?"

Timessa said perfunctorily, "The toxin. Chura's infected."

Arethusa added, "We hacked the MIT internal forum. It links the life science labs. It's used for jokes, announcements, or rumors about the latest breakthroughs. About an hour ago, all hell broke loose."

Timessa interjected, "Dr. Chura raged through her lab, throwing equipment at assistants, smashing stuff that had been in the works for years … The toxin hasn't weakened. It may even be more potent. Chura started yelling that everyone was an agent of the NSA. Twenty or thirty trials destroyed. Security wrestled her down —"

Arethusa said, "There are eyewitness accounts. Hundreds of texts."

Laine grinned. "She'll never be allowed near an experiment again." Laine looked hot, her blouse sticking to her belly. She said, "Now, we lie low —"

Only Arethusa appeared serene, her heartbeat even. She caught my eye and opened her mind. I was not surprised: tranquility, stillness, calm. She might have been an ancient being who'd seen this scene replayed before. Her eyes pierced mine.

I turned away, filled with uneasiness and a premonition. Chura was about to be destroyed.

CHAPTER 52

That afternoon I tried to sleep on my office couch. I rarely took naps but felt exhausted. I knew the reasons. And I worried: why had none of the male gods materialized? There seemed no explanation. They had not "reanimated," and I was the sole male. Although I had ridiculous capabilities — godlike, I slowly admitted — was I truly one of them? If so, was I, too, as vulnerable? And I had other concerns. Were we safe from the inevitable investigations that would start with a fury once someone, in some country, found a commonality in the outbreak of madness among scientists worldwide?

And what the hell was Laine's endgame? Was it simply extirpation? I thought of the dozens of deaths to come. When Nobel laureates dropped in succession —

I rose after twenty minutes, uncertain I had slept. As I stood, the door opened and Arethusa entered. She half-smiled. "May I speak, sir?"

"Of course." I gestured toward the same chair Timessa typically used. Her clothes: a light skirt and a simple black silk blouse. She wore a discrete necklace, and the top buttons of her blouse were undone. Her image was of a self-confident, perhaps wealthy, socialite. Yet, she was a nymph.

She frowned. "The goddess Lachesis is not aware I am here."

"No nymph hides her thoughts."

She fidgeted, glancing at her hands. As she did, I found her impenetrable, which itself was remarkable. She whispered, "I convey what I wish. She sees what … I allow."

As in Laine's office, she opened. Her thoughts were transparent. As she felt me probing, she smiled. *See? Layers. There are endless layers and I hide them as I choose. For you, they all unlock.*

It appeared true. Looking at me pointedly, she crossed her legs and sighed. I wasn't sure how to proceed. I smiled, "I hardly know you. What do you prefer as a name?"

"What do you mean?"

"Dolphin's awkward."

"That goes way back. I've never shaken it. Most of the girls have nicknames." She laughed. "I'll come, whatever you call me."

"Then I'll call you Danaë."

She flushed. "Why?"

"Dolphin is clunky. Danaë has half the syllables of Arethusa —" I paused. "And besides, it suits you, given you're cooped up with Artemis, and your namesake was similarly shut away."

"You know that story?" she asked.

"Clo recited it awhile ago. That Danaë's father, a king, shut her away so no man could impregnate her, as an oracle had predicted her son would kill the king."

From Arethusa's reaction, I knew I had the story right. "Danaë remained hidden in her father's chamber, like you with your goddess, until the greatest of the gods desired her. Zeus took her one afternoon as a golden rain. The child from the union became the warrior Perseus, who eventually killed the king … Danaë is as lovely a name as the girl before me …"

She laughed. "You surprise me!"

I continued, "Or I could call you Danaë-Arethusa."

Neither of us spoke for moments. She seemed comfortable in the silence and I said, "Why are you here?"

She stayed open as I watched her. Her mind was almost meditative and her heart as slow as someone asleep. She said charmingly, "I like you. That's reason enough."

"Danaë, do we have time for this? Won't the goddess wonder where you are?"

"Ah well, then, goodbye." She stood, smiling, offering her hand in an archaic gesture, a princess' offering. I gently took her wrist, guiding her to the door. As she stepped into the hall, she said, "I see into the future. You should know we —"

"We what —?"

Her eyes were enigmatic. her thoughts closed. She placed a finger on my lips, smiled and left.

ॐ

Sometime later, Laine saw me in the hall and said, "Sorry. No walk today. Too chaotic here."

"Are you sure? We'd both benefit from getting out."

"Impossible. But take one of the girls."

"Tag Arethusa. I know her least of all."

I watched Laine for reaction. But she nodded and turned to leave. "Fine, I'll send her about two."

"She may not want to go, but if she agrees, get her out of that skirt."

"You surprise me, Jack. I'd hardly looked at her today. Now you're objecting to a girl who's *à la mode*? You've been checking out the help."

Laine tapped my cheek. I understood: I should be a careful boy. Her attitude was increasingly demeaning: I could take the girl but should behave. James, Kline and his assistant, Singapore, Chura's madness — Laine was now wielding a blooded scythe.

I sighed, thinking of her promises: love, *forever*, the terms now seemed farcical. The understanding struck me instantly. At an earlier time, I might have anguished for weeks before being certain. Now I knew she was lost. I wondered about the weeks ahead: I had never sought this outcome nor asked to be who I had become.

A few minutes after two, Danaë-Arethusa knocked. She was in a simple tunic. A thin strip of leather below her small breasts cinched the dress and her golden hair fell free. In all her confidence, she still gave me a self-effacing smile. "I've come to walk."

She was astoundingly beautiful and I knew she knew.

ॐ

As we traversed the trail, a mile from the house, I said, "Danaë?"

"Sir?"

"When we're alone, use 'Jack,' or 'Hey you.' Never 'sir'."

She smiled openly. "Explanation?"

"I suspect you understand."

She nodded. "Yes, but not why you invited me to hike."

"Instinct, impulse … or your face filling my eyes every night for the last week as I try to sleep."

"Oh, do I do that?" She blinked innocently.

"Yes."

She stopped, saying, "Jack —" Her hesitation was conscious. "There's so much I haven't said."

I put my hands on her waist, the contact utterly improper, yet entirely correct. She stunned me, slipping into my arms. Unlike Timessa, she projected no sense of being needy. Instead, she conveyed a luxurious sense of nonchalance, or of belonging.

"Whatever hasn't been said, say it now —"

"I'll be quick," she smiled.

"Or be slow."

With a nod, she took my hand as if we were old friends, and gestured for us to walk. "I told you at that party I worked with Poseidon?"

"The sea-god."

"What do you know of him?"

"A flowing beard, a trident spear."

She appeared delighted. "Yes! Don't laugh but …"

She stopped again and observed me, evaluating whether to proceed. She said, "Okay, don't make fun. I more than worked with him. He's my father." She paused. "I spent years beside him before he sent me to minister to distant waters and springs. There is truth to the dolphin nickname. They often surrounded me as guardians —"

"My woods estate has become a magical wonderland, filled with fantastical characters, each with a wilder story than the last."

"You doubt me?"

"Come on, your father's Poseidon?"

Bright-eyed she said, "You can be thankful we're high and dry. If we were at sea, you'd have been killed for merely touching me."

"Are you accusing me of molestation?"

She nodded through her obvious happiness.

I smiled. "I was admiring you only. I'm honorable in that regard, believe it or not."

She blushed and whispered, "My father was one of the gods who didn't return."

"I'm so sorry. You're not a nymph at all, are you?"

"No. Some call me a naiad, a water nymph. But I'm more —"

"Is the daughter of a god a princess?"

"Better than that." She had an impish smile. "I'm a demigod. Actually, a demigoddess."

"Demi — a half-god?"

"Yes." She had an unusual radiance, holding my eyes steadily.

"You say you sought protection with Artemis —"

"I wanted to tell you earlier when I barged in."

"Now there's all the time in the world."

She laughed. "Little do you know."

We had come to the clearing and I motioned her toward the bench. Hesitant, she sat, hands folded in her lap.

"That topic —" she said, "Aphrodite's theme the other night —" Her eyes softened.

I said, "Virginity? I've grown weary of it. The topic creates an instant firestorm."

"Which is why I want to talk," she said.

I stared at her. "Danaë, you say you're a demigoddess. Yet, you run with Artemis' girls —"

"I am grateful for her protection."

"So you, too, are a virgin."

"I have so represented myself."

Sunlight wove through the trees overhead and forced us to shade our eyes. I looked around. The old shed at the edge of the clearing waited, Laine's refuge. "Let's retreat to the shed. Shade — and privacy —"

"Oh —" she looked surprised. "I've seen it but never been inside. Isn't that the goddess' retreat?"

"Once. Once long ago in a fairy tale." I took her hand.

As we entered, I swept my hands around and said, "Le Maison. It's somewhat shabby and lacks plumbing. But I swept out the cobwebs a month ago."

She seemed delighted and we sat at the table. She tucked one leg under the other. I said casually, as if an attorney, "From your, 'I have so represented myself' comment, I take it you're not really one of Artemis' virgins."

"No, I was taken advantage of. Once."

"'Taken'? In what way — and why tell me?

"Do you know that demigoddesses cannot lie?"

"No, you're the first I've met."

"Then, you're lucky. I'm special, as you'll see." She grinned. For a girl offering to reveal secrets, she was amazingly comfortable.

"Be aware Artemis told me your story this morning."

"Her version. Now mine ..." She covered my hand. "Once, before I sought Artemis' shelter, I guarded a spring in what is now Sicily. I was only fifteen, doing as my father wished. Unbeknown to me, the river god Alpheus, emerged a short distance away and, seeing me, fell in love."

"At first sight?"

She looked at me as if I was an idiot. "Of course."

"It had to be your hair."

"I was naked. And I'm beautiful."

I laughed at her ingenuousness. Danaë frowned. "There's more. What you don't know is that Alpheus was a shapeshifter like us —"

"*Us?*"

"Yes, I am as well —" The light around her seemed to slide in a small refraction, then a young boy of five or six sat before me. Dressed in navy shorts and a dirty tee, he surveyed me incuriously, placed an index finger in his ear and twisted it. Pulling it out, he looked. "Gross!" He glanced at me, his eyes amused.

Then the light shifted again, the thin chromas a prism's rainbow, except the light was confined to an area no greater than a square foot: Danaë reappeared with a mischievous smile.

"Impressive. What else can you become?"

"Anything. You can do the same."

"Yes, maybe, but I'm far less confident."

"You and I, Athene and Aphrodite — we're the only ones. And best of all," she said excitedly, "no one's aware of me."

I sighed. "Our secret. Let's refocus on you at that spring, with Alpiss —"

"Alpheus."

"The river god is stalking you. What happens?"

"He knew he would terrify me, so he became a water current. He flowed around me and swirled between my legs. I remember the intense warmth, the sudden rush of the column up my thighs …"

"He took you like that?"

She nodded. "I fled and he pursued me. Artemis hunted nearby. I found her encampment and begged for protection. I've been with her ever since."

"I thought she only accepted virgins."

In the silence between us she said, "You alone, only you know the truth … And my thoughts can appear transparent when they're not. Artemis knows nothing."

I paused. Her eyes were a darker gold than her hair. "Danaë, why tell me this?"

"Why? Why not?" she pouted. She turned her head and saw the leather cot. "Oh, is it soft?" She threw herself atop the bedding, on her back, languidly gazing at me. She seemed to have no more sense of propriety than the nymphs.

She was far more beautiful than Clo or Laine. *Beauty*, I thought, *we're programmed to worship it*. Irrationally I accepted her as a sea-god's daughter, child of a dark salt-sea. Her arms relaxed above her head, and she said, "Is this how the goddess lies on her love-bed when the two of you are here?"

"Your voice is mocking."

She motioned and said, "Come sit."

I joined her, putting a hand on her stomach. Almost imperceptibly, her belly rose and fell. She left her loose arms overhead, her hair hanging off the side. I pinned her wrists where she left them and said, "I should kiss you for being impudent."

"I'm not." Then, she laughed. "But you should."

"Why would I want to do that?"

"Love at first sight."

"Like that river god? I wasn't aware."

"Men are slow."

I put my mouth on hers: softness, endless warmth. Her kiss had none of the sisters' feverishness. After seconds, I said, "Oh my. From now on I kiss only demigoddesses."

She whimpered and whispered, "You've been through a succession of girls, one prettier than the next. I won't be an infatuation. I'm much more."

"Oh? What will you be?"

She pretended to struggle against my grip, turning her head softly from side to side. I said more firmly, "And if not one of my casual affairs, one of my throwaway girls, what will you be?"

She closed her eyes and then, opening them with the smallest of smiles, said, "After that kiss, do you not understand?"

"Danaë, if not another girl, what will you be?"

She pulled me down and we kissed again. "The planets in the heavens are watching you, Jack Night."

"If not another of my throwaway girls —?"

"Our bond is immortal."

"I've heard that before. One last time … if not one of my throwaway girls —?"

In the silence she whispered, "I will be your wife."

I let go of her wrists as if stung. She allowed me to see her thoughts. Danaë radiated only love. She whispered, "We will have three sons and you will love me more than you have loved anyone before —"

Then she whispered, "Put your hand on my heart."

I did, conscious of the soft rise of her breast below my palm. Wife — was she mad? In a millisecond, I scanned her every thought: I saw no subterfuge.

She whispered, "Demigoddesses cannot lie. My love is immutable, not insatiable; abiding, not ephemeral."

CHAPTER 53

My hand still above her heart, I ran my free hand into the nape of
her neck, my fingers in her hair. I was like a blindman who must
touch and taste to understand. She said nothing as I did, her dark eyes on
mine, tears appearing. Minutes passed; we exchanged absurd endear-
ments I could not have foreseen — I had never felt the overwhelming
fondness for anyone I did at that moment for her — and she said, "As
Poseidon's daughter, as the woman who will give you sons, I pledge
myself, Jackson Night."

Give you sons — the phrase itself archaic. My avowal in response,
however ineloquent as it was in my discombobulation, echoed hers. Of
course it made no sense — all an utter impossibility — and although her
beauty was immense, it seemed a mere divertissement for something else.
I sensed more, a burning — love not as competition, but as an oblation.
And I remained illogically convinced her confession — "You will love me
more than you have loved anyone before" — to be unvarnished. And
what of timing? The girl had caught me as I spun away from Laine, an
outcast moon careening from its planet's gravitation. Coincidence, or did
she wait until Laine and I had failed?

As much as I had seen in the last year and a half, none of it, however
extraordinary, had prepared me for this. I thought briefly of Laine — yes,
I had been "tested" and had succeeded beyond their expectations. But in

the thin spaces between my challenges, a veil had been ripped away —
the full extent of Laine's dissimulations and manipulations obvious. And
shocking.

Danaë read my thoughts and said, "No, no anger. That's over now."

I studied her, relieved that her eyes were merely golden brown, her
skin un-freckled. I scanned her and found no barriers, and when I
touched, she gave herself without condition — perhaps even as destiny
— trusting that I grasped the immensity of her gift. The audacity of her
declaration astounded me.

"Yet," she said as we stood, "I want to be your wildness, your
untouched beach. Because of that river god, I cannot be."

"Danaë, if you believe you lost your virginity to some rush of water,
think again. He took as much from you as a peeping Tom with binoculars
takes from a girl he spies undressing. At best, it's a pitiful act. You're as
pristine as any untouched beach —"

"You don't care?"

"We are open now. Tell me, do I care?" I held her as she cried, my
hands protecting her from millennia of self-reproach. "Make it gone," I
said. "It's meaningless."

Late in the afternoon, we wandered from the shed, blinking in the
afternoon sun. A dozen nymphs hid within seventy-five feet. I said,
"You're aware we've been watched?"

"Artemis would never leave me unguarded, even here with you."

"I'll have to talk to her."

She giggled. "Let's turn into birds and fly away!"

Yet, I could see she was already anticipating what lay ahead, readying
herself for Laine's machinations. "Jack, we have twenty minutes to talk
about her plans. More acorns will be mailed in a couple days. I'm
supposed to help. I don't know if I can —"

I took her arm. "Do you believe in what she's doing?"

"No."

"She's as crazy as the unfortunate Dr. Chura?"

"Crazier."

"Then there are two heretics. You and I." We hiked back. Before we
had gone a couple hundred feet, Orthrus appeared ahead. He maintained an identical distance from us whether we stopped or ran. "Serious
security today."

"Yes. I apologize."

"Use the same discretion with the goddess as you have with Artemis."

"Jack, once I was utterly open to my father — only to him. Then that incident occurred, and I hid myself to survive. Now, with you, I open again, but only you —"

She stopped for a kiss. We continued.

Several hundred feet before the meadow, we saw a woman straddling the trail: Laine. As we approached, the goddess said loudly, "An hour walk turned into two. Or was it three?"

Danaë looked down. "Goddess, I'm sorry. Time got away — "

I interjected, "I wasn't aware of time constraints. Arethusa has endless stories. I'm grateful for her openness …"

Laine put a hand on each of our shoulders and gazed at length into Danaë's eyes. She cocked her head and tapped a finger twice on Danaë's cheek: a warning. At last, she nodded blandly and said, "I'm glad the two of you get along so well. Arethusa, we're working into the night. Now come along —"

She took a strand of Danaë's hair, and as if tugging a child, led her back.

❧

After a dinner bereft of levity, Laine's cadre returned to work, captives for the night. I had neither been invited nor uninvited to her office so I wandered in. Laine glanced up. "Don't expect me later. I'll be here all night."

Timessa sat at Laine's computer, while Laine was hunched in a swivel chair, flipping through folders. Danaë knelt at a low table with dozens of glass containers laid in rows. She shot me an open smile.

Asking no one in particular, I said, "Need help?"

Chloé, sitting to Danaë's left, said, "We may have a delivery before eleven tonight. A package from overseas. Needs a signature."

I didn't have to ask: the acorns.

Timessa said, "Box should have a return address of Artemida, a town northeast of Athens. I've been tracking it. Sir."

"Fine. I'll shift my work to the living room." I noticed Aisa asleep on a blanket beside Chloé. She wore a pink jumper, her mouth open and hair sweaty.

Without glancing up, Chloé said, "She's fine." She worked on a large rectangle of cardboard scribed in lines — eight rows and four columns, 32 squares, each about four-inches wide, the lines drawn with precision in black marker. Each square was numbered, one through eight in the first row, nine through sixteen in the second, and so on to thirty-two. The rows themselves were lettered A, B ...

"What's the purpose of the board?"

T said, "Organization, sir. Once Arethusa has scrubbed the containers of fingerprints —"

"Each gets a square," Chloé said. "Tomorrow morning we fill them. The cards are personalized, boxes are sealed and the first batch goes out."

"Not all? I thought it was critical these go in a single shot."

T continued, "Logistics. Thirty-two boxes mailed from post offices scattered throughout the region on the same day? We'd need an army of us, and a half dozen nondescript cars. So instead, they'll go out in batches of eight, on back-to-back days. Sir."

"But that drags it out almost a week." Timessa nodded in acknowledgment.

I turned to leave. "I'll be upstairs. If the package arrives, I'll bring it down."

Danaë looked over and said, "Or yell and I'll come."

❦

I stood in the living room, gazing into the darkness, thinking about Danaë. We hadn't made love, yet our rapport seemed as deep as any time-earned intimacy. I alternated between reveling in the new relationship and wondering at its suddenness.

I reminded myself that I was always under my own harsh scrutiny. As I shifted restlessly, headlights wove up the driveway — a van. Within moments it pulled into the entrance and honked once. The driver opened the rear, grabbing a box. I met him at the door. I must have looked odd as I wore a pair of gardening gloves. He handed me the package. The return label read, *Mt. Olympus Assoc., Artemida, Hellenic Republic.*

He left and I set the box down. Two corners were bent, but the box undamaged. I took a plastic garbage bag and, before alerting anyone to its arrival, pulled the bag over the box, flipped it over without touching it and closed the top with a twist tie. I thought briefly of its contents—that this was an opportunity to derail Laine's plans. I could vanish it as I had done the birds. But I cautioned myself: Laine might be more powerful than me. Destroying the acorns seemed far too obvious. I walked to the stairway, yelling, "Box has come!"

Within moments, I heard light footsteps and knew at once: Danaë, her hair a rush of light. Our embrace lasted briefly. I took her shoulders and pushed her back, smiling. "Do demigoddesses have to sleep?"

"What?"

"Goddesses often go without. Nymphs only need a couple hours."

"A couple hours works."

"I'll tuck you in tonight after I've put Timessa down."

She pouted. "Timessa first?"

"Yes, so I'll have you longer. Long enough to bother and molest."

She teased, "Do you plan to fondle me?"

We looked at each other and I said, "I wrapped the box so you don't have to handle it directly."

She sighed. "Thanks. Now I return to the labyrinth."

"The snake pit."

"The labyrinthian snake pit." She half-smiled, took the bag and left.

Around two that morning, I checked in. Timessa used my visit as an excuse to quit. Danaë said, "I'm exhausted, too." Laine glanced at Chloé and said, "We'll stay." I noticed Aisa sitting to Chloé's right, waving a magic marker in circles. As I glanced at her, she stared back. After seconds, she slammed the marker against the floor, her eyes never leaving mine.

I said to Laine, "No break?"

She shook her head. I left, following Danaë and T. As T opened the door to her room, I said, "See if you can get to sleep tonight without my help."

"Unlikely. You know that, sir." Danaë stopped to watch.

"I'll be focused on something of importance tonight. If you can't sleep, let me know quickly." The girl nodded, closing her door.

Danaë stood a few feet from me and smiled. I stepped closer and ran a hand down her arm; we linked fingers. "I trust the goddess has set you up with clothes?"

She said, "I have nothing."

"Follow me —" Danaë and I went to my room. Aware our conversation might be overheard, I pointed at Laine's dresser and said, "Middle drawer."

She was no more than a half minute and bunched something up in her hand. "I'll tell the goddess tomorrow what I took —"

She left. Predictably, minutes later T looked in. "Sir?" I followed her to her room. There, she slipped into bed, waiting. I sat beside her, stroking her waist, and she said sadly, "I haven't been a good muse. Sir."

She sighed again and fell asleep. I left for Danaë's room. Her door was cracked, the room dark. A nightlight barely illuminated the bed and she lay covered with a sheet. I sat beside her. "Can't sleep?"

Mimicking Timessa, she said, "'Impossible. Sir.'"

"This may help." Our kiss felt boundless, and her hunger was obvious. She slipped her hands into my hair and rocked her mouth against mine.

"Is this how you put your girls to bed?" Then she said in a hushed voice, "Pull the sheet down and look —"

I did. She wore one of Laine's demi bras, red with an expensive lace sewn along the tops of the low cups, her areolas half exposed — the slightest nudge would have freed her breasts.

I gazed into her dark eyes. She was shocked as I straightened and said angrily, "Take it off. Not you, not this —"

CHAPTER 54

I had castigated myself for months for being typical, beguiled by Chloé with her lingerie, then in turn by Laine. In my belated realization, I rejected it all. The silk and camis and crinoline — the demi bras — had been like a red *muleta*, a matador's cape flashed before my eyes. I had been beguiled. Now I knew, yet Danaë could not have.

Avoiding my eyes she reached back and unhooked the bra, throwing it aside. She turned on her stomach and buried her face in the pillow.

"Danaë, I'm sorry. I was too harsh —"

Between her sobs she said, "The goddess' drawer is filled with that."

"Yes, a demi bra for a demigoddess. But the lingerie's been part of their artifice."

We were silent in the warm darkness. She turned on her side. "I don't understand."

"It's me, not you. I apologize. In the last year I've been ... maneuvered, conned —"

She touched me. "And your reptile brain reacted."

Watching her, I felt an overwhelming love: Danaë-Arethusa. *Absurd, and yet* ... I studied her eyes, then kissed her. She snaked an arm around my neck and held me. "Someone tomorrow morning will ask why we spent so much time together here."

I felt her breath and said, "I'll say, 'She's impossible to put to sleep.'

I'll theorize it must have been the unfamiliar bed. I'll say you'd have done better sleeping in the grass outside. With the dog."

She giggled. "I'll say, 'He was kind to stay so long. That he treats all the nymphs so well.' " Mimicking Timessa, she said, "Sir."

We finally acknowledged that all hell would break loose if I stayed much longer. I rose and walked to her window. A slivered moon glimmered above the treetops. Danaë whispered, "*Bella luna —*"

"Indeed." I turned and smiled. "Bella Danaë."

She wrinkled her nose. "I'm closing my eyes and you better be gone when I open them or I'll tie you to my bed and never let you go."

For the first time, I didn't sleep. At dawn I felt refreshed, but wary. Laine, Chloé and Aisa had never left the office. I pulled the blinds back abruptly. To my surprise, the bronze tripod stood beside the altar and smoke tumbled from its bowl. Surely Artemis was not at play? Weren't we through with games?

Before going upstairs, I leaned into their office. Aisa slept and the sisters ignored me, although Chloé used my intrusion to stand, saying, "Got to wash up."

I said to Laine, "Come to the kitchen if you want to eat."

Silence. I closed the door.

Upstairs I found T and Danaë. Timessa had her back turned and cheerily called out, "'Morning!" I smelled coffee. "Five stars to whoever made the brew."

"I did!" Danaë volunteered. "I want my stars."

T turned and observed us. "Sir, what does she get?"

I took Danaë's arm and, spinning her away from me, whacked her bottom. She squealed. "Star one. I'll take the other four however I want." Danaë rubbed her bottom and grinned.

T shook her head. "You've never done that with me."

"Arethusa has not been a good girl like you." T looked confused and turned back to washing strawberries. I said, "Warning: this may be the totality of our amusement for the day. When does the first batch go out?"

T volunteered, "Today, if all goes well."

"You're transferring the acorns into the containers?"

"Yes, sir. We bought tongs so I won't have to handle them."

"And the caps are glued?"

"Yesterday. They've had the night to set." She sounded officious. "I'll need the car. Sir."

"You can really drive?"

Excitedly, she said, "Yes. I even have a license." She caught herself. "Well, a good fake anyway. The whole run will take five hours."

"The postal clerks will ask if you're mailing anything hazardous."

"And I'll lie, sir." In a seductive plea, she asked, "Will you come?"

Danaë glanced and I shook my head. "Not this round, T. And remember disguises. A new one at every spot. You'll want to check the car for gas."

We sat to eat and Laine walked in. T pointed at the counter and said, "Coffee's on."

Laine poured a cup and walked out. T and Danaë exchanged glances. The table fell silent and we ate. T rose first, saying, "We're almost there!" Danaë looked away. "Dolphin, you're psyched, right?"

"Psyched is the wrong word," Danaë said. "I didn't sleep well last night. I dreamt I was in a room surrounded by girls, all about eight years old. Human girls, and they all pointed at me, shouting, 'Murderer!' I guess seeing the kill list did it."

"But this is what we have to do!" T's voice rose. "This is the only way —"

I stood and helped Danaë up. I said, "The end justifies the means, right?"

Timessa said, "What?"

"An old idea. It's a way for murderers to rationalize their deed."

She studied us, turned and left. After seconds, I walked to the windows. Nothing. Even Orthrus was gone. But the smoke from the tripod persisted. I saw no fuel, yet flames leaped, sparks drifting up and sideways onto the altar and grass. I was tempted to snuff it out with a thought, but didn't. I turned to Danaë. " 'Sorry about your dream."

"If you'd held me, they'd have all been sweet."

We hugged and almost simultaneously, Chloé appeared with the child. "Jack, Jack, Jack," she said from the doorway. "Always a new girl."

Laine had once called the meadow an *epikentros*, a power center. Perhaps.
To a greater extent it felt like a violence-attractant. Or a volcano, its
magma poised to extinguish the best minds of a generation.

Danaë had gone downstairs, and I soon followed. I had weaponry to
draw upon, but far too little experience to predict the victor. The brief
equanimity I had felt was lost, replaced by disquiet. I cloaked my premo-
nitions, carefully projecting neutrality and walked into Laine's office. "On
track?"

T said, "On track." As she turned away, she said hurriedly to the
room, "A notice on the MIT forum: Chura has died. A memorial service
is scheduled."

Chloé remarked, "That was fast."

Laine stood and walked to the windows overlooking the meadow. She
said in a monotone, "The toxin's mutated. It's more virulent than we
knew." She turned to Timessa. "Handling protocols are imperative."

I noticed the squares on the cardboard panel were now filled with
perfectly centered glass containers—thirty-two, each vial weighted on the
bottom with a tiny pillow awaiting its ovary. Thirty-two pawns set for war,
four times more than arrayed in chess.

I stepped closer. "Will all of these be filled at once, or batch by
batch?"

T said, "All at once, sir." As she spoke, she gingerly moved the box of
acorns from a corner of the room to the floor beside the panel.

For the first time I noticed Aisa. She sat, waving her arms overhead
randomly and rolling her eyes. She sang,

La-la la-la la la —

Her voice was high and grating. At the end she stared at me, shook
her head and cried, "Now dance!" I ignored her little comedy.

Timessa looked away, turned to her desk and pulled a pair of nitrile
gloves from a box. Through this, Danaë said nothing, quietly working. I
said, "I'll be down the hall."

I paused as T, using tongs, lifted acorns from the box and dropped
them into containers. She robotically lowered each onto an indented
pillow. As I turned to leave, Danaë said, "I'll come for the car keys, sir."

An email arrived that morning from my attorney stating the closing documents were complete. I wrote Ketchum, noting I wanted to close by Friday. Almost at once, she messaged back. She recommended 2 p.m. Thursday. I was aware her fee would be over a million, a windfall. I called my banker, requesting a cashier's check for the amount of the purchase. Later that morning, I received an email from Mrs. James' maintenance super, Alec. I had been too preoccupied with events to remember him.

Dear Mr. Night,

I have been informed you become the estate's owner late this week. We have not discussed the status of my employment. As I mentioned when I had the pleasure of meeting you, most of my short career has been spent maintaining this property. I would be honored to continue in that role. If you wish to discuss this matter, my phone is —

I emailed that I had not made a decision and, at least temporarily, I would like him to stay month-to-month. We would discuss something more permanent in time.

Taking a short break, I stepped into the meadow. Artemis had precipitated all prior phenomenon; today I had no sense of her, no indication of nymphs or even wildlife. Yet, the air around the fiery tripod smelled of burnt hair, the altar covered in ash.

I started to go inside, then saw movement as Orthrus sauntered into the meadow. It settled at the edge of the meadow, blinking its eyes rapidly and then stopped. I found myself fantasizing about fleeing to an island, taking the demigoddess with me. Belize, Santorini, Vanuatu. Absurd thoughts, given an hour earlier I had confirmed closing on the new estate.

I squatted in the knee-high grass, my arms braced on my thighs. The morning sun was warm, the humidity pleasant. Shaken from my musing by Orthrus as it barked twice, I stood and threw a stick at the hound. Orthrus lazily dodged it. Tiring of the theatre, I walked to the tripod and shook the structure. Sparks cascaded and Orthrus growled. I stopped, looked at the beast and went into the house. Instead of returning to my office, on impulse I went to the bedroom.

Danaë lay on the bed. "I knew I'd draw you in."

"Aren't you in danger here?"

"We're on break. The goddess is in conference with Klotho. And Timessa is putting the first batch in bags. I'm safe for now ..." She sat and opened her arms.

I joined her, all caution gone. "I need hours with you, not minutes —"

"You'll have me forever, soon."

I shook my head. "I've heard forever from others."

"*My* forever is for all time, forevermore." She smiled. "What do I say about demigoddesses?"

"They never lie."

CHAPTER 55

Later in the hallway, I found Timessa holding two unmarked bags. I frowned. "Four boxes per bag?"

She nodded.

"You got the keys from Arethusa?"

"Yes. Sure you can't come? Sir."

"Not today. Drive carefully. No speeding. What's your itinerary?"

"Birdsboro, Pottstown, St. Peters, Reading, Womelsdorf, Bernville, Leesport and Lyons." She grinned and left.

Downstairs, the door to Laine's office was open. I saw Aisa and Clo. Danaë shot me a smile, while Laine stood at the windows.

"Jack, not now," Laine said, her back to me, her voice a rasp. "Go away."

Clo sat at Laine's computer, looking at the screen. I made a face at Danaë and left. I considered taking a walk alone. I might check the back James property, or follow one of the many trails branching off from Artemis' grove. It would be mine soon and I wanted to see the amphitheatre again. On a whim I returned to Laine's office, saying, "Can I borrow Arethusa for a walk? She knows the back trails on James' land. I'll be exploring there —"

Waving her hand dismissively, the goddess sighed. "Yes, but be back on time."

Danaë stood, glanced at both sisters and skipped over. I pointed down the hall and followed her. We walked through the bedroom and into the meadow. The fire in the tripod still burned, its intensity unchanged. Against the side of the altar, Orthrus watched as I scanned the site.

I felt a rush of pleasure seeing Danaë, the sun washing through her hair. As I began to speak, she put a finger to her lips. I nodded and said, "Let's go. Be my woodland guide."

She curtsied. "Of course, sir."

The trunks of the old pines shone black from rain the night before. Ground cover — ferns, Canada mayflower, sedge — glistened in a raw beauty. About a quarter mile into the woods, she stopped and placed her hands on my shoulders. "We're beyond their hearing."

I laughed. "I wonder. I've been half-listening to Clo and the goddess chatting since we left." I paused. "I can still hear small talk."

"Your powers are greater," she said with unusual intensity.

"And how do you measure the extent of my powers?"

"I'm not certain. But I do. Some people's minds are like a haze — oily, impenetrable. Yours is like an open sky."

I said, " 'Glad you're on my side."

"I am."

"Danaë?"

"Yes?"

"Who are you?"

"The one who walks with you now, who will for all remaining time."

Within twenty minutes, we jumped the stonewall between my property and James', and passed the sacred grove. Danaë took the same path Filly had led me down for the trial. I was surprised at her pace, and she kept turning and saying, "Come on, come on!"

Ahead I saw the clearing for the amphitheatre, and as we advanced, the vast walls of the circular structure yawned above us. We entered the center portal and stopped at the proscenium. She said, "You didn't see me at the trial, did you?"

"No."

"Just another girl in the audience."

"The pretty one?"

She pushed me and pointed. "Look! Overhead." We glanced at camo netting now covering the entire opening. Jute and coconut fibers in the net appeared dense enough to fool a drone or surveillance plane. Artemis was saving this space, yet a fine dust covered the slabs as if it hadn't been used in centuries. Danaë pulled me toward one of the exits. "Come on, there's more to see —"

Almost on a run across a series of paths I'd never seen, she cried, "Come on, come on!" We were a blur, covering distances with ease. Danaë stopped as we approached dense trees and motioned with her arm. "Here is the most sacred of our places." Before us lay another grove, substantially larger than the one surrounding the pool. Ancient trees circled the area and the interior appeared a warren of enclosures. Girls as young as seven and as old as twenty crowded the area. I always imagined Artemis with forty to fifty nymphs; I now doubled the number.

In the center of the grove stood a slightly larger dwelling, which I surmised as Artemis'. Smoke swirled from a source near the dwelling. Danaë said, "She knows we're here."

We wove through a chaos of girls, many of whom stopped and hugged Danaë happily. I was surprised that the girls also fell to their knees, dropping their heads as I passed. Danaë's face remained solemn, her posture straight as we approached the center structure. It, like all the dwellings, had no sides. Forty feet to the right of the dwelling stood an altar identical to the one in the meadow, fire rising from an identical tripod.

Then with a shimmer of light, Artemis stood beside us. Danaë fell to a knee and bowed. The goddess placed her palm on the back of Danaë's head, and said, "Up, most lovely."

As Danaë rose, the goddess turned to me with her palms out — the double-handed greeting, which I mirrored. "I have never been comfortable with your name, Jack. It should be something more nuanced. Maybe Thales. Or Ikarious."

I smiled cautiously. The goddess wore her usual tunic with a leather belt embedded with coin-size gold circlets cinched below her breasts, her hair pulled back under a modest diadem and matted as if she had been hunting.

"Arethusa is mad about you." She smiled.

"You are kind."

"The girl has been a daughter." Artemis put her arm around Danaë, her eyes on me. "I am aware you will guard her now forevermore."

Thirty or more nymphs gathered around us, many grappling with each other to get a better view. Whispering in high voices, they pushed and grabbed each other's hair. The goddess turned and said, "Hush. You may listen, but be polite!" Their voices quieted, and she looked at me.

"If you seek my blessings, they are yours. Be aware, I give you rare perfection." The little girls broke out in applause.

Artemis said, "Tell me what you see at the house."

I focused briefly. "What I see is fanaticism. I see the Fates' jubilation."

Her gaze became distant. Then she spoke. "None of us imagined this."

"Perhaps I am speaking for myself," I said. "But I see weeks of executions — assassinations, murders, whatever you wish to call them. So far there have been twenty-one, including Singapore. If today's packages succeed, the number jumps to twenty-nine. A day later, thirty-seven, then forty-five, then fifty ... and we should expect more. Family or colleagues will handle the acorns ...

"The result? The world's best geneticists dead in a month." I felt my anger spike. "Is Gaia herself so weak? The creator of volcanoes, earthquakes, hurricanes, and tornadoes — somehow Nature can't survive without this intervention?"

Artemis met my eyes calmly. I continued, "Lachesis is what humans call a psychopath, however brilliant. She's expanded her ancient role, and worse, we've abetted her crimes."

Putting her hand up to stop me, she looked at Danaë. "And you agree?"

"I do."

Artemis turned to me. "Use your vision. Were the boxes mailed?"

I located Timessa driving home. She was playing music and singing along.

"From all appearances," I said to the goddess.

CHAPTER 56

Artemis gripped our arms. "You must return."

Danaë groaned, "Not me. How can I go back?"

They held each other's eyes, and the goddess said, "I see." She turned to me. "She may stay if you concur."

Danaë took my hand. "What will you say if I don't return?"

The goddess bent and kissed her forehead. "We will not speak less than the truth. Our existence is predicated on that. We are guided by the old ways —"

I interjected, "Which are—?"

"In this case, a prohibition," Danaë said. "The murder of beings who are not even aware of doing wrong is not allowed."

Artemis added, "Lachesis' targets are scientists who understand nothing of ethics, virtue, history —"

Danaë said, "They view themselves as heroic explorers in search of youth."

Artemis concluded, "Yes, let's end this … calamity." She turned and pointed to a nymph standing at the edge of the girls: Filly. I hadn't noticed.

"Philippa, tonight you contact Timessa. Go to Jack's house. Get a copy of the master list of contacts and return."

The goddess offered her hand to Danaë. As they touched, Artemis said, "And you will contact each target before their gifts arrive. I will dictate a precise message. Texts, emails, calls if necessary —"

The goddess scrutinized me. "Last, shipments must end. How do we do so?"

I said, "'Something I've already considered. Remember the birds on the wire?"

Artemis half-smiled.

"I'll vanish the acorns identically."

"Good. But there will be instant war between you and the Fates —"

"I'm suggesting deceit, not something overt … Tomorrow morning, as they finish the second batch, I wait until the eight new boxes are sealed. Only then do I vanish the acorns, leaving the boxes untouched. Unknowingly, they'll mail empty packages."

Danaë whispered, "Devious."

"And I'll repeat the procedure for batches three and four on the following days."

"Yes," the goddess said. "Deceptively simple. And what will you do with the acorns?"

"The bay is nearby. A saltwater bath will kill the toxin."

She nodded and sighed. "So we go to battle, and we use our wiles first, our weapons last. Chicanery, Jack — I never guessed you capable."

"Chicanery? Betrayal."

"War is often treachery." Then Artemis gripped my arm. "I'm still uncertain of the end game, but we will win the first skirmishes."

"We'll win the end game too."

She paused. "Careful. Go now. Much time has passed."

Danaë and I hugged. Artemis added, "Filly will arrive after midnight for Timessa. Please block knowledge of her presence from the others."

I nodded, kissed Danaë's forehead — marveling at her constant radiance — and left on a mad, exhilarating run.

⁂

Laine, Chloé and Timessa worked steadily. Pausing in the hallway, I observed the activity but was ignored. At this point I accepted that I was an irritant at best — I'd been discarded. Jettisoned or not, I felt it wise to check in. Timessa looked up.

"All boxes mailed?" She nodded shyly. As neither Clo nor Laine turned, I winked at her, as if we were conspirators, and closed the door on them. Half-amused, half-offended, I left. Why the obvious affront?

Around 10:15 that night my door opened. T peered in and said, "Work's done for today. At least for me."

"An early night. Is it going well?"

"Yes, sir. And I'm free."

"You should get something to eat, take a bath —"

"We could spend some time together. Sir."

"No." She looked disappointed. I said "Filly will visit you tonight." She flushed. I continued, "You're to say nothing about this, before or after — now go."

I spent the remaining hours alone, reading and too frequently rehearsing the next day's actions, although they seemed, no matter how I gamed them, to be sound. Around midnight I detected Filly signaling Timessa, and sensed T slipping out. I masked them from the Fates.

At dawn, I fell into an unsettled sleep and had an almost instantaneous dream. In the back meadow, Laine lay atop a high platform. It rose at least five feet off the ground. She was on her side, eyes closed, dressed in a gown. A hawk perched nearby in an oak — it was the hawk that seemed to exist only in my most fretful dreams. As I watched, its head revolved as if on a turret, its eyes obsidian. Suddenly, it lifted above the branches, then swept down on a diagonal toward us.

At first, I thought I was its target. Then I realized its prey: the bird spread its claws and descended over Laine, hovering, grasping her gown. I saw the material go taunt. Effortlessly, the hawk levitated, its claws bunched, rising higher, lifting her, beating its wings. Through all of this, she slept. The bird turned abruptly and swept with its divine payload toward a vast pyre in the gloom.

Above the flames, the hawk hung with its divinity, taunting me far more than pondering whether to release her. I knew exactly what would occur — then, with a deafening shriek, lifting its head and opening its claws, it dropped her. As she hit the pyre, in a dream-slow descent, she opened her eyes and gazed at me, emotionless, the lovely blue of her eyes now a mirror's silver emptiness. She struck the fire and tumbled into the tinder, rolling as her gown burst into flame.

When I woke Laine stood at the foot of the bed. She was no longer my lover. I said, "My dear, you haven't slept in days."

She replied, "And you no longer believe."

"I once thought you brilliant."

"Now you think I'm mad."

"Or a murderer."

She laughed. "Oh, what shall I do with you?"

"Or I with you?"

She turned sideways, coyly. "Would you unzip my dress?"

"No."

"I'll let you have me. You know you want your virgin girl."

"No. And you're not that. You're closer to a chimera —"

"What a funny word. Let me remember: part goat, serpent's tail and whore?"

"Yes, a divine monster."

"Is that really what you think?"

I yawned. The conversation had become sophomoric. "Are you here to say that coffee's on?"

"Jack, your eyes are wary."

"I prefer *cautious*."

"Cautious?"

"You are not what you pretend."

She shrugged, "Where's the new apple of your eye, lovely Arethusa?"

"She's not returning. Not her type of scene."

Laine stared, then left, slamming the door. Minutes later, I dressed, aware of being high on a strange omnipotence. I remembered Artemis' caution about overconfidence. Yet I felt invincible. I wandered into the hallway and found Timessa. So she had returned last night. I walked up and took her arm. She seemed heavy-hearted.

I said, "Yes?"

"Yes." She kept her eyes down. I let her go without warning, almost abusively. She looked at me, hurt and confused.

I paused, saying, "Everything now happens suddenly. Be on guard."

CHAPTER 57

I softened my voice. "Come on ... I don't know about you, but I can use a cup of something strong."

She whispered, "Would you come with me today? Please! If you drive I'll be your navigator. Sir."

I shook my head. "Not possible. I'll give you a couple twenties for gas." I guided her up the stairs.

We sat at the table, alone and with little to say. I drank coffee and Timessa orange juice, the house silent. The sun's light slanted through the kitchen blinds. I had my back to it, but the rays hit T. After a minute, she got up and sat beside me with a whispered, "Headache-ville."

"Not Margaritaville?" The deep violet of her irises was darker than Chloé's. I thought of her dolphin tattoo, and felt an aching for Danaë. "You saw Filly last night?"

"Yes."

"What did she say?"

"That she needed the master list —"

I put a finger to my lips and shook my head. "Nothing else?"

"Only this." She pulled the strap of her tunic down to expose the soft skin just above her breast. I saw a deep bite, slightly inflamed.

"What the hell?"

"A warning. A shark bite."

"Filly?" She nodded. "Why?"

Shrugging she said, "It means, *Be loyal or* —"

"Or what?"

"Or else. Like, I may be culled out."

"From the tribe?"

"Uh-huh. I don't understand why she did it. As I turned to leave, to hug her, she pulled my strap down and … bit me."

"Filly's decision?"

"Artemis. Nymphs deliver the warning, but Artemis orders the bite." She looked away. "I'm fucking scared. I don't know why I'm being warned."

I took her face in my hands, and kissed her forehead. "You're safe —"

"Safe? From what?"

"From all the monsters and beasts that roam the woods."

She shook her head in confusion. "Why? What have I done?"

She was no more than an Amazon carrying out orders that, on their face, seemed virtuous. I put my hands on her shoulders and lightly dug my fingers into her tight muscles. The bite was turning purple.

"At the trial, Filly pushed me to use powers I wasn't aware I had," I said. "There are more. Close your eyes —" As she did I bent and kissed the wound, her skin fragrant, a confection of musk and salt and burnt sugar. I let my lips linger on the bite until I felt a small electrical shift. Then, I released her.

The bite lightened, the redness blanching, becoming pink. Before Timessa could touch it with her fingers, Filly's teeth marks disappeared entirely. She looked up and said, "Only gods have such power."

I put a finger to her lips. "Now go downstairs. Be impeccable. Be the brilliant girl who's majoring in molecular whatever. Be the one chosen by Lachesis for her intelligence."

She stood, covering what was left of the wound. "Thanks for all of this," she said. I said nothing and she whispered, "I owe you. Sir."

"No. We couldn't risk one of the sisters discovering the bite."

She left. Without a glance to the back meadow, I saw how the chess pieces moved: Orthrus beside the altar, crows across the field, smoke from the tripod, trout rising in the shallow pools of Pegasus, a young rabbit hidden in the shrubs beside the stream.

Nowhere did I detect Danaë, but she was safe. Artemis protected her and that was enough. I wondered if Timessa knew too much, enough to endanger the mission. Artemis had conveyed a warning, but T wasn't certain of what to avoid.

ﻬ

I sat in my office, blocking the three from my thoughts. The closing was two days off. I reminded myself I'd intended the purchase as a gift to Laine. Now I cursed my decision. And how would such a mansion otherwise be used? Thousands of square feet was absurd, and I had rationalized it by romantically imagining the structure as perfect for a tribe of extraordinary beings — and yes, with me as a benign country squire in their midst.

In my office, playing out alternatives, I thought of Danaë — the two of us in such a home, remarking idly as we gazed out a window about the depth of water in our moat, counting the koi hovering along the banks, or critiquing the gardens surrounding the maze. Now all of it seemed hallucinatory, a cruel deception.

I pondered walking away from the purchase. What were the consequences? Impulsively, I called my attorney and asked her to check. She worried about deposits and put me on hold to examine the contract; when she reconnected she noted the penalty clause. I would lose my downpayment—15% of the purchase price—and could anticipate a suit.

I glanced at the hour: 10:20. Almost time to check in across the hall. I had a few minutes. If on schedule, the boxes for the second batch would be sealed soon. I put off a decision on the closing.

Observing a small lamp in my office, I decided to vanish it. The shade had always bothered me. I raised my hand, palm open: it disappeared. Yet, the gesture struck me as ridiculous. Seeking subtlety, I repeated the act on an old paperweight, vanishing it without moving. A mere thought sufficed. Enough. The power was intact.

I walked into Laine's office. Aisa idly practiced pirouettes beside a chair. She pointed at me, giggling. Timessa looked up and smiled. To T's left, the cardboard panel held sixteen glass containers, each with an acorn set precisely in a square. T had already set aside eight boxes on the floor. Aisa spun awkwardly.

Pulling up a chair beside T, I asked, "Ready for today's run?"

"I have to double-check the labels, but otherwise, yes, sir."

I reached into my pants and found bills. "Here's money for gas."

Then, I focused on the eight sealed boxes, narrowing my scan to the individual acorns nestled in each. Without hesitation, I vanished the entirety en masse. Doing so was effortless and I briefly wondered about my limitations. Could I vanish thirty, or seventy-five as easily?

Dismissing these thoughts, I shifted the eight to the Delaware Bay. Dropped, they spun like waterlogged tops. The briny water enveloped the acorns, coating each shell in a soft phosphorescence. The glow from the contact of salt and toxin shimmered for seconds, then dimmed.

I checked the sisters. No cognizance. Laine finished a cigarette, an ashtray beside her elbow overflowing with butts. T knelt and, wearing gloves, placed four boxes in each bag. Chloé spun in her chair and handed T a printout.

"Here, today's stops with addresses. I calculated travel time: assume five and a third hours end to end." Timessa nodded.

A tiny movement caught my eye. Aisa still balanced on one foot, her arms out and wavering. She looked at Timessa and laughed. T waved to her and took a bag in each hand. Laine never acknowledged me. I wasn't surprised and said to T, "I'll walk you out." As I stood, I scanned the checkerboard of remaining containers. The bottom rows looked symmetrical: sixteen, unsealed, each with an acorn. We left.

I waved as T pulled out of the driveway. Instead of returning, I walked around the house to the meadow. I needed to see Danaë and report the day's events to Artemis. For the first time, rather than shutting off discrete layers of thought, I shut myself off entirely. In effect, I vanished. In seconds, I crossed the meadow and jumped Pegasus, entering the woods. After 1,000 feet I spotted Filly on the path.

❧

She said, "Arethusa is down the path, at the clearing, waiting. First, the goddess wants a full report."

We walked down the trail, ever farther from the house. I related the morning's activities, asking her about last night's meeting with Timessa — Filly had told T only that Artemis demanded the list. I mentioned nothing about the bite. Our conversation was factual; we reached the clearing and she pointed: Arethusa.

Danaë sat on the bench, her back to us. Although within hearing, she never turned. Waves of hair fell across her back, shimmering with hints of gold. Instead of her woods tunic, she wore what appeared to be a sundress, her hair held back by a silver diadem.

Filly took my hand and whispered, "Till later —" and left on a run. I stood on the edge of the clearing, observing the young woman on the bench. "Danaë …?"

She turned her head and had been crying. When she saw me, she stood. "I talked myself into believing you didn't care!"

She was almost frantic, smothering my neck and cheeks with kisses. I took her face in my hands and held her, whispering, "Now, no more until …"

I stopped speaking and she said, "What? Until what?!"

"Until you tell me about our sons."

She laughed joyously, taking one of my hands and dragging it over her cheek, down her neck, and over a breast where she pressed her hand against mine. "There will be three or more, all healthy and strong. The oldest you will name Ajax —"

"Not Edward?"

"Silly. And I will name the next boy, Belos."

"That's terrible. We'll call him Bob."

"And we'll call our third son Chryses."

"A, B, C. They will be the butt of every joke in school."

"They won't go to school. You and I will teach them everything." She put her arms around my neck, pressing against me, saying, "Hold me, hold me, hold me —"

After minutes, I took her shoulders and nudged her back. The sundress was cut immodestly, the swell of her breasts caught in a shaft of light. The dress was tight at her waist and hips, flaring below. I smiled, "Who dressed you, girl? You're all candy and confection."

"The goddess conjured up this piece. She warned me you'd want to rip it off."

"Sundresses are not supposed to be seductive. And Artemis is a couturier?"

"She only wants the best for us."

"Close your eyes." Danaë did and I lifted her dress slightly and ran a hand up the inside of her thigh, finding an edge of panty, stroking her softly.

She sighed, "Silk. A first for me. Please say that you approve —"

We spent the next hours in the shed off the clearing. As I removed her dress, I asked her to send away the nymphs hiding in the woods. She giggled and said, "How many do you see?" I named the number and location. She put her hand to her forehead, stayed silent for a second and said happily, "They're gone."

"Why she imagines you need to be guarded is beyond me."

She teased, "You know why. And she's now given me to you. It's official —" She winked.

"You needed permission?"

"If she'd refused, I'd still be yours."

"Love at first sight?"

"No, I've loved you forever. But I had to wait for you. All the diversions …"

"Klotho, Lachesis?"

"Yes."

I stood in one of the yellowed windows, viewing the clearing. I thought of Dr. Kline and his associate shooting each other, of Laine's reaction to the murders — her demand I touch her amidst the violence. Sex and death, the primordial cogs. Danaë stood at my side. "Where do we go now, girl?"

"Nowhere. We're already here. No more wandering at last."

"That sounds like demigoddess talk."

She whispered, "Jackson, I've been saved for you. For this minute, this love. Artemis knew."

It broke my heart to ask, but I said, "You're sure I'm the one?"

"Remember I told you I know certain things? And I can read certain people? What I didn't say is that my certainty opens like a flower only when the one I love has come.

"You're the one," she continued. "You fit me, your hands in my hair make me sing. When you stroke my thighs, my softness cries, *He's the one.* When our eyes meet, they shine. When you're gone, even if it's only hours, I'm in tears."

Speech seemed unnecessary. We were, and nothing else mattered. She shrugged charmingly, as if she hadn't shattered me. And so we spent our time, alone and in enough privacy that her cries and mewls were ours alone. As much as I remember those precious hours, throughout we spoke fewer than a dozen words. Touch sufficed.

After making love repeatedly, we opened wine and crackers. A great change had occurred that afternoon: I became hers, my endless self-doubt, my reservations and endless cynicism vanishing like Nyx's odious birds, gone like the acorns.

Near the end she whispered, "I'm filled with you, pollinated, stung to the quick by my honey bee."

"Sated?"

"My woodland god, my satyr." She kissed my cheek. "I can take no more." Her eyes clouded, "But now you must return."

"To the little war? It's winding up. It's almost done."

I sat on the edge of the cot, readying myself. I found myself talking about the James property, about my reasoning, however confused, my waffling, that if I bought it, it would drain almost half my fortune. After I had gone on too long, Danaë surprised me. "Jackson, the house was never meant to be the Fates'."

Her certainty surprised me. I said, "Perhaps. I admit I wasn't sure its purpose. But I bought it anyway."

"You bought it for us."

I laughed. "*Us?*"

"Remember the statue in the maze?" I nodded. "And the sculptor's name?"

"Pi-something."

"Phidias."

"Yes, but what's your point?"

Aphrodite is the goddess of what —?"

"Love."

She made a face and said, "Don't you understand?" She knelt beside me. I looked at her, still marveling, then lifted her onto my lap. Her hair shifted lazily; the sundress she'd pulled on swept up her thighs. She slipped her arms around my neck, saying, "Aphrodite. Love."

"Who needs statues? I've met the real thing."

"Yes, and when Artemis acted shocked at seeing the statue in the maze, she wasn't. That's her gift to us. Not something some old man bought —"

"Placed there after his death?"

"Of course. After his wife left for New York. It's a present from the goddess who celebrates our love."

"Slowly, slowly, girl. You're telling me the Phidias statue is a gift to us from Artemis?"

"You can't imagine how important we are to her."

We gazed at each other. She was solemn, almost stern. I whispered, "Why would she place a rare statue — in her own words, possibly the world's rarest — in the backyard of some garden I don't even own?"

"Because she knows. It will be our home. The house is too big for us, but all those boys will need a place to run and race and hide." Her somber eyes now twinkled. "So my advice, Jackson Night, is that you buy the house. Besides, Artemis says I'll love the master bedroom." She kissed me lightly. "Is she right?"

I casually ran my fingers through her hair. It seemed my turn to be solemn. I slipped one strap down her arm, and then the other. I used both hands to lower the sundress. "You asked me if Artemis is right?"

She whispered, "About the master bedroom." She closed her eyes. I kissed each swell, then said, "Look at me and ask again."

Opening her eyes she said, "My heart is going crazy!" She glanced away, breathing deeply, clearly calming herself, saying softly, "Okay, Jackson Night, is the goddess Artemis correct?"

"Yes. And you needn't have asked. As demigoddesses never lie, Artemis never errs."

For the first time in years, I felt no doubt.

CHAPTER 58

As we stepped into the clearing, a chorale of cacophonous birds quarreled overhead. She said, "We should celebrate."

"A coming out?"

"Oh, something bigger. Artemis can tell us what to do. No one in the tribe has ever joined —" She paused. "It'll be splendid!" Then, without further explanation she sent me off.

Back at the mansion I saw Timessa first — she had mailed all the boxes. As I stepped into the snake pit, Clo was finishing cards for the third batch. Everything appeared front-loaded. Only final packing remained.

Laine excused everyone early, saying she would continue alone. Shortly after, I sent an email to my attorney. I'd meant to do so earlier. "Forget my vacillation. We're on. Thanks."

The rest of the day was uneventful. Perhaps I should have been more insightful that night, but I wasn't. There were no precursors, no harbingers of the next morning's catastrophe.

Dawn was lovely, crisp. The day started routinely. I spent a few hours in my office, attempting half-heartedly to attend to business. Fortunately, whenever I worked, I did so at hyper-speed. Before checking activities in Laine's office, I sent a half dozen messages to clients.

I glanced into the meadow: blue skies, a light breeze stirring through the arching grass in the meadow. Somewhat to my surprise, the field was quiet. Although I couldn't see the beast, I knew precisely where it lay. Three wild trout tailed in the small pool I'd created weeks before. A snake — a black racer — lay sunning beside the altar.

As I opened the door to the Fates' office, I noticed Aisa sitting on the floor near Laine, cross-legged, smoking one of the goddess' cigarettes. She was only eight months old, but now the size of a three-year-old. When Aisa saw me, she released a ring of smoke, smirking at my expression.

I said, "Clo, she's too young for that."

"You know we aren't affected."

As I watched, Aisa robotically dragged on the cigarette, exhaling, dragging on it again, blowing smoke into the room, imitating Laine. I found the act outrageous. "I don't believe it. She's still a child —"

Chloé sighed, "Stop."

Laine swiveled in her chair and hissed, "Just fuck off, Jack."

Aisa laughed at the comment and waggled her arms like an airplane, the cigarette neatly wedged between her first and second fingers. I was reminded of my father's gesture on his last flight, the yellow plane rocking its wings. My anger rose.

As I turned back to Aisa, she struggled to her feet and stood swaying uneasily. Nicotine, I thought: no effect on goddesses, none whatsoever. Laine swiveled toward her computer monitor, and Chloé smiled as if that was that.

I said quietly, "Now *dance*, Aisa." She sat hard, looked away and took another drag.

At 10:42 I returned. The containers for batches three and four remained unsealed. T looked up and smiled cautiously. Neither Clo nor Laine turned. Aisa no longer smoked. Instead, she stood awkwardly on one foot, performing a version of Laine's pirouette, positioned beside the cardboard panel with her arms out horizontally. Timessa whispered to her, "Turn on your toes. It's easier —"

Aisa rose on one foot, trying to steady herself. Timessa seemed charmed and stifled a giggle. Aisa grinned for her small audience as she tottered back and forth. Then, she lost her footing. With a cry, she lurched backward and sideways, her arms flailing.

From the moment she tilted, I knew the outcome. Although the sisters were oblivious, T watched, mouth open as Aisa twisted in an absurd attempt to right herself. Her left hand hit the edge of the cardboard panel, then her shoulders hit the center and simultaneously, her head. The sound created by the shattering glass was a bright tintinnabulation. Several of the cylinders spiraled lazily into the room as if shot from catapults. The acorns themselves shook free, rolling across the floor. Pericarps spiraled off. Aisa ended the fall screaming angrily, wedged between the sawhorses, the cardboard bent in a V.

Chloé lurched toward the child and at the same moment Laine turned and roared, "No!" She dropped to her knees, frantically gathering acorns. At first, Laine cupped them in her palm, but they kept rolling off. Clo grabbed an empty box and said, "Here!" and they began tossing the acorns into it. Even Aisa had recovered and knelt to help.

In a strained voice, Timessa cried, "Don't touch them!" to which Laine responded, "We're not affected by this shit!" I noticed Aisa stuffing one of the cap-less acorns into her mouth. Clo pried her fingers into the child's mouth, and tossed the acorn into the box. Laine shook her head. "Count them — how many —?"

"Five, seven, twelve, fifteen —" She paused and said angrily, "Fuck. One missing." She looked up and said, "Timessa, get your ass down here —"

I stepped into the chaos, scooping T into my arms. Without a word, I stepped back to the doorway and released her onto her feet, pushing her into the hall. Laine was stunned. "What the hell are you doing —?"

"Saving the innocent."

She didn't reply, instead returning to her hunt. Clo had frozen in place on her knees. Aisa stood crying. I wondered if Chloé understood. Glancing around the room aimlessly, Laine said, "This'll kill a day."

I took T by the wrist and forcefully walked her to the kitchen, turning her to face me. "You touched nothing, right?"

"Nothing."

"Stay here." I walked to the window, shoving the blinds aside. If I had seen an apocalyptic landscape, I would not have been surprised, but the meadow lay asleep.

Laine's office was silent. When I returned Chloé was on her knees, her forehead on the floor. Laine sat on her haunches, and as I watched, picked up the box of acorns, shook it and set it down. She said, "I haven't had a bath in days."

Clo said, "Aisa put one in her mouth —"

Laine stood. "I saw it. We should wash."

Aisa lay on the floor tossing restlessly.

I returned to T, who sat at the kitchen table. "Did you drink beer at Vassar?"

She started crying. Taking two bottles I said, "Follow me —"

We walked into the field. I looked for somewhere to sit, then gestured for her to follow. We walked around the house to the front and sat on a bench. I handed her a beer. "No talk. Just drink."

She nodded, the midday sun pleasant. I noticed for the first time that the older maple trees were turning, gold and orange leaves scattered through the green matrix overhead. After awhile, we breathed normally. T wore one of her old tunics and had tear-stained cheeks. She seemed weary, and yawned.

I said to T, "Sorry it's so boring around here."

She leaned into me and whispered, "It isn't. It's insane. Everyone's demented. Kiss, sir?"

I said no, then sensed a presence. I swiveled right: Danaë, unexpected and a joy.

Dressed simply, she said, "Timessa, if you ever hit on him again, I'll cut out your tongue." Then she looked at me pleasantly.

"I never sensed you here," I said.

"'Sorry. I masked myself until the craziness in there ended —" she gestured toward the house, "Didn't mean to surprise you."

Then without warning, she grabbed T's hair, pulling her off the bench. With a shove, she yelled, "I meant every word! Go on —!"

Timessa stumbled off, saying, "Go where?"

"Back to Artemis," Danaë said. "It's over here."

She smiled at me, then whispered, "Now, what's going on in there?"

I focused on the three. Clo stood in a window, incognizant. Aisa lay on the floor. And Laine had not moved, except now she wiped her hands together repeatedly, her eyes blinking rapidly. Danaë shook me, whispering, "What?"

"Like they've all taken a hallucinogen."

CHAPTER 59

After a moment, Danaë said, "I sensed chaos. Tell me."
I told her about Aisa smoking, their mockery of my concern, the child's fall — and the aftermath. I told her the three sisters had all handled the acorns, and I had not allowed Timessa to do so. I told her about Aisa mouthing one as if it were a dollop of chocolate, and Chloé prying it from her mouth. I told her one was missing.

After a moment of hesitation, Danaë admitted to an ongoing debate within the small goddess clique about the actual toxicity of the virus and whether it had mutated over thousands of years.

"You mean, into something lethal enough to kill the divine?"

She looked at me solemnly. "Yes, that strong. Artemis thought it possible. Dr. Chura went too fast. Based on our experience, she should have shown symptoms after a few days, then really lost it after a couple weeks — but no one expected what happened."

"T tried to stop them from touching the acorns. Laine shouted, 'We aren't affected by this shit —' "

"That's sounds like the goddess. If she's wrong and things are falling apart in there, none of us can help. *None* of us. We can only wait."

I had no response; she was correct.

"Jackson, let's go to Artemis." She pulled me up and turned. I followed with trepidation, hesitant to leave. About halfway to Artemis' village, far down the trail, I stopped and said, "Yesterday you said we're important to Artemis — I still don't understand."

"What if I won't tell you?"

"Hmm, I have multiple ways of extracting the truth."

She slipped her arm into mine. Neither of us spoke. We leaped the stonewall separating the properties and she pointed. "The pool. We'll talk there —"

She beat me to its edge, and pulled off her tunic. "Come on!" She was almost in the middle with the water over her hips. I stood on the bank, removed my clothes and joined her. "You're the first male among us in 1,600 years. Lachesis must be thanked for that."

She turned away, her back to me. Waves of hair drifted across her shoulders, golden as the flecks of light sparkling on her arms. I let my palms slip over the flat of her belly. She put her hands on mine, quieting my exploration. "Listen, here's what's so important ... Artemis has long said we have no counterbalance."

"What's counterbalance?"

"She wants boys around. She says that would make us sturdier —"

"Make you coarse and hairy."

She laughed. "Sir, I beg your pardon! That's not it at all."

The pool was shaded, yet splinters of light sparkled off its surface. Overwhelmed to be near her, I said, "You, Arethusa, are so beautiful."

"'Arethusa'? You *are* serious —"

"Is that counterbalance Artemis seeks a man?"

"Only partly, Jackson. Our boys will help, and then their sons." She blinked innocently. "And we may have more sons than three. And they grow so fast —"

Her eyes held mine. Then I understood — and I was dumbstruck. "Danaë ... you're saying we're like an Adam and Eve."

"Well, they were a myth. But, with love — with our immense love — we'll repopulate the divine tribe." She quieted. "And that's why we're so precious to her. And to others you still have not met —"

"Others?"

"Athene, Hestia, Themis — all of whom appear shortly."

"Only Athene is familiar — the goddess of wisdom?"

"Yes, and once the guardian of Athens. Hestia protects households.

Themis was the goddess-mother of Achilles, and spins prophecies. She's partly to thank for my gift."

Absurd, yet my heart beat wildly. She caught the madness in my eyes, fit her hips against mine and cupped my cheeks in her hands in the manner that a girl might hold a small bird. She said, "No, you cannot have me here."

She knew I was tamed, saying, "I love your imprudent heart. I love that I can make you mad like this." Then she took my hand and led me to the bank. As she pulled her tunic on, sunlight danced on her and she said, "Gather yourself. We have much to tell."

The walk to the village took minutes. I was relieved to hear the high voices. We quickly briefed Artemis on events. With our concurrence, she called a summit for late afternoon to include Aphrodite, Hestia, Themis, and Athene — a rare gathering. Such a meeting had not occurred for centuries.

She selected a dozen nymphs to accompany us. Looking back and forth between us, she said, "Arethusa, may I speak to him alone?"

"My goddess, I am his and he is mine. We are one."

Artemis smiled graciously. "A proper answer. Stay, of course." She gripped my arm. "Do not be offended, but at the summit I will address you as Jackson. In fact, I will never address you otherwise. You must realize your familiar name is now unsuitable —

"In addition, for today's gathering you are to wear a warrior's clothes. They are called chitons and are similar to our tunics. Arethusa can help you dress before we meet. That is all." She turned and left.

Danaë whispered, "I've been using 'Jackson' too. She's correct. And you'll be handsome in uniform. We'd stored Apollo's garments for his return. Alas … His chiton is made from gold threads and the finest lamb's wool. His will now be yours."

I knew that being clothed in something Artemis' brother, Apollo, had worn was an immense honor. I turned and saw young nymphs sitting in a semi-circle, as close to us as they risked. When they saw me, they turned away, half-smiling, unwilling to meet my eyes. Danaë said, "Come, my Priapos, we must elude this gaggle. I am to dress you now. Let's see if Apollo's clothing fits my man."

"Priapos?"

My back to the nymphs, she put her hand on my crotch. Giggling she said, "See? Priapos was one of Aphrodite's sons. He always had a giant erection." She whispered slyly, "Like you. But he was a running joke."

"You're comparing us?"

"No. Every time he tried, he couldn't keep it up. Not your problem." Ignoring the nymphs, she leaned in for a kiss, her fingers brushing me.

CHAPTER 60

anaë and I were the first to the grove. She wore a formal tunic and I Apollo's chiton. The grove was silent, its only sound the murmur of water flowing through stones at the foot of the pool.

As we stood on its banks, Danaë whispered, "Jackson!" A young woman appeared ten feet away, clothed in diaphanous material that might have been made from woven cloud. Danaë whispered, "Themis!" She fell to her knees and said, "Goddess, we are honored you have come —"

Themis waved her hand distractedly. "This is, I presume, Jackson?"

"Yes, honored one."

The late afternoon sun spun a vague, ochre-colored luminosity across the waters of the pool. As if carried by the faint breeze, Artemis suddenly appeared with another young woman. Artemis introduced her as the goddess Hestia. She radiated compassion, her eyes effusive in approval. Then in a shimmer of particulate, a slight shift of silver light, Aphrodite appeared. She laughed as she took us in. "A gathering of the beautiful!"

Finally, almost simultaneously, in a silken, rustling sound, a seventh being appeared at Aphrodite's side. Unlike the others, she emanated a radiance that would have been, if not gentle, blinding. She cradled a small owl in one hand. Before Danaë spoke, I knew. *Athene*!

Her eyes gleamed, vast and spacious. Athene ignored the others, observing me closely. Danaë stepped aside. Athene said warmly, "Apollo's chiton. You wear it well."

I bowed slightly and replied, "I am honored."

She inclined her head, then turned to the goddesses, lifting her hand. "A divine congress. Let us begin."

A table with stools had been placed near the pool's edge and we sat. None of us appeared to be over twenty-five. Artemis nodded to me, a cue to explain the morning's events. After doing so, I responded to a number of questions, notably from Athene. She asked me to repeat exactly what I'd seen when Aisa put the acorn in her mouth. She wanted to know how many acorns Chloé and Lachesis had handled, and when the pericarps had decoupled. I finished and the two skilled in prophesy, Danaë and Themis, were asked what they foresaw. Their comments were somber: shadows and darkness, a gloaming, dusk without dawn.

Artemis gave me a sharp look. "And you, Jackson?" I scanned the mansion. "They appear to be in shock. Whether physical or something else, I'm not sure. I detect no activity. But I will return tonight, as I normally would."

The goddesses agreed. But Athene said, "If you find the toxin affected them only briefly, we still must stop their work. Vanishing the acorns behind their backs is ingenious, foolproof. But Lachesis will then try something new."

"And if so?" Hestia asked. "The Fates are more powerful than any one of us."

Athene smiled, "Yes, but not more powerful than all of us combined." She motioned toward me. "And Jackson may be more powerful than even Lachesis. When she spun his DNA, she created something unexpected —" She turned, "I catch myself speaking of you in the third person. My apologies."

I said, "Are you sure I'm the colossus you imply?"

"Yes. The goddess knows not what she did. Do not be offended, but you were intended to be a toy, something to entertain her on long nights. She made mistakes — let's say she crossed a fortuitous wire here and there. Your talents, and possibly your lifespan, may now exceed our own."

I was silent. The extent of my powers remained unknown to me. I lacked her confidence, and imagined overreaching at a critical moment.

Reading my thoughts, Athene said, "When this meeting ends, we will talk. I may accelerate your understanding." She glanced at Danaë. "You will facilitate."

❧

When the others left, Athene said, "Aphrodite might have been the more suitable of us to conduct this exploration, as the remaining power is unlocked by love." We listened and she said, "Jackson, do you agree we must always be fully alive?"

"You refer to living in the present?"

She nodded. "Real love lives neither in the past nor future. It simply is."

Without obvious cause, Danaë came and stood next to me, slipping an arm around my waist. I felt her nuzzle my neck, kissing me as she played. I put an arm around her, and said, "Of course."

I was not aware she and Athene were silent partners, or that I was once again being tested — that Athene was measuring the extent of my love. "Now," Athene said, "let us list the powers you've perceived. First, there is augmented hearing, and with that, the awareness of all sentient beings within an extraordinarily wide radius …

"Too, you can easily modulate massive amounts of data, a measure of your increased intelligence …

"There is the ability to reveal what you choose to those who might read your thoughts. And like me, you can change your appearance at will …"

"Yes," I said, "all of that."

"There is enhanced physical prowess. And, in addition, the power you discovered in a recent dream — you can reconstruct objects after their destruction. This power may seem vacuous, even frivolous. It is not …

"What else? You can heal yourself and others, and you can make all things disappear at will, effortlessly, in fact. You can vanish them into atoms; or you can vanish them intact to precise locations."

"Yes," I said. "I also discerned Artemis' illusions. The amphitheatre is an example."

Danaë continued to nuzzle my neck, casually but consistently shifting her hips against mine in an almost imperceptible motion. Her actions, I learned later, were guided silently by Athene. I whispered to Danaë, "You've not become one of those cats in heat?" She smiled, then lightly bit my shoulder.

Athene continued, "What we have compiled are powers you know, although you have not explored their limits. Now let's untangle what remains."

She stepped closer, weaving her fingers through Danaë's hair. "In a few short days, we will conduct the coupling ceremony —"

"And that is?"

"The two of you have been marked as eternal lovers, although you, Jackson, knew not. The ceremony will celebrate the joining —

"Let us," Athene said, "go on with today's exploration. Arethusa's love for you and yours for her is pivotal."

She pointed toward the pool. There, on the mossy bank, I saw four or five duvets, stacked one upon another, all in soft colors. Together the duvets rose a foot high. A single white sheet topped the quilts. Athene whispered, "Arethusa, for you —"

Danaë nodded and walked to the bed. She smiled shyly and pulled off her tunic, tossing it aside. Athene gestured for her to recline, and she did, laying on her stomach. I smiled, knowing their immense fondness for these theatrics. Athene whispered, "She needs your love."

"She has that and she knows."

"She seeks authentication."

"What would you have me do?"

"Show her. Kisses, touches, love."

"And you will watch?"

"I will observe and weigh the *pathos*." She pointed to the girl. I viewed Danaë's long legs and followed her spine up her back; its sinuosity was like an acquiescent river. Her vertebra merged with the waves of hair covering her shoulders.

Athene whispered, "Kisses, touches, love."

I removed Apollo's chiton, knelt beside her and said softly, "Danaë." I moved my hands across her as if stroking silk, pausing here and there, circling her sacrum, kneading her thighs and calves. She moaned and I bent lower and planted kisses across her as I stroked her legs. My passion soared, and as I tasted her, I murmured, "Danaë, Danaë," aware her ardor matched my own.

My divine onlooker, Athene, dropped from my consciousness. Desire canceled every sense. And as I was swept away in her fire, Danaë turned sideways, slowly rolling onto her back. There, she kissed me with a fever at least equal to my own.

Athene softly cried, startling me, "A love so grand —" whispering,

The hinges are undone, the bolts pried free.
Both of you: Close your eyes and rest in equanimity.
As you share your love without constraint,
You will share knowledge of the things that await.

It felt right, I remember, hovering inches from Danaë's lips, sensing the pulse in her stomach at my touch, and closing our eyes as one. Our thoughts joined, and as suddenly, I recognized my remaining power. Athene said, "You know. Now stand."

I did so, taking Danaë's hand. She smiled blissfully, as if post-orgasmic. Athene stood beside us and said, "Tell me what you perceive."

I laughed. "The Fates are powerful because their cards are dealt from the deck of death. Death is their leverage, their power —"

"And?"

"And I now know I can reverse that, reverse death itself. Whoever dies I can revive. Whomever they condemn to death, I can liberate."

Unexpected confidence surged through me. I'd been shot with adrenaline; this was not Eros' doing, not his cloying potion. My breath was replaced with fire, and Athene — the goddess with gleaming eyes — scanned my face in delight.

CHAPTER 61

I n less than five hours, I'd heard Danaë's prophesy that our coupling would repopulate a divine, forgotten tribe. And the goddess Athene — who had suddenly revealed herself — exposed my remaining gift. I had been vetted, the remaining impediment rolled away.

During the last two years, I had known Eros' lust and infatuation, but never real love. This love, unlike any before, was extraordinary. Danaë's love had revealed love itself — and through that love, I could reverse death. Satisfied at the authentication, Athene smiled and vanished.

As Danaë had said, our uniting was destined, and the time we spent together after Athene left a validation. As we reluctantly parted at the pool's edge, Danaë whispered, "We celebrate our coupling Saturday at noon."

I simply whispered her name. The mere sound now evoked the cosmos itself. I was lost — it was the love Athene had sought to confirm.

At sunset I left for the house, treating the return as a trial run to test my speed. As I approached the meadow, I traversed the distance in a third the usual time. The house was silent and I paused: The three were upstairs. I sensed instantly that their consciousnesses were no longer linked.

I entered through the back and continued upstairs. Laine sat by herself in the kitchen, a cigarette in her hand. She didn't appear to notice

me. Chloé and Aisa were in the adjacent sitting room. Clo lay on a couch
stroking the child, who lay on the floor.

Clo, like Laine, didn't look up, saying simply, "Fever."

"You?"

"Everyone."

I knelt beside her and she said, "Don't touch!"

"What is her temp?"

"104 hours ago. Now 106."

"That's high."

"You know nothing about our babies."

Our babies. "Perhaps I don't, but 106 indicates an immune system
fighting like hell. Bodies are bodies." Clo said nothing. Her eyes appeared
almost ceramic, darkly melancholic, fear clearly mixed with anger.

I went to the kitchen, and sat down across from Laine. Minutes
passed. I waited. I had all night. She finally said, "Timessa's working
downstairs?"

"No. She's gone."

Laine, too, was a tangle of disjointed thoughts that bloomed and
dissolved, sparks that rose and fell in a strange, fluttering darkness. I sat
patiently until she hissed, "We don't need her."

"No, we don't."

"We can rebuild tomorrow. Two batches left."

"You or Chloé will make mail runs?"

She cocked her head. "You'll drive."

She failed to block any portion of her thoughts, a first. Her analytic
functions fluctuated wildly. I knew she hadn't slept in a week. And from
her appearance, I guessed she hadn't glanced in a mirror for as long.
"Laine, it's time to reevaluate your plans."

She poured herself a drink, frowned and tried to take a draw from
the cold cigarette. In frustration, she smashed the butt into a plate. "I
don't know what you're talking about."

She stood, then sat again and leaned toward me, saying conspiratorially, "Chloé believes this place is bugged."

"Why?"

"She does. That you did it. To watch us."

Without warning, as she leaned closer I felt her probing. Her probes
came as small taps — I would never have been aware of them earlier.

Now they showed up as plainly as blinking LEDs. I quietly blocked them, parrying each thrust. Feint, counter, dodge.

She frowned. "You've vanished, Jack. You're a zero." She spoke in the vexing, little girl's voice I hadn't heard in weeks. "I've missed you — missed loving you."

I allowed seconds to pass, then said, "No, you haven't." Although at the conclave we hadn't discussed how to end Laine's gambit — the goddesses deferred to my supposed cunning — I sensed now any prolongation would be an error.

"Laine?"

"Um?"

"It's over."

She shook her head and squinted. "What?"

"Whoever you are, it's time to leave. Perhaps you can go back to being a brilliant geneticist."

She put her face in her hands, sighing. Her eyes flashed as she looked up. "Giving us the boot? That's it?"

"You can go as suddenly as you came."

She laughed. "Hmm, I'll think about it."

"No, you'll leave with your sisters. Tomorrow."

She turned, showing me her profile and drank. At the first sip, she made a face. "The pinot's turned. Nasty sludge."

"Check out here is 11 a.m. No exceptions allowed."

Without moving her head, she said, "I can change you back to what you were." She set her glass aside and studied her hands. "Yes. I was a fool to do what I did."

She turned, smiling. At that instant, I felt the probes again. They tapped like sharp needles and I countered each. At first they were lazy intrusions, almost exploratory. As I blocked each, she probed faster. Our maneuvering steadily increased in pace, reminding me of speed chess — each move instantaneous, parried by the next, the stakes, I knew, unimaginably high.

Throughout, her eyes never blinked. My grim reaper, the Angel of Death come to take me and strip me as clean as James' old carcass. Her thoughts were singular: *You are inconsequential ...*

Yet, she failed. I thwarted each attempt. She had inadvertently made me at least her equal. I knew now I existed beyond her reach; deconstruction was not possible. She had mentioned once, in the early days, that she had killed gods in the past, that the Fates were invincible. I knew it was inconceivable to her, but she now faced a being before whom she was impotent.

She walked to the windows that overlooked the field, standing unsteadily. When she turned to look at me, her face was blank. Then, with a sudden, sharp exhalation, she drove her right fist through the window, crying out in fury —

She froze, her fingers extended into the night, splayed apart like a starfish. Then, as abruptly, she drew her arm back, her fingers and wrist lacerating, blood running freely. She lifted her arm to view it. The bleeding should have ended in moments, but it did not. "Heal it," I said.

She turned to me, shaking her head in pain, her eyes vacant —

Then, in silence she left, the trail of blood a betrayal of her ancient divinity. Any human would faint from the massive loss. I took a step toward her, and she pointed the bloody hand at me, saying, "Traitor. Don't come near me!" I left the kitchen, shaken by what I'd seen.

In my office, I calmed myself, while at a complete loss about how to proceed. I checked messages, an action which in these circumstances felt bizarre. The only one of note was from my attorney reiterating I should appear the coming day to sign documents at a certain law office. Darkness approached, and a low fire from sunset hovered interminably on a fringe of the horizon. *Red sky at night.* For any sailor on this bloodied ship, the journey would be no delight.

I had not expected to spend the evening at the house. On the other hand, I was expected to resolve the crisis. Wandering back to the kitchen, I noted dried blood splattered over the floor. Chloé entered alone, more a waif than goddess. I turned in time to see her stagger at the doorframe. She stared, bewildered.

"How is Aisa?"

She shrugged. Since I had returned from the goddess convocation, neither Clo nor Laine had been cogent for more than moments. Was their behavior due to the toxin? The accident had happened only hours earlier. Such a reaction seemed impossible. Even Chura's symptoms, which had spread like wildfire, were gradual in comparison. The Fates were beings with a far greater vitality; they essentially healed themselves when harmed.

I found a half casserole in the refrigerator, and returned with it to my office. I expected to see Laine at any moment. She would negotiate before giving up. And as expected, the door opened and she entered. The lacerations across her arm were swollen, although no longer bleeding. She looked more like a wounded animal escaped from a hunter's steel trap than a divinity.

As she sat carefully, I said, "Your arm looks terrible."

She crossed her legs and shook her head. "A bad day. I've seen worse."

We knew the unhealed wounds as an impossibility. Still, she posed as seductive, willing. I said, "Have you discussed leaving with the other two?"

In a soft voice, she said, "I know you're kidding, Jack."

I shook my head. "I'm not."

"I've missed our nights together. I've missed your touch." She tossed her hair off her shoulders and smiled.

"Is there anything I can do to help you pack?"

She said nothing, then shifted subtly, grimacing. "You see," she said. "I've been considering … virginity. And I was wrong." She stood. "Wrong. Aphrodite … right."

"Laine, we're way beyond that now."

When she said, "So then you're fucking Timessa," I realized how little she knew. All of us had assumed her omnipotence. As I watched, her thoughts tumbled into chaos again. She pressed her arm against herself, scowling, then stood to leave.

Pausing in the doorway, she held her forehead. Then, with a sharp inhalation, she opened her palms to the empty hallway. Her eyes were vacant. As if she had forgotten me — and only after she had smiled to herself — she wandered off.

CHAPTER 62

That night I monitored Laine. She paced repeatedly in our bedroom. I sensed her heart racing. Her thoughts at times were rash; she planned elaborate, wildly risible exploits, rejecting each, however brilliant they seemed upon conception. Every option was repudiated, every thought rebuffed. Several times, she fell to her knees, choking, cursing the room's insentience, the cosmos' silence.

Decoupling from her angst, I thought, *Carpe noctem. Seize the night, Jack. Otherwise, she'll bring you down.*

In my office, as a distraction, I played mental chess with myself, now able to visualize the board and remember without error every move I and my phantom opponent made.

Close to dawn, I was startled when Laine ripped out the bedroom blinds, reveling briefly in the aluminum slats clattering against the floor. She stared into the meadow at Orthrus, now sitting on its haunches, its red eyes afire. She stretched her hands out to it, thinking, *I've been abandoned!* but it never blinked. She tried, *You know me — Lachesis, Lachesis of the Fates*—but it watched her silently. Slumping to her knees, she imagined fierce bats swirling around her head, explosions of light before her eyes, feral cats smashing themselves against the windows.

I went into her office. The sun had broken above the trees, and light flooded the room. As I had expected, the chaos from the previous morning remained. Glass was scattered across the floor. A diagonal of sunlight struck one side of the box used to hold the acorns. Watching my step, I carefully counted its contents: fifteen glistening acorns. One was missing.

Then I knew: Aisa. She'd swallowed it. After the first acorn, she had tried a second. It was the one Clo had noticed and pried from her mouth.

I had stupidly ignored Chloé and the child through the night, engrossed in Laine's angst. Now I tried to connect to either. As I feared, Clo appeared largely comatose; she showed little neural activity and her wave oscillations were barely detectable. Worse, Aisa seemed utterly insensate, her heartbeat less than twenty beats a minute. I had no way of detecting fever, but she lay without thought, all of her crackling fury gone.

I opened the windows and blinds of Laine's office: the light was honeyed. I guessed the time to be 7:30. Orthrus faced the house, lying now with its eyes closed, its head in its paws. The tripod beside the altar was cold. Wishing it so, I watched it burst into flame. Orthrus' eyes snapped open.

I turned to the acorns, loath to touch the box. I didn't need to do so as I easily pictured their exact placement. *Mirabile dictu.* I made them vanish, then reappear outside, hanging head-high in a tight snake in the morning air. Each touched the next in an invisible chain, a poisonous fifteen-acorn python in the sky. Then, I propelled them as if shot into the flames of the tripod.

A sharp flare occurred as they hit the fire. Sparks erupted, ascending violently, then flickering out. Explosions shook the tripod. Then, after moments, the fire returned to its indolent state.

Alchemy. I'd turned toxigenicity into something inert. Throughout, Orthrus watched. As the flames calmed, the beast turned its eyes toward me and barked. I nodded to it, knowing Artemis would soon have details.

Then, I sensed smoke in the house and ran to the bedroom, opening the door. Laine was on her knees. In the center of the room, a foot from where she knelt, a sheaf of papers burned on the floor. She held a match and turned to me. An unlit cigarette hung from her mouth. "Jack!"

"What the hell are you doing?"

"Saying adieu to genius!" Her voice was merry. "Goodbye, Poet X!"

"You might burn down the house."

"No, the world."

I opened the windows and the door to the meadow. The papers were charred; smoke hovered on the ceiling. A scrap of one of the poems was still legible.

All then lost
the groves burnt
the oaks axed, tossed out …

Taking a glass of water from the nightstand, I threw it at what remained. Ashes sizzled, paper remnants scattered in a wet, sullied blotch. Shaking her head, laughing, she slowly reclined onto her side, beside the disarray, legs drawn up against her chest.

Then, she slept. After a moment, I left her to check on the others. Chloé lay unconscious, her thoughts more chaotic than Laine's, flashes of sullen reds and small bursts of fragmented words scrolling across her cerebellum. I couldn't tell if Aisa lived. The child had become a cipher.

I could no more touch them than touch Laine, knowing the toxin's virulence. And calling for help would be disastrous. Medical science was unprepared to deal with these beings — gods, conspirators and revolutionaries do not turn to authorities.

I returned to Laine who, to my surprise, now sat, arms around her knees, rocking and singing quietly,

Eros, pathos, death …

Pathos. Squatting beside her, I said inanely, "Any better?"

She looked with blank eyes, the lovely blue now a silver-gray, unfocused and far away. She whispered, "I was born a virgin birth."

"As the child of Nyx?"

Rolling onto her side again, she curled up, exhaling, then said plainly, shaking her head, "Something has eaten the gods —"

I wanted to stroke her hair, but could not. Her eyes closed. In moments, she entered a dark, narrowing coma, the time about 8 a.m. Squatting, I shifted silently into a semblance of Athene, one of her oldest friends, a trusted ally. I knew my appearance was literal and I carefully masked my thoughts. If she woke, she might be comforted.

As Athene had done for thousands of her supplicants throughout millennia — suffering young mothers and dying children throughout Attica — I conjured a cloak and laid it across her body, leaving her face exposed. Her red hair lay like a stilled wave on the floor. She sighed, an index finger flicking restlessly.

Retreating soundlessly, still as Athene, I returned to Clo and the child, covering both in cloaks as well. Chloé's eyes rolled open as she felt the weight, their silver emptiness unsettling. In Athene's voice, I whispered, "Klotho —" and she went slack, her eyes fluttering.

Unable even now to accept my observations, I, Athene, hovered in my solemnity, then silently walked out to the open meadow where I stood in the grass facing the sun, arms up, as if a *kolossos*, a mighty statue placed to commemorate some tragedy. As I emptied myself, opening to the solar fire above, the hound settled itself at my ankles, sighing in its infinite lassitude.

Later, I reentered the house, still impersonating the goddess. I confirmed that none of the three had moved. Aisa had died first, and probably within an hour of her death, her mother. Still, the fearsome Lachesis lingered on, lying with her eyes and mouth agape. Through the silvered cataracts, I could see her pupils enlarging, then lazily narrowing, over and over — the only physical sign she lived. Like Chloé earlier, her thoughts had become clotted, a thick cream of random letters, electronic screeches, colors washing across molten seas.

A mirage-hawk now sat before her, blinking. It was the final thing Laine grasped: her hawk had come, a thing of feather, salt and finally flame, cruelly extinguishing itself before her silvered eyes in a long emanation of scattering atoms.

Then her brain activity ceased except for flashes of red, her heartbeat undetectable. Still, she persisted. As I squatted beside her, I thought of Danaë and Laine. One woman celebrated life, while another spiraled toward death.

Days before, Athene had identified my greatest power: bringing the dead back to life. I remembered saying to her, "Whoever dies, I can revive." Yet, now I caught myself. Bringing the Fates back would be reprehensible. I wondered: would I betray my gift if I turned my back?

I walked to the kitchen and shifted back to myself. I possessed keys to life, and rather than turn them in death's lock … I made coffee. As it brewed, I gazed out the window into the meadow, searching myself for empathy. Instead, I saw movement. Filly leaped the brook and gestured. I waved for her to come ahead. In moments, she bounded the stairs.

"Sir?"

"Filly."

"I have a question, sir."

"You're here at Artemis' bidding?"

"And Arethusa's." She stepped closer and put a palm on my chest, her eyes direct. "Where are the Fates?"

I covered her hand with mine. "Two are dead, the last one soon."

She fell to her knees and whispered, "The acorns —?"

"I disposed of them."

"Who lives?"

"Lachesis."

"Maybe she'll recover —?"

"No." I raised Filly to her feet and took her face in my hands, trying to calm her terror. "Philippa, we'll be okay ..."

She shook her head. "This was not supposed to be."

"Go back and tell Arethusa — and Artemis. Say, too, I've destroyed the acorns that remained."

In tears she covered her face. I sensed her desolation, thinking to myself, *Why am I not suffering more? I have even lost a child.*

I caught myself. *No, no sentimentalizing —*

Filly studied my eyes. Who knows what she saw, but she turned and left, stumbling from the kitchen backward, then ran down the stairs.

CHAPTER 63

In the silence, I again scanned the house. Nothing. I returned to my room, pausing briefly to shift to Athene's visage. Lachesis lay inert, her open eyes obscured by an odd, ocular clouding. Both her iris and pupil had turned an identical silver, mimicking a marble statue's polished eyes. I thought, *No, not silver — quicksilver, mercury.*

I got off my knees, sensing a presence: Athene. She stood at my back. "Goddess —"

"You are me. Even our gowns match."

With a tiny flash, I returned to myself, half-bowing.

She smiled. "Should I be honored to be appropriated?"

"I could think of no one, if Lachesis woke, that she would trust as fully."

She glanced down at the body. "Her eyes are the eyes of every dead god or goddess. The other two are the same?"

"Yes." Athene seemed taller than I remembered, resplendent, carefully factual. I thought of Filly's reaction and continued, "All dead. You're not disturbed?"

"There are issues to adjudicate. Whether justice was served, the cause of death, how these deaths effect our equilibrium. None of this, I assure you, was anticipated."

She left herself open. I reciprocated. With some disgust, she said, "A dishonorable ending." Then she sighed. "Artemis will come shortly. And Arethusa." She stepped closer, saying, "Tomorrow we celebrate your coupling, and shortly after, we mourn these deaths." She paused briefly, then touched my arm. "Jackson, move on from all of this. What was here is no longer —" In an almost indiscernible flash, she vanished.

The room was stifling, a faint acrid smell lingering. With a shudder, I returned to the meadow, hoping the sun might warm me once again.

In minutes, Danaë appeared on the far side of the brook, then behind her, Artemis and several nymphs. As they leaped the stream, I raised my hands in the usual greeting. None of us spoke and Danaë slipped under my arm.

We stood in a small circle, seven of us, a thin wind coming off the trees. Artemis said, "You have forgotten. You have business in town. Take Arethusa."

I looked at Danaë. She wore a white blouse and black skirt, and Artemis' gold necklace. I had forgotten the closing. "Of course."

"Then go."

"You're sure?"

The goddess nodded. Regret, loss, tenderheartedness: I detected none from her, no attachment or remorse. She exuded an emptiness that, inexplicably, pulsated with intelligence and life.

We were all parties to a conflagration. It was as if the meadow we stood in had become a platform overlooking a vast field burned to naught. Fire, the force that fused the atoms of the cosmos. *Fire.* Through Orthrus' eyes I looked into the beginning, and in the same instant, the end. And I understood.

Danaë nudged me. I nodded, and we walked from the small group to the car. We said nothing about the deaths. Within ten minutes, we arrived at the attorney's office. The entire closing took minutes. At the end I was presented with statements and a ring with labeled keys, *Front Door, Rear Door 1, Rear 2, Rear 3, Side Right, Wine Cellar, Safe Room, Guest Cottage*, ad nauseam.

Outside the office Danaë took my arm. I saw a pub across the street and we wandered over, slipping into a booth. To my relief — anything to avoid revisiting the night — she described the plan for the coupling. After our second drink, I said, half-humorously, "But wait. I never proposed and you never accepted."

"The girl decides the match —"

I took her hand. "Indulge me for a minute. Levity is a bit difficult ... What will be done with the three?"

"They will have been removed by now. There's no need for preservation. The bodies of gods do not decompose for weeks."

"And they will be buried?"

"Burned, as it has always been. Somewhere on the estate."

I thought of my recent dream — the large hawk dropping Lachesis into a massive pyre, her eyes empty as she fell. "Let me guess: a pyre?"

"Yes. But first," she said, "the three will be set out under the stars. Artemis favors the sacred grove —"

I shuddered, thinking of coyotes. "What about animals?"

"There will be guards. The custom is an ancient one."

On our return drive, she leaned into me, her hand higher up my thigh and whispered, "Oh — the night before the coupling, the girl sleeps with her chosen and the two become as one —"

"I have a perfect location," I said.

"Please. Not your house."

"No —" I made a right turn a quarter mile away and drove up a narrow road. After two minutes, I made a hard left into a winding driveway: the new estate. As we pulled into the front, she squealed and jumped out before I'd stopped.

"Look at this crazy place! It's huge!"

I jiggled the keys, wondering if Alec had left for the day. Indeed, the house was empty and our voices echoed as she wandered from room to room. After some time, she said, "Show me the master bedroom." Then she lowered her voice. "Take me there."

I led her into the suite that overlooked the acres of gardens in the rear and she laughed. "Here's where we sleep!"

The car had emergency blankets and a sleeping bag in the trunk, and we used those for bedding. A half an hour remained before dusk and she insisted on visiting the Phidias Aphrodite, magnificent as a red dusk set the statue afire. She knelt, motioning me to stand near. I heard her speaking quietly.

"What are you saying?"

"I'm praying to the goddess." She looked up. "Praying my man will sing his love tonight and fill me with his song." She blushed and I knew with certainty that, although much in my preceding life had been grace-less, inept and subject to reproof, our coupling was not.

I ordered takeout and in thirty minutes we ate Chinese noodles and drank beer, cross-legged on the floor of the empty dining room. As I shared her enthusiasm, I thought: *Hours earlier I'd observed death at work. Now at dusk on the same day, I sat beside a girl blushing at every double entendre, at the humor I spun freely.* Every word was a talisman against the swirl of death.

Athene may have wanted time to pass before judgment was rendered on what occurred, but I knew Lachesis' hubris, her psychosis — had precipitated her end. And now in the evening of the same day, Danaë and I laughed on the oak floor of a vast new home. I thought to myself, *Not mourning is not indifference. No, it's living without grief.*

The girl's charm was an incantation that extinguished all past and peripheral things. And I was thankful for it, as I would have otherwise relived the last days.

Later in our new bedroom, I watched as Danaë undressed. Her words as we shared the sleeping bag: "Lighten your heart. I am yours. Tonight we celebrate —"

As we fell asleep in the last hours of night, a storm swept the area. I remember stirring at the sound of rain — and listening with my arm around her. I wondered if the bodies were exposed and shuddered at the thought.

෴

We woke at dawn, diurnal creatures intertwined. We made love again, Danaë unconcerned about privacy. After, she seemed as buoyant as the night before and frowned only briefly when I asked if she would show me how to find the grove where the goddesses lay.

"Of course," she said. "There's a path from the maze — a brief walk."

"Probably," I said, "the access James used to spy on Artemis." She said nothing. We dressed and left, the path wide enough for us to walk and hold hands. The ground was soaked. Within moments we entered the sacred grove. Six older nymphs stood at guard and knelt when they saw us enter. Three daises were set in a line on the opposite bank. Each stood about four feet high.

As we walked closer, the nymphs stepped aside. The goddesses had been left exposed to the sky. Only Aisa was covered, and then with a thin sheet ending at her neck; Chloé and Lachesis lay naked, their bodies glistening, rainwater still pooled on their bellies. They stared into the sky with mercury-eyes, their hair soaked.

"No one closed their eyes."

"The eyes of the divine are always open."

"How long do they lie here?"

"Until tomorrow. There will be a final rite at dusk."

Chloé and Lachesis seemed placid, their mouths slightly open, while Aisa appeared angry, her face knotted up even in death. I saw something glitter on one of Chloé's fingers: the Tiffany ring. She'd worn it until the end.

We stayed only another minute before I nudged Danaë: "Enough."

CHAPTER 64

E *t in Arcadia ego.* Even in paradise, death is inevitable.
Or was this not paradise, but an archaic Ēdēn, with wheels of fire in the sky? An angry god stalking the night and counting his stars in Pleiades to ensure that each hot sun still spins?

As I returned to the wide lawns surrounding the property, I marveled at the expanse and the reflection of light across the moat. I felt a strange reverence as sunlight illuminated the Aphrodite statue. One of my priorities would be finding a covered location for it, possibly in the house. Several of the rooms had vaulted ceilings.

I felt an unexpected optimism — the sisters' end had severed my months-long sense of impending doom. Clearly, my disquiet had been a foreshadowing. Entering the mansion, I bounded up a rear stairwell that led to an upper floor. There, I met Alec. He looked startled, but composed himself. He wore the same beret from our first meeting. "Mr. Night, I hadn't expected you. Welcome home."

Instinctively, I didn't like this man. He would go. But I would ask questions, learn as much as I could and deal with his dismissal in the coming weeks. He could not be allowed to meet any of the beings who inhabited the backwoods. I intended for them to use this building freely.

"Good morning." We shook hands, his grip delicate. "What are your usual hours?"

"7:30 to four. I stay late," he responded, "if requested."

"And what does your job entail?"

A smile, a hint of superciliousness. "I keep this place ticking. For instance, the moat has four recirculating pumps. It's amazing how often one goes. The a/c system is massive. There are six zoned units that I'm always tweaking. I manage the grounds crew —"

"A crew?"

"Subcontractors, landscape people who come regularly. We have housecleaners, six women part-time, several days a week."

"So, you're basically like a caretaker."

"More like a plant supervisor." He smiled.

"Overhead costs are significant —?"

"I'll go over the books when you want." He frowned, his skin oddly porcelain. "You weren't told any of this?"

"No, but I'll admit I didn't ask …" For the first time, I scanned him; his thoughts were diffused and oddly blurred. "What's your full name?"

"Alec a'Aleixo." He lowered his voice. "May I speak frankly?"

"Yes."

"I sense distrust …"

"You sense that, and I sense duplicity."

"It's time," Alec said, "that I come clean."

He had become sycophantic, obsequious. Shrugging, Alec pulled off the beret. Shoulder-length hair came tumbling out. He unzipped his jacket and opened it — a woman's modest breasts swelled a cotton shirt. His voice softened, becoming melodic. "My real name is Alecta. I serve Artemis … and now the two of you."

"A woman! And why are your thoughts so opaque?"

"The goddess thought it best."

I laughed. "You were introduced a month ago as Mrs. James' super, the man who ran this place …"

The fawning voice faded, became more confident. "I've only been on board five weeks."

"I don't get it."

"The goddess anticipated you would buy the house. She wanted the transition to go smoothly — and she wanted you to have good help."

"She knew I'd buy it a week before the listing?" Alecta shrugged. I asked, "Are you good at this?"

Her voice was almost subvocal. "I'll stay if you want, sir."

Sir. "Alecta, confess: Are you one of the nymphs?"

"Yes, sir."

"Let me see your teeth —"

She showed me a half smile, her teeth rectangular, and said, "Caps, sir."

My regard for Artemis soared. "Okay, superintendent, you're on board."

She looked thrilled. I said sternly, "I have two hours at most. Show me around."

❦

We toured the infrastructure. Ninety minutes later a moving van pulled into the driveway. Alecta said without surprise, "Oh, on schedule, sir. Basic furniture and food ... if you'll excuse me."

Soon, the master bedroom contained a bed, bureaus, lamps and linens, the dining room a table, chairs and dishes. Provisions sufficient for several weeks were added to pantries and freezers. Drinks included cases of wine and sparkling water. At the end of the frenetic unloading, two nymphs appeared and made the bed in the master bedroom. I guessed their age at about thirteen. Upon finishing, they opened a cedar chest filled with rose petals and spread them across the bed and floor.

They, too, left. Alecta spread her arms expansively, saying, "Artemis would never allow you to come back to an empty home!"

We finished the tour and I complimented her thoroughness. Artemis' choice of personnel was flawless. I asked, "You and Arethusa know each other?"

She blushed. "We're good friends, sir."

"Is she aware of these preparations?"

"No —"

"I trust you're coming to this afternoon's coupling?"

"With your permission, sir."

I gave her the afternoon off, noting that calling me "sir" was now forbidden. She smiled shyly and said, "I am to prepare you for the celebration." She went on to note she'd been given my "raiments," and that I was to dress properly. She led me to the master bedroom and opened a box: Apollo's hallowed chiton. She shook it out. "Please dress and I will turn away."

I took off my clothes and pulled on the chiton. After a moment she turned and studied my appearance. Then, she lifted its hem. "The boxers must go."

"No underwear?" Stoic, she nodded. I pulled them off.

"Oh," she said. "And I forgot —" She grabbed a smaller box and handed me a pair of bull-skin sandals. Gold roundels ran up the strapping.

I tied them on. "Apollo's, too?"

She nodded. "Now, it's time. You will be escorted there —"

Moments later as I walked out a backdoor, I spotted a tall nymph standing in the distance, her back to the house. As I got closer I knew. "Filly!"

She turned and bowed. "Sir."

"I'm glad you're here. And no more 'sirs' from any of you."

She smiled broadly, her shark's teeth bright. We followed the path Danaë had taken me down a day earlier, bypassing the grove on a secondary trail, avoiding, I presumed, the bodies. I followed her at a rapid pace. She wore a dress made from a thin material tied tightly at her waist — the dress floated away like a mist as it descended from her hips. A few ribbons were woven in her hair. At one point she whispered, "This is a very, very, *very* festive day."

To our right, thousands of birds swarmed near the village, their shape a sinuous, slithering S, a murmuration. Filly looked up, saying, "An intelligence drives their behavior. It's neither divine nor conscious." I tried to guess the species. Starlings? They were black and an iridescence glinted off the wings. The sky was clotted with them.

Abruptly. she said, "Oh, first, I am to tell you that all eight scientists were alerted to the mailings. I understand several universities have launched investigations. Authorities in this country and others are attempting to trace the origin. That will not be possible. It'll go down as an unsolved mystery — a one-off hatched by an ingenious crank. Artemis says we did what we had to do." She stared, confirming my satisfaction, then continued down the trail at a faster pace.

We approached the village and veered off on a new path. The trail rose toward a low hillock. We walked a narrow path between head-high mountain laurel and small cedars. At the top, I saw an opening, an unexpected meadow in the woods. Filly stopped with a finger to her lips: "Shhh —"

From the rise, we viewed a field covered in low grasses and wildflowers. A rectangular platform stood to the right at the end. No one appeared. Overhead, the murmuration fragmented, birds descending endlessly into the surrounding woods.

Then, I saw movement coming from the left. A girl, perhaps five or six, danced into the meadow. She skipped with abandon into the center of the field, giggling, in a blue dress, blond ribboned hair. She stopped, looked our way and began a slow pirouette which became a blur, the ribbons in her hair a slurry. She spun faster and faster — then, laughing, vanished in a flash of glitter that fell slowly like stardust in the rays of sun.

She was the little dream-girl who'd appeared repeatedly at night a year and a half ago, now, here in the light. "Filly — who is she?"

Filly whispered, "One who shows herself only to the blessed. She is the spirit that animates our tribe, that animates this world. Her appearances are auspicious —"

"Does she have a name?"

"She is Ge, or Gaia."

"Earth herself?" I was stunned. *Gaia?*

Filly nodded. "The oldest of the old gods." She whispered, "Artemis was always outraged that Lachesis imitated Gaia's dance. She thought it blasphemous."

"I saw it many times."

"It was whispered that Lachesis fancied herself Gaia's equal. After reanimation, Gaia never showed herself to the Fates. Lachesis presumed her dead."

"So she usurped Gaia's routine?"

"Yes, her ..." She searched for a word. "Her dance. But Gaia knew of the appropriation. She'd gone nowhere. And waited. That she has appeared before us now — on this festive day — is propitious."

"She used to appear to me in dreams."

Filly looked at me. "Then her appearance was a harbinger that you would become who you are. That you would become one of us."

As we spoke, young nymphs in single file entered the meadow. All wore frocks like Filly's. Thirty-five or 40 strode toward the platform and split off left and right facing the stage. A group of older girls followed, all with ribboned hair.

Filly took my hand and led me away to yet a smaller path skirting the meadow. We walked to a point close to the platform, still hidden from those in the field.

The meadow was now filled with nymphs, all standing. I guessed the entirety of the tribe had come. There were at least a hundred girls. None of the goddesses had appeared, nor did I see Danaë. From the rear of the platform, six nymphs stepped onto the stage. All held instruments — golden lyres, tambourines, painted rattles —and played a happy, simple tune.

A small flash in the center of the platform preceded the appearance of a new structure, a pergola and bed with linens. Growing through the pergola's cross-beams was a dense network of vines. Grapes, I guessed. A nod to Dionysos, the god of drink?

Then, Timessa appeared on stage, straightening sheets and arranging pillows. She pulled a rectangular case from under the bed and opened it, reaching in and throwing petals around the bed and on the stairs leading to the platform, her actions almost meditative. When she finished, she left using rear stairs. The musicians played a new tune, livelier and more complex than the last. The nymph playing the gourds raised the rattles above her head, swaying.

With a suddenness I found surprising, a tall blond appeared on stage and advanced toward the bower. Aphrodite, barefoot, wore a white gown that brushed along the floorboards. Her waist was circled by a golden sash, and her dress started below her breasts, which were uncovered and rouged. *Minoan.* She could have held writhing snakes in her hands, but instead stopped beside the bed and turned to face the meadow. The music quieted, and she rose dramatically as she raised her arms.

"You know me," she said loudly as she raked her fingers through her hair. "I often say my beauty surpasses that of all gods and mortals. Yet, there is one whose beauty mirrors mine. You know her, but she is not who you think she is —"

She paused to allow the words to make an impact.

"I speak of Arethusa."

I heard small outcries and gasps.

"She is a daughter of the god Poseidon. Yes, you were unaware. She is a demigoddess. You supposed her one of you."

The nymphs broke into applause.

"We gather now for her and for the rarest of events: a coupling!"

She raised her arms high. Many of the nymphs swayed and undulated, their voices excited, melodious.

"I announce the lovely Arethusa!"

From the back of the meadow, Danaë appeared, dancing with a fluid, whirling grace. Unlike Aphrodite, whose dress fell to her ankles, Danaë's ended mid-thigh, the gown white with yellow ribbons matching the waves of her hair. She danced her way to the stage, through the grasses, stepping without hesitation in lovely patterns. Filly whispered, "We call it *khoreia*. When done solo, it is a devotional for a beloved. It's her coupling dance for you —"

Danaë ended her dance at the stairs and turned toward her audience with a small, self-effacing smile. As quickly, she flitted up the stairs and into Aphrodite's arms. They held for seconds, then the goddess led her to the pergola. Danaë swung herself up into the bed. She sat against the headboard in a sea of pillows and closed her eyes.

Aphrodite cried, "Now, the man with whom she mates!"

Filly touched my arm. I felt a slight shift and suddenly stood on the stage beside Aphrodite, Artemis and Athene. Aphrodite exclaimed, "She has chosen this one as is her wont, declared in an ancient time and by prophesy!"

Jumping up and down, the nymphs applauded.

"Standing beside me now, Jackson Night —"

I felt an alarming tingling through my thighs, a warmth growing in my groin. Aphrodite waved expansively. "The two come before us to affirm their love."

The girls broke into wild applause. I felt that if I viewed myself, my thighs would be flushed. Worse, I felt myself tenting the tunic. I knew Danaë would be mortified.

"We call ourselves amoral," Aphrodite continued. "We are without the veneer of society. And what is society? A human community whose morals change by the day. Amorality, in contrast, is a timeless thing."

She gestured for Timessa, standing to the side of the musicians. T bowed and approached the bed, drawing Danaë's gown up over her thighs and to her waist. Danaë wore nothing under and lazily complied. She met my eyes briefly, joyfully.

Then, the nymph swiveled and without warning took the hem of my tunic and pulled it up, tucking it into Apollo's belt. I stood fully exposed, aware that I had an immense erection.

Aphrodite said as an aside to the crowd, "Be not mistaken! Jackson is no Priapos! That god, my son, was always ready, but couldn't keep it up, an embarrassment and mocked by all. This man is his opposite."

She paused, scanning her audience, then gestured casually toward me. "What you see is a child-maker who has come among us to bring you boys who will grow to men, males to repopulate our tribe —"

The cheering became deafening. Athene stepped forward, her palms out, motioning for the nymphs to restrain themselves. Like a politician, Aphrodite's voice rose alluringly. "Arethusa's boys will all need mates. We will be relaxing rules, allowing many of you to couple as these two do today —"

Through this I stood exposed, my embarrassment increasing. I expected at any moment Aphrodite would have Danaë and me making love before the throng. But instead, the goddess slyly put an arm around me and whispered, "We cannot have you mating here. These girls are far too young. Instead, we'll nod to the prophesy …"

The goddess' eyes were liquid, a sensuous sky-blue. I said, "What prophesy?"

She looked at Danaë and whispered, "You are to will her to open. Then, create a veil of golden flecks to rain upon her, filling her with love. You will continue this ravishment until she cries in joy. This Zeus did to an earlier Arethusa."

I knew the old story and understood. I simply had to visualize the act. I stepped closer to my delirious demigoddess. With the slightest smile, I willed her open. She made a sumptuous movement of her legs. I ensured her offering to be an act of love — at once titillating, yet decorous.

Noting the approval in Aphrodite's eyes, I willed streams of sun-struck flecks, slick and small as dancing motes, down, listening to her moan as I guided the golden cascade womb-deep. The flow filled her, then I slowed the restless probing rain, throttling the deluge as she cried in joy.

In the end, a shimmering light, a halo, surrounded the pergola.

Danaë, ecstatic and enveloped in the lightest of rainbows, opened her eyes to mine. In rapture, arms wide, she said loud enough for every nymph to hear, "Now take me to our home —"

I picked her up, turned, and left toward the woods with the girl. As I stopped at the meadow's edge, the raucous sound of voices, hoots, lyres, and gourds descended on us.

CHAPTER 65

I woke in the morning, Danaë in my arms. Dense clouds built in the west. The sun flooding the estate might be short-lived.

Danaë whispered, "You succeeded."

"At what, beautiful?"

"Consummating." She had a mischievous smile. "But all-nighters leave me hungry. Do you ever feed your girls?"

"Alecta left provisions. Coffee? Strawberries?"

"All of that." I got up, pulling on shirt and pants. From the window, the Phidias statue shone in the early light. And in a distant meadow, I noticed dozens of fat sheep and with them, a lone herder — a girl. She drove them into the rising sun, shading her eyes. Two hawks circled above the maze, drifting aimlessly on currents of air. I turned to Danaë, saying, "Sheep. Something that came with the estate?"

"They're from Artemis' herds. Several of the nymphs make wool. Others weave. The old ways are treasured. Notice the sheep are large — they're a rare variant she breeds." She pulled on a gown. Shaking out her hair she stretched, then shuddered. "I had forgotten. We meet at the amphitheatre at dusk."

I was too well aware. "Details?"

"A pyre in the theatre. That's all I know."

We made breakfast. As we ate, we gazed at each other for a long moment, touching fingertips. She leaned across the table and gave me a sloppy kiss, saying, "Love …"

We spent several delirious hours arm-in-arm walking through the landscaped gardens. Of the 186 acres, more than thirty were carefully manicured. On a slope we found an orchard of old apple trees. Then we stopped to look across a field of lavender, its aroma overwhelming. To its side was another field with flowers. Danaë asked, "What are these?"

Alecta appeared and said, "The flowers are cosmos. They'll be gone in the first hard freeze."

I thought, *October. The wind's already turned.* I glanced at the sky. Now three hawks circled, wheeling against the distant storm, spiraling far above us. We wandered back to the house. Alecta smiled, "Was the bed … adequate?"

Danaë curtsied. Then, in a rush she said, "It was perfect!" Obviously they were old friends. Excusing herself, Alecta said, "Workmen coming soon —"

The day passed in a lethargic flow. We made love before lunch, then again later. Danaë changed into a dark dress. The funeral was an hour off. I wondered what would happen if it rained. At about six o'clock we left and started the fifteen-minute walk to the amphitheatre. More hawks had gathered in the sky. I counted eight, then nine.

"Have you noticed the birds? We saw a murmuration at our coupling, and now this —"

Danaë glanced up and grimaced. "A kettle, or a cauldron. They're on the thermal updrafts. I see a couple crows and grackles, too —"

"I've never seen so many at one time."

"It's not coincidence. Think of your dreams. Always hawks, hawks. In the back meadow, a hawk. Lachesis attracted them all. Maybe they're here to say goodbye."

She snuggled against me as we walked, then asked, "Do you miss the three?"

I spoke carefully. "At first I was a loyalist. We all were. Enlisted to save the world, Lachesis' dutiful soldiers. But we unwittingly became her pawns …"

She tugged me along and in moments we entered the amphitheatre. The camouflage had been rolled back. A buzz of high voices from the nymphs echoed off the proscenium. And dozens of hawks reeled above.

In the center, three pyres rose like witches' hats. Each had a slot at the base large enough for a body. The pyramids were at least forty feet tall, dark with tinder and resinous pine stumps. A nymph stood at each holding a torch. I felt impatient. *Do it. Strike the matches, make it so*—but the bodies were missing.

Danaë and I found seating. I noticed goddesses scattered among the nymphs. Aphrodite wore a black rose in her hair; Artemis looked grim. I saw no mourning or evidence of a vigil and whispered to Danaë, "Will there be an elegy or lament?"

"They died in dishonor. The pyres are their due; more would be intemperance."

I'd begun to recognize the faces of the musicians. This afternoon they waited close to the righthand pyre, in a line, holding conch shells. At an unseen signal, the six raised the shells. From the rear of the proscenium, the bodies were carried in on litters, a nymph at each corner. As they walked onto stage center, the nymphs halted briefly — the shells were blown once — before proceeding toward the pyres.

Lachesis and Klotho were naked. Black squares of cloth now covered their faces from chin to forehead, but otherwise they were unclothed. Laine's red hair hung from the litter. I thought, but only briefly, that this could be yet another play, Artemis' most enigmatic tragedy.

Behind them, Aisa was carried in, covered head to foot in a white sheet, a concession, I supposed, to her age. With the litters in place, each beside a pyre, one of the musicians raised her conch and blew a wavering note. The litter-bearers stooped and robotically slid the corpses into the openings, then joined the audience.

Through all of this, hawks, now in the hundreds, orbited the amphitheatre. I noticed a large one drifting lower. It plunged and, claws out, landed on a high limb on the pyre that held Lachesis' corpse, shaking its wings and rolling its head around the amphitheatre. Athene sat to our left. The hawk's eyes were orange — and the two locked eyes. Without a sound and as if on cue, Athene stood and clapped her hands.

Each nymph guarding a pyre bent and threw her torch into the tinder. The torches thudded into the fuel, smoked brightly, and the cones burst into flames. As the pyres exploded, the hawk above Lachesis lifted itself nonchalantly, flapping its wings against the heat. It shrieked once and with insouciance, lofted higher.

The pyres merged into a single howling inferno. As I watched, the corpses turned ashen, the hair on their heads snarling in sparks and small flares, the bodies quickly lost in the conflagration. To my astonishment, the dense smoke lifted as high as the top of the amphitheatre and vanished, clear sky above it. Danaë leaned against me, saying, "Artemis controls the smoke. Otherwise, it would be seen for miles."

The heat was so intense that we raised our hands as shields; watching became impossible. Danaë put her arms around me and turned away. I stroked her, feeling the heat pound her skin. The pyres burned faster than I would have guessed. The crackling — a modulated roar punctuated by pops like gunshots — was magnified by wails from the nymphs, the cacophony unnerving. At its end, I saw only charred debris in soft, smoking spirals. Smoke meandered into and among the marble benches in a gaseous sinuosity that left us coughing.

The smoke thinned. The musicians blew their shells repeatedly. Then they suddenly stopped, turned stiffly and exited.

Artemis rose first, catching my eye, quietly asking, "May we gather at the house?"

I nodded. Rain began to fall, light at first, then in torrents. The divine and the semi-divine, the smoking cinders, the unidentifiable ashes of the Fates, and high above us, the whirling birds of prey — all were washed in Gaia's grim deliverance. I thought of a poem from Epicurus:

> *Death is nothing to us,*
> *since when we are,*
> *death has not come,*
> *and when death has come,*
> *we are not.*

CHAPTER 66

S ex and death. And fire. I have read that early philosophers believed all things are composed of four elements — fire, earth, water, air — and of the four, they called fire the most bestial. A strange word, bestial. Artemis said once, "No god gave birth to earth: on the contrary, it was borne of fiery debris, magma and gases. It spun for billions of years in flame, only slowly coalescing. When life first appeared, when the fires cooled, only then did Ge, the glittering Gaia, begin to dance."

Now, as I finish this work, Danaë and I have been together (if I honor the atomic clock of linear time) for five years. She has borne us sons. The first — Ajax — is now five, conceived on the afternoon of our coupling from the golden shower I loosed as the crowd of nymphs heard Danaë cry in joy.

In the last year, I came upon an illustration of a Gustave Klimt painting, astonishingly titled *Danaë*. Painted at the turn of the 20th century, it depicts the same act I performed at our coupling. Klimt's Danaë lies on her back, lips open in ecstasy, one breast undone, legs up, head tilted sideways in coitus as a shower of gold rains down. Fascinated, I found Rembrandt, Titian and others had painted similar scenes.

When I showed Danaë the illustration, she asked about the original. Her birthday was coming and I discovered it hung in the Galerie

Würthle in Vienna, on loan from a wealthy family in Austria. After months of haggling, I bought it through a New York dealer.

Public outcry occupied Austrian media for weeks, along with demands it be repatriated. The sales agreement included a nondisclosure clause; the piece was presumed to have been purchased by an oligarch or a foreign billionaire. The controversy quieted. It's small — about 31 inches square — and now hangs above our bed.

If you walk from the master bedroom downstairs to one of the large rooms facing the gardens, you encounter the Phidias. I had it moved to the vaulted center of the room. The two pieces complement each other. Aphrodite's kind comment when she saw the two was, *Yet, neither compares to Arethusa's beauty —*

I've wondered if, in this same room, Marlene Dietrich lounged in meditation trying to escape her celebrity. I imagine I can smell her cigarettes, and inevitably think of Laine.

Ah, Laine. A half decade has passed since the Day of the Pyres, and throughout those years I have reflected on the events that begin this book. I am tempted, of course, to emphasize the role of the sisters, and to stress their role as the Fates. Chloé alone was truly innocent.

But this story is not about Chloé or any one of them as much as it is about transformations. Little did I suspect Gaia was always there, the little girl doing joyful cartwheels and pirouettes. As a child — her preferred incarnation — she is, in her essence, vivacity.

And Arethusa? Without her wit and intelligence, I am uncertain where I would be today. In the last week, I wrestled with a difficult section of this work. Reflecting out loud on the recklessness of Laine's maneuvering, I expressed my usual disbelief. Danaë laughed, saying, "A bite from a cunning shark leaves no trace of blood."

She wouldn't elaborate, but by that I suspect she meant their mission had lost its subtlety. The sisters jettisoned their primordial principles. Like so many zealots, Laine sacrificed the honorable for the expeditious.

That same evening Danaë added, "Never forget: we are amoral, but ethical."

But I have sidetracked. Danaë has pointed me repeatedly toward Gaia's importance. Life is, she says, a struggle against decline. Entropy, when it prevails, triggers an inexorable descent into death.

Gaia not only reveres life, she is its source, and consequently, its ultimate protectress. When the three sisters were lost, many in the tribe feared the old cycles would collapse, that time-driven birth and death would implode. But that has not occurred. If, as Laine once told me, the Fates truly created a life-death algorithm, it continues on. Its creators are gone, but like an automaton, the algorithmic reaper still sweeps its scythe to the old rhythms. Death hardly retired at their demise.

And as to Laine's assertion that scientists would break the sacred life-death cycle with some sleight of hand, Danaë assures me Gaia has no such concerns. During billions of years, species have come and gone, flourished and perished. Humans are no more unique than dinosaurs. Gaia, I am informed, favors no species over another. If the human race overshoots itself, tumbling to its demise, she will remain present at the birth of every hummingbird, firefly or salamander, treasuring each as she does us all today.

Two nights ago I observed an old buck wandering like an aimless Zen monk through our maze. The maze center now hosts a sundial. In the fading light of dusk, the buck appeared undeterred by the cul-de-sacs and twists of hedge we find so ingenious. Now that the nymphs come and go openly, I was not surprised to see two girls in tunics stop and watch the stag. Although it glanced at them briefly, it continued its amble toward one of the exits.

I had seen this deer before, the dark rub marks on its antlers a give-away. It was one of Artemis' spirit deer. Danaë once told me these majestic beasts are taken by the huntress' arrows, but reappear the next morning.

At first, I struggled believing Gaia's extreme antiquity. Based on contemporary science, for her to have appeared at the dawn of life, she would be billions of years old. The timeframe is unthinkable. Still, I accept her eminence.

I know as well that Lachesis reappeared in this modern time as a flawed and broken thing. Her state of insatiability should have warned her. Instead, she delighted in her new sensuousness, blind to her blind-ness, rationalizing all.

I do not mean to suggest sensuousness is wrong or is a thing to avoid.

To be hedonistic is merely to have heightened sensory affection, to live fully. And it must be noted that throughout the increasing intrigues of the sisters, Gaia watched with immense patience, amused, I suspect, that her persona had been arrogated. (I have wondered on occasion if Gaia herself amplified the Sessile acorn's toxin so that the Fates could not resist its blooded claws.)

I dreamed two nights ago that Gaia appeared as I drank coffee in the room with the Phidias. Perhaps it wasn't a dream, as the girl is a trickster. At dawn the glistering little girl cartwheeled in, spun, stopped and looked at me mischievously, saying, "Now that you are who you are, remember that you happen to the world, not otherwise."

"Happen?"

Yes, the world no longer happens to you.

Her appearance was her first since the afternoon of the coupling. I cocked my head. She laughed delightedly. And for the first time, she stepped closer, putting her hand on mine, her palm warm — and I sensed fondness. Her body appeared to be slightly translucent — perhaps 30 percent or more — her eyes limpid, her mouth amused.

Squeezing my hand, she vanished in an almost imperceptible shift of color. But I speak of what occurred last night. As I write, Ajax wanders in. The boy is a towhead and Danaë refuses to cut his locks. He stops, observes me and says, "What are you doing?"

"Writing things down so I don't forget."

"What things?"

I can tell his mind is already flitting about. He has no patience for my meditations. Instead of replying, I give his bottom a small whack and send him off. He squeals and runs off, arms out, pretending to be a bird. Of course, shadowing the child, Danaë appears. She smiles, "You —"

As she sits in my lap, I kiss her neck. She pushes me away and says, "Last night I looked at the stars, pulsing. Did you see?"

"Of course. They hang suspended in the sea of night —"

She smiles. "Are you describing my father's ancient seas?"

"Yes, I regret never meeting him."

"He was called the Kind-Hearted One, as are you, my love."

AFTERWORD

During the years I raised Chloé, my life, as vital as it seemed at the time, was no more than a fantastical construct. I played father, then lover, then repeated the folly with a second girl. Love was a chimera. And a lie.

Yet, I survived, washed onto Danaë's shore. When she found me, I was a humbled traveler, chastened and dark. She pulled me from the tidal wash, the tangled wrack, combing broken shells from my hair. Her light is luminous. Through her I am, for the first time, whole.

In the last five years, I fenced the entirety of the two properties, merging them into a single tract. The original house — the site of the Fates' demise — has been largely unoccupied. Artemis has hosted day parties there. I appeared at one or two, but recognized myself as peripheral. And the house holds memories.

After the Day of the Pyres, I wondered if the remaining goddesses would leave. Yet, they did not, purportedly staying to oversee my transition. Now half a decade has passed and they remain.

On the fifth year post-coupling, Artemis, Athene and Aphrodite met with us at the main house to discuss their future. I idly wondered if Themis and Hestia — even the monstrous Nyx — might show, but they did not.

The rendezvous followed an informal lunch. One of the nymphs watched Belos, our second son, while Ajax — whom I had nicknamed AJ

— roamed the backwoods with a half dozen girls his age. He is often gone for hours, stalking the spirit deer and climbing trees. Danaë and I can pinpoint his location and condition, so he is free to play anywhere within the enclave. Several of the girls have, amusingly, already declared he will grow up to be their mate and run at his side.

We met in the large room with the Phidias, among scattered rattan chairs and couches. With the afternoon sun casting its thin fire on the walls, the location seemed rich with past spirits. As everyone sat, Danaë led a young nymph into the room. The girl carried a panpipe, the Greek flute made from cane tubes. She raised it to her lips, looking up into the vault of the ceiling, and whispered, "To Orpheus, Hermes and all the lost Satyrs —" and played.

Another nymph filled glasses, and Artemis rose, saying with unnecessary formality, "Our goal, before sunset, is to decide our future domicile. For years Jackson has been accommodating. Too much so."

As she spoke she paced, pausing for emphasis. "Hestia says we have become caged animals. Once we had vast countryside to roam, mountain ranges, crystalline rivers. No more —"

Aphrodite raised her glass in affirmation. Artemis paused and said, "When we decided to retreat from beloved Greece, perhaps we erred. Yet, mankind had gone mad. Once revered, we were mocked." She ran her hands through her hair. "You remember it well. We all do. And in the years following our withdrawal, while we decamped to wildlands, mankind became more voracious."

"So what?" Athene interjected, "Gaia would shrug. Although she loves us, she simply watches. Her mission is the preservation of life — not ours, or the lives of humans, or of rare birds. She ensures only that animation and sentience, in some form, persists. She tends the fire, not the coals." Athene smiled. "We focus, do we not, too much on ourselves."

Danaë interrupted, noting that less than a decade ago, the tribe had been in crisis. Now there is hope. She reminded them that goddesses and demigoddesses had given birth in the past — and she was a confirmation they would again.

Athene interjected, "Well and good. But aren't the real questions, Where do we go from here? And what is next?"

I stood. "This small preserve has proven itself a refuge. I'd prefer it to be hundreds of times larger. But we lack for nothing, and although the local climate can't compete with the Aegean, its winters are only slightly harsher than those of Greece."

Artemis laughed. "Yes, better than what we endured for millennia in the backwoods of Spain and France."

"We are off topic," Athene said. Her gray owl had appeared, and sat yellow-eyed in her palm, its head pivoting.

Artemis nodded. "We can blend in as humans if we wish. We can blink twice and be in Greece. Or Istanbul. The Levant. Or Iowa. We can send our girls to universities. But I view all that as diversion. Here our culture remains pure, our girls virtuous, our traditions superlative."

Then she became irate. "And admit it: if we scatter ourselves throughout the world again, we are lost! Look at the other bands in other lands: all subsiding, all denying their decline ...

"Here in Aegle no one knows we live. But in a few short decades, the tribe will grow. There will be more couplings and children."

Danaë surprised me, slipping her arms around my neck and kissing me tenderly. In any other gathering, the length of her kiss would have been embarrassing. Here it brought applause.

Artemis continued, "In Aegle we have no wars. We need no physicians. We have no politicians, so are free from lies. We need no army. Our only need is sustaining ourselves — and we have made that turn."

"Jackson?" Athene interrupted, her owl swiveling its head toward me. "We are not using the houses well. This mansion — you and Arethusa and the children are its only occupants. And the first house — it's smaller, but largely unused. The winters have been harsh on the younger nymphs."

"I offered shelter years ago and —" I gestured toward Artemis. "— you said you preferred the old way."

Artemis grimaced. "The weather doesn't effect *us*, but, yes, the girls are often cold."

After looking at me, Danaë said, "Whatever you need. Our home is yours."

Artemis walked to a mandevilla vine in the window. The plant was in a final riot of flowers as its season ended. She idly ran a finger down its twisting stems. "We have reached a deflection point, haven't we? And we agree."

"Yes," Athene affirmed, "Aegle will remain our home for now. At least until Arethusa's boys are men."

The afternoon retreat turned into a party. Word went out to the nymphs in Artemis' village and those scattered through the estate to gather at the big house. Within a short time, we had dozens of girls throughout the ground floor.

AJ came home with three of the girls, all dirty from running. He was excited and I kept calming him down. The energy level among the children seemed extraordinary, although they were simply delighted to be together without assignments, knowing nothing of our decisions.

As the party wound down, I observed Danaë paired with Aphrodite, the two of them passing a nautilus shell back and forth, giggling. When I asked, the goddess said, "She won't admit its curves are like a woman's. She thinks I'm always single-minded." They smirked and I graciously filled their glasses.

Recently, I have been occupied with a side interest of some importance. As the sole male, I have never shaken my disquiet that none of the gods reanimated. Although at the sisters' demise I chose not to reverse the Fates' death, I am exploring using that power otherwise. Restoring Dionysos, Apollo, Hermes, and even Danaë's father, Poseidon, would affirm that gender was not, as Laine avowed, the cause of their failure to wake. As time has passed, I have even wondered if she purposely left them comatose. The gods would have been direct competition, which she disdained.

I imagine inviting Danaë down to the Phidias room for a drink and watching her surprise as she finds her father, trident in one hand and stiff drink in the other. I am optimistic.

As snow and cold begin to mark the season once again, my view of the back estate is one of gardens, stone walkways, the moat and maze, and fountains (which are turned off because of the cold). I have glimpses of the winding path that leads to the woods.

It's the same path used by Filly to take me to the grove where the goddesses lay, and the same James walked in his last hour. In this season, the gardens are covered with snow, and only dark footsteps indicate the path's location.

Moments ago, Danaë brought me coffee. AJ stopped in to tell me an endless story about his morning, of the two girls he ran beside and how one has beautiful hair. I said, "As nice as yours?"

He stared quizzically and said, grinning maniacally, "Better! It's a *girl's* hair!"

As I struggle to be lucid with this summation, Danaë comes again to fill my cup. I had asked her last night to skim the last few pages of my narrative. "What did you think?" I asked.

She sets the carafe down, saying, "Yes, yes, you're close ... but there's something you've passed over."

I pause, looking into her quiet eyes. "Tell me."

She says, "Even after five years, you haven't shaken your fury."

"That I was betrayed."

"Yes, used by Laine. Poisoned by Eros."

"Of course. It lives on."

"Unlike the Fates."

I took a breath, finally saying, "Imagine losing Chloé, someone you thought for twenty years was your daughter — served up like a tart and then destroyed. Aisa, too. She was always the grim reaper, and she never had a chance."

"You were a devoted family man. As you are now."

"I was used. Yet I participated."

"You didn't know. You were human ..." She paused. "Do you ever wish you hadn't met them?"

"If I had not, I would not have met you."

"That's true ... Still ..." she whispers.

Trying to lighten the moment, I say, "At least I know enough *now* to know that my rage has softened into ... mere anger."

"We must both accept," she said, "that some things endure."

"Yes," I say, touching her cheek, "like our love."

"I told you once," she smiled. "*My* forever is for all time, forevermore."

As if this is all self-evident, she leaves.

I look out into the gardens and marvel at the gusting wind. The temperature is close to freezing. Still, a half dozen nymphs play near the maze. Even in this cold, they are barefoot and bare-assed. I have never lost my sense of amusement when one bends over, or in the case of today's games, the wind lifts their tunics high.

Indeed, in the beginning is sex, the wildfire that in its wet heat drives conception. Things are made and unmade. Fate is unpredictable. Gaia dances and fire endures.

❖ The End ❖

GLOSSARY

All names are those of classic Greek divinities.

❧

Aphrodite The goddess of erotic love, beauty and sensuality.
Apollo The god of music and arts, an archer, and Artemis' brother.
Arethusa In this novel, a demigoddess and the daughter of Poseidon; some sources attribute her parentage to Nereus and Doris, making her a naiad.
Artemis The virgin goddess of wild animals, protectress of girls and Apollo's sister.
Athene A virgin goddess celebrated for her cunning, wisdom, and intelligence; the co-founder, along with Poseidon, of Athens.
Fates Three sisters who controlled the life spans of mortals and gods alike, and were, consequently, the most powerful of the Greek gods.
Gaia One of the earliest goddesses who, from herself, created Earth.
Nyx An early goddess and mother of the Fates, Death, Dreams, and other children.
Orthrus A divine dog known as the Two-Headed One for its ability to see the past and future simultaneously.
Poseidon God of the sea and other waters, of earthquakes and horses.

ABOUT THE AUTHOR

Patrick Garner is a writer, artist and podcaster, in addition to his other pursuits. He has written stage plays and cofounded the off-Broadway Bright Lights Theatre company in Providence, Rhode Island. He was honored by the American Theater Critics Association when one of his plays was selected for a reading.

He published *A Series of Days of Change* and *Four Elements* (poetry), *Playing with Fire* and *D Is for Dingley* (biographies), as well as numerous articles and reviews in national magazines. His paintings and etchings are in museums, universities and private collections. Narrator and host of the breakout podcast, *Garner's Greek Mythology*, he lives in New England.

Made in the USA
Thornton, CO
06/07/24 20:55:13

9245bb40-6965-4213-86b2-2ebb00a72f9eR01